ARRANGED DECEPTION

USA TODAY BESTSELLING AUTHOR

CC MONROE

Her deception is my demise, *or is it?*

To us women.
Fuck the patriarchy.

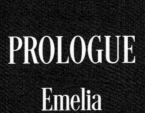

PROLOGUE

Emelia

"It's not a marriage of choice, Emelia. You have a duty to this family. Do you want to be the demise of it, or do you want us to reign?" my father seethes, his teeth clenching and spit flying from his lips.

Today is my twenty-second birthday, after four years of me flying under the radar. Most women in the mafia, or bratva, or any such bloodline are married off at eighteen. But there had been no threat. Not one. We had made peace with all the families in the other outfits.

Until now.

The Seattle boss has made himself known and is now the last standing enemy of my father and his reign. Nico Dante Valiente—the most ruthless man of his generation. Word has it, it only takes something as simple as looking at him or his men just a little too closely for him to make a bullseye of your temple.

Now, my father, Giuseppe Notelli, wants me to marry that dangerous man. But not to unite the families. Oh, no—no, that would be too easy. But better, he wants me to marry him as an informant, so my father can end their control in their territory and overtake it. Once they get me in, I'm to find out all the most intimate details, and they'll kill Valiente, so my youngest brother, Sal, can take over, since he would be next in line.

Because women cannot reign.

But as the widow of the boss, my family would take over if Valiente doesn't have any other family to claim his outfit.

"How will it be Sal who takes over if you take the man's entire empire? He could have family, Father," I address him, but not without some robustness.

My father has always beaten me, treated me like a human punching bag at times, and I've decided to run with the most popular motto around here—"If I go down, I'll go down swinging."

His eyes darken, narrowing on me. "You must learn to control your tone, Emelia Rene. He has one rule for marrying you." My father pauses, lighting his cigar and stepping up to me.

As he exhales the smoke in my face, I hold very still, my expression remaining stoic. I will not let him see me crack.

"And what is that, *Father*," I mock.

I see it coming but don't move in time to avoid it. The back of his hand connects with my cheek, my entire head jerking sideways. This has me whimpering, and I hate that I let the sound out.

Never have I hated anyone more than I hate my father. He is no dad. He's a beast, a monster, a phantom who haunts my days and my dreams. Once, the beating was so bad I had to be hospitalized, and when the staff started to question me, I was removed by my father and left to heal on my own at home. In fact, my broken wrist never did; the bone on the outer side still protrudes. You can see it never healed right, and it aches more frequently than not.

Holding my cheek where the skin is hot and most likely now bruised and scraped from the family crescent ring he always wears, I ask him, "What is the rule, Father?"

He laughs from deep in his gut. "That in the event of his death, you are never to remarry. He doesn't like to share. Even in death."

Those words make bile rise. I know I would be stupid to think my father would let me marry anyone outside of this world, but part of me hoped that maybe one day I would find a knight. The ones in all the fairy tales, they slay beasts, like my father. Maybe one would whisk me away to save me from the dangers that fall over my house—over my life. He would spoil me. Protect me. Guard me from the monsters in the night.

But alas, now I know that will never happen.

There was *one* who did for a time... but he got away.

I shake away the memory of my lost love, not ready to ruminate on that heartache.

"If his entire bloodline were dead, why would we need to live up to that?" I ask, my hand dropping and my eyes following its trail. Cowering, that's what I'm doing, and I wish I could pull myself out of it.

"Because if other outfits see us not following a post-mortem rule of the fallen boss, then we would be labeled traitors, causing strife we don't need. So, you will marry this man. He's coming tomorrow to meet you. Cover the bruise and skip the meals between now and then. You'll be lucky if he decides to still go through with it when he sees you."

With that, he turns, and my eyes well with tears.

Why couldn't I have a father who loves me?

One thing about the Italian mafia, it is nothing like the movies or what you read in books—at least my family isn't. Not all men and fathers believe in protecting honor when it comes to women. Some do, but most... most treat us as if we are collateral damage or a means to an end.

"Yes, sir." With all I have in me, I try not to let that come out snarky.

I was born the daughter of Giuseppe and Isabelle Notelli, with two brothers, Salvatore and Lorenzo. They took after my father, treating me like a rag doll, never stepping in when Father would hurt me and even sometimes joining. My mother—that woman makes all other women look like saints, because she is the worst of the worst, the rotten root of the tree. Mother wouldn't enjoy watching, but never did she step in to protect her daughter. Father used to beat her, but then I came along, and got to pass on two things: her looks and the burden of my father's heavy hand.

I'm shorter than her though, 5'4" with a fuller frame. My parents deemed I was fat from a young age, because I didn't look like the women in our world.

I, however, love my body, and no matter how hard my parents have tried to bring me down, that love for myself never wavered. Because of them, my life was built around vanity, not brains or ambition. I wanted to go to college, get a degree, have a mind of my own, but that was never my fate.

It's clearly to be the wife of a homicidal egomaniac.

I graduated high school at eighteen, then I became captive to the gym, this home, and my room. The most interaction I have is when I talk to the other daughters of the outfit at balls, auctions, and luxurious events. Shopping sprees with the spawns of Satan— my parents—hardly count as free time. They ridicule me and press hard on me with their heavy thumbs.

There is a life outside of these walls that I wanted to explore. But now? Now, I will be used as a ploy and be passed on like a used puppet to a new string master.

One who might even be worse than those I currently live with.

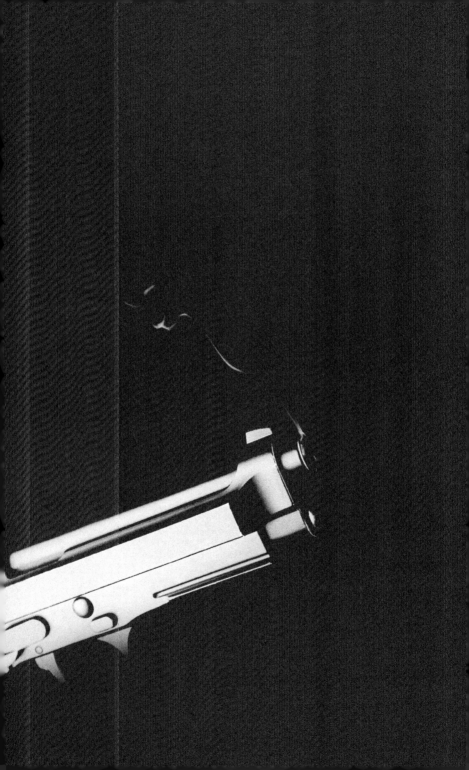

CHAPTER ONE

Nico

"You're telling me that he took off with an entire shipment of goods, Levetti?" I place my hands in my pockets, my stance dominating, my feet planted as I tilt my head to the side and assess the men who are supposed to be professionals. Men I trusted to keep my business solid. And now they cower in front of me—because they've failed me.

I see the fear in their eyes, the sweat beading on their foreheads. They know all too well what happens to men who cost me money and have stolen property. What's mine is mine, and anything taken from me only leaves the thief good as dead.

"Giulio, can you tell these men what happens when something of mine is taken?"

My right-hand man, the *only* man to date who has not let me down, nods.

"Tell or show?" he questions, and this has me clicking my tongue and smirking.

"Tell them today. I'm short on men and need all the working kneecaps I can get."

With that, he steps in front of the men, who are all lined up.

"Find the shipment, or not only will the cargo be missing," he whispers, his Italian accent thick, "but so will your bodies."

I turn and walk away, listening to him provide one swift blow to Levetti's stomach. Pulling my phone from my suit pocket, I see New York calling.

"Giuseppe. What is it? I'm working." Annoyed, I ask the father of my betrothed this while checking my watch to see I have to catch my red-eye to New York to meet my new bride. One I don't care to marry but know it must be done to bring the last two outfits at war together as allies.

At least, that's what Giuseppe thinks. I have my own fucking agenda. To him, I was just the kid who grew up and went to school with his son. So stupid. He is the lousiest man I have ever met, the most ill-witted man alive. He has no idea that I know everything he's planned.

This marriage is for revenge, the complete opposite of what he thinks it to be.

However, the marriage won't just aid me in my plot for revenge, because there is the fact that I'm not getting any younger. I need an heir, someone to take over the name after I'm old, dead, and gone. In order to make all three things happen, I need to marry Notelli's only daughter, Emelia.

"Nico. So harsh. We are to be family soon, and you're taking my daughter all the way to Seattle. We must be able to break bread and do so frequently," he drawls, and I roll my eyes, unlocking the Maserati and climbing in. "You know, to keep in touch with our sweet Emelia."

Her name matches her beauty, but that is all there is to her. No educational background, no hobbies, nothing. When I did my research on her, I was disappointed to see she will be good for nothing but breeding and wearing on my arm.

I had one rule to ensure the safety of my outfit. That she will never remarry. Granted, I plan to build my empire with heirs and die at an old age, but in my line of work, I'm a walking target at all times. I will not let my men and my Seattle reign be brought down. The only options in my absence are either my child or my wife's brother. Yet the latter will never happen, not when I'm done. I haven't even told Giulio, my underboss, my plans for this marriage, and I intend to keep it that way until it's time to put the pedal to the metal.

Tomorrow, I will meet her. And by the end of the week, she will be Mrs. Valiente, wife of the ruthless mafia boss, Nico Dante Valiente. Poor woman, she will never see it coming—what it means for me to be her husband and her my wife. She is a pawn, and there's no guilt within me knowing this. I have no conscience. My dead father, God rest his soul, taught me to be a merciless leader, a man everyone quakes in the presence of. He always knew I would be his shadow and grow to be the best made man he trained me to be.

"What can I help you with?" I rev the engine.

"Listen, my daughter may have a little bit of snark to her, and as a man, I felt it was appropriate to come to you and let you know she can be easily—" He hesitates, and the skin around my green eyes tightens. Where is he going with this?"—placed back into submission with the right amount of force."

Is he calling me to tell me not only does he beat my future bride, but that I must do the same? The nerve. The egotism. Who does he think he is to call and tell me this? And secondly, who is he to tell me how I will handle my own wife when she is disobedient to me?

Running one hand through my black hair, I shake my head, my tongue grazing my top teeth.

"Giuseppe, I mean this with the most disrespect one man can probably produce. If you ever touch my wife in that manner again or tell me *I* should, I won't hesitate to show you the same treatment. This arrangement doesn't keep you safe from my wrath if you fuck with anything that is mine," I growl.

There is a moment of silence that follows, and I await his coming statement, ready to defend what needs to be.

"You're right. I'm sorry. I would never want another man to tell me how to handle *my* wife. We will see you tomorrow, and we look forward to the joining of our families. Goodbye, Valiente."

I grunt, annoyed, and end the call on my dashboard screen.

How fucking dare he? Now I know my wife is submissive and meek. A weak woman. Which I cannot have if she is to be mine. Men all over are looking for a way to get in, and if anyone or anything looks too afraid, they just might get in and use that weakness for their gain. The only thing that brings me hope is the fact that he said there's a bit of snark to her. Which means there is a small flame I can maybe fan into something wilder, something stronger.

But what really pisses me the fuck off, another man simply trying to tell me what to do, that makes me see red.

Hardened and without mercy, I will not let anyone or anything break me down or boss me around. Ever.

STEPPING OFF MY PRIVATE JET, I BUTTON MY SUIT JACKET and put my sunglasses on, blocking the mid-morning glare. Giulio stands beside me, scanning the area around us as the black SUV pulls up. He steps in front, opens the door, and gestures for me to enter. Sliding in, I pull out my phone and check the status back in Seattle.

"They found the shipment. I need to focus on today and some of the wedding shit. You handle the perpetrators. I want proof. Pictures. Names and burial coordinates," I tell him, now moving on to look at the emails pertaining to my underground club, Dante's. I run a sex club, very elite with a high price tag. My members are mostly from the outfit, but there are lots of Seattle businessmen who own gold memberships. Every night is completely booked solid, and the line to get in to the upstairs nightclub—a front to keep the men in uniforms away—is wrapped around the building. Not that it would matter, because I have a lot of them on my payroll.

I answer the emails, then peer out the window, waiting for Giulio to finish the call I asked him to make.

"They are working on it, boss," he confirms, ending the call.

"Good. What's the status with the new models they're producing in Spain?" I ask, referring to the new guns. These are custom works, never been made before, and I will be the only one to have access to them. I've spent so much time behind the scenes, dealing with the missing shipments, henchmen fucking up, and more, that I haven't been on the front line. I worry some of my men think I've gotten soft. This thought alone infuriates me, because I can't let the men who fall under my command think they can slip through the cracks or let things happen that shouldn't.

After my travels and this arrangement are finalized, I can get back to work, leading the men the way they need to be. Which will be with a quiver in their knees and a chill in their spines. If my men don't fear me, then the other outfits will see me as the weak link. This is not the fate that will make me fall.

"They are in the early stages of mass production, but the samples were sent."

My jaw tightens."How much time will that take?" I growl.

"Six months, sir," he replies, and there's no mistaking the fact that he knows how this is going to make me react.

"Six fucking months! In that amount of time, anyone withing the chain could break the nondisclosure agreement. Others will be onto it, and they could gather more buyers. These are my creations! I fucking designed them, and they could be exposed for all other outfits to fucking copy. They will bring in more money than any other weapon we trade. Did you tell them I can call off the deal at any time?" I bark.

"Yes. They said they will do their best to put a rush on the production line. They promised they wouldn't sell to anyone else, sir."

I glare at him and, through gritted teeth, give my response. "First, the shipment of imported cocaine was taken. Now, you're telling me there is going to be a long waiting period for the weapons I paid to produce and be done with already? What the fuck is going on, Giulio? If I focus on the wedding for one fucking week, will my outfit fall apart?"

If my looks could kill, he would be dead. He is supposed to pick up where I leave things in the interim when I'm needed elsewhere.

"You're right, and I take responsibility for this, sir. If anymore shipments go missing, you can take my hand as payback. I shouldn't have let this happen." He lays himself on the chopping block, like any well-trained underboss would.

Taking a deep breath, I try to calm myself down, because at this time, Giulio is the only one I can trust completely, and I need him focused. If he runs around like a chicken with his head detached, it will get messy.

The rest of the drive is silent, and Giulio makes no more attempts to talk to me. He knows what I need from him, and I trust he will get shit done.

He clears his throat. "Boss, we're here."

We pull up through the security gates and up a gravel road, leading to a large mansion. It's an almost Southern style, with white columns lining the steps, and gray shutters. Funny, since we're in upstate New York. You can tell they made it look as wholesome as they could. Old-money-looking, versus dirty money. Keep enemies at bay and neighbors unsuspicious. The house is surrounded by a twelve-foot wrought-iron fence, curling at the top to give a polished look.

The front door opens when we pull up, and Giuseppe steps out first, followed by his wife. He gives a nod, and Isabelle greets me with a smile, then from behind them, I see Salvatore and Lorenzo appear, the sons. I expect Salvatore to give some acknowledgment of our history, but he ignores it more than his father does.

All right, that's fair. Play it cool; don't draw attention to the past. How fitting that he doesn't see how that draws more attention to what lingers between us. The secret they think they hold. But the truth… I already know it. It's spelled out so clearly. In fact, it's ingrained in me and will be my driving force in this marriage. Payback is a bitch, and I'm the reaper who will deal it out with great pride.

Lastly, the blonde-haired, brown-eyed daughter with the most miserable look a woman could possibly wear appears, and that puts my attention back on the here and now. She doesn't look at me, and I want to yell at her and demand she greet me with eye contact and respect, but we will save that for the day she becomes my property. I'll break her into the perfect boss's wife. This is a transaction, not a fairy tale or story that will progress into love. It is a business deal to keep the peace until I get my revenge.

That sweet fucking revenge.

However, I am a man. And I can appreciate the assets that will be mine. She is beautiful. She is curvy in all the places a male like me appreciates—full, wide hips, palm-filling breasts, and a thick waist that will overflow my hands as I control her body. Aware that I'm zoning out and becoming hard instead of focusing on the task at hand, I make my way up the steps, taking a mental note that she still won't look at me. Maybe it's not defiance I'm sensing, but more accurate, misery. Arranged marriages tend to have that effect.

"Nico—" Giuseppe starts, but I quickly interrupt him.

"You can call me Mr. Valiente." My bark is equally as ferocious as my bite.

"Then you may call me Mr. Notelli."

A sly grin takes over my face as he puffs out his chest in defense.

21

"Deflate that ego. You and I both know I won't be treated with anything but respect. Don't dare spit on my shoe, Giuseppe. This deal is at my mercy. Don't fuck it up." This gains Emelia's attention, and that's when our eyes lock. I take notice of her cut cheek, and my shoulders square.

"Giuseppe, is that a mark on my future wife's face just days before we are to be wed?" I step up to her, and she retreats when my hand extends to touch her cheek. Our eyes lock, her brown ones a stark contrast to my green ones.

"What's this on your face?" I grip her chin and tilt her head to fit directly in line with my gaze.

"If she gets a little out of line, a heavy hand will do the trick, like I told you on the phone," her father responds, and it's in a tone that stokes my rage—a simple statement as if repeating the weather.

Did he not heed my warning?

Emelia's eyes never waver from mine, and I see her own raging storm behind them, millions of secrets she holds—tales she could tell of how awful her father is to her or the horrors this house has seen. All of which could be used for my selfish agenda.

This provokes me. One thing I have always stood by, and most call it old fashioned, is you don't fuck with women who are members of the familia. I keep her chin in my hand, assessing the mark, from the thin laceration to the bruising around it, shades of yellow, purple, and blue.

My words finally come. "I do not care if you are her father. You see—arranged or not, she is going to be the wife of the most dangerous boss this country has ever seen, and you are not excluded from his wrath. It only builds the strike against you that I find myself having to repeat this, as you didn't hear me clearly the first time." I let go of her chin, not leaving my spot in front of her.

"Hit the queen of my outfit ever again, and you will see exactly why I'm so feared. Don't touch what is mine," I growl, my jaw tightening, then releasing repeatedly as I pull my gaze from my betrothed and adjust only my head to stare at her father.

Giuseppe tries to hide the gulp, but I've observed the fear of God in so many eyes that I know it when I see it. Turning my expensive pointed shoes, I step up to him.

"Lastly, don't ever tell me how to handle my wife. You must have grown impaired with your memory, since I told you this once before."

He nods, a gesture I didn't expect. Being a boss, you don't let others come into your home and bark demands or insults. I've done both in less than five minutes. But then again, I have too many people who will take my side in this war if he and I were to get into one. The man would be wise to politely break bread with me.

I glance back at Emelia, and I don't miss the way she looks at me, like I'm a damn mystery. To her, I'm a stranger. While I will not love or treat her like some treasure, I won't let others hurt her. If she is weak-looking or poorly represented, then that becomes a reflection on me.

"The arrangement hasn't started yet. You are showing a hefty amount of disrespect to the head of this house and this state." He attempts to sound bigger than his nod let on moments ago.

I put my hands in my pockets and lift my shoulders. I suspected after that moment of submission that he wouldn't say anything back. I will give him some points for finally standing tall in his own establishment. But I will always have more to say, in order to get the last word. Call it a character flaw that I have.

"Then we shall call it off and continue to build alliances against one another. Why not? I like a little fucking chaos."

He swallows thickly, his eyelids tightening, and I watch him hold back all the things he wants to say to me. All of which he knows I wouldn't tolerate.

"Honey, let's not square off. We're here to celebrate the joining of states. Please, let's not spoil dinner." His wife, Isabelle—a wise woman, clearly—steps in and pats his chest softly. With one more look of pure disdain, he turns and gestures for us to go inside.

"Future Mrs. Valiente, lead the way," I tell Emelia. When she continues to just eye me fiercely with so much focus and interest, I drop my chin and raise my brows.

"Oh yes, sorry. This way," she stammers, staggering a bit as she moves into place. She wears a white sundress, and it hugs her body nicely as her hips sway while she walks.

I'm not disappointed with the extra prize I get with this deal. I'm a red-blooded male. I am feral and like to fuck that way. She will break and mold for me. My own personal toy. One I can fuck whenever and however I want.

Emelia's hips—they're perfect and thick enough to grab, control, and help throw her around like a rag doll. Rough touches, heady fucking, with screams of pure ecstasy is how I like it.

The trick will be coming to terms with having a wife. Being tied down isn't for men like me. Yet, I don't think I will ever truly be tied down, even when I'm married. I could still have women on the side. Emelia is an arrangement, a way to bear an heir.

We both know the rules. She doesn't seem like a stupid woman who would think there will only ever be her for as long as my cock is still functioning. However, if she enjoys the way we fuck, I wouldn't complain having that body under me at all times of the fucking day.

As we walk, she peers at me over her shoulder, her brown orbs admiring me. And although I have no lack in confidence, I still appreciate it.

Stepping into the dining room, I see the table set with a feast meant for dozens of men. It is a typical Italian meal, with many types of pasta, wine, cheese, and cannoli.

"This spot is meant for you," Emelia speaks, and her voice is a raspy one. It's feminine but has this spice to it that makes her sound sensual. It will be fucking intoxicating coming from her lips when we're in the throes of passion.

"I expect you to sit next to me," I tell her as she moves more toward where her family sits across the table. She drops her head in submission and nods.

"Head up, Emelia. I won't have a wife who acts small amongst others."

Her head snaps up, and she glares at me.

There she is.

I know she's a firecracker waiting to be lit, to skyrocket into a spiral. To fly free from her confines and let whoever is in her way feel years of pent-up wrath.

She steps up to the seat next to me, and with attitude behind her movements, she sits and scoots in, loudly dragging the chair with her to emphasize her annoyance.

"Emelia. Enough!" her father hollers, and my fiancée's back seizes, her hands going to her lap and her head dropping once more.

Interesting.

This will be interesting.

Because I don't think I'll be able to handle this dinner until his mouth is full, as he chokes on the barrel of my fucking gun.

CHAPTER TWO

Emelia

I HATE MY FATHER. HATE THAT HE MAKES ME COWER and docile around others. Wanting for years to have a voice, freedom, and a place where I don't need to fight for respect and lose it so easily was a futile dream. I stand no chance.

But Nico, he makes me so angry, confused yet intrigued. It's a hot and cold type of behavior I can't decipher. One second, he is telling my father I am someone he needs to respect, then he's bossing me around. Basically, I'm to be respected by others but still treated like property by my husband-to-be. History repeats itself, and this is the most abhorrent part of it all.

We pray—the young women in this life—that we will be able to break free, but we're just passed on to another power-hungry man with no regard for us as humans. We are made to kneel at their feet, used to fuck like we are nothing but holes and have their children. All while we play the perfect submissive wife, turning blind eyes to so many different things, including their indiscretions with their mistresses.

I won't lie when I say it felt good and truly amazing to watch my father cower in front of another man. To feel just a small dose of what I do when he talks down to me. Nico is a good bit older than me at thirty-two, and he has experienced a lot of men infected with power trips, I'm sure. Himself included. Does he ever get annoyed by his own arrogance?

He's beautiful. That is the worst part. He must be 6'2" at least. His hair is midnight-black and trimmed nicely, showing a slight hint of gray just at the temples. His smile, the cocky one he showed earlier, is perfect and white. It almost makes him seem human and not at all the monster dressed up nice in an expensive suit.

How many men has he killed while wearing that suit and smile? Those broody green eyes—how many times have they watched life leave someone at his command?

More than hundreds, I'm sure. I did research. His father died when he was just nineteen.

He became a boss at nineteen.

This almost—not completely, but almost—has me feeling sorry for him. That's too young an age to take on such a responsibility. A life of crime, violence, and killing. No wonder he's hardened and callous—ruthless and cruel. That's what he is. Everything I learned about him led me to one conclusion.

I'm marrying a monster. An asshole. A man with no restraint. The most dangerous men in our history have been like this. And the women at their side? They have been the most miserable and misplaced women in all the world.

I hope I never have a daughter. Knowing part of this deal is to have a child makes me the sickest.

I've always wanted to be a mother, but to a child who wouldn't be born into blood so vile, with a man who loved me and who I loved. That was the fairy tale I believed in and never had a chance to have. I never made it out like very few women in our world did. No one ever came and saved me.

The only one who has, this one, is another man who wants to lock me up in a cage and pluck out the few feathers I have left. I'll be naked and bare soon, stripped to nothing but shame, misery, and captivity.

This is a fate I never want a daughter to have to suffer. Maybe I will be barren, and then I won't have to bring any children into this dreaded life.

"The reception will be here in our ballroom, proceeding the ceremony at the church. We have everything in place. Many made men are coming, and we want it to be perfect. The planner can show you everything." My mother's voice comes through my haze, and I bring my eyes up and look at her, then glance at Nico before landing on my plate.

"No need. I just want the guest list. I need to make note of everyone in attendance and make sure we aren't missing anyone," he says, taking a sip of his wine. I watch in my peripherals the way his jaw works and his throat bobs as he swallows.

"Sure thing. You don't want to know the colors? Theme? Anything?" my mother questions with a surprised tone as her voice moves across the table to where we are.

"No. You can tell my underboss, Giulio, this information, and I will make sure I have the things I need."

"The colors are white and soft gold," I whisper.

Nico turns toward me, his gaze hot where it lingers on the side of my face.

"Look at me when you speak, Emelia," he demands, and I want to slap him so hard in that moment for basically scolding me in front of my father. Do I not suffer enough humiliation because of that man?

Nico demands respect but lacks it when it comes to giving it to me.

"You demand such respect while also ordering me to hold my head high. Which is it? Where is yours, Nico Valiente?" I ask matter-of-factly, looking him directly in the eye.

"Emelia Rene Notelli!" my mother hollers as my father slams

his fist down.

"Damn you, child. Watch your mouth," he yells.

Nico lifts two fingers to my father and mother, never taking his eyes off me.

"Both. But you have to *earn* my respect. It won't be given freely like everyone else will have to because of your upcoming title. Show me you are worthy of me."

I scoff. "Worthy of you? You're a mafia king—a boss and a terrible man who does awful, wicked things. It is *you* who needs to earn mine." I stand and scoot the chair back, throwing down the cloth napkin as I go.

"Excuse me while I go off and learn to be an obedient wife." I take off and run out the door, listening to my father call after me and the guards to follow me.

But I didn't miss the way Nico looked—impressed by my response, yet angry and filled with the compelling need to subdue me.

If I'm going down, I'll do so swinging. I just wanted love.

I wanted what I had with *him*.

God... what I had with *him*.

"Damian," I whisper his name as I fall to the ground and cry, now far enough from the house to feel alone but still surrounded by bars. Trapped.

I was in love once. With a man who promised to save me. The first man to love me, to protect me, to touch me with a gentle hand. Damian. One of my father's guards. He was assigned to watch me when I turned nineteen, and we fell fast and hard.

It was reckless, dangerous, but beautiful. He promised me an out. A way out of this world, a way to have the world I always wanted, with a man who wanted to protect, love, and cherish me.

Then he left. Like a thief in the night, he was gone, taking my heart, my innocence, and every bit of hope with him.

When I asked why I was assigned new security, my father said

Damian was offered a new job. I didn't believe it for one moment. Though no one knew about us, I think Damian ran off scared. That is the only thing that makes sense, knowing that if we were caught and tried to escape, he and I would be good as dead.

I feel him then, his touch, the whispers in my ear, the touches of passion and love in middle of the night. And it *was* love. At least he made it feel that way. Suddenly, that feeling is replaced with a chill up my spine when I feel someone behind me.

"Emelia. Stand. Now," Nico says in a deep baritone, a quiet but powerful demand.

I wipe at my tears, refusing to let him see me mourning the most intimate loss I ever experienced. Standing, I right my dress, lift my chin, and square my shoulders. I turn, and he towers over me.

"What?" I sniff, doing a terrible job at hiding my emotions.

"I don't want this either. Trust me. Marriage was the last thing on my agenda. But you have to learn to control these emotions you're having." He gestures at me up and down, and I feel the heat on my neck rising.

"These emotions? The ones where I despise you just as much as my father, you mean?"

He eyes me over. "You've known your destiny for long enough. I would have expected you to come to terms with it by now. We will get married in two days, and you will smile at that wedding. You will not show any disrespect toward me. We won't become targets just because you can't handle yourself."

Just like that, I snap. I reach out and slap him so hard my hand burns. His head turns, but he doesn't move it back. Nico stays looking to the left, his jaw tightening, and I brace myself for the impact from his retaliation. The slap was worth it. I hate this man.

"You ever lay your hands on your future husband like that again, and I will smack your ass so red you won't sit right for weeks. Get your shit together. Are we clear?" He finally looks at me, and

I gulp. The image of me over his knee and receiving painful slaps comes rushing in, and I want to slap him again.

"Whatever you say, *husband*." The emphasis makes him smile at me evilly.

"Good. Now, back inside."

We look at each other one more time, and it's the start of a war between husband and wife. What a world, what a life this will be. I finally move and make a mental note to never forget the hatred I feel in this moment for this man.

WEDDING DAY

I LOOK MYSELF OVER IN THE MIRROR. MY HAIR IS STYLED in a slicked back bun that falls just above the nape of my neck. My eyelids are a smokey color, and my lips are stained a glossy red. I look like a stranger.

My dress, though I wish I was wearing it for someone I want to walk down the aisle to, is beautiful. It's a mermaid gown, all silk with a lace overlay, off-the-shoulder with a sweetheart neckline, and the sleeves match the lace, connected by a thin piece of fabric under my armpit. The lace goes all the way down my arms and ends over the back of my hand in a point with a piece of elastic around my middle finger.

My brown eyes look large, and they're filled with sadness. I don't want to do this. I don't. I look down at my white satin heels, and a tear falls.

"Shit," I say under my breath.

Damian should be here. It should have been him. I hate him in this very moment for breaking all those whispered promises made in the meadow, the lies given against my skin as he kissed away the bruises my father left me.

"You can't be crying. You will ruin your makeup, and if your father sees that, he will be very angry, Emelia. Please, let's not set him off today. All types of men from other outfits are here, and we don't need the scene. Can you just marry Nico with a smile on your face?" My mother enters the room like a mouse—quiet yet a disgusting creature you don't want to come near you. If I could, I would jump on a table and scream as I try to get away from her.

"Yes, Mother. I will go out there with a smile on my face and pretend everything is okay," I tell her with the least bit of pleasure.

"Good. It's time. Your father is waiting at the chapel doors. Let's go." With one last look in the mirror, fixing my makeup with the tissue my mother gave me, I turn and make my way toward my new life. A life I already existed in but may just end up being ten times worse. Tomorrow morning, I will fly to Seattle with a stranger I was forced to marry just so my father can get intel and take down Valiente.

Meeting my father at the doors, he takes my arm but says nothing. No "you look beautiful" or "I'm so proud of you." I get absolutely nothing that a bride would normally hear from a doting dad. He takes my arm, stands tall, and the doors slowly open. Everyone stands, and all the men are dressed head to toe in all black, as if it's a funeral.

And isn't it?

It's the death of the last bit of freedom I had. I know none of these men but do know there are a lot of murderers in the pews of my wedding ceremony. What an eerie thing to think of. I smile politely like I've been trained to do, and when my eyes finally meet Nico's, his face is stone-cold.

Neither of us wants to do this. Difference is, he will still get to live his life the way he sees fit, and there will most likely be other women, ones he could fall for. Where I will never be able to even talk to others without his permission. How 1940s of the mafia.

Making it to the altar, my father lifts my veil, grabs my shoulders with force, and leans in to kiss my cheek. To onlookers, it must seem sweet, but they don't hear what he whispers.

"Obey and know your place, Emelia. Get the job done." With that, he hands me off, one devil to the next.

I see Damian in my head then, smiling at me, whispering to me how beautiful I look. That's not the case with Nico, but never did I think it would be, nor want it to be. But the image of Damian being the one standing across from me makes this bearable.

Besides, Nico will be dead soon. I must remember this is a job, and one day I will be a made woman alone and won't have to answer to anyone. I'll take my money and live in a house by myself with a couple of dogs and my own emotional scars, drowning in my trauma from the life I was born into.

Nico takes my hand, and I must admit this gesture shocks me. I didn't expect him to touch me at all. When the pastor begins to talk, I look from him to Nico and see he's intensely staring at me. His jaw tight, his eyes focused on me, it's more than intimidating.

Why does he look like he wants to have my head?

I'm behaving, aren't I?

I almost roll my eyes at the idea.

"I do," he says, then it's my turn.

I make my promises to obey and cherish my husband, and it's like signing my own death warrant. "I do."

We lean in and kiss, and it's brief but telling. His lips are soft, full, and if I were interested in him, I would say I like the feel of them against mine. There is power, control, and experience, and I can tell all that from the simple peck. If he ever kisses me deeper, I can only imagine what that would be like.

I push that image to the back of my head.

This isn't love. No. This is a transaction, and I'm the product. The church pews fill with cheers, whistles, and applause, but inside, I am petrified. This has to be a nightmare I will wake up from and not be trapped in anymore. It just has to be.

The birdseeds are thrown, the applause is loud, and handshakes continue for Nico as we make our way out of the chapel and into the limo. Once inside, it's as if the noise is turned off, and we're in a cone of silence. The lack of ruckus is eerie. Nico sits on the opposite side of the bench as he checks his phone and avoids any contact with me. God, this really is the saddest, most pitiful wedding day.

His phone rings, and he answers it. "Yes. Is my jet ready?"

The person on the other end says something, but I can't make it out. It's quiet inside here, but his volume isn't high enough to make out their response.

"Good. Emelia and I will be leaving right after the reception. I have business I need to tend to."

I gulp. We'll be leaving for Seattle tonight? Why does this seem so jarring? It's not like there's anything here that makes me want to stay. This place is hell's armpit.

"See you then." He ends the call, and we continue to sit in silence.

Finally, I can't take it anymore, and I speak. "We have to present the sheets." I inwardly cringe, disgusted by the ancient tradition of proving the marriage has been consummated. But I'm more afraid to tell him what I'm about to.

"I'm aware. We will do that before the flight. We don't need to wait until morning."

I shiver. I'm not ready to make love—well, be fucked by Nico. Especially when I have to tell him I'm not a virgin. How will he react? Is he going to break off the deal? That is one thing men in the mafia expect of their wives—to be pure and virginal.

"Nico, I have to tell you something."

"What?" he asks, not looking up from his phone, because he can't be bothered to stop answering messages. Maybe if I just say it while he's distracted, he won't be too upset.

"I'm not a virgin," I blurt out, and I immediately realize I was wrong.

This sure as hell gets his attention. His jaw clenches, and he wraps his fist so tightly around the phone I'm convinced it's going to dissolve.

Shit.

"Who?" he asks, and I shake my head, confused by his question.

"Who what?"

"What was the name of the man who felt he had a right to my wife?" There is a sharp edge to his voice. It's dangerous, and it even has me shivering with fear. He sounds murderous.

Most likely because he is, Emelia, I scold myself.

"No. I'm not telling you that. It's between him and me. The one I should have married." My remark was meant to be snide, and I know it's one that could really set him off. Father did forewarn me and made it abundantly clear what his thoughts were on sharing. That he doesn't like it.

"Really?" He turns his head slowly, glaring holes into my soul, and it's filling me with anxiousness. "You will tell me in time who it is, Emelia, and if I'm feeling forgiving, I might just let him walk around with only a broken knee cap. If it's a good day, that is." He clicks a number in his phone and demands someone "bring the kit" with them.

What in the hell is the kit?

I gulp. Watching him make threats and hearing them leave his mouth in regard to Damian makes me petrified. I shouldn't have said the second comment, maybe just left it as "I slept with someone random and don't remember or know their name," but I had to go and run my mouth. Drive the point home, didn't I? Great.

"Also, I want you to do a full workup of anyone who has been in my bride's life in the past... let's say seven years." He looks over at me, and my jaw drops.

"You prick. What does it matter that I had someone before this marriage? You don't care about me, so why is it a problem?" I raise my voice, appalled by his behavior.

"I don't know what your father told you, seeing as he may be one of the most useless men in the entire mafia familia, but I don't need threats. I don't need surprises showing up. And lastly, I don't like sharing. I don't have to give a fuck about you in order to not want people touching you."

"You will not treat me like this. You will not treat me like I am some piece of property. I've done that my entire life. You're jealous of my past, while I'm sure you have a list much longer than mine. You stay away from Damian!" I slap my hand over my mouth, and he gives me a sideways smirk, tsking at me.

"Oh, principessa, your rage is so uncontrolled. Poor man may not be able to walk tomorrow. Or breathe. We shall see."

My blood runs cold."I hate you, and I will make this marriage something you dread. You think the world fears you? That you have all this intimidation and power? You haven't seen anything. I will be your match, and you will regret ever saying yes to this arrangement. You arrogant son of a bitch."

I throw open the door as we pull up to my house for the reception. I round the back of the limo and make my way up the stairs, passing his underboss, Giulio. I don't even say a thing to him, trying to get as far away from the man I'm now wedded to. Before I open the door, my arm is yanked back, and my front is turned and slammed into a hard wall of muscle. *My husband.*

His eyes bore into me, his face stoic yet filled with unmistakable rage. The veins in his neck and his forehead protrude.

"You will never talk to me like that again. Do not play games with me, Emelia. I will not tolerate it. If you want to *attempt* to have some type of enjoyment or freedom in your new life, you will treat me with more respect," he grits out through his teeth. "Now, put on the act and let's get through this goddamn reception."

Angry tears well in my eyes, the ones you get when you are overly furious but can't do anything. I'm not sad. Or afraid. I'm mad. Raging. Fuming with pure hatred.

"How romantic. Why don't you *attempt* to look like you can be a decent fucking human?" I give it right back.

"Gah, fuck!" he hollers, turning and punching the frame of the entryway. "Enough, Emelia. This is your life now! Stop acting like a child and fulfill your responsibilities!"

So stupid of me to even get upset. My responsibilities, yes. His demise. Soon, I will never have to look this man in the eyes if I just do the job I dreaded at first.

My demeanor changes, and I know he thinks it's all him, but really, it's me. All me. The holder of his fate. "Lead the way, *husband*," I say snidely, and he runs his hand through his hair, then rights his tuxedo jacket.

"Good. Let's go. I don't have to be the enemy here, Emelia. If you obey and respect me, I can do the same. So stop making me angry any chance you get. We can work together. You can be the queen, or you can be the downfall of your own narrative. You decide."

He takes my hand, and I let his words resonate. If I want him to let me in on all the things I need to know, I do need to start playing the part. And now, if I want to keep Damian safe, I will have to be the doting, submissive wife.

It's temporary. This will only be temporary, I remind myself as I plaster on a fake smile and make my way into the ballroom.

Everyone stands and welcomes us, and I skim over the guests before stopping dead in my tracks.

Damian.

He sits at a table toward the head of the room.

No. He can't be here. How could he come to this after leaving me behind?

He looks just as handsome as I remember. Now thirty, he looks no different than the twenty-seven-year-old who was head-over-heels for me. Who I loved in return.

Who abandoned me.

I grasp impulsively onto Nico, and he looks down at me.

"What is it?" he asks, sounding annoyed.

"Nothing. I just got a cramp in my leg. That's all," I lie.

He stops and then drops to his haunches, and I gulp.

"What are you doing?" I ask, gasping when he lifts my dress a bit and rubs my leg.

"Putting on a show. We have to convince the masses, Emelia." He takes his calloused hands and runs them up my legs, gaining hoots and whistles from the made men all over the room.

I look over to Damian and see how angry his expression is. He tightens his fists at his sides, and I decide the best way to pay him back for leaving me is to lean in to the show. Put on an act that he will feel in his heart for years to come.

It's only fair.

I loved him, and I wouldn't be here if he would have fulfilled his promise of getting me out. Regardless of how much I miss him, it doesn't mean anything when I'm now married to a man I hate. This is just as much his fault as anyone else's.

Looking down at Nico, I bite my lip and laugh as his strong, thick, vein-lined hands run up my leg, and when he reaches my thigh, he wraps his finger around my garter and pulls it down. He licks his lips, and if I weren't aware of the act he's putting on, I would say he's enjoying this. And something in the way he looks at me and smiles...? I hate that the arousal between my legs builds, and a dull ache forms.

Shit. No. I can't let his charm and looks get in the way of what he really is. A terrible man.

Standing, he tosses the garter into the crowds of men at the tables. I peek over at Damian, and he shakes his head at me.

That's when my chin is grabbed.

"You invited him to our wedding? Not a smart move, wife." Nico leans in and kisses me. It's not like the altar kiss, no. This one has a purpose. He bruises my lips, bites and nips, and I let our tongues slide against one another. He tastes like toothpaste and a new flavor I've never tasted before. Him. *His* flavor—and it pains me to admit—tastes like lust and desire, and I give into it. But he puts an abrupt stop to our kiss, and I lose my footing a bit, nearly stumbling forward.

"I don't think he'll need his kneecaps broken. Watching him watch you take me so well just might do. The idea that I will—and believe me, I will—fuck you so damn good that he'll never be able to compare might be better than ordering his death. Lifelong suffering sounds like the best fucking revenge."

He grips my chin again. "Don't you *ever* bring him into our lives again."

He leaves me then and lets me greet one side of the room as he works the other. I stumble to it, in shock over what just happened. In fact, it takes me nearly three tables before my equilibrium returns.

When I get to Damian's table, I look over at Nico, and he watches me over the edge of a whiskey glass from where he's chatting with a few men. His eyes are intense, and of course my body decides to play horny little bitch and be terrified but aroused. I'm in the lion's den, and I'm afraid of what that means.

"How could you let him kiss you like that?" Damian asks, his eyes searching mine.

"Because you left me behind."

His question is upsetting. How dare he have the audacity to ask me this, as if I still belong to him? He abandoned me. He walked away without a goodbye. He broke all our promises. Now, he wants to ask me how I could let another man—my husband, might I add—kiss me like that?

"I had no choice. I knew your father was going to find out. It was either leave or die. I'm here; I came back for you. I will get you out of this marriage. I'll save you now."

Each time he speaks, it only offends me more.

Truly? Now? When it's too late? How dare he do this to me right now!

I would slap him, but if I did that, Nico would be over here so fast, and I would have caused a scene. One thing I have learned— do not cause a scene in a room filled with the mafia. Blood will always be shed.

"If you know what is wise, you will walk away. Nico is dangerous, and he knows about you now. Just leave." With those last words, I walk away and head to the front of the ballroom, where the bride and groom's seats are, and take my place.

I'm getting a headache from the stress of this day, the tight, slicked-back bun in my hair, and the mess of my ex being here and Nico putting on the show of a lifetime. I'm tired. Exhausted, actually, and ready to go to sleep. Can this event just be over? I never wanted this day, and now I am fucking drowning in it.

"What did he say to you?" Nico joins me, the music and the talking from partygoers giving us some privacy.

"Nothing. He just said hello and that he wanted to see me on my special day," I lie through my teeth.

"Sure. I will get the real answer out of you. We aren't staying here long. I let your father know we'll present the sheets and will be leaving." I gulp, not over the fact that I don't want to have sex with him, but from not having the slightest idea how we will fake my nonexistent virginity being taken.

"Don't worry. I have no plans to touch you. I have some deals I want to complete before we start for a child. And I'll take care of the sheets. Just let me handle it." He leans in when the photographer starts to approach us, and he kisses my neck, before whispering in my ear, "If you lied to me and he has plans to fuck with what now belongs to me, you will both pay. In different—*much* different— ways."

A chill runs up my spine.

Will he kill me?

Would he do that to me?

"Nico," I whisper. "Please don't hurt me. That's all I ask in this marriage, that you not lay a hand on me in anger. My body and soul can't handle much more." I show him an ounce of vulnerability, and I hate it, but the exhaustion, the shock and awe of Damian, and the show Nico is putting on are all fighting against the hidden independent woman who just wants... to breathe.

I excuse myself to go to the restroom before he can say anything back to me. I need a minute, and I should touch up my makeup before my mother has an aneurysm.

I can feel Nico and Damian's eyes on me the whole time I make my way through the ballroom until I head up the stairs. Making it to my bedroom, I see my suitcases on the bed, and I take a moment to look around the room. I take everything in and consume the first moment of quiet time I've had today.

"Baby." Damian's voice fills the room, and I turn, my breath catching as I do.

"Damian, you need to leave. Nico will not be okay with you being in here. He will kill you." My words rush out, terrified to be alone with him in this room, in a house filled with dangerous men.

"No, he won't. He doesn't love you. He would thank me for taking you off his hands."

"No, that's not the case. He doesn't love me. He hates me, but he is a very possessive, jealous man. If he knows someone else is after what belongs to him, it will lead to bloodshed. I'm not a human to him. I'm just a piece of property. Please, go, and do *not* contact me. Not now. Let me reach out when it's safe."

"Brave man, aren't you?" Nico steps into the room, one hand in his pocket as the other one shuts the door. He's cool, calm, and collected. More dangerous than any other emotions in this world, if you ask me.

"Nico, he was just leaving."

"Tsk, tsk. See, wife? You told me there was nothing to worry about, yet I found you alone with an ex-lover on our wedding night." He pauses, coming to stand in front of me, stopping within inches of my shaking, unsteady frame.

"Nico...," I whisper, when he moves his unbuttoned tux jacket to the side and shows me his gun in its back harness.

"When will it be safe to call him, Emelia?" It's a rhetorical yet terrifying question. "Because we made a deal. He stays away, we have no problem. But this man has the nerve to disrespect a boss on his fucking wedding day and be alone in a room with his bride. The room said boss plans to fuck you senseless in." He turns and faces Damian, and I think on my toes.

Think quick; it's all I have.

Men like Nico, they like submission and being praised like gods.

"Nico, I don't want him. I married you. You are my husband, and I will obey anything you ask me to," I tell him as I reach out and ever so slightly touch his shoulder. It's taut, tense. "Please, just let him go, and I will never speak about him again. And if he dares to reach out to me, I will tell you. I will not hide secrets from you. Please, my boss. My husband. As your wife, please respect this one thing I ask of you," I plead.

No matter how angry I am at Damian, I loved... *love* him. And I don't want to see him dead because of me.

"Leave the room. Now. You come near what's mine again, and I will watch the life drain from you. I *never* grant fucking mercy," he growls. "Run."

The threat is so imminent even I feel it, and without one look at me, Damian leaves, and I release a deep breath as tears threaten to fall.

The intensity within that moment was far too much for me to take.

"You think I'm stupid. I know that was all an act. But clearly you value his life more than I will allow. You won't play me. You understand?" he asks, gripping my chin in his hand.

"It was nothing. I told him to leave. He wouldn't listen." I glare up at him. "Besides, I don't have to explain my life to you. I put on the 'bride smitten by the mafia king' act. Now get your hands off me." I push away his arm, and I move, but he is on me faster than I can make it out of the room. Slamming the door shut next to my head, he closes me in. My breath catches, and beads of sweat form as he cages me with his entire body.

"On the bed, now," he demands, and I snap my head to the side and see I'm within inches of his. So close I can smell the whiskey.

"No, I'm not having sex with you. You can't—"

"We aren't having sex. I'm going to teach you obedience and what happens when you don't take my threats seriously. As if they're empty." He gesture slightly in the air around him.

"You can't treat me like a fucking dog. I will make your life hell, Nico."

Grabbing my upper arm with enough force to get my attention, he moves us to the bed. I sit, and he stands back, removing his jacket, his holster, then slowly unbuttoning his shirt. Each button reveals tight, smooth skin that I hate to admit is attractive. Not just attractive, but truly erotic. He looks like a god among men.

There are some marks on his chest, and the more he exposes, I can see each ab, oblique, and muscle in all their glorious definition. Removing his crisp-white shirt completely, he towers over me, looking down on me. Reaching into his pocket, he pulls out a knife, and suddenly I'm not looking at his body. I focus on the blade shining in his hand.

Is he going to hurt me?

What is he going to do with that blade?

"I-I'm sorry. I won't do it again. Please don't hurt me." I hate that he's instilling fear in me. A stranger. The scariest stranger. The man I hate but am married to now. The fact of the matter is, I'm at his mercy.

"I may have no respect for most men and will kill for even a wrong look, but I will not hurt you. Real men don't stoop low enough to hurt women."

Lifting his left arm, he takes the blade and begins to drag it along the taut bicep.

"What the hell are you doing!" I try to stand, but he growls at me.

"I told you to stay away from him. I don't have to love you, Emelia, to own you. You belong to me now. You think this is crazy? You don't want to see what will happen if you talk to him again." Moving the knife away, he wipes off the blood, and that's when I see he carved an E into his arm. I'm stunned silent, shocked, and truly disturbed. He moves to the bed, throws back the comforter, and wipes the blood on the sheet.

That's when it hits me.

That's how he's going to present the sheets.

Relief floods me, even though I just watched a sociopath carve my initial into his skin.

Why?

How can someone look at ownership so animalistically?

I have nothing to offer. I'm not someone he knows. Definitely not someone he loves. Why are mafia men so beyond the definition of psychotic?

I gulp when he pulls out some sort of kit from his dress pants. Opening it, he pulls out a band-aid and covers up the wound.

"There. Now we can present the sheets, have our first dance, and leave. I will be having your *ex-lover* removed from our wedding," he emphasizes, and I implore more.

"He doesn't deserve to be killed. You have me as your wife. There is no out for me, and I know what my fate would be if I were ever to cheat. I was raised by a made man. I know the rules. No other men." He buttons up his shirt, tucks it in, and puts his holster back on. Sliding on his perfectly fitted tux jacket, he rights the lapels and buttons it. I jolt a bit when he reaches around me and grabs my hair in its bun, pulling tightly. It stings, and I cry out in pain.

"Nico, that hurts. What the hell?" I push him hard, but he doesn't move.

"Stop!" he hollers, and I go rigid. He starts to mess with my hair, then lets my curls fall free, and I'm completely taken aback when he takes his thumb and drags it against my red lips. This makes my lipstick smear, I'm sure, and that's when it hits me. He's making me look like he just fucked me. This animal. My miniscule sense of dignity is stripped from me.

"Good. Now remember, just like you said, you're my wife now." Taking out his phone, I assume he calls Giulio, and I stay stunned into silence over the scene that just played out.

The knife.

My initial.

The blood.

The mussing me up.

He's thought of everything.

"The sheets are ready. Bring in the men." He helps me stand, the shock still penetrating me.

What is happening?

Just what den did I get locked in?

I married the villain, or the real-life beast of every fairy tale.

"You need to cling to me, look pleased. They need to believe we fucked."

His crass words sting me. I jolt when the door opens, and I cling to him like he ordered, placing my hand on his hard abs. He places his hand on the back of my neck, kneading the knots that have started forming from stress and exhaustion. This helps me lean into him more, at least. Damn the sensations, and damn them for feeling nice. He brings his lips to my forehead, and I watch my father step in, as well as some of his men and Giulio. They look at the sheet, then to us.

My face grows red, as if I really did have sex. How humiliating this tradition is. It's dehumanizing and vile.

Nico kisses my temple, moving his hands all over my neck for the sole purpose of adding to the act. But I won't lie—it feels so. Damn. Good.

"Well done. We will meet you down there for the final dance and send-off." My father nods curtly before he leaves, with all the men in tow.

Giulio and Nico share a knowing look, and then he's gone. The second they are out of sight, Nico is off me.

"You do what you need to do to come out there and look like a happy, pleased wife, so we can have our dance and leave. I have business tomorrow, and Seattle is a long flight away. Try not to be too damn long." He slides out the door so effortlessly you would think he vanished into thin air.

Turning, I take a look at my reflection in the mirror.

"You got this. Infiltrate his life. Get the information. And bring him down. Then you will be free," I remind myself over and over, repeating it what feels like a million times.

Finally, I am able to pull myself together and fix my hair and makeup before leaving the room. Giulio meets me down the hall and stops me.

"Your bags are all packed. I will take them to the car. Mr. Valiente will have other necessary items bought and placed in your new home when you get to Seattle."

"Oh, okay. Thank you, Giulio." There is a kindness to this man, and I truly believe he hides it well, but I know he has it in him. There is something in his eyes. A way about him that makes me feel bad that he has to harden himself to keep his cruel boss pleased.

Maybe he's like me, born into a life we both never wanted?

Who knows. I guess we will see soon enough.

CHAPTER THREE

Nico

WE DANCE TOGETHER, AND SHE SLIPS IN AN OCCASIONAL smile, masking her hatred for me well. An actress. I've learned some things about her so far that just might work in my favor, if I can just keep her on the right side of my preferences.

Emelia drives me mad—truly and utterly mad. How can she be so quick to talk back, have a backbone with me, but then the second I show authority, she backs down? It's maddening. I can't tell when she will be hotheaded or docile. If I can't break her into being exactly one thing, this is going to be one of my hardest jobs yet. And that's saying a lot, given my line of business. I want her to have a backbone, but not to use it *against* me. I want her respect. That's it. Yet she defies me any chance she gets.

Taking her hand once the dance is over, I lead her out of the ballroom and straight to the waiting car. Her parents give her a pitiful half hug, her brother Sal and Lorenzo as well, but there is no emotion from them for her departure. It's as if they couldn't wait to send her off.

I don't miss the way that hurts her either. The longing she has for her parents to just love her is prevalent and evident.

We don't talk in the car while we make our way to the airport that is less than thirty minutes away. If I don't leave the ground soon, I will miss important meetings. I plan to have a honeymoon later, since our marriage took place during many big deals to complete.

If I'm being truthful, a honeymoon isn't really needed. Honeymoons are for lovers, not arranged marriages between two people who couldn't care less about being in one another's company.

We get to the tarmac and rush up the steps and into the plane. The last thirty minutes are rushed, so I can be in the air on time.

Emelia takes time to look around the plane, taking in the dark mahogany wood accents and the cream-colored seats. There is a door to the back room, and I point it out to her. "Your bags are in there. Feel free to change. It's a long flight."

Moving, I grab the decanter of whiskey and pour it into a tumbler.

Once again, she leaves, swaying her hips and showing me the temptation of her round, luscious ass. I have to fight the urge to go back there and just fuck her out of my system.

She returns twenty minutes later, wearing leggings, an oversized shirt, and some long socks. Her hair is down and falls in loose curls, tossed to one side. I admire her the same way I did when she was dolled up in her wedding dress. She can make anything look good.

Siren.

Not saying a word, she sits next to me, brings her knees to her chest, and leans her head against the window.

"I have one request," she finally speaks after ten minutes.

"What is that, Emelia?"

"When we do decide to have children, whatever whores you're with need to be put on hold. And you need to be checked. I won't be put at risk just because you can't be a faithful husband."

There she is, the more headstrong woman I've caught glimpses

50

of. Unafraid to call me on my shit. The one that drives me up the wall with something I can't place.

But it's a feeling I think I like.

"I can do that."

She looks hurt at my answer.

"What?" I question, intertwining my fingers and placing my hands in my lap.

"Nothing. Just glad we can agree." She keeps her eyes fixated on the window.

"Tell me what you were thinking, Emelia."

Shaking her head, she looks over at me, her eyes boring holes into mine."I never thought I would marry a man who I not only hate, but fear *and* have to share. It's horrible, and I hate that I have to be a captive in your home, alone, knowing every night you are going to be out with other women. But if I dare talk to a man I once loved and who loved me, I am threatened." She scoffs. "Men. Made men. You're all the same, and you're the downfall of *real* men." With that, she stands and leaves me there.

Her insult still lingers in the air.

The downfall of real men?

I debate going after her, but I'm tired of arguing with my new bride. This is her life now, and the sooner she pouts, then comes to terms with it, the better off she will be.

"Emelia, we're here." I stand over her sleeping form on the bed in the back room. She slowly stirs and looks around the room as she sits up. Finally, her eyes meet mine, and she rubs the sleep from them.

"What time is it?" Scooting to the end of the mattress, she stretches, and I watch her intently. I can't fucking help but watch her, fascinated by the way she just simply exists.

"Six in the morning. I need to move fast. I have an eight a.m. meeting, and it's an hour drive to my penthouse."

She nods, moving without a response. I leave her to it and

head to the front of the plane. If I didn't get out of there, I would just watch her like a fucking madman, and that wouldn't do us any good. I'm just horny, and she has all the things needed to satiate that. That's it. It has to be.

I don't know if I'm trying to convince myself or bargain with myself. Either way, I go in search of a distraction.

"Giulio, when she gets settled, I want you to make a list of anything Emelia may need and have it ordered and delivered. Also, I want her tracker placed. Call the doctor."

"Sir, I want to let you know that I mean no disrespect, but maybe you should talk to her first. This is a lot for her as well, and if you want her to respect you—"

I cut him off. "I appreciate you as my right-hand man, Giulio, but I will handle my woman how I see fit. Now, make sure she has everything she needs. I don't care about the price. If she needs it, get it. Make her as comfortable as she can be."

This comes out of nowhere.

She doesn't need more than the basics, but there has to be some give and take if I want to gain her trust, so she can give me what I need.

I need a woman in charge. Being a mafia wife is a scary title to hold. They are constant targets, and in order to keep her safe, we have to have a solid relationship. And with how things are going, we have a long way to go. But most importantly, if I want to take down her father, I can't do it without her on my side.

"Ready," she announces, stepping out with her many bags in her hands.

"Giulio, bags," I bark.

"I've got them. It's no big deal." She shrugs, and I shoot her a look.

"Giulio, get her bags. I don't want her carrying anything down the steep stairs." He grabs some, and I reach out and take two. She rolls her eyes but lets us have this victory. She must be just as tired as I am of fighting.

I lead the way. Giulio lets her go next, and he follows right after her. Loading up the car, I round the trunk and open the door for her to slide in. I take the driver seat, and Giulio takes the passenger. He and I make small talk, being sure to leave out any information too sensitive that she has no business knowing. I will not talk shop in front of Emelia, not while we are still enemies and at each other's throat, playing a childish game of tit for tat.

The drive back to my penthouse located in downtown Seattle is silent on her end. She doesn't say a damn word. Maybe a clearing of her throat or a hushed yawn, but other than that, she is as quiet as if her presence were nonexistent. Makes me more curious to know if she is channeling her rage and preparing to hit me with it the second we're alone in my fortress. Pulling into my spot in the parking garage, I peer at her through the rear-view mirror. She looks at me briefly, then back out the window.

"This is it then?" she whispers.

"Is this what, Emelia?" I ask her, my voice heavily laced in annoyance. I really don't have the patience to deal with a bratty wife.

"Your place. I don't need pity, Nico. I'm not a damsel." She pauses, opening the door, and before she gets out, she halts, purposely making eye contact with me in the mirror. "As far as I'm concerned, this will be a step up from where I was. Especially if you follow your promise and I follow mine. I just expected the place to be bigger." She shrugs, and my eyes narrow at her trivial remark.

Like I said, it is a back-and-forth game with her of who can hit with a lower blow.

A sly, confidence-boosting grin splays across her face. "For a man so powerful and strong, it seems... underwhelming." She gets out and slams the door, and I grit my teeth. I so badly want to get out of this car, spank her, and place my hands around that thin, gorgeous neck, subdue her.

"Giulio," I bark.

"Yes, sir." He stops his movements at the back of the car where he is getting her luggage.

"Take her up. I need to be at the club. Meet me there once she's settled." My meeting will take place there, and I know if I go upstairs with her and she says one more wrong thing to me, I just may do something she won't be able to handle.

"Yes, sir," he repeats.

"What club?" she asks, coming to stand next to Giulio.

Oh, this will be gold. Cat-and-mouse games no longer. I'm the fucking monster, and she is the beauty.

"The sex club I own. I have to test out some of the new merchandise."

Giulio shuts the back of the SUV, and I don't miss the way she looks both angry and dare I say hurt by me throwing that in her face. She bared her weakness to me, and if she wants to attempt to play the puppeteer when she's under my command, then I will take anything that can break her and use it at my will. I will exploit her insecurities. I will not be made a fool in my own home and, more importantly, in my outfit.

I run Seattle.

It fears me, and so will she.

The women dance and put on a show, while I survey the rest of the club from above. The meeting I had is finished, and I plan to have the rest of my day here in my upstairs office before my next meeting.

"Nico, baby." A low rasp pulls me from my own thoughts. I see Kelara, the woman I hired a month back, stepped into my office without a sound. I have spent far too much time with her these past few weeks, and now she has grown overly clingy, like flies to fucking honey.

Staying on guard, I keep my hands in my pockets and look her over. She's naked, head to toe, not a scrap of fabric on her. Her skin is slightly flushed, telling me she must have just finished with a client. Kelara's hair is a dark-brown, and her eyes are the shade of honey, highlighting her intentions clearly. Approaching me, she touches my shoulder, and I glare down at her.

"What do you need? If this is business related, you can speak to Giulio." Coldly, I start shutting her down. I'm not a changed man. I'm not doing this because I have a gorgeous wife at home who I love, but I don't want to put my cock where my business is, when there is a lot at stake with this new arrangement.

I already fucked her one too many times, and look at how she's behaving. The way she waltzed into my office like she had some sort of right to me. If word were to spread that I'm sleeping around, then Emelia may get wind, and that could lead to not only a war in the marriage that has already been hinted at, but also between our now blended families. One day, I will satisfy my needs, but not when I'm only one day into marriage.

I'm not a dumb man. That's for immature boys who can't control their urges.

"You." She slinks to me, and I push her away with just enough force to jolt her backward. "What was that?" she asks, seeming affronted.

"Nothing. I'm not interested in this at all. If I want you, I will pay for it," I insult. She felt it, and her jaw tics, but it's really in her eyes, and if they could slice me down the center, they would.

"You're an ass." Moving to grab her, I'm stopped by Giulio's interruption.

"Sir. The Irish are here."

Wanting to tell her to never disrespect me again, I fight against it, because I don't have the time. Kelara is lucky my second meeting showed up early. I roll out my shoulders and my neck, tugging on the lapels of my suit jacket at the same time, trying to get my head level again and gain back my focus.

"You need this job. I will make you kiss my shoes and then

kick you out on the street if you ever disrespect me in here again," I threaten her, because it's all I have time for. And she knows it.

Cowering under my harsh tone, she drops her head and whispers, "Yes, Dante."

"Mr. Valiente. You address me as Mr. Valiente." I leave her with that.

Moments later, she is out of my sight, and Giulio and I make our way down the hall to the conference room.

"How did Emelia react to her new detail?" I ask.

I hired two men to look after her, for both safety reasons and also the glaring fact that I can't trust her yet. There are two in the penthouse for the times that I am unable to be there—which will be a lot. I felt two was being generous to her, seeing as I *wanted* to put two more outside. But there is building security, and I decided to cut her some slack.

"She wasn't..." He pauses, and I stop and look him directly in the eyes, urging him to go on with just the lift of my brows. "Pleased. We will be replacing some of the dishware. Let's just say some plates were thrown."

This gets my blood boiling, and I can't just sit here and let her get away with being so irrational. Defiant little shit. Grabbing my phone, I select her number and press Call.

"Oh, my dearest husband, to what do I owe this wonderful pleasure?" The word "pleasure" holds such disdain, and I mimic it.

"You little brat. Do you have to turn everything into a fucking show?"

She laughs. "Aw, were the plates your best friends? Do they talk to you and keep you company? Is your little heart as broken as they are?"

"You're getting on my last nerve. If you want to act like a fucking child, I will treat you as such. Do not keep fucking with me. You want a war, principessa, I can give it to you."

"Good. I have years of pent-up rage from bullshit handed to

me by men like you that I am looking to unload, and you're the perfect candidate."

Looking at Giulio, I glare. He steps into the room and gives me a minute out in the hall.

"You either play the part, or I will call your father, and we can call off this deal. I can make the arrangements, and I will start building alliances against one another once again. You want that, wife?" I enunciate the last word, making sure she feels that shit in her goddamn chest. Even though that is the last thing I want to do, because it could get in the way of my pre-made plans, I still use it as a threat. Because I know she hates her family more than she could ever hate me.

Emelia may feel close to that type of hatred, but I haven't hit that peak yet.

"If it means it would be your downfall, then I wouldn't give a care in the world. Also, I just want you to know—it's only him. It will always be *him*. I'll never stop loving Damian."

This statement. This enrages me. What the fuck did she just say to me? To make such bold announcements. Does she think she even has a chance to be with him again? We'll see how much she wants him ones I flay his skin from his very bones.

"You have no idea what I'm capable of. Hold tight, Emelia. This has only just begun." I end the call, making sure I have the last word.

The rest of the evening dragged on, meetings, business deals, and another fucking letdown. I had to handle a man myself, leaving him with more fingers cut off than attached.

That's what I do when you steal from me. You'd think everyone would learn after hearing the horror stories on the street about what happens when you take from me. But this just goes to show, you must reinstate force and give reminders of your power. You have to re-terrify those who have forgotten just what you are capable of.

What's worse? I thought about her all damn day. Grew angrier with each passing second. She makes me want to bend her over my knee and spank her into submission. But with her, I can't. Why? I fear I would like it. But that would be my red-blooded male desire—not love. And I don't need her ever feeling like this could be love.

Did her mentioning Damian nearly make me call to have him taken out? Yes. But I don't need her thinking it mattered to me that much or that her words hold any power over me. Because they don't.

He doesn't have any chance of getting into her life. I would shut that down before he ever got the opportunity to do such a thing.

By the time I'm home, it is nearing midnight. Stepping inside, I smell the dinner I had my chef make and leave in the oven for me, but I see not one broken dish. However, I do see the empty-as-all-fuck cupboards and more.

My staff had to place an order for new dishes, and that embarrasses me. *No one* embarrasses me. Preparing to turn on my heels and finally unleash my wrath on this maddening brat, I'm stopped by her presence in the doorway. She leans against it in barely-there lingerie.

I do all I can to not choke on my own tongue. Her breasts are full, her pink nipples peeking through the white fabric. Her pussy is shaved, those lips begging to be stretched and brutalized by my thick, long, and angry-looking cock.

I may hate her. Loathe her. Even want to wrap my hands around her throat both in the throes of passion and in an act of rage, but I am a man, and she is all woman. A goddamn sexual creature sculpted by the gods. She will never know I think that though. I refuse to let her know.

"Welcome home, *husband*," she hisses out the title.

"You're a spoiled fucking brat, and I won't let you act like that in my home."

She saunters toward me with a sly smirk plastered on her face. "Don't you mean *our* home? You married me, made me move here, filled the closet with clothes I didn't want. Stocked the bathroom with items you knew I'd need. Wouldn't this be our home, husband dearest?"

My hands clench at my sides, because I want to rip her apart. I want to take each inch of her and redden her skin with spankings, bites, lashes from my whips.

"This is your home, but I have a staff. A staff who had to pick up after you and order new items. I pegged you for a defiant woman, but an entitled asshole with no regards for others—that, I didn't think you would be."

There is something that changes in her eyes. She looks as though she may feel some sort of guilt. She doesn't have a soft spot for me, but my staff seems to matter, because she's filled with instant, obvious regret.

"You have men here watching me. I don't need your henchmen breathing down my neck and reporting everything to you."

"So, you dressed like a whore after breaking my things and disrupting my staff... for what? Some cock?"

Once again, I am met with a sharp slap, the sting lingering as my face stays turned to the side.

"I wore this for myself. Make no mistake, Nico Dante Valiente. I will never do anything for anyone but myself again. I married you to escape my father, not to become someone else's doormat." She steps up to me, and I slowly turn my head back to its original place and bore holes into her eyes with mine. I match her flames with just as much fuel. "You talked about war, and I will gladly bring it to your doorstep. Don't ever call me a whore again." She leaves, a gust of wind in her wake.

"Goddammit, Emelia!" I holler, my skin crawling and heating instantly.

"Fuck you, Nico!"

I'm on her in an instant. Grabbing her elbow, I spin her fast, and her expression matches mine, two lions facing off.

"You will respect me. And tomorrow, *wife*," I mock her back, "you will be getting a tracker put in you, and if you fight that or pull a stunt like today, I won't stop at that. You belong to me now."

I expect her to fight, but to my surprise, she doesn't. Instead, she yanks her arm from me, and she leaves. I make no mistake though. I saw the indignation in her eyes.

She may have walked away from me today, but tomorrow, she will put up a fight. I will have to deal with that then. I already have a war to fight with the world outside these doors. I don't need to worry about the war in my home until the problems arise, and I know this vixen will have many she plans to bring to the table.

My phone rings as I move back toward the kitchen to find my dinner. I take it out of my pocket, my appetite suddenly lost. "What?" I holler into the mouthpiece.

"Sorry, sir. There been an incident at the club. One of the girls was attacked, and two of our guards were gunned down."

"Fuck." I'm already fucking agitated, and now I have to go to the club and handle business. No rest for the wicked, and no sleep for the reaper. "On my way." I end the call, ready to make my next one.

Knowing Emelia's security are in the apartment just a few floors down, I call for them to come back up here. Next, I call for my car to be pulled around outside, and without another word, I leave. I don't miss Emelia watching me from her place on the couch as I go. She doesn't need to know where I'm going, and I don't plan to start telling her now.

I call Giulio, knowing he's the one most likely holding the gunmen captive if they were caught, as my driver gets me there as fast as possible.

"Did you get the men?" I ask, looking out at the Seattle nightlife.

"One. The other two got away. We have ears and eyes out for them now."

"Good. I want them now, or someone is going to pay. Someone always pays when they fuck with me, Giulio."

"Yes. Sure thing, sir. I will give them to you as soon as I can. Until then, I have the one waiting here. The main perpetrator."

"Good. My gun. Get it from my desk." I have a preferred weapon when I dole out punishment. It's the most efficient kind. And rest assured, I enjoy the hunger being fed by the punishments. Their flesh taking abuse, retribution for whatever wrong made against me, my outfit, or anyone in the familia.

Most shudder in the face of violence, but I lean into it, relishing it. And tonight, I will unleash my wrath, make them pay for their wrongdoing, and—the cherry on top—release the anger I'm holding against my brat of a wife.

They will be sorry.

CHAPTER FOUR

Emelia

FORGET A WOMAN SCORNED. HELL HATH NO FURY LIKE a mafia wife. Nico made the color red seem too dull for what I saw. He made me so angry my vision filled with an inferno of flames. I'm failing my parents terribly, and in brief moments, I remember that. But it's shot straight to shit when what's supposed to be my teammate in the ring does something so wrong I want to gouge out his eyes with the tips of my well-manicured nails.

When his two henchmen showed up, I felt a pit grow inside me, which quickly filled with bitterness toward Nico.

That bitterness morphed from a thunderstorm to a full-blown tornado spiraling all around me. I grabbed every damn plate, cup, or any glass thing I could find, and I brought it down like a hurricane. My storm circled, collected anything in its path, and Nico's things were the casualties in the calamity. Up until he got home and reminded me that others had to clean up my mess and not him, I felt a sense of retribution. For years, I was punished and told I needed to stay silent. Breaking free from those confines gave me a sense of false courage, but yet again, I was reminded that I am in a cage. It's just a different man holding the key.

When he left tonight, I knew where he was going. He thinks only he knows things about me. Joke's on him. I know who he is, what he does for business. I overheard my father talking about that club he runs. Or more accurate, the women he runs. What a typical sick, sadistic man, exploiting women for money. Doesn't he have enough from his reign as a mafia boss? From the drugs and guns and other things he sells?

No. He's so greedy he has to also sell women to old, disgusting, desperate men.

There was still a pain in my stomach though, and I won't lie about that. I don't love him, but knowing he is with other women... hurts. I know his life and all the vile, criminal things he does, but I thought if he could do one good thing and one good thing only, it would be the act of being a faithful husband.

I'm standing at the floor-to-ceiling glass windows, when the elevator suddenly opens behind me, and I see in the reflection the two men who had me riled up in the first place. I roll my eyes and turn.

"Did your daddy send you here, boys?"

They don't say anything, ignoring my snide remark as they step out and take their places on the left and right sides of the elevator. They both stand so stoic, almost rehearsed, and it's even more annoying. I decide then I will call it a night. I'm tired. I hate to admit it, but fuck me, I am just so freaking tired. I've spent the past few days fighting a battle that I will undoubtedly lose, and I just can't anymore. Even I need to rest. Regain the strength to refocus my priorities.

"Goodnight, daddy's boys." I flip them off as I walk past, and I feel the eyes of one of them on me. Suddenly, it makes my skin crawl. I'm aware I'm wearing nothing but lingerie, but I know one thing—henchmen don't look at their bosses' wives unless they have no will to live.

Rushing now, I hurry to the bedroom and slam the door. I

help myself to one of Nico's large shirts and lock the door before crawling into bed. My phone rings, and I see it's my father. Rolling my eyes, I know I need to answer this time. Ignoring him for a third time today will only rouse his obnoxious, overbearing personality more.

"Yes?"

"You think you're just going to ignore me, Emelia?" The demands start already. The berating and harassment. Even on opposite ends of the country, he still tries to control me.

"I've been here for twenty-four hours, Dad. You expect me to have a rundown of his entire operation already? You're comical."

My father can't hit me, and I cling to that and talk freely.

"You little bitch. You watch your goddamn mouth."

I roll my eyes, knowing he can't see it and punish me for it.

"I'm not his keeper. For a boss, you seem—" I pause. "—misguided."

"You better remember who you're speaking to, Emelia."

I knew that would elicit that response. I want to get under his skin and make him angry. Knowing he can't touch me from his place all those miles away adds so much fire under me that I run with it. It's years of anger, of torture—of malice and regret for never sticking up for myself—rearing her beautiful head.

"And you remember this. I am now the one in charge of what happens. You reap what you sow." I end the call, feeling empowered. I don't know what was in the air on the flight here, or the switching of times zones, or hell, even in the water, but there's a side of me that stayed so deeply buried now peeking through that I can't help but push her out, pulling her from inside me, and unleash her to the cruel world that used to drown her with its misery.

I do all but toss my phone across the room. Feeling this overwhelming surge of retribution, I smile, dragging my tongue across my teeth.

My phone chimes, interrupting me from my moment of glory,

and I see his name.

Damian.

Opening the text, my eyes dance along each line.

DAMIAN

> I miss you. I shouldn't have let someone else come in and claim what I should have kept all to myself.

Tears. I feel tears welling in my eyes. I still hate him for leaving, but I crave his affection. The only man who made me feel loved and adored. Sexual and the beautiful kind of love, the one that only happens once in a lifetime.

I debate what to say. How do I tell him I hate him but need him again? That living with a husband who will never love me makes me want to claw my way out of my own flesh to erase the life I was born and sworn into?

EMELIA

> You don't get to tell me these things. Not now. And IF you valued your life, you would leave me alone.

As much as I want to lean on him and feel that connection again, I can't. I shouldn't.

Should I?

DAMIAN

> I value what we had, and I want it.
> Your father told me what your plan is.
> I will come back for you, Emelia.

EMELIA

> You're working with him? Tell me you're not.

DAMIAN

> Leave that to me. You just hold on, princess. I'm coming for you.

Suddenly, I err on the side of caution.

EMELIA

Nico is the worst man there is, and you have no idea
what you stand to lose. You think you and my father
can just come in with a mediocre plan and have Nico
killed? Well, you can't, and you're going to be the
only ones in body bags. I have to go. Do yourself
a favor and stay far away from me and anything
that has to do with the downfall of Nico Valiente.

DAMIAN

You know I was never good at listening.

Talk to you soon, my love.

I grip the phone. Flashbacks of him inside me, telling me I was his love, come flooding in, pulling me under like a riptide. Damian knows what he's doing, and I'm just supposed to sit here and pretend it's not happening? Why would I ever do that? As much as he hurt me, I still love him, and I don't want him mixed up in my father's plan.

Infiltrate Nico's life, find out all I can, get to his Achilles' heel, and end him. We're all at risk, and I don't think I have it in me for Damian to be included in that risk because of me. The more people brought into this, the more casualties there will be. I grew up with soulless and heartless people, but those are tracks I've never followed in, nor do I intend to in the future.

I crawl into bed, one I will most likely be alone in all night.

There's no need to be jealous, but aren't we all by nature? Knowing that we don't love each other is fine. Marrying for love or with the intent to fall in love wasn't part of this plan, but still, couldn't he be faithful? This will most likely be a loveless marriage like my parents have, but why can't he give me the courtesy of monogamy?

Stupid girl, you've known for years men in this life see no reason for any of that.

So why do I suddenly want Nico to be that way with me?

"Doesn't matter anyway. He will most likely be dead in weeks," I say to the empty room. Until then, I will get in his head, cut the underbelly of the beast, and handle what needs to be done.

The bed dips, causing me to stir from my sleep. When I open my eyes, the room is mostly dark, but the city lights illuminate the surrounding walls. He smells like shower gel. It's a scent I have to admit is appealing. Staying as still as possible, I wait for him to settle in and fall asleep.

"We have a ball next week. You are being fitted for a dress tomorrow. Be up and ready by nine a.m."

So, I wasn't sly enough.

"How did you know I was awake?" I ask, my voice a bit above a whisper.

"Your breathing changed."

I nod, and it's silent for a while. But my headspace is suddenly filled with curiosity again.

"The club you own. You said it's a sex club?"

Nico is smart. Arrogant and blatantly cocky, but he is smart.

"I do. Why?"

I shrug, that ping happening in my gut again. There is no way I will let him make me feel like I'm not good enough to have a faithful husband. No. No way in fucking hell.

"Curious. That's all."

He releases a deep sigh. "Emelia. You drive me up the fucking wall. In fact, I have the thought to call off this deal every second you act like you did earlier. But... I am not fucking any other woman."

There is a sudden ease that comes over me, and I would physically kick my own ass if I could for being relieved.

Relieved, but not ignorant.

"You don't have to be such a prick. I didn't want to marry you either. I would rather be physically tortured than deal with you." I scoot closer to the edge of the bed.

"Coming home to you is going to be a fucking delight every night, isn't it?"

I debate what to say. Finally, I release a big sigh. "I will wave the white flag now. What good will it do if we're just constantly at each other's throat?"

"Good. It would do nothing but make this that much more unbearable. Go to bed, Emelia."

"Don't you think we should talk? Get to know one another a bit?"

"What do you want to know?" He blows out a breath as he moves a bit.

I make sure to keep my back turned to him. It feels safe. Keeps the vulnerability at a minimum. "Do you have any hobbies? Other than sex clubs, weapons, drugs, and murder."

This has a small laugh leaving him, and I smile at the sound. It's warm, his laugh. It's the deep kind, the one that comes from low in the chest.

"You think that's all I do?"

"Isn't it? Tell me the last time you did something morally ethical in your day-to-day?"

He doesn't speak for a moment.

"Fair. But being moral doesn't really fit in with my lifestyle. Or maybe I find what I do very ethical to my own morals."

Rolling my eyes, I scoff. "That is such a mafia response. Hiding behind that wall of yours seems very lonely. You should think about lowering it. Get some hobbies. Oh! Maybe even some friends," I tease.

"I have friends, Emelia."

"Henchmen aren't friends; they're employees." I can practically feel the eye roll he probably just gave me.

"No one needs friends. Especially when they have a wife like you. I'm too busy just trying to cope and live with you. There is no room for more."

This has me turning toward him. "That's rude. You have no idea who I am or what I'm like. I could be the most interesting person you've ever met."

"Or the most stubborn." He looks at me, and I see his position now, the city lights helping my eyes adjust to the darkness. He looks comfortable, relaxed, and his body... wow. He is shirtless, the sheet pulled up to just beneath his belly button. The flesh exposed is taught and defined with some scarring and, surprisingly, only a few tattoos.

"Stubborn, or just the only person who won't put up with your shit attitude?" Taking my focus off him, I get back to my original topic.

"I don't have an attitude, Emelia. I have authority. Don't mistake it."

"Okay, stubborn, or thinks your authority needs to be knocked down a few pegs?"

Dishing it right back, he smirks. We aren't fighting, and the banter is something I don't think he would ever have with anyone else.

Aren't I the lucky one?

Not.

"I don't need friends. You are stubborn. And I feel morally sound. Anything else?" He changes course.

Pursing my lips and thinking hard, I decide to keep harping on him, but I change the question.

"Well, Nico, thank you for asking about me. I'm Emelia. I like to read. Sometimes, I like nature—if it doesn't bite me. And I love ice skating," I admit.

"Ice skating? Why that?"

"Don't sound so shocked. It's ice skating. You kill people for a living. I think you take the trophy for shock factor, my friend."

"I'm just curious. Why skating?"

"Because it makes me feel like I'm..." I think about this.

What's the best way to describe freedom to a man who has never had to worry about it his entire life. The ice is the only place I ever thrived—the only safety net I could fall into when I needed someone to catch me. "Free," I come out with it. Sugar-coating it seems pointless and, quite frankly, unnecessary.

"Free. You feel free on the ice?"

I nod, adjusting so my head is atop my stacked hands.

He waits a beat or two before asking,"Does it keep you in good spirits? Is it a place for you to blow off... steam?"

"Yes. I grew up with an abusive father and a mother who called me fat every chance she got. I held a lot of resentment for those people," I admit.

"When did he start hitting you?"

I watch a shift in his eyes. They don't sparkle like they did from the city lights. It's as if they darkened, and he's suddenly no longer human.

"Um, sorry. Uh...." His demeanor has thrown me off. I can feel the tension and anger radiating off him.

"When did the abuse start, Emelia?" His repeated question is far more intense this time.

"I was eight when he first slapped me. I was playing with the neighborhood kids, and when the streetlights came on, I didn't come home right away. This earned me my first-ever punishment." I gulp, and I swear it echoes around entire room.

"How often did they abuse you? Mentally, emotionally, physically, all of it."

"Daily. If it wasn't a slap, it was an insult. If it wasn't an insult, it was the silent treatment. Everything always accompanied by ignorance."

"Ignorance?" he questions, and this time, I turn to lay flat on my back and peer up at the ceiling.

"My brothers are just as bad as my parents. They failed to protect me, acted as if the abuse was no big deal. In fact, they acted like it never happened at all. They were ignorant." Every bit of my hatred is evident in each strewn together word.

"Cowards. Men and women who abuse their family, they are cowards," Nico says, and I look at him.

"Does that mean you *really* don't plan to ever hit me or verbally abuse me?" I question—a small amount of vulnerability peeking through.

"No, even though you are the most difficult, complicated pain in my ass. And it hasn't even been a week."

I try to hide my smile. This man sees criminals, perpetrators, enemies, and more every day, and I won the title as his biggest complication. Good. Victory is slowly becoming mine.

"Maybe one day you'll figure out how to deserve my less hostile side," I add.

"Most women submit. You're not like most women."

"That's an insult. All women are powerful and strong. We just get bulldozed by men with too much power, who think we are too much or too little. So when you think about it, men are the root of all things wrong with the world."

This leaves the room eerily silent, but my mind is filled with pride. This got me in trouble a lot, but it never completely stifled the woman who knew and wanted to roar.

"You're going to make me go mad one day. Sleep now. Tomorrow is a big day."

I remember him telling me about the dress fitting, and I think, *That? That's not much of a big day.* But I stay silent.

We left off on a high note.

So maybe he will slowly learn after all.

"That son of a bitch!"

He didn't learn a damn thing. I slap away the doctor's arm, and I go to stand.

"Farren," I call one of the men hired to watch over me.

"Yes, ma'am?" he answers, stepping up to my fuming form.

"Get that bastard on the phone." He doesn't need me to elaborate.

"Yes, ma'am." And within thirty seconds, I'm yelling into the cell.

"You're a piece of work. I am not...I repeat, and hear me loud and clear, Nico Dante—I am *not* getting a goddamn tracker implanted in my arm so you can keep tabs on me!"

Yes, he had the nerve to send a doctor over after the fitting to casually slip in and tell me he was inserting a tracker into my arm. My *arm*. Through my actual goddamn skin!

"Emelia. This is not up for debate. Sit the hell down and let the man put in your tracker," he barks back, but I jut out my chest more, ready to fight this one until one of us folds. And when I say one of us, I mean him.

"No." It's slow, low, and drawn out. I want Nico to feel how mad I am. How annoyed and disgusted he has made me.

"You are a weapon now. A pawn in my world. And as much as you and I don't see eye-to-eye, I need to make sure you are safe. Everyone and anyone can be after you at any given time, Emelia, and God forbid the day it happens and you don't have me!" He matches my tone from earlier. Shouting into the phone, he makes me jump a bit. Bastard.

All eyes are on me in the room, and I've never felt more embarrassed than I do right now. He humiliated me, springing this on me and allowing others to do his dirty work. And I vow to make sure the payback is just as good.

"Emelia?" he barks, and I jump again.

His reasoning finally sinks in, and I can understand it. I just wish he would've explained it to me first instead of sending some stranger in to confront me with it.

"Yes, Nico. I'll get the tracker." I drop my head like a child who has just been disciplined. But I make a promise that my revenge will be so much sweeter, and everyone here witnessing my embarrassment will witness his.

"Goddammit," he rushes out. "I have a serious matter at the club to attend to. No more interruptions unless it's an emergency." With that, he ends the call.

I place the phone down, closing the few steps between the doctor and me, and I hold out my arm.

"Do it," I growl, and I await the burn, the pain, the betrayal, and the revenge.

Later that night, I'm sitting in the bedroom, dressed in an all-black silk gown. It hugs my curves, the softness of my stomach, and the roundness of my hips. The bodice is a short corset, holding my chest up high, and it's see-through with the exception of the black cups. My blonde hair is wavy, in a vintage style collected on one side, cascading down my shoulder. My makeup is a classic smokey eye but more blown out, with my lips painted fire-engine red, a matte color that compliments my skin tone. My black Louboutin's are covered in crystals and have a strap that reminds me of a snake, wrapping around my ankles and going a few inches up my calves.

"You ready?" Nico walks in, and I peer up, doing my best to not let him see just how mad I still am from what happened earlier. If he sees even an ounce of it, he just might spot a hint of my planned revenge.

"Yes."

He wears a three-piece suit, looking stoic, and once again, I'm reminded of how annoyingly handsome he is. There is no denying Nico is attractive. Not even a little bit.

"You look lovely, Emelia. Now, stand. I have something I would like you to wear."

I do as he says, hesitant as to what he has planned, but stand nonetheless.

"These pearls were my mother's. I expect you to wear them at any event or ball we attend."

He's giving me his mother's pearls? That seems like too intimate of a thing to just give me.

"Token of ownership, I suppose," I mumble under my breath, and he catches my jaw between his hands and forces me to look up at him. His eyes pierce mine with ferocity.

"You have to get your shit in order, Emelia. We talked about our white flag, and today you've seemed to do nothing but stomp on it. We are a united front, and my tracker may have pissed you off, but it's truly for your protection. You should be thanking me for thinking of your safety."

I scoff, crossing my arms and taking a step back.

"Again, I'm not a damsel, Nico. I saved myself by marrying you and getting out of the monster's lair. And what, you want praise for doing psychotic things and offering the bare minimum outside of that? Your mother's pearls are supposed to make me swoon or something?"

Placing his hands in his pockets, he cocks his head to the side and looks me over. A strange expression passes over his face, and I can't quite pin what it means, but it flashes so quickly it's like it didn't even happen.

"That's exactly what I expect. Think you can manage a simple task, wife?"

"Call me Emelia. Wife implies love or, hell, even just an ounce of respect, dignity, and self-identity, which you have stripped away." I push past him, and he grabs my elbow. His touch is hot, and it sends an electric bolt through me.

"You will be on your best behavior tonight, Emelia. You will."

Oh, I will—over-the-top will. Will painstakingly be a thorn in his ass.

"Yes, Nico. I *will* be," I emphasize and then yank back my arm, storming off before he can say another word.

We ride the elevator down in silence, and I feel the thick tension in the air. But he must feel it too, because he is fuming, his aggravation felt from here, as if he were shaking and boiling to a tipping point. Stepping out onto the street, we are about to slip into the car, when shots ring out. The sound is so piercing I can't help but scream and cover my ears.

"Giulio! Cover! Farren, get Emelia inside! Now!" I try to look back at the scene, but I'm practically overtaken by my bodyguard and rushed into the building. We make it to the elevator, and I hear Nico ask, "Is she shot? Is my wife shot!" That's when I spot the trail of blood that followed behind us.

"No, sir, it's me. It's just a flesh wound on my arm," Farren confirms, and I look at Nico, seeing a flash in his eyes that I can't place, but he looks somewhat...relieved.

And the way he yelled out, asking if I—his wife—was shot? It held so much fear, protectiveness, and more. It was palpable. The doors shut, my sight of Nico cut off, and the elevator rises.

"Are you okay, Farren?" I ask, turning to check on him. My throat is tight, and my adrenaline is seizing the blood in my veins, but I feel awful he took a bullet while protecting me.

Suddenly, I feel terrified and alone, scared of what is going to happen next. Who attacked us? It wouldn't be my father; he wouldn't risk me getting shot...would he?

"Yes, I'm doing just fine. Not my first time. Are you all right, Mrs. Valiente?" he inquires, and I nod.

"Um... yeah, sure. And please... Emelia. Call me Emelia," I tell him in a whisper.

Would my father really try so soon and so brazenly to shoot my husband with me in the crossfire?

No. He couldn't. I refuse to believe it. I have to.

The next thirty minutes pass in a blur. I start to worry about Nico and Giulio. Are they okay? What happened? Do they know? I have some of Farren's blood on me, and I want a shower, then take something to knock me out. My adrenaline won't settle, and the spike in anxiety is making it impossible to calm myself down. I think about showering, but something in me can't get past waiting until someone comes in here and tells me what is happening.

"I don't care what it was or who. I want them dead. Whoever that was made one of my men bleed, and they nearly got Emelia. I will have their blood and flesh for payment!" Nico yells into the phone as he steps off the elevator. His shirt is covered in red. Blood. His blood? Giulio's? My heart lurches, but then I see Giulio step out, and I'm instantly relieved.

"Nico. What happened? Who did this?" I am up and on him in just a few strides. I'm assessing his body and trying to see if it's his blood or someone else's.

"We were attacked, Emelia. Someone is out for us."

I swallow back the guilt and knowledge that I already knew there was no peace. Also knowing who it is who wants to see Nico's reign end the most.

"Oh my hell, Nico, you were shot!" I see the bullet wound on his left bicep, and I reach down, grab the bottom hem of my dress, and rip. I fold the cloth up and add pressure. Turning my head, I tell Giulio to call the doctor, the same man who placed my tracker implant.

"Yes, Mrs. Valiente."

I don't correct him as I focus on Nico's bleeding arm.

"I don't need you tending to me. I have been hurt worse than this before," he tells me, and it comes out more as a fact than something condescending or disrespectful.

"I get that, but I know how to keep you from bleeding out, so just let me help. But it serves you right after tracking me like an animal." I use my earlier anger without an ounce of shame.

"Fine. Giulio, send Dr. Fontelo into our room." He nods toward our bedroom, and we walk there as I keep pressure on the bleeding wound. I will need more cloth, as it's already soaking through the fabric of my dress. I tug him toward the bathroom, and I search for towels or anything else I can find.

"Right side, second drawer down," Nico tells me as if he reads my mind.

Hurrying, I grab the washcloths and rush back, grabbing his arm once again.

"Nico, they got you good. We might need to take you to the hospital." Saying this earns me a scoff.

"I'm fine, Emelia. Seriously, I've had worse. Dr. Fontelo will be able to remove the bullet and stitch me up just fine."

"Stubborn," I grumble.

"Pain in the ass," he retorts.

We lock eyes then, and I see that look again. "What?"

"They came after what was mine, Emelia. I told you I don't take kindly to it."

I gulp. "I know people coming after your men must be hard, but doesn't that happen often?" How can he be this upset or shocked that people came after his outfit? He and his guards must be shot at on occasion.

"No. They came after *you*. They tried to touch what they know is off limits," he says through gritted teeth, and I feel like I just got whiplash.

"What does that matter, Nico? If I get hit? Your pain in the ass would be handled, and you wouldn't have to deal with me." I change the cloth again. I seriously think he may bleed out if the doctor doesn't hurry his ass up. "You and I both know this is only an arrangement."

"Business deal or not, you are my wife, and I won't let them attack you. You are not up for fucking grabs. No woman in the outfit should be, especially not mine."

I almost say something, but he's quick to speak again.

"I want you home. You are not allowed to leave here unless you're with me. We will leave in a few days for the honeymoon, while my men investigate the shooting."

"Okay." I'm still fixated on the statement he made moments ago. And the fact that Nico is trying to act so unfazed by his feelings. My safety means something to him, so *I* have to mean something to him. Right?

Oh God, I have no idea why I'm even entertaining this idea right now.

"Good."

We don't speak for a while after that. I'm thankful for this, because if I'm being truly honest, I don't want this to be anything other than a simple conversation. I don't want to read into it, and I'm sure he doesn't either. This is all really messy and overly confusing.

What have the last couple of days of my life been—a cruel fucking joke?

Is someone just out to see me shake and cringe, while I simultaneously become a victim of the hot and cold tension between Nico and me?

My life has never been less than chaotic, but this is a whole new level of crazy. I'm a different person now with a whole new life. Will I ever get to experience "normal"? When will I be able to ice skate, read books, bake, and just exist like a normal person, instead of being controlled by power-hungry men and dodging bullets in a high-crime world?

Oh yeah.

Never.

"You think you know who it could be?" I finally ask, hoping it's not my father's name he spits out.

What would that mean for me, if he found out about my father and me?

Death. He would kill me... end me for sure. I just know it.

"Chicago, maybe. Last we heard, there were some insiders who turned against their boss. Maybe they wanted to prove dominance, and seeing as they were the last once before New York who we made peace with, maybe they picked us."

I inwardly sigh in relief. Nico isn't onto us yet. That's all I need to breathe a little easier.

So why does this make me feel guilty? I'm the middle man in this battle, and I'm doing all the dirty work—well, supposed to be.

That's why. Aren't I just as evil for being a spy against my new husband? To know, with just the right insight, I will end this man and his entire outfit?

I can feel the blood on my hands suddenly. It's ironic and cynical at the same time. I'm patching his wounds, my hands literally covered in his blood in this moment, when soon, his death, his undoing, will be because of me. His blood will then stain my hands for the rest of my life.

And just as suddenly, I realize... I can't do this. No matter how much I hate Nico, I can't be like my father. I *never* want to be.

But how will I escape that? Should I stay with Nico and let my father kill me, or betray Nico and have him killed? Either way, death happens, and I have to make a choice on who is more important.

Nico or me?

CHAPTER FIVE

Nico

IT HAS TO BE CHICAGO. THEY WERE THE LAST ONES WE made peace with, and knowing they had insiders turn bad, it just makes sense. I demanded Giulio to investigate it.

They got away before we could catch them, so the only thing we can do is lie low and be stealthy with our movements. For now, I'm sitting in my bedroom being stitched up by Dr. Fontelo and going over every detail I can remember from the shootout. But the only thing I can seem to recall is Emelia. Seeing her in the crossfire of whatever war some unknown force is waging on me.

I look to where Emelia sits in her ripped and bloody silk dress, the material not hiding any part of her curves, softness, or weight that I salivate over. She is the bane of my existence, yet all I could think about was her safety. Even after she pissed me off when I gave her the pearls.

My mother's pearls.

Emelia doesn't know that was a meaningful gesture in response to her saying she was waving the white flag. I was stupid to think she really would, and the realization she lied was solidified when she didn't say thank you for giving her such a gift.

My mother was a fucking saint, and I handed her most precious jewelry over to someone who couldn't care less. What was I thinking? I'm a fucking idiot for letting her have something that was once so special to my mom, and one of the only items of hers that I kept. I'm a fucking fool, and I slapped that label on all by myself. When Emelia brushed off my gift, I wanted to yank the pearls from her neck, but that would have broken the prized possession, and I couldn't do that to my mother.

Looking at Emelia shouldn't be something I want to do right now, but I can't fucking help it. I'm drawn to her lustfully. I crave her and want to have her, all while I hate that she's even in the same room as me. My mind tells me to throw her to the wolves, but my body is telling me to feed her to the beast inside me.

She's a temptress, and I think she knows that. I see the way she admires me the same way I admire her assets, yet we do nothing about it. Because then she and I might start to believe this means something more than lust.

But I need it. That craving. That addiction I keep at bay. The hunger that never seems to be completely fed, and if I didn't just say my vows, I would be fucking the endless options at my club. One every night, or multiples every day. I have an... insatiable need that has to at least attempt to be met, or the world I run can become far harder for everyone under my reign. I don't do well with so much pent-up need.

"You are good to go. Take the antibiotic so it doesn't get infected, okay?" the good doctor tells me, and I agree with a nod. Taking the pills, I open the bottle, dump two in my hand, and throw them back with a dry swallow. I eye Emelia while he packs up and she just stares back, her eyes wide with wonderment, and that is my snapping point.

There isn't room in my head to play out the logistics of what this means or how we will navigate. I can't fight the urge to have Emelia anymore. I just can't. That thirst in her eyes and the way she licks her lips while watching me is all I need to seal the deal.

"Doc. I need you out. Now." Fuck it. We are married, and I need to have her. To subdue her in some way. I can't seem to do it outside the bedroom, so maybe I can *inside* it. I need to fuck Emelia, or I just might cut off my own damn cock and hand it to her on a platter. That's what her sassy attitude and fucking challenging ways are doing to me.

And the body.

Fuck me, the body on her. She's not like the women I've had before. No, Emelia is gifted with a roundness I crave to fucking destroy. I want to grab the extra skin, lick the marks, and bite that damn cellulite. Because they are exactly what my palette wants.

Hating her doesn't hurt either.

Yes, I want to hate-fuck my wife. Want to show her what it's like to get in bed with a dangerous man who has needs that seem to be insatiable and rarely close to being met.

"Yes. I will be on my way."

As he leaves, I notice the way her breathing increases, and I can see her swallow past the thickness in her throat. I can smell her arousal, practically fucking taste it.She wants all this too.

Did I luck out and marry a woman who might actually meet my desires?

I could have lost her tonight. Before I ever got to taste her. Before I could have gotten to know if there was more to her than a woman with a need to drive me mad.

That's all this is.

The way I'm feeling—there is no love. Not even an ounce. But there is lust. A very annoying hankering for her. The second I hear our bedroom door close, I stand, and she does too, our bodies moving of their own accord. We are riled up and aroused, and tonight, I will really make her my wife.

"Nico...." She trails off as her legs rub together.

"You have been getting under my skin. Driving me so goddamn

mad with the way you test me. But I think it's time you learn just what this does to me. Your lack of respecting me has taken my lust to its highest peak, Emelia."

She gulps and slowly backs up as I take slow, measured steps toward her.

"I still hate you," she admits, and my sly grin widens, showing her my teeth.

"I don't have to love you to fuck you. We can hate each other all we want, but that just makes the sex better."

"I hate you," she repeats, but this is more of a promise, a declaration, a threat. The kind she wants to say repeatedly until it makes me snap and take her like a wild animal.

"I fucking hate you too, Emelia." And with that, we collide, and I do mean *collide*. Our bodies slam together, and our lips connect. A mess of tongues, teeth, lips, and breath. Sucking and fucking one another's mouth doesn't even come close to explaining what this kiss is like.

"Oh God," she moans into my mouth when I easily pick her up. I've always kept my physique in top form, so carrying her and controlling her body will be fucking effortless. She needs a real man who can do things only real men can. Take every inch of that gorgeous body and ravish it like the five-course meal it is.

"You don't mind the weight?" she questions, wrapping her legs around my waist as I carry her to the bed.

"No, principessa, I fucking welcome it. And tonight, you're going to let me mark it, bite the places where it dips and curves. You're going to let me fuck this body made by the gods."

Emelia doesn't seem like the type to have ever let her body bother her. And that confidence is a bonus for me.

"Do whatever you want. Just make me feel good. Please."

"Such a good girl. So fucking damaged. You need me, little mess, don't you? Need this cock?"

"Fuck, yes," she cries, grinding against me. I will learn something tonight, and that's if Emelia likes to be controlled in the bedroom.

"Then lie on the bed, open your slutty legs, and offer me your cunt."

The whimper that escapes her lips... beautiful. So damn good. Who knew those lips could express anything other than defiance?

When I place her on her feet, she looks up at me, and I grab the bodice of her dress, where the swells of her breasts meet, and I yank, pulling it apart and down to her hips, exposing her body to me.

"No bra and no panties," I growl. When the dress falls to the floor, she looks up at me, and there is a question in her eyes, one I can't place. "What, Emelia?"

"Degrade me. Really make me feel like filth to you," she states, knocking me on my fucking ass.

"You want to feel filthy? Why, baby?" I grab her chin, and I do it with force, my grip locking her into place.

"Because it makes me feel bad, which makes me feel *so good*. Are you not up for the task?" she challenges, and I tsk at her.

When I throw her down on the bed, she yelps, and I climb over her. Without warning, I jerk her legs apart and slam two fingers into her tight, wet center.

Holy shit, that's going to feel incredible wrapped so tightly around my cock.

"This pussy is mine now. I will have it when I want and how I want, and you're going to be a good little whore for your husband, aren't you, Emelia?"

She doesn't answer, and I flick her clit hard with my thumb.

She screams, "Yes. Oh God, yes!"

"God isn't here, baby. It's only your personal devil. Call me your boss."

"My boss," she breathes.

"Your keeper." I slowly lock my two fingers against her G-spot and rub circles.

"Keeper," she parrots on a husky sigh.

"Husband." I dare her to admit it. Admit that I own her in all forms.

"Husband. All of it, Nico. Please, just fuck me," she cries.

"You've wanted this, haven't you? The minute you saw me, you saw past the situation and spotted just who you were marrying. You've been soaked for me, haven't you?"

"Yes, it's the only thing about you that I found worth the arrangement. I knew you would at least fuck me like I would want it."

"You're about to be broken. Damaged. Ruined beyond repair. Are you sure you're ready for what that means?"

She laughs through a moan, the sound musical.

"Get this one thing, Nico. Don't ask me—take me. Do things to me. Degrade me. Praise me. And be the man who can do what I won't let you outside this bedroom. Which is in control of me."

Never has a woman made me so infuriated that I get pleasure and aroused by it. Never has a woman made me feel like I want to consume her and burn her with my words like I do with Emelia. A challenging woman with so much to offer, yet it's been wasted by her parents. Hiding her and silencing her. What would become of Emelia if I were to give her some semblance of power in our home?

"Nico, I'm aching. Please. Don't make me beg anymore." She pulls me back in from the thoughts that were carrying my mind away from what's right in front of me.

"You look enticing when you beg me, Emelia. Truly a delicacy."

"I can beg you some other time. Until then, I need you."

"Yes. Yes, you do." Standing back, I undress, watching her watch me reveal inch after inch of skin. I let my eyes wander lazily up and down her body, from her temptress eyes, all the way to the pink on her toes. But the most tantalizing place I want to look is between those thick thighs.

Her thighs are marked with pink lines, and they have dents

that look damn near deadly with how much I want to taste them. I want to lick and bite those marks, so hard one wouldn't be able to tell which were already there or made by my teeth.

"Show me how you play with yourself, baby. Give that slutty clit some attention," I order, dropping my pants and grabbing my hard shaft. The engorged head is leaking precum already.

"Fuck," she moans, looking at my cock and eagerly reaching between her legs. The second she makes contact, it's like an explosion. She comes with a shudder, liquid shooting from her.

I nearly come right along with her, learning I have myself a generous sharer.

I've been with all kinds of women, but the ones who can give you gratitude in the form of squirting? Those are women sent from the gods.

"Lick your fingers clean. Now," I growl.

I'm warped, my mind wrapped in lust and overtaken by what her body is going to offer me tonight. Uncensored fucking. Her body will be used by me, a personal house of worship where sinners beg for penance. We will do things that would make even the saints turn away.

Bringing her fingers lazily to her lips, she licks them, making a show out of it, one that makes my cock that much harder.

"God, I taste good. You want to try some, Valiente?" Emelia quips and taunts me so well that I don't wait a moment longer. She may think she's able to tease me, but I don't like being toyed with. She wants it, she gets it, but in my own way.

Grabbing her ankles, I flip her over, roughly grip her hips, and pull her up on her knees. Before her yelp completely dissipates, I dip low and lick her engorged clit, following up with such a harsh bite to her pussy lips she lurches forward. I grab her hips violently and pull her slit back to me.

"I'm not done with you. Move away again, and I won't give you the foreplay. And trust me, you need it for what I have planned."

Gulping loud enough I hear it, she nods, and I slap her ass so hard the skin and fat reverberate, and the sight has my cock throbbing. I love a body that gives me more than just a hole to empty into. I need depth, in body and in life. She has both, and I loathe but welcome it at the same time.

I do not love her, but slowly, I can see myself not despising her.

"Yes, sir. Please, make me come," Emelia begs. I don't respond as I let that plea replay in my mind while lazily licking her clit and up her center. Looking up the long line of her back, I see her trying to look back at me while I lap at her. But she fails, this position making it impossible.

"Left, princess. Look left... in the mirror, while my tongue fucks this tempting little asshole." I point my tongue and plunge it into her backside, the puckered hole stealing my attention. I rub at her clit with the intention to make her come so hard she will be wet enough to take me all the way. I'm large and thick. There's no way she'll be able to take me without enough preparation.

"God, Nico, that feels.... Fuck! Oh!"

I'll admit that loud lovers were never my thing, but Emelia? She makes it sound like music. I will fuck this asshole, and her mouth, and her pussy. All of it. The jealous man in me will erase any lover before me. Because no one, and I mean no one, can compare to Nico Dante Valiente. I'm arrogant, prideful, and cocky, the worst traits any man can possess, but I do it so fucking well, and she will beg for it.

"Come again, Emelia. Reward me. You owe me a thank-you." I slap her clit.

"Oh fuck! Fuck you!" She detonates around my plunging fingers, cursing me while she does.

"Good girl. Now, be a good wife and hate-fuck me, Emelia, because we all know you want my well-trained cock." I drop onto my back, positioning myself on the pillows, placing my hands behind my head. I watch her breathe heavily, trying to regain control.

"Condom?" she asks, finally moving and straddling me. What a sight. Beautiful, full breast, a soft stomach, and thick thighs so deliciously wrapped around me.

"We don't use them. You are my wife, and we will never have sex with condoms," I tell her.

Her eyes penetrate me."I'm on the pill, but how do I know you're clean?"

"I tested before the wedding. You're fine. Now what are you going to do, Emelia? I'm growing impatient, and I'm ready for my wife to show me what a dirty slut she can be." Her thighs clench, and she audibly whimpers, a failed attempt to hide her obvious arousal from me.

"Ride me, wife. Become the official *regina* of this outfit."

The queen.

My match has been made. And we are about to dance on the graves of those before us.

Slowly, she lowers herself on me, hissing as she takes each inch, and I let her have full control. Watching her take pleasure is like the high that comes with an illicit drug. Euphoric. Each inch. And she fits me tightly—oh *fuck*, the tightness.

"Am I doing okay?" Her eyes go doe-like, and I know what she's wanting.

"So good. You're taking me so well, principessa."

"Yeah, does it feel good for you?"

As she lowers herself nearly to the hilt, I eye her deeply.

What is she doing?

How have I never experienced this type of lover in the bedroom? Submissive and needy? A turn-off to some, but for me— this is exactly what I want, right here and right now.

"Feels like you need to roll those hips and ride me."

Throwing her head back, she does just that. And part of me instantly gets blood-boiling angry, filled with jealousy. She fucks good, and that means Damian had enough time to teach her.

I should have been her first.

"Faster and harder. Take it, Emelia. Don't be shy," I demand, grabbing her hips and helping her bounce, then drop all the way to circle her hips. But it's not enough. I want to fuck the anger and jealously swirling in my stomach right out of me.

"Fuck this." I move us swiftly, turning us so that I'm now on top of her. Taking her hands, I pin them above her head and start to thrust into her, trying to split her up the middle.

"Oh! Uh! Nico! Right there. That feels...." Her eyes roll back as I hit the perfect spot in her repeatedly.

"Yeah, no one has ever fucked you like this, have they?"

She doesn't answer, and I'm sure it's because the pleasure is overstimulating, but I won't take just her moans as obvious satisfaction.

"I want words."

"No. No one has. Ever! I'm coming! Nico, I'm coming. Tell me to!" she screams, and my chest swells with pride.

"Come for your husband. Be my little slut and come for me."

"Yes! Yes! Yes!" She explodes around me, reaching her peak, and the vice grip her cunt has on my cock makes me join her just a few thrusts behind. I orgasm, spilling into her until she can't take anymore. I keep at her until she's begging me to stop, her core too sensitive.

In time, I finally and reluctantly let up. Rolling over, I look up at the ceiling and let nothing but our breathing carry throughout the room.

When enough time passes, I move first. Standing, I head to the bathroom, grab a warm washcloth, and bring it back to her.

"Open your legs, Emelia." Shakily, she does as she's told. "Good girl." Taking the towel, I go to clean her, but something more sinister comes over me.

Leaning down and placing my knuckles on the bed next to her

head, I whisper, "Just so we're clear, that act made you irrevocably mine. I will not share you. Ever. Make sure you never forget that." I place two fingers on her thigh and collect the come dripping from her. I move slowly upward, then slide those fingers inside her. "Keep every damn drop of me inside your snug pussy where it belongs."

I own Emelia, and I don't care what she fights me on. She will learn to love it. She licks her lips as she watches the action and hears my words. I can see that storm brewing again, this little sex fiend. She's nowhere near done. She wants more. So much more. But I won't give it to her. Making her sit at the edge of her seat while we bicker will be the best foreplay for the next hate-fuck session we have.

"Not tonight. I have a lot to do tomorrow. Relax and let me clean you up." I do just that, and when I finish, I go to the bathroom and shower.

Halfway through, I see her enter without saying a word to me. Emelia moves toward the bath and lifts the handle. As the water starts filling the tub, I watch as she looks at the salts I had brought in for her. Dumping in one that smells of lavender and honeysuckle, she climbs in, and once she's settled, she turns and looks out the floor-to-ceiling window at the city.

Keeping her eyes there, she doesn't even peer over at me once. But I, however, can't stop watching her, wondering what is going through her mind. Wiping the glass, I get a better look through the steamed-up shower.

"I promise to find the men who organized the shooting tonight. Is that what you're worried about?" I ask, placing both palms against the glass and waiting for her to make eye contact with me.

"Yes, I don't know what I was expecting. It's not like I thought my life would suddenly be different and I'd be safe." Emelia still peers out the window, laying her head back on the curved lip of the tub.

"It's going to be the opposite, Emelia. You're now going to be at *more* events and social gatherings. You are the wife of a mafia king; your life is in significantly more danger. But I won't let anyone hurt you. That is one thing I can guarantee. That's why I have men with you all the time and insisted on the tracker."

She goes to speak, but I stop her.

"I know you want to argue over the tracker, but tonight is not the night to do that. Okay? After today's event, I could snap at any moment. Let's not make this night end on a bad note."

I don't miss the way she rolls her eyes as she looks back at me.

"Damian would have never done this to me."

There it is. I snap. Turning off the water and throwing open the shower door, I grab the towel. Wiping off my face in a haste, I tie the towel around my waist, and I tower over her.

"You will not speak his name in my house. You keep using him to get to me, and I will use him to get to you."

"What does that mean?" she seethes.

"You know exactly what that fucking means, Emelia. You are a lot of things, but a stupid woman isn't one of them." I leave the room before I say worse. I'm already at my limit, and I need a place to blow off steam.

Looks like I'll be sleeping in the other room. Being near her when she has the nerve to test me like that will lead to me being a madman on a mission.

I should have killed him. Sparing him just for her was pointless. Because now, I plan to kill him, and that will be the first fucking thing I do when I get back from our honeymoon. Sure, I could have one of my men do it, but I want to. It has to be me who sees his life end and his eyes go lifeless. That fucking son of a bitch.

Dressing fast, I leave the room, slamming the door so she knows just how much she angered me. The submissive is gone, and the pain in my ass has returned with a vengeance.

Got off just to be pissed off.

Stepping into the guest bedroom, I call Giulio.

"Sir?"

"I want a full run-up of Damian Fuccenli. Phone records included."

"Will do. I'll have it soon."

"Good." I end the call and lie on the bed. Looking up at the ceiling, I think of Emelia in the other room, still mad, but what's worse is I'm thinking about the space between her legs.

What we just shared.

The way she sucked my cock dry with her voodoo pussy.

Maybe having sex wasn't the best idea, because quite frankly, I'm going to crave it all the time now. Feel it, taste it, want it, and need it. She created a monster, put a spell on me.

I need to focus on work. On new enemies. On the weapons that keep getting intercepted and new rivals doing dealings on my docks. But instead, I'm lost in a vicious cycle.

It's aggravating.

"Nico?" Her voice fills the room, and I sit up on my elbows. She stands in some silk night own that leaves nothing to the imagination, and her hair is wet and pulled around to one side.

"Yes, Emelia." There's no attempt to make my voice sound anything less than irritated.

"I'm sorry. That was too far. I didn't mean to bring him into this. We agreed to wave a white flag, and that was a low blow." She fidgets her hands, moving her wedding ring around her finger.

"Listen, I know this life is more than one step farther than what you wanted, but I can't keep doing this with you. Either you get on my side, Emelia, or we will have to end this. That's all there is to it."

"I know. I get that. Just... please don't be upset. Tonight was scary for us both. Well, for me at least. I've never been shot at before." Being voluntarily vulnerable is new for her; I can tell. Though she is being forthcoming, her body language is riddled with an unwelcome feeling.

"I'm used to it, but I'm a man of my word. You follow the rules, put some trust in me, and all will be fine. I won't let anyone hurt you, okay?" I tell her this, sitting all the way up and looking at her.

"Okay. I just wanted to come in and say sorry."

Is this part of what her father did to her? Her mother? There are so many layers to Emelia. I peel back one, and another's edge comes loose. It's hard to decipher, but so am I. Two complicated people, living in a complicated world.

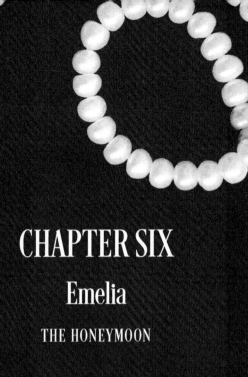

CHAPTER SIX

Emelia

THE HONEYMOON

Nico wasn't kidding when he said we needed to get to our honeymoon. After we had sex, we had an argument, I apologized, and then the next day we were on a jet. The flight was extremely long and filled with rest, light conversation, and two rounds of intense fucking.

That's the one thing I can say about this marriage—the sex will always be enjoyable.

I don't think Nico is someone I can see myself relishing the company of, but he isn't the worst conversationalist. In fact, it was more than tolerable this entire flight. He is highly intelligent and has a plethora of interesting stories from his well-lived life in the mafia. I would say it extends past the definition of wild. Actually, I would dare even say he's had a tormented and damaged life. Made men don't seem haunted or affected by the life they have led, but no normal person with an ounce of humanity in their body can say this life doesn't affect them at all.

There were moments, especially when he briefly shared a snippet of his life with me—one where his father and mother played the main characters of the story—that I saw something. A glimpse of pain? Disparage? The possibility of freedom from this life?

Who am I kidding? We are not free and never will be, and this marriage only solidified our destiny. Being in the mafia comes with one thing that is always guaranteed—you don't know freedom. The chosen ones may have more privileges and can move about as they please, but it still comes with limitations and duties.

Then there are people like me who are born to be tools. We are the damned.

And right now, I can't tell which one Nico truly is. Is he really one of the chosen, or part of the damned?

The jet lands and I stand, reaching for my small overnight bag, and Nico snaps his fingers. I nearly tell him to pick someone else to snap at like a dog, when I look up and see he was actually doing it at one of the guards he brought to watch over us. The tall, blond-haired man rushes to me, takes the bag from my hand, and gestures for me to follow Nico. The second my body is blanketed by the hot sun, I smell the salt water and freshness of the air. You don't get that in the city.

Nico descends first, his suit crisp and unwrinkled. You would think he just stepped into the expensive outfit and hadn't spent hours sitting on a plane. My dress is white with thin straps that tie atop my shoulders, and the bodice is made up of lines and curves that mimic a corset. At my hips, it A-lines into a flowy sundress.

My hair is curled, and my makeup is light with sunscreen, mascara, and lip gloss. I knew we would spend most of our time on the sands of Greece and hopefully in the deep blue waters.

"Emelia?" His sharp voice whips through the wind, and I look at Nico.

"Sorry. Just taking in the view. In a rush or something?" I ask, continuing my descent.

"Yes, I would like to get to the yacht before I'm ancient."

"A yacht? We're in Greece. Don't you think a resort would be more enjoyable?" So I won't be spending as much time on the beach as I thought. I'll be on a boat. Trapped at sea with a man I enjoy fucking and having small bouts of conversation with. Great.

"Safety, wife. The yacht will add an extra layer of safety for now. But I will make sure to take you to spend time on land, if you insist. Now, let's move before dawn comes and we miss dinner."

The time change will definitely kick my ass, but I won't complain. I have always wanted to see Greece; therefore, I don't mind losing some sleep. I will joyfully push through the heaps of exhaustion in order to see all the things this beautiful place has to offer. Besides, I believe they say the best thing for jet lag is to stay up until the next day starts, then sleep when night comes.

Maybe I made that up.

Who knows and who cares, because I'm in Greece!

Nico spends his time with his eyes glued to his phone, checking God knows what business, as I take in the city. We drive around the curves and bends of the mountain and into the small towns with uneven cobblestone roads and filled with locals. Our giant SUV could barely jolt to the left or right and cause havoc, and the driver is clearly aware of that, because he drives with steady caution.

Looking over at Nico, my eyes narrow and I click my tongue. "You know, if you look up, you would see and possibly enjoy what all that business on your phone buys you. You're missing the sights."

He releases a deep breath, giving me a sideways glance before locking his phone and looking up.

"I've been here before. I have seen enough. And money isn't a worry of mine, Emelia, if you can't tell."

Shaking my head, I look out the window when we pass an alleyway. There are children kicking a ball around, and I smile over the simplicity.

"You know, there is this thing that men have been programmed to believe." I wait.

He huffs. "Great, let's hear this one."

I smirk discreetly."That all women are wowed by money. That power and expendable amounts of money make us go all weak in the knees. That's a lie. Made up by men—for men."

"So, my money and my experience in this world doesn't get that beautiful cunt just a little wet?"

Any other man could say that word to me, and I would cringe, but he says it so smoothly, almost like it's a word he invented to describe the beauty of a woman, and I nearly purr. Twisted, no?

God, yes, 100 percent, Emelia. What the hell is wrong with you?

But here I am. Enjoying the fuck yet only tolerating the fucker. However, at least there is *something* pleasing coming from this relationship. A woman should never be ashamed to get hers. Men have been doing it for years, so why shouldn't we?

"Money has been around my whole life. Yours is no different. Don't overinflate your ego; it's already spilling over."

"Oh, how mighty of you, Emelia. I would debate that out of the two us, your ego is the one overflowing."

My eyes burn holes into his, but Nico doesn't crack. I try to out-stare him, but the tension in the car grows, and the way he looks at me—like he's fucking me with his eyes—is enough to have me backing down first. I hate that.

I mentally scold myself as I continue to look out the window. I'm sure I'll have time to get him back with a snide remark, maybe prolong his orgasm, and for sure test his limits. Might as well make this fun while it lasts.

The only two things we have in common—we find joy in pissing each other off and fucking each other madly.

Minutes later, we arrive at the port, and I see the yacht a ways out, kissing where the water meets the sun. I hurry to open my door and meet him on his side, since I know he was going to try to open my door so his guards would think he's the one in charge. I take a mental tally of points. That was for sure a hit to his ego.

He mumbles under his breath, then blurts out orders for his men to grab the luggage and move it to the dinghy. Even the small boat meant for quick transport from the dock to the yacht is nice. Nico really is a man who is overly proud of his money. You would think men like him wouldn't flash their money around like it's nothing. Rich men with real power don't have to brag.

I shrug to myself, and he lowers his glasses from his eyes, looking at me.

"What?"

"Nothing, Nico. Just thinking all kinds of things that would piss you off. Nice boat. Let's go." I step ahead of him, and he grabs my elbow firmly and pulls my back harshly to his front.

"Listen. The jabs are useless and unbecoming of a boss's wife. Shape up, Emelia, or you will spend every moment of this honeymoon alone," he sneers.

"What a dream," I retort, smiling wickedly. I peer up and back at him, and he growls again before I yank my arm away. He stays there for a bit, and I all but skip to the boat with pride swelling wildly in my chest.

I know I re-waved the white flag during my apology last night, but this banter is all in good fun. We're on our honeymoon, after all, and this shit is like foreplay for us.

I sit at the back and rest my arms on the rail of the boat, peering at the coastline. He takes the front, and I enjoy that space. I've spent my entire life in silence, and when I can be alone and not under the thumb of someone, it's peaceful. Every damn second.

The boat glides along the water, the coast fading, and the turquoise sea turns to deeper shades of blue. It's a color I can't describe, but it's breathtaking. The wind whips my hair and nearly becomes one with it, and my skin prickles with the right mix of chill from the wind and kiss of the sun.

I remove my sunglasses so I can really enjoy the sights encompassing me. There are cliffs, the shore, the water, even random clusters of small mountains emerging from the sea. My father traveled a lot with my mother, and other times with my brothers, but I never went. I wasn't jumping and begging to go anywhere with him, but it would have been nice if I could've gone alone at least and seen some of the world. Being sheltered makes moments like this worth one's weight in gold.

I sneak a look at Nico, and our eyes meet. But just like that, they break contact, and we resume the standoff. It's so hard to read this man. If I'm supposed to report back to my father about all-things Nico, I will have to crack him and get inside his mind. And sure, the banter is fun and leads to the best sex, but every once in a while, I spot that look on him, of intrigued desire to see what would be if we could just get along.

Maybe this is the best way to get in. Keep up the back and forth and the moods that make his brows furrow as he clenches his jaw.

Some would say that I'm a mastermind, and others would say I'm a fool who is willingly chancing my own death. The hard truth is that I'm dead to my father if I don't betray Nico, and I'm dead if Nico finds out. I just have to decide which one I would rather be the one who takes my life.

In the past two days, I've been swayed to let it be the cocky, arrogant husband I was forced to marry, instead of the man who tormented me emotionally, mentally, and physically my entire life.

Approaching the yacht, we do a few circles, and I shout to Nico, "Are we playing a game of ring around the boat?"

"No, Emelia. The security team is still making sure it's safe. Including the divers."

I snort. "The divers? What is this, the secret service?"

"It's like you were locked in a tower or bumped your head, principessa. You want to get on a glaring target, then be my guest.

I, however, still have business to conduct." Gesturing toward the boat, he tries to make his point clearer.

I roll my eyes, like he makes me do so very often, but I keep my mouth shut.

"Wow, no rebuttal. Who knew the sound of silence could be so sweet."

I turn and look at him, crossing my legs and resting my chin on my hand as my elbow balances on my knee. With my other hand, I lift my sunglasses and smirk. "You know, a not-so-wise man told me once that jabs are useless and unbecoming." I tilt my head as I use his own words against him, and he cracks, his jaw starting to tic in response.

Boom.

"Enough. Get us on the boat. My wife must be craving a lesson," he growls, hatred that can't mask the arousal seeping out of him. The expression that perfect combination creates on his handsome face calls to the most feminine parts of me. The spot between my legs feels it first, then it spreads throughout my body, hitting every nerve ending.

But there is an even deeper desire in me. To resist him. With each bit of information I learn, the more I will let him have me. He doesn't need to know that, and yes, it may be hard for me to resist, but there is a job to be done here. And there is a line I have to draw somewhere.

If I give him everything just because I have the same insatiable desire, what bargaining tool will I have after that?

There must be a line in the sand, a place in this marriage where I have control. And this is the way to do it, his Achilles' heel—his lust.

CHAPTER SEVEN

Nico

THE ENTIRE DRIVE, BOAT RIDE, AND THEN HER SNIDE little remarks had my palms aching to grab onto pounds of her flesh and bruise them with my hateful fucking. There are these moments that I see her thinking she runs the marriage, and while it's good she does it with her shoulders squared, Emelia needs to know and learn balance. She must understand that her boldness can be mistaken for disrespect toward me.

I want her to be controlled and aware, not pompous and disrespectful. Not just in public, but also behind closed doors. If she were one of my men in the outfit, I would have her kiss my fucking shoes, or worse.

We get on the boat, and I grab the inner part of her bicep and start pulling her to the bedroom. She resists, putting her heels in the floor, but she is no match for my strength.

"No!" she screams, and I halt.

"No?" I question her.

"I said no. If you want to yell or punish me, go for it. But I control my body. I have full autonomy over it, and you will not get any of it unless I let you." Her voice is controlled and low, every word packing a thousand punches. I drop her arm and lift my chin. I'm a bastard, but I'm not that kind.

"Fine. Then you can go to the cabin and come up when dinner is ready. Until then, enjoy your solitude."

Her grin is malicious. "Gladly."

Emelia thinks she's won. That's cute. But she has done everything *but* that. I lead the way and show her where our room is. She steps in and looks around, the walls nearly barren, with only one large window showing the ocean and its depths.

"What a beautiful room to be away from you," she gloats.

"I'm glad. Because you won't leave it until you're ready to learn a lesson. You don't speak to me like that in front of any of my men. You broke a rule today, Emelia, and now you can sit with it."

I shut the door and take out my key, quickly locking it behind me. Could she unlock any other door? Yes, but for safety reasons, I made this door a key lock on both sides. You need a key whether you're inside or outside this room.

I hear her laugh and listen to her steps as she comes up to the door. I cross my arms, now reciprocating her gloating, and I wait for whatever she has to spit at me.

"Oh, so scary. Good thing I can just open the door and lea—"

The handle jiggles lightly at first, but it quickly turns into frantic tugging and twisting.

"Nico! Open the door! What the hell is this?" Emelia screams, slamming her fist against the wood. My teeth show as I smile wildly, knowing I have her locked away and she can't leave. She will have to beg me to let her out. But until she decides to lessen her pride and do that, I have work to do.

Walking away, I puff out my chest, the sounds of her yelling blending with the banging on the door gradually fading with each step I take. Coming to the kitchen, I ask the chef what the menu is for the night, just to make sure my orders were followed.

"Steak, with mashed red potatoes and a savory gravy, and

steamed carrots. Dessert is the tiramisu you requested, sir," Ricardo, my personal chef for all occasions, including my meals at home, reads the menu I had Giulio send over.

"Thank you, Ricardo. I would like a variety of red and white wines and some champagne as well." Giulio let me know what things my new bride enjoyed, and I made sure to accommodate that. But after her little bout of attitude back there, I'm thinking I should just make her drink what I'm drinking, and she will just have to deal with it.

Suddenly, the image of her peering up at me with her mouth open comes to mind, me taking a sip of my whiskey and spitting it onto her waiting tongue.

I am snapped back to reality when Ricardo speaks. "Will do, sir."

My eyes go to my phone in my hand as I leave the kitchen and make my way up to the deck. I need to call some contacts and check in on things at home. The staff ignores Emelia's pleas, trained to know better than to interfere with anything I haven't instructed them on.

Emelia will learn from this.

The phone trills before my underboss answers.

"Giulio," I say, and we get lost in conversation. We haven't been able to find the entirety of the stolen goods, but Giulio has been working on it. There is someone out there who is fucking with me, and while that is not uncommon in my line of business, it hasn't happened often. In fact, it'd been quiet in my outfit before now. The businesses were running smoothly, our deals were going unperturbed, and the money was coming in large waves.

Until now.

My marriage seemed to make people out there think my guard is down. But little do the enemies know I'm more vigilant and aware than ever before.

"Chicago is out? You're sure?" I question, taking a drink of my water.

"Still, yes, but I have an eye on all their docks, sir."

I release a deep breath and run my hand through my hair.

"Fine." I can't believe I'm asking this, but there is only one more place to look. The last enemy we had up until recently. "New York. Check into the Notellis."

"Sir. You married Mrs. Valiente to ensure they would no longer be enemies."

"Exactly, Giulio. Enemies are enemies. They may make deals to become your allies, but you can never trust them fully. Check into them. Keep tabs and get back to me." I haven't even told Giulio that I have plans to get close to my new bride in order to take down her family after what they did to mine. Because this information is safest close to the vest.

"Sir, I don't think that's—"

"I would think twice before questioning me and my demands. I'd hate to think we need to look into you. Do I need to worry about my underboss, Giulio?" I let the threat roll off my tongue like it's the only language I speak. Giulio was made my second in command just shy of a year after I took over as Seattle's king. I picked him, because his father was my father's right hand. There has never been a time I've questioned his loyalty, but right now, no one is safe. I'm smart enough to know that our most trusted companions have the highest risk of becoming our biggest betrayers.

Giulio is dedicated, hardworking, ruthless, and loyal, yet he has a tendency to give certain people the benefit of the doubt. That is one thing I've had to teach him *not* to do. But when it comes to women... he has a soft spot, and it surprises me that he hasn't found a bride—or a life partner, for that matter. Hell, I don't even know what sexual orientation he is, since he hasn't dated in the years we've been close.

"No, sir. You have my word. I will keep an eye on Chicago *and* New York."

I cut the call and look out over the water, trying to think about what could be happening. I have to get ahead of this.

My new bride's family could very well be in on this. They were the last ones we needed to make peace with. But marrying Emelia could have been what they believed was a good distraction while they made their moves.

Is it the most likely of possibilities? No. But it will always be one. No one is safe at war in our world. Every outfit has traitors, and every boss has enemies. Until business resumes as it was before, I will keep every fucking avenue open.

The chiming of my phone draws my attention back to it. Fuck, I hate being away from Seattle. I spend all my time on my phone checking in on business versus being there and on the scene. Whoever said doing remote jobs was ideal lied. This is fucking miserable.

I see her name and just know I'm about to read something vulgar, sexual, or annoying, possibly all three wrapped with a goddamn bow.

NATALIA

I miss you. Your wedding looked nice.
I couldn't bring myself to come.

Natalia is a former fuck buddy of mine. Nothing more. The moment I realized it was something more to her, I cut her off. She was a good time but not a permanent thing. I told her in the beginning that the only way I would marry a woman who wasn't through an arrangement would be if I had the capability to love.

Spoiler—I don't.

So I had only one possibility left, and that meant marriage to Emelia. The stubborn, voluptuous, smart-mouthed blonde I can barely tolerate, all while simultaneously being unable to keep my hands off her.

NICO

Natalia.

It's a warning. She knows me well enough to know what I'm

trying to convey in that single-word message. She was grossly and annoyingly obsessed with me. Dissected all my actions, tried decoding all my moods, and questioned me beyond what I could fucking handle.

NATALIA

What? Can we not talk anymore? Is that off limits?

NICO

I can talk to anyone at any time, but I like to pick those conversations wisely. If you're going to message me about my marriage and missing me, it's useless. I don't have time for this.

NATALIA

A blonde? And I never pictured you marrying a fat girl.

Tilting my head, I crack my neck, clenching my phone while holding it as if it were her neck. How dare she talk about my wife in any way, but especially like that? I don't care if I don't love Emelia or if she is a pain in my ass; I won't let anyone—*anyone*—disrespect what's mine.

NICO

Jealousy is ugly. You should know I think it's the most disgusting trait in a woman. Maybe you took me fucking you to mean you were more to me than just a hole. Obviously, since you now think it's your place to disrespect anyone or anything that belongs to me. But you were very wrong in that assumption. She is my wife, and if you ever find yourself in the same room as her, I suggest you remember who she belongs to and what power she now has. Not only do I have the privilege of getting rid of problems permanently. Now, she does too.

NATALIA

I'm sorry. I just don't get it. Why wasn't it me? You loved being with me.

If I didn't need the phone, I'd toss it into the fucking deep. Between my eyes being stuck on it for hours at a time, multiple times a day, and hating the desperation and the false narrative she created, I'd love to be rid of the device.

I think of Emelia then. Her body. She's not thin. She's thick, and there is nothing about that fact that bothers me. I've never been one to discriminate. Most men in our world do, but to me, Emelia's body is perfect. Artists have been drawing the female form for centuries, and I've never seen one that encapsulates the perfection of my wife's. The thick thighs, covered in lines and dents. The extra pounds of flesh on her hips, and her stomach—that's my favorite part. I can admit that biting that flesh and marking it has the potential to become my favorite pastime. Her insides might be my biggest hang-up, but her body? That's art. That's perfection made by God's hands.

I'd never admit this to her. Her ego is already big enough. But I'm a man, and I know what I like physically, and Emelia fits my desires more than just well enough.

Natalia messages me a few more times before I decide enough is enough and block the number. There is no place for her in my life, and she is a bother at this point.

A few hours pass, and I look to see Emelia still hasn't messaged me, and the sun is now setting. Ricardo is setting up the table, and I nod when it's all complete. Debating if I should eat alone and make her wait until I come back to our room for the night, I decide against that. Maybe she's learned her lesson now.

I stand, button my suit jacket, and make my way back down to the bedroom. Taking the key from my pocket, I unlock the door. Either she will lunge at me, or she will be asleep; those are my two guesses. With this in mind, I prepare myself and open the door slowly.

I don't see her at first, and the bed is empty. The room is dark, but the light from the hall behind me shines in, and I see her sitting in the corner. Emelia's legs are pulled up in the oversized chair, and she's wiping at her face.

I flip on the light and see she's been crying, her face pink and marked with darker blotches. I place my hands in my pockets and eye her over, waiting for her to say something. But she doesn't.

"Are you ready to show me some respect?"

She wipes at her last tear as if it's a bother, her face turning cold. "Respect? No. I'm not even ready to *pretend* to." She stands and moves toward her luggage.

"You need to learn—"

She snaps then, turning on me and cutting off my words. "I know fucking respect, Nico! And I also know who deserves it. I have yet to meet a man in this world who has earned it. You are all the same. You take, take, take. You blister over with lack of control, and then when you snap, you do it. You *take*. Take freedom, control, self-respect, and any dignity."

I open my mouth, but she keeps going. "I've lived my whole life under the thumb of a man like you. I didn't ask to marry you. I begged to not be sold off to you like a fucking animal. I am a woman. A person. And *I* deserve respect. You claim that the world we are in owes me and must respect me because of my position. But you? You're exempt, right? You can mock me, ridicule me, push my buttons, and lock me in a fucking room like a caged animal. And *you* can just... exist." Her last word is spoken softly, a stark difference from every other word in that rant.

I stay put, letting her have the floor. No one is around. And if she needs to get it off her chest, then she can. Part of me feels a dash of guilt, but I brush that away, because I don't feel bad for people. That's the furthest thing from my damn DNA.

"So no, Nico, I don't need to learn respect. But I've now been taught how much I despise the man you are. I would ask if your father would be proud, but he's the coward who raised you, so I'm assuming he's just as pathetic."

That's the last tick of the time bomb, and I explode.

"Enough! You—" I gain on her, moving until I have her backed into a wall. "—are never to speak about my parents again. You can call me whatever, Emelia, tell me what a prick I am, but if you say any ill words like that about my father again, I will lock you in the penthouse, and you will never see freedom again!" I yell and punch the wall next to her head.

Emelia jumps, her shoulders lifting and her head burrowing between them, scared that it's her who will catch my fist. I breathe in and out deeply, my chest rising and falling harshly, and I give her one final look of disgust before I hastily pull back and leave the room, slamming the door behind me.

How dare she? My father was many things, but he was not pathetic nor a coward. My parents are the one subject I take zero shit about. You disrespect them, then you might as well be spitting in my fucking face. And if that were anyone other than her, I would have put a bullet between their eyes.

I get to the top deck, and I take my whiskey off the table and down the glass before I refill it. I sit down at the table, and I stare out at the blackness of the night sky. The lights from the yacht make it hard to see the stars. I'm trying to calm down, trying to let what she said go, but I can't. I want to hurt something, break someone's face, and make them pay for what she said.

And then I let out an incredulous laugh.

Of course I'm in the middle of the fucking ocean with no one around to do just that.

"Nico?" Emelia's soft voice comes from behind me.

Closing my eyes, I grit my teeth. "What, Emelia?"

I listen to her move, her bare feet making nearly no sound. Rounding the table, she stands over me. I don't look up. If I look at her, I may flip the goddamn table.

"I'm sorry. Parents are off limits. I crossed a line. It's you I'm mad at, and it's below me to attack others like that. Especially those who have passed."

My fist tightens, the reminder that they are gone, hitting me. Still, I stay silent.

"I would like to have dinner and not argue."

Is she asking me for permission?

I look up at her finally and see that's exactly what she's doing.

"Sit," I order. Taking her seat, she waits. "Eat, it's getting cold."

Picking up my knife, I cut into the steak and take a bite. I'm starving and ready to enjoy a hot fucking shower and a long night of sleep. Might as well take advantage of being too far away to handle business myself. I can't remember the last time I got decent sleep.

She picks at her food, pushing it around and taking occasional bites.

"What's wrong with the food?"

"Nothing. It's great, thank you."

"What is it, Emelia?" I can tell she wants to ask me something. She's practically falling out of her seat from her leg rapidly bouncing up and down.

"Nothing."

"Emelia," I warn, my voice sharpening.

"Okay, I just thought maybe you could tell me a little bit about your parents."

This is a joke. It must be. She calls my dad a pathetic coward and then wants to ask me about them after I put my fucking fist through the wall. Does she like living on the edge? Does she not feel fear?

"No. We aren't talking about them. You haven't earned it. Just like I haven't earned your respect." I use her words against her, something we are both very well-versed in.

"Fair. So, what do we talk about? Are we just supposed to coexist and fuck when you're horny?" she asks, setting her fork down.

"Precisely. You can be arm candy occasionally when we have

events, but yes. You exist, and I exist—separately, unless we both want to fuck." I'm crass with my words, but Emelia has proven she can handle more than a bit of bad language.

"Thrilling. Am I allowed to have friends?"

I nod. "Other wives, mistresses, and girlfriends in the outfit, yes. Outsiders, no. Too risky."

"Mistresses? I'll skip that one." She takes a sip of her wine.

"It's normal in this life. You should know. Your father has multiple." I did my work and research. I know how much that old man enjoys the company of escorts and private dancers.

"No. If you don't have to talk about your family, mine is off limits too. They may be the reason we had to marry, but I don't want to talk about them. And I don't care how common it is. I will not be friends with mistresses. Speaking of..." She pauses and takes another sip. Placing the glass down, she looks out into the dark night. "You plan to have one, I assume?"

"I already answered this," I tell her, setting down my fork, and a member of my staff comes and takes my empty plate.

"You said there are no other women now. And while I want to say I can trust anything that comes out of your mouth, I don't. And each minute spent with you is like whiplash."

"Yeah? And who's the one driving that car, Emelia?" The insult is clear.

"I only go hot and cold when you do."

"Well, look at that. Something in common. Maybe we should both set some rules. Some things that will not and cannot happen in this marriage," I suggest, leaning forward and grabbing the wine decanter, pouring myself and her some more.

"I think that's not the worst idea. You first."

"I insist, ladies first." I tilt my head.

"Fine. I want to be able to have my own room. I don't want to sleep next to you at night. We can do what is needed, then I would like to have my space to retreat to."

"No." I instantly shut that down.

"And why is that, Nico?" She huffs, rubbing at her temples.

"Because I want access to you at all times. I don't want to waste time coming to your room to fuck you when we're both needy in the middle of the night."

Her breath hitches. We eye each other over, her lip getting caught between her teeth. She can't hide her arousal; I don't even think she notices her thighs rubbing together or her nipples puckering. What a sight.

"You can call me, and I will come to you, if it's that big of an inconvenience to walk a few doors down."

I shake my head. "No. You are in my bed. You're my wife, and you will sleep in the same bed as me. And when I need your tight cunt on my cock and you need my cock to fuck that pretty pussy, neither of us will want a couple of doors between us."

"Nico," she breathes out, raspy and needy.

"Next rule." I'll get her under me soon, but right now, I want to make her wait for it. Make her hurt and ache for it.

"Fine. I want to be able to ice skate. It's my one hobby, and I don't want to lose it."

Interesting fact: I don't recall that being in her portfolio Giulio gave me. It surprised me when she told me how much she loved it.

"Consider that arranged."

"Thank you." She tucks her hair behind her ear, the wind catching it and giving me a glimpse of her perfect, delectable neck. I want to mark it up.

"What else?"

"I would like for you to be someone approachable. Not so cold, calculated, and angry. For hell's sake, you have to find joy somewhere in this life."

This makes me smiling a little. "What does that entail?"

"Maybe you can tell me some parts of your day. I've heard it all, so it's not like you can scare me off. I just think it would be nice to have some rapport."

"Expand," I tell her.

"I don't know, Nico. You're a smart man. How about, 'Hey, Emelia, how was your day? Oh me? Great, yeah. I shot a guy!'"

This has me laughing out loud.

"Well, who knew? It laughs!" She chuckles along with me. "I'm serious though, you don't have to tell me who all the Tom, Dick, and Harrys are, but you could at least just tell me how your day was. I don't plan to make too many friends with the other women. So, it's just you and me and that ridiculously large penthouse in Seattle. Give me something."

Our laughter settles, and I agree to give her that one. "Fine. I can let you know how my overall day went. Anything else?"

"Yes, can we get to know something about one another every once in a while?"

"What? Like favorite colors or trivial things like that?"

"Yes, exactly, and what is that color?"

Oh, she was serious. I was thinking this was one of those moments Emelia was teasing.

"I would say blue."

"Huh, I would have thought you would say something like gray. Moody and lifeless."

"Funny," I retort. "Yours?"

"Easy, yellow."

I cough through my laugh. "You? Yellow?"

"What? It's a great color. It's bright and happy and reminds me of sunshine."

"Emelia." She's fucking with me right now.

"What? I'm serious."

I wave my hand at her, not buying it for a second.

"Nico, I'm serious. It's my favorite. If I could, I would paint every wall in your penthouse yellow."

"Not going to happen."

"Why is it so hard to believe I like that color?"

My brows lift. "Really?"

"Yes, Nico, really."

"I don't peg you for rainbows and butterflies and all things happy. You are often cold." I can tell that hurt her.

Her brows furrow a bit before she mumbles, "It's one thing that could possibly bring me light in my darkness there."

I almost—just almost—say something.

But that's enough for now.

"My turn?"

Shaking her head, she gives a small smile."Yes. Your rules."

"I want you to show me respect in front of people."

"Same," she cuts in, but I continue.

"If we respect each other in public, great. Now, if you're mad or want to take something out on me, you have the right to do that in the privacy of our home. I won't ask this again. I have too many times already."

She nods."Fair."

"Second. Your body is mine now, Emelia, and I know you have a past with your ex, but that has ended. If I find out you're sharing yourself with others, they die. This is also my last warning. I don't share."

She gulps, not saying anything, but nodding slowly, she agrees.

"Lastly, you will always come to me if there is something or someone bothering you. If you are ever threatened, blackmailed, or in danger, you tell me. I don't care what the risk is. I'm unhinged and a man who can be quite careless, but your safety is something I will take seriously. You are my wife; you will be the mother of my children. It is my priority to keep you alive and safe."

"Yes. I can do that." Her eyes seem to be void, like she's not sure about that last rule, and I take note of that.

"Emelia, I am serious. This is non-negotiable."

"Non-negotiable. I get it."

"Then why do you look like you aren't going to follow this rule?"

Dropping her head, she shakes it."I'm just..." She pauses, playing with her hands in her lap. "I just haven't had anyone really care if I die or live, who put my safety first."

Her words enrage me. That is the one thing about the world we live in that I do not accept. My father protected and provided for my mother, even though she was strong enough to do it on her own, and in today's world, it's not like that. The men in our world treat women as collateral, and no matter if this was love or arranged, I will protect Emelia at all costs.

A flashback of my father hits me then.

"Take care of your mother for me, son, and remember when you marry to protect your bride with honor."

I shake my head, not wanting to remember my father in that state. Death looming over him and a goodbye staring back at me when I was just a young man. Watching my father die the way he did is a great regret I will carry with me the rest of my life. And remembering the way my mother crumbled to nothing as he took his last breath is a haunting no exorcism could cure.

"Nico?"

Suddenly, I'm aware I left the moment, slipped away, and Emelia is calling out to me.

"Sorry, let's have dessert, and then we can call it a night." My mood shifts drastically. I don't want to talk. Don't want to fuck. Don't want to make conversation or play nice. I'm officially checked out, and that's why talking about my parents is off limits.

"Okay." Emelia doesn't push me, and for that I silently thank her. I don't have it in me to fight with her again. It's been a decent dinner, and I would like to end the evening on a high note.

We make it through dessert and head to our cabin for the night. I let Emelia have the shower first, and I take one next. Letting the hot water scorch my skin, redden it, and burn it to the point that all I can focus on is the pain. No one prepares you when you're young for what it's like to lose the only life you ever knew, or how to carry on the legacy while mourning the greatest people you have ever known. By the time I make it to bed, Emelia is on her side, her eyes closed, and the comforter is pulled all the way up to her chin. I don't hear the sound of her deep breathing, but I assume she is drifting.

I listen to the waves slosh and sway outside the window, and I stare blankly at the ceiling, waiting for the night to take me. When it finally does, I see it then—the life leaving my mother's eyes.

My alarm wakes me, and my eyes open one at a time, the sun on the horizon peeking through the window. I reach over, stop the alarm, and see my messages waiting for me, most from Giulio. I ignore them for now and run my hands over my face.

I turn to see if Emelia is still asleep, but she isn't there. Listening closely, I see if I can hear her in the bathroom, but it's eerily silent. Standing, I put on a black tee and some gray sweats. I'm starving and in desperate need of coffee, my head pounding. It's been a hell of a week with work, and add the travel and all the bickering with my new bride, my head takes the brunt of it all. I can't remember the last time I had a migraine.

Figures Emelia would be the one to conjure one. Yesterday was... confusing, to say the least. Making my way out of the cabin and up the steps, I walk into the glass-surrounded living room area of the boat. I look for my wife, and when my eyes land on her, my breath halts. She's lying in the rays of the morning sun on a lounge chair on the deck, a coffee mug in her hand, and she is facing the mountains.

She's fucking beautiful.

I grab a mug, pouring myself some black coffee, and Ricardo appears from the kitchen.

"Morning, sir. Mrs. Valiente said she would take yogurt and fruit. Would you like the same or something else?"

I roll my eyes, a gesture way beneath a man my age, yet I do it.My wife must be rubbing off on me. "I would like bacon and eggs benedict. And make her the same. Thank you."

"Yes, sir."

I nod, then take a sip of the hot liquid. It moves down my throat, and I can feel it warm my body in just the right way to take the edge off my migraine. I pray it wakes me up and prepares me for whatever mood Emelia may be in.

Last night after dinner, we didn't talk more than just to compliment the chef on the delicious meal, but she seemed to feel better after we had that small conversation. It didn't end perfectly, but it was the first time we truly didn't go for each other's jugular.

"Emelia," I greet, stepping into the sun. It's warm, but the wind makes it the perfect temperature.

"Nico." She matches my tone. Neutral.

That is where we are, and it's not a bad place to start. I would like to take her to the beach today, and in order to do that, it would be ideal for us to be on a level playing field. I bring men to their knees and have them begging me to not end their lives, but here is Emelia, making me gauge what mood she's in so I can tell what kind of day we are going to have.

However, I can't treat her like she's one of my men. That is one lesson I need to learn, and I do it grudgingly.

"I want to go ashore today, enjoy the beach, maybe walk around town and shop a bit."

"You like to shop?" A smirk lights up her face, and it's fucking adorable.

I run my hand through my sleep-tousled hair."No, but I assume you do."

She snorts around her coffee."Just because I am a woman, you think I like shopping. Sexist."

"Am I wrong?"

She hesitates."No, but still. I only like to because I enjoy

123

collecting little trinkets."

"I won't make you apologize for that one." I sit next to her, running my thumb over the rim of the coffee mug. Her eyes are steady on the water, and I take in her profile. It's perfect. Her nose slightly curves up at the tip, and her lips are the most enticing fucking pout. I want my cock between them so damn badly, and I plan to do that tonight.

Her curves are being hugged beautifully by a silky material. It's a nightgown with lace trim and a slit up the thigh. Looking at it, I can't help what I do. It's as if I'm a man possessed as I lean down and nip at the thick flesh, then I stand after she gives me a satisfying yelp.

"Nico?"

"I want your body tonight. I want you to fucking suffocate me between those thighs."

She gasps, and I reach down for her hand and grab it as she watches me with lustful eyes. Placing it on my hard cock over my gray sweats, I jerk in her palm when she lets out a gasp, and the distinct moan that follows it makes my cock twitch once again.

"Be a good girl, and we can have a really good night, principessa."

"Maybe I want it now and don't want to wait," she purrs.

I grin devilishly at my insatiable bride. "Good girls wait, and good girls get rewarded. Are you going to behave today, wife?"

Nodding eagerly, she bites her lip.

Reaching up, I pull her lip free. "Be gentle with that mouth for now. I will be fucking you so hard tonight you'll bite it to the point of bleeding."

Her thighs rub together. "I'll behave, *il mio re*."

Emelia calls me her king in Italian, and she has no idea I am diesel right now, and she's carelessly playing with fire. My desire is going to burn us both alive. Add in the anger we use to fuck, along with the layers upon layers of need, and we just can't get enough.

I've fucked in dirty ways, but with Emelia, it's almost like we try to one-up the kinkiest thing we did the time before. I want to fucking destroy her, and she wants to wreck me.

What a beautiful damn disaster we are.

I walk away from Emelia before the entire staff gets to witness me fuck her, because then I would have to put bullets between their eyes for seeing her that way. We make our way to the breakfast table inside the glass observation deck, the breeze of the morning still coming in through the opening. It's going to be a nice day, the perfect setting for a day on land shopping and eating the finest cuisine.

And as if my thoughts conjured him, my chef sets our plates in front of us.

"Oh, thank you, Ricardo, but I'll just stick with what I originally wanted," Emelia tells him.

"No, you need food. Whatever diet you're on, you can kick that shit."

Looking at me affronted, she crosses her arms. "I get nauseous easily in the morning. I have for years, so I've always eaten a light breakfast. It's not for dieting. Nice way to assume because I'm a bigger woman that I consume diet culture."

Shaking my head and releasing a deep breath, I realize I went too far and she has a fucking point. "That's not what I meant, and it has nothing to do with your weight, Emelia."

"Really? Do explain. I'm dying to hear how you'll dig yourself out of this one." She sits back, arms still crossed, and I bring my fist up to the top of the table, an ironclad grip on my control.

I don't answer to people, and now I'm challenged at every corner, fighting with someone I secretly want to ravish at every turn. I once killed a man because he laughed at my table. Laughed at something I said that had no humor. In fact, it was a very serious meeting. We cut the dinner short, because the food and table were suddenly covered with fragments of his brain and copious amounts of blood.

I then attended his funeral and shook the trembling hands of his parents. Grieving while shaking with fear, because I showed up to watch them bury the man I killed.

"All women are dieting," I finally say.

"My hell, you truly are sexist." She clicks her tongue. "Can't say I'm shocked, but you really are dense and stupid for a person who claims to be the most cunning and intelligent man in our world."

"Waving the white flag clearly isn't the case this morning, so what version of you am I getting today, Emelia? The cocky, snippy one, or the tolerable one who graced me with her presence last night at dinner with less hostility?" I lift my brows and wait for her to respond.

"Same question for you. Am I going to get the hotheaded, sexist, controlling megalomaniac?"

I tilt my head back, look to the ceiling to somehow find clarity in the woodgrain, and ignore her question. I see her in my peripherals, watching me, but I don't give her the satisfaction of even a glare, grunt, growl, or spark of male rage.

And as if the gods heard my silent plea for control, they send me a distraction. My phone rings, and Giulio's name comes up.

"Yes," I answer.

"Boss. The new shipment of drugs came in. It was fake. The seller sent it, but somewhere in transit, it was switched."

"What the fuck, Giulio!" I slam my fist on the table, causing Emelia to jump. What the hell is happening in my outfit?

"I know, sir. I'm doing my best to find out who keeps interfering. I have Chicago, Los Angeles, and New York under watch, and so far they've been minding their own business. No interference."

I pinch the bridge of my nose. Being so far from home makes me that much more enraged.

"Clearly your best is not enough. You are the underboss. You are supposed to be performing at my level when I'm not there. Do

I need to come home and do your job *and* mine?" I yell.

"No. No, sir. I will get to the bottom of this."

"You said that yesterday." I slide my chair back and head out on the deck.

"How much money did we lose on this?"

"Sir," he tries to defer, warning me with as much respect as he can.

"How much!"

"Over a million with the guns and the drugs."

"I want a meeting set up first thing when I get back. All bosses. Someone is fucking with my goddamn business, Giulio, and I want to look each son of a bitch in the eyes and see who fucking bluffs." I watch the crew arriving with the boat that will take us ashore, and I look over my shoulder at Emelia.

"Keep an eye on the Notellis. Something tells me they know something or have a hand in this."

"Him marrying off his daughter to you doesn't kick him off your radar?" Giulio asks.

"I told you earlier. I find it interesting that this all began when I made the arrangement to marry his daughter. This could have been a stealth attack and not a fucking alliance."

"Will do, sir." He stops then, and I know something clicked in his head.

I don't even give him a goodbye. I end the call and make my way back toward the bedroom, passing Emelia without a word.

"Rough day at the office?" She comes in a few moments after me as I pull out my clothes.

"Every day is a rough day, Emelia." I pause for a second and eye her over as she starts to pick her outfit. My anger starts to mold into something deeper, like it's searching for an outlet, and before I can stop myself, I'm on her, my hand gripping her neck with enough force to keep her still and show her my authority.

"Nico!" she gasps.

"You listen to me, and you better not lie to me, Emelia. I would hate for you to end up being a newlywed who didn't even make it through her honeymoon."

She gulps, and I feel it against the palm of my hand. Her eyes widen, and this is the first time I see true fear there. It's not the kind I saw when I nearly killed her pathetic ex.

"You think hard about this, wife. And I mean really hard and pick your next words wisely."

She claws at my hands, and a tear falls, so I loosen my grip. It's not my touch causing her tears though; it's the fear of God in my eyes burning into hers.

"Wh-What?" she stutters.

"Is your father fucking with my outfit, and did he send his walking siren of a daughter as a distraction? Was this an alliance, or are you a fucking decoy, Emelia?"

Her eyes search mine, as mine do hers, and there is no sign of deception. I can smell, see, and sense that shit from a mile away. Like sharks smell blood in water.

"No, he didn't. I was sold off to you so you two could shake hands and be allies, Nico. I swear." Her words are rushed.

Is this fear talking? Or is it blatantly obvious that she's lying, and I can't decipher between the two?

"Emelia!" I yell, my face inches from hers, and my free hand comes up and punches the wall next to her head.

"Nico, I swear it. I know nothing. My father said this was a deal to end the war between you two. He feared you and knew his sons would be too weak to keep up the war. They would have died at your hands, and you would have taken over his outfit. So here I am, the treaty between two families. That's all I know."

I release her.

That's real fear.

Even if her father has a plan of deception, why would he tell her that? Notelli treats his daughter worse than a rabid dog. Why would she know anything?

That doesn't mean it hasn't been his plan this entire time though. And if this is the case, when we uncover it and can prove it's true, will Emelia choose me or her family?

Because if she doesn't choose me, she becomes the enemy.

And I *need* her to choose me.

If nothing but to make my victory even sweeter.

"Fine. We will invite your family to our place when we get home, and we will see just how true that is. I really hope your father isn't fucking with my business, Emelia. That would be a shame, wouldn't you agree?"

She gulps, rubbing at her neck.

"Yes," she whispers.

"Louder, shoulders back, Emelia."

"Yes. I said yes," she hisses, and I step back, grabbing my things and moving to the master bathroom to get dressed.

"Be ready in an hour." Shutting the door, I lean over the sink before bringing my face close to the mirror. My hands grip the lip of the counter hard. My face is red, the veins in my neck are protruding, and I can feel that burning feeling in my stomach, the need to take what calms me and brings temporary relief. The urge to hurt, to take someone and release that anger upon them, is bubbling hot inside me.

There is a part of me I keep cornered until I need to unleash it. I keep it dormant, reserve it, because once I let it free, it's unmatched, untouchable, and unstoppable.

I am the reaper, an unhinged madman with no regard for others. The most dangerous type of man there is, and I would hate for this to turn into a bloodbath.

I suddenly imagine Emelia covered in blood, and something else churns in my stomach, and I really look myself over.

What the fuck was that?

I brush it off, physically. I shake my head and turn on the

scalding-hot water of the sink to splash it on my face, enjoying the pain and letting it rattle through me, all the way down to my bones.

Emelia isn't anything more than an arranged marriage, a device I obtained to use in her father's demise, and a really good fuck. That's all she will ever be.

Unless she becomes my fucking enemy.

CHAPTER EIGHT

Emelia

I HAVE NEVER FELT SO MUCH FEAR IN MY LIFE.

Why would he ask me that? I haven't even tried to figure out the details my father demanded. This man has seen me so intimately, and yet he just showed me I am nothing to him in one glimpse.

I'm not falling in love, and I am no better than him, since I'm practically a spy planted in his life. But that look, the way his eyes blackened, the way he put my life in his hands just to show me that he has the power to keep it or end it, scared me more than knocking on death's door myself.

Being his wife only grants me immunity if I take his side and never betray him. But if I don't betray him, that means going against my family. Yet again, I'm reminded I must decide who I would rather have kill me, my own father or the man I married. Either way, I'm dead. They both made that perfectly clear.

I don't dare cry as I listen to the running water in the bathroom. If I do, it would show him my weakness and vulnerability, and the image I've portrayed as a strong, cold bitch in front of him is the only thing left to my name.

I was stripped of my rights, my future, my pride, and my

fucking dignity. I won't give up control of the most intimate parts of me that make me human.

I wipe at the tears and rush to my makeup bag to find my concealer and powder. The heat in my cheeks and the tears that fought me and lost have made me all blotchy. I pull my blonde hair back, slicking the front down and letting my curls fall loosely down my back. I cover my face with sunscreen, foundation, and concealer, trying not to do it too fast and with too much pressure, as that will only make my face redder.

Thank God I finish blending it just as he comes out. I put on some mascara and avoid eye contact with him. He moves around the space like a bull waiting to be let loose. He demands the room, takes control of it, and I do my best to not get in the way.

I slide my cut-off shorts and an oversized button-up on over a black two-piece swimsuit, slipping on my sandals. When he finally leaves the room, I release a deep breath.

I want nothing more than to dive headfirst off this boat and swim off into the damn horizon so I can escape this world, but instead, I just look in the mirror. My brown eyes are a lighter shade now that my tears have dissipated, and I say out loud, "This is your life. Born into it and will die in it. Only death will set you free, Emelia."

With that, I spray on some perfume, grab my sunglasses, and head up to the deck. Nico is in a similar shirt to mine, a lightweight button-up, with darker jeans and some white casual shoes. Seeing him dressed down almost makes him seem like an everyday guy, but the second he turns and looks at me, I'm hit with the realization he is anything but a normal man. His black hair, light eyes, and James Dean look hits me, and I realize he is a god among men.

No, more like the devil.

He is untouchable, a walking daydream.

A casually dressed nightmare.

"Let's go." He's sharp in his tone, and I nod. I'm tired of fighting the man, and quite frankly, I don't dare try after what happened back there. He showed me how he could be when he caught me with Damian—merciful, but the tables turned on me fast, and he showed me that I can easily become a casualty in his wars.

My desire for him? Gone.

The wondering if we could make something of this? Gone.

Any bit of humanity I was starting to see in him and cling to? Gone.

He is once again just my captor. Sex was all we had, and now we won't have that. I won't let him touch me anymore. Not when I'm clearly not as safe as I thought I was in his hands.

God, who am I kidding?

I'm no freaking better. He was giving me himself, while I was preparing to betray him. We were both sleeping with the enemy.

I follow him to the boat, and I take the same spot I did when we took it here to the yacht yesterday. Expecting him to do the same, I'm shocked when he sits next to me. Purposefully, I keep my eyes on everything but him. Nico doesn't talk for a minute or so, but then his hand possessively grabs my thigh. I freeze, and my back stiffens.

Leaning into me, his lips touch my ear. "Don't try anything stupid, Emelia. I see that look in your eye. You fear me now, and if you try to run, I will find you. Anywhere you fucking go, I will hunt you down and bring you back."

Swallowing, I nod. This side of him is different. He is eerily controlled, but there is a storm under there, and anyone who can contain that with such finesse and grace—those are the ones to fear. Those are the people who make up nightmares. They are the enemies you never want to have. Today showed me the tip of the iceberg of just how dangerous a man I'm in bed with.

I choose him.

In this moment, I choose Nico.

My father wouldn't torture me for betraying him. No, he's too much of a coward to do that. He would be quick.

But Nico? He would be ruthless, and I don't want to suffer through my death. I want it to be painless and quick, so it's Nico I choose to be loyal to.

I realize I didn't respond, and quickly, I nod, keeping my eyes forward and holding back any snide remark that would make him angrier. I've now met the devil in his human form, and I never want to strip the flesh and meet the real him.

When my father comes, I will tell him I'm no longer his inside man, and he can do what he needs with that information. But it will not be me who helps him take down Nico.

My husband keeps a tight grip on my thigh and goes back to taking in the sights. He releases a deep breath and says into the open, "What a beautiful day, isn't it, Emelia?" His smile is cunning and all knowing. He acts as if he isn't practically paralyzing me with dread.

"Very."

"We will shop a little, then enjoy some lunch. Then we can relax on the beach," he states.

I'm not sure what to say, so I go with the easiest thing I think up quickly. "Thank you."

"Of course, my bride. It's our honeymoon."

Another chill tingles up my spine. What the fuck is he doing, and how do I get it to stop? I'd rather take his anger than these false niceties that intensify and solidify his power and control over himself and me.

The boat docks, and he stands, taking my hand and gripping it painfully. I wince, and he looks back at me.

"What's wrong?" he asks.

I look at the bodyguards and lower my voice. "You're hurting me."

His eyes search mine, and I hold my breath, terrified of his response. But he just loosens his grip, kissing my knuckles before interlocking our fingers.

This gesture throws me off, and when I finally feel somewhat steady again, I look up and give him a soft smile. "Thank you."

He grunts, and that's that. We head toward the Grecian streets, and he never lets go of my hand.

He's placed his guards strategically, two in front of us and two behind. The tension is still there, and I just want to breathe and focus on something else, so I window shop, seeing all the beautiful things this town has to offer.

We pass a jewelry shop, and as we continue forward, I do a double-take at the piece of artwork they have in the window made up of a string of gorgeous diamonds.

"Would you like to stop and look in there, Emelia?" Nico asks, his first words since the boat.

"Oh, no. I just saw this pretty choker. They're stunning, but I've never owned one. Never thought chokers would look good on me."

"And why is that?" We keep walking.

I shrug. "I don't have the neckline for it. That's what my mother says anyway."

"When has your mother ever told you anything that held the truth? You couldn't just buy one on your own? Wear it for yourself when she wasn't around?" We cross the street, him looking both ways and guiding us.

"Never, now that you mention it. And I was never allowed to buy things they didn't approve of. Besides, I wanted my grandmother's. They were special," I confess, seeing my sweet grandmother's face in my head.

"Did she leave them for your mother?" he asks.

I shake my head. "No, for me. But Mother kept them for herself, and that's when she told me chokers are not meant for women with larger frames, like me."

His hand tightens briefly, then loosens, and I sneak a look up at him. His eyes are covered in Ray Bans, so I can't tell what emotion they hold, but his jaw is stiff.

"They body-shamed you? Real winners. You didn't believe them, did you, Emelia?" He stops us then, in the middle of the sidewalk, and people just move around us. You would think they'd seem annoyed by him stopping—us two and his four large bodyguards—but now that I'm conscious of it, every person has moved briskly and avoided Nico and me.

Lucky bastards. I wish I could fly under the radar, or run and hide. Anything to get away from this terrifying man. I almost want to whisper "help me" to each passerby, but I don't want to be responsible for the death of an entire village.

"What? About my body?" I clarify.

He nods, and the sun hits his face just right so that I can see his eyes through his sunglasses. There is a softness to them, but I don't let that fool me. There is nothing soft or caring about this man. He's most likely playing the same game I was married off to do, attempting to beat me at it. Nico is smart enough to test if I know what my father had us married for, seeing if I'll crack.

"No. I have never been ashamed of my body, Nico. I'm a fat woman, and that isn't something I will ever be shy about."

"You're beautiful."

"Did I say I wasn't?" Why is that always something people follow up with when you bring up your weight? *But you're still beautiful.* I never doubted that. But we aren't talking about beauty. We're talking about weight.

"No."

"Society has steered so many people wrong. Anyway, no, I don't believe what she says, Nico." I don't care to get into the politics of how society has ruined the minds of people and their perception of women like me. He can look it up if he wants to know. I'm not his guide to what or what not to say to a fat woman. I claim that word, and I'm proud of it. I stopped listening to my parents and the world a long, long time ago.

"Good. Tell me about your grandmother." What in the actual fuck is happening? Are we supposed to act like this morning didn't happen and that he didn't threaten to kill me? Or how he chillingly told me he would hunt me down if I ever left? Not to mention the stunt he pulled last night, locking me in the cabin. This man is the definition of a sociopath. Nico isn't even from this planet. He is from hell itself. The gates opened wide and spit him out, and he took on the world with bitterness that even the underworld rejected him.

"Um, her name was Marjorie." I start out simple and gauge his reaction.

"Beautiful name. You two get along well?"

"We did. When she died..." I pause. Sharing information with him about the one stable relationship I've ever had doesn't interest me one bit, so I keep it vague. "I was really torn up about it. She was a great person. Taught me a lot."

We stop by a store; it's an art gallery, and it piques my interest. Catching on, he opens the door and gestures for me to go in. I do and turn to wait for him. He tells his guards to wait outside the door.

"Welcome! I'm Rhea. I run the gallery. Would either of you like some champagne while you browse?"

I would love nothing more than to get shitfaced so I can already forget today, and it's not even noon yet. I'm thankful we cut the conversation about my grandmother short. I really don't want to give him parts of me that I wish to keep private and safe.

"Um... yes, please. Nico?" I turn while he finishes talking to his men.

"Yes?"

"Rhea owns the gallery and wants to know if you want some champagne," I tell him.

He closes the door and steps up behind me. I turn back and

watch Rhea take in the full appearance of Nico, seeing her release a hushed gasp as her cheeks turn red.

Yes, he is beautiful. I get it. Which makes this ten times more infuriating. Couldn't the man I married be hideous, like an actual beast? Instead, I get a handsome husband who is ridiculously good in bed, but that doesn't take away his arrogance or his lack of redeeming qualities.

He is 6'3", muscular, his hair is a deep black, and his eyes a stunning green that darken with his moods. His jawline is like something out of a fairy tale. A ping of possessiveness hits me as I watch her practically eye-fuck my husband.

Stop that, I curse myself, remembering just what he did and what he said less than a couple hours ago.

"No, I will have water. Thank you," he replies.

I start to walk while she stumbles over her words, very much wanting to remove myself from the scene playing out in front of me. I'm sure I'll get used to women gawking at him.

The art is stunning. It ranges from abstract to scenes of Greece. Stealthy, without me noticing, Nico is back at my side. I look at the third painting, and my eyes widen. The picture is of a woman's body. She has dips and skin that folds over above her hip, her stomach rounded. Even the details of the stretch marks and the cellulite are highlighted. The painting is half of the woman in great detail, and the other side is the opposite half of a colorful butterfly. I want so badly to touch it; however I refrain. What's more, I want to cry.

I feel the parallels between the muse in the picture and me. A woman trapped in a world where she is broken down to nothing but her bare self, while the inside of her wants to break free and fly away to be her authentic self.

"Your champagne and water," Rhea announces when she returns. I take the glass, but I keep my eyes on the painting, eyeing every intricate detail. "You like this one?" she queries.

"It's beautiful. I have never seen anything like this before. How much?"

"We will take it," Nico hurriedly inserts before Rhea can even tell us the price.

"It's very expensive. It's—"

"I have enough money to buy everything here more times over than you could imagine. My wife would like the image."

"Oh. Very well then. I'll get that settled for you."

I turn and look at him. "You don't have to get it. I don't have the money to repay you."

He laughs deep in his chest. "Emelia. Do you still not understand what being the boss's wife means?"

I take a sip of the champagne. "No. I mean, my mother had an allowance, but she had to earn it." I shiver, but not in a good way. I knew how she had to earn it, and it disgusted me to think about it.

"I'm not your father. Thank fucking hell. But you get what you want, Emelia."

I give him a onceover. "You want to spend an ungodly amount on a painting for me... after you had your hands around my throat and accused me of being the enemy?"

"I don't think you are. That doesn't absolve your family though. I don't think you have anything to do with the possibility that your father is the one meddling in my business."

Is my father really doing that? If he is, then what did he need me for? I'm so confused right now. Did I fall and hit my head and am in a coma, dreaming all this up?

"What happened?" I take another sip and turn my body toward him.

"No, no. You don't get to know about the business, Emelia. It doesn't concern you."

"It does if my father is involved." And when *I* was supposed to be involved. It's only been a recent decision to not do what my father asked, but still, the wound is still fresh.

"No, it doesn't. If your father is the one behind the things going on back in Seattle, he will be dealt with. And you, Emelia, will decide to either join me or join him, and we both know which one would be the wiser choice."

I shake my head. I want to yell so loudly that I *did* choose him, and not because I care about him, but so I can rub it in his arrogant fucking face that I had a secret.

"I hate it when you threaten me." I'll be dying when we get home anyway. Might as well go out with a fucking bang.

"It's not a threat. More of a reminder."

"That's a threat, Nico." I scoff, shocked that he really thought that one was going to work.

"You know, I want to go home. I don't want a honeymoon. I don't want to be near you, and I don't want to pretend anymore. Take me home. I want to go home, and that is that. Then you can call my father over and persecute him." I walk out, and he hollers after me. I ignore him, and when I step out, the guards look at me, gauging me, and my body chooses flight.

I make a run for it. I don't look back. I can hear them calling after me, and I hear Nico, but I just keep running. I find an alleyway and take it, and when I glance back, I don't see the guards, but I can hear them coming, so I hide. Squeezing behind a stack of wooden pallets, I hold my breath as I hear them talking.

"Boss, she couldn't have gone this way. It's a dead end." Then they keep running. I slowly emerge and see they're gone. I walk back toward the entrance to make sure they're out of sight. I don't want them to spot me leaving and be back on my trail.

Where do I plan to run? I don't know, but here we are. I almost make it to the end of the alley, when I'm stopped in place, my body responding instantly to the deep voice in a small alcove I haven't quite reached yet just inside the alley.

"You tried. You lost. Now what, principessa?" Nico emerges then, like a demon from the shadows, lurking and ready to take what he's been hunting.

Still trying to catch my breath, I watch him while my body faces the street.

"Nico, please." I step back slowly as he moves closer.

"Oh, baby, beg me again. Better yet. Run. We can make this really fun," he taunts, stalking me, making my pulse rise.

I try to think fast about what to do, but I can't get past him. He would catch me with one outstretched arm, and the alley is a dead end.

"Nico, I want to go home. I'll behave; just let me go home. Please."

He runs his hand over his five o'clock shadow while looking me up and down. Whatever he's thinking, it's laced with danger and... desire. It's almost a physical entity that radiates off him.

Did it turn him on when I ran from him?

Did it turn *me* on?

The throbbing between my legs and the puckering of my nipples tell me it did. I can't hide it or ignore it, and part of me wants to run again so he can catch me. Yet that would go against everything I decided today. That I wouldn't let him have me physically, because I fear him, and I don't want him to have any form of power over me.

Who am I kidding? Nico has all the power over my wildest desires. My body aches for him, while my head curses at me, waving red flags and caution tape. But the touch of Nico—that is something that no amount of intelligence can deny. I toed the line constantly, since he walked into my home that night, between sanity and lust. And right now, the lust is smashing my sanity in its deadly, cold hands.

I don't know who I am in this very moment. I've never been at such an impasse in my life.

Who am I anymore? I thought I was going from one life to the same one, just in a different state. That couldn't be farther from the truth. Nico is mercurial. Hot then cold. Arousing then terrorizing. At least with my family I knew the minefields to avoid and exactly where I stood. When I came into this marriage, I had a job to do, and now I've abandoned it. Thrust into this life with Nico has been nothing like I expected, and I don't know how to live and exist in his world.

I have to ignore the lust. Leave it behind and respect what little shred of sanity I have left. Which is a thread still burning, and each single strand is withering away the more we're within feet of one another.

"No, do not touch me, Nico. Take me back to the boat and back to Seattle. I want to be far away from you." This time, the tears refuse to be dammed. My voice trembles, and that vulnerability I said I would cling to? Yeah, that's shot to shit. I'm tired, and I just want out. I want to be free from everything restraining me at this very moment.

He stops, his face turning serious, all deviousness disappearing in the blink of an eye.

"Fine. We will go home." And just like that, he takes out his phone, calls the guards, and gestures for me to walk ahead of him. I'm dumbfounded, honestly. I would have thought he would fight me on this. Tell me I had no choice and keep me captive on the boat for the remainder of the honeymoon. It takes me a few moments, but I set into motion, occasionally looking over my shoulder at him. Nico stays a few feet back as we walk toward the dock.

This is the last thing I remember clearly. This is when my battery drains to empty and I move on autopilot. Everything from leaving Greece to getting home is a blur.

And when I get home, my sleeping pills help keep me practically comatose.

For three whole weeks, I ignore Nico. I ignore my parents. And most of all, I ignore my own inner thoughts.

I just want to disappear into a silent place inside myself.

The last real conversation we had was more or less mechanical and required. Every night, he would come to bed after I closed my eyes, and he was gone before they opened again. Can't complain. I wanted to be as far away from him as I could get, and I got that.

Then it comes. The arrangement my ever-so-loving husband planned. My family is coming to Seattle so they can be interrogated.

He may just find what he's searching for, and the bloodbath will begin. I just hope I'm the first one down and can finally say goodbye to this bullshit.

Or maybe I can sneak out and run for the hills. Maybe even a different country. Start a new life with a new identity and say "fuck you all" and have a great life.

Would I be found in time? Probably. But then again, there is a chance I could live the rest of my life under the radar.

Doesn't that sound fucking beautiful?

Everything from my so-called honeymoon up until the meeting with my parents is ridden with self-pity and great remorse for the shit show that is and will most likely always be my life.

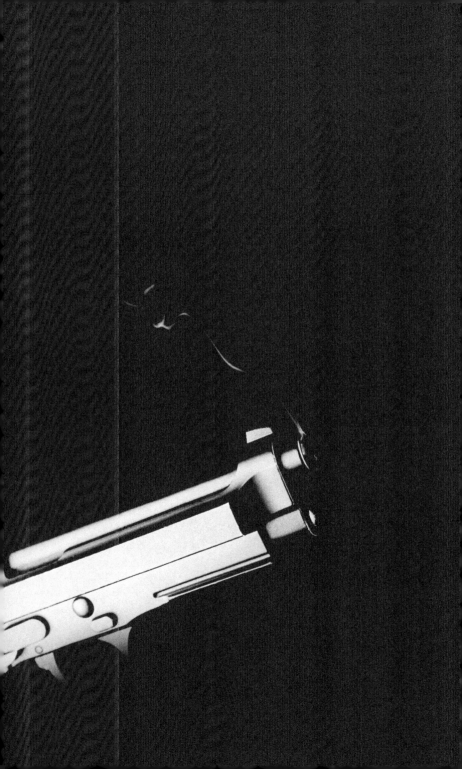

CHAPTER NINE

Nico

EMELIA WENT SILENT THAT DAY. IT'S BEEN THREE WEEKS since we came home from our overnight trip. No one would call that a honeymoon. She walks the penthouse, silent and moving like she's on empty. Giulio and I have spent time in meetings with all the outfits we've made alliances with, and I stayed at the club most nights until I knew she was asleep.

I'd check the bedroom camera, and the second her head hit the pillow, I would head home, sneak into bed, and slip out before she woke. I was able to get work done and put all my effort back into knowing what was going on in my city. My knuckles became bloody again, my barrel was emptied multiple times, and I was finding outlets for my rage again.

I was angry for the way Emelia handled what was supposed to be our time away together, and the way she turned into this shell of a person. There is nothing to say, and it's not in me to try to nurture her or make her feel better for this life. I make no apologies for who I am. But the life I am providing her is paved in gold compared to what she had at home.

Emelia is infuriating. She is selfish. And self-centered. She should be thanking me and falling in fucking line.

Tonight, however, will prove to be an interesting one, I'm sure. Her family is coming to dinner. Well... stepping into my kingdom, so I can look her old fuck of a father in the eye and make sure he isn't trying to low ball me and fuck around in my world. If he is, that's the most idiotic thing he could ever do. I will not give Emelia back to him, and I will kill him. I won't hold back. Giuseppe Notelli was my father's enemy, and that makes him mine as well.

Especially after what he did. What he and his brainless fuck of a son planned and executed. I will hate him until I can kill him, and the best part is having his daughter. He will watch me take her and build an empire to overrule him no matter the size of his army. Then, I will kill him. I will do what I've been planning to do for a long time.

Does Emelia know that? That her father and mine were enemies? Did she know about the decades-long war they rained on one another? There is no way she knows what my plans are and that the war never ended, that I just carried it on. She thinks this was all about joining families, when really it was the demise of hers.

Emelia may be in a fog now, but I do know her enough to understand she isn't a dumb woman, and she wouldn't have agreed to marry me if she knew that.

"Sir, the Notellis have arrived," Giulio informs me.

Looking up at him from where I'm sitting at my desk in the office, I give a nod. "Emelia?"

"I will let her know."

"Have her come here first. And have the Notellis seated and get them whatever drink they want. My wife and I will be down in a moment." He nods and slips out the door almost soundlessly. Finishing up the work I was doing, I stand and right my tux. I dressed the part for tonight, and I made sure Emelia would too.

Just as I button my jacket, she steps in. Her head is low, and she whispers, "You wanted to see me?"

She looks so fucking beautiful. Her body is wrapped in a dress that clings perfectly to her. The material hugs her curves just right, but the neckline scoops, hanging loose, showing off her full breasts.

God, I want her. Want to bend her over my desk and take her. Fuck my cock into her cunt and make her remember who owns that perfectly sculpted body.

Her blonde hair is down and in loose curls, contrasting prettily against the emerald-green dress. The black heels wrap around her ankles and up her calves, where they're tied in a bow. I haven't even seen her face yet, and I am salivating.

"Emelia, lift your head. They want to see you weak. Don't give him the power." Slowly, her head lifts, and her eyes bore into mine.

"And you care why? *You* like seeing me weak," she states.

"I never said that. You act surprised that I care. How many times do we have to go over this? Surely you knew you weren't marrying Prince Charming, but again, you are mine. No one can fuck with what's mine except me."

Dragging her tongue along her lip, she then bites it before letting it pop free, and I watch it closely.

My lip. I want it. *My* fucking wife.

"I didn't expect you to be a prince, but I didn't expect you to be just like my father. I would have rather you ignore me and go on as if I don't exist. You were supposed to be a place I could run to and escape him. But I ran from one den to another."

She turns to leave, but I grab her arm, doing my best to not lash out. Not just my best—it takes *a lot* of effort, every damn ounce I have.

"Listen. We will get to a point where we can talk, and we will work on things enough to tolerate one another, but you aren't the only one who is adjusting. I didn't plan on having a wife."

Yanking her arm from me, she steps back. My palms twitch to break or hit something.

"I will go with my head held high, because I hate the people out there. But I will not act like I'm your doting wife." She leaves, and I all but scream.

"Fuck," I growl and take a few deep breaths.

What am I going to do with her? We can't be like this all day, every damn day. I'm the master of standoffs, and I enjoy a lengthy negotiation, but this is too fucking much. It's been over a month, and I swear it feels like we are hitting the seven-year mark and I still know nothing about her. Other than she's sassy, great in bed, hates her family, and had a close relationship with her grandma.

We have to give and take somewhere. But when is she going to let that happen? Emelia wants to fight me at every corner. It's like she's getting back at her father by taking it out on me. Years and years of pent-up hatred and resentment being thrown at me, because at the end of the day, no matter how angry she is, I will never hit her. Ever.

Snapping back to it, I make my way to the hall and catch up with her. I take her hand, and she doesn't fight it. I don't need her to dote on me, but we do need to look like an alliance. I will grill her father, and she knows him better than I do. She will be able to tell me if he's lying and if I've cracked him.

Entering the dining area, her hand suddenly grips mine tight, and I look down at her. Her lip trembles, but she doesn't drop her head. Following her eyes, I see they're on her father, and he is staring straight back. That look is a scare tactic. He wants her to fear him still. Is he checking to see if I've made her unbreakable, or is he making sure he's still in control of her?

Not on my watch.

I notice Giuseppe is seated at the opposite end of where I sit. What a stupid man.

"That is Emelia's seat. Take any other seat at the table," I order him, and he has the audacity to laugh.

"Hilarious. The heads of table are for the men."

My eyes shoot daggers, and I watch him swallow thickly, his

pompous smile falling.

"Not in my house. That is for the queen of the Seattle outfit, and seeing as you attended the lavish wedding a mere month ago, you're very much aware that is now Emelia. Take another seat."

"Nico, it's fine. I can sit beside you," she whispers, pulling at my arm.

"Then I can't look at my wife and admire her while we enjoy our meal. You will sit at your rightful place at our table, Emelia. This is *our* home."

She gulps, and her chest rises fast before she clears her throat. "Yes, Nico." She leaves my side and slowly walks past her mother and two brothers. "Mother. Sal. Lorenzo."

They don't acknowledge her, and she continues to her place.

Well, that just won't do.

Flashbacks of Sal and me when we were younger come back, along with the knowledge of what he did, and I say what I do next with more wickedness than anything.

"Isabelle, your daughter said hello. Haven't you missed her?"

Giving me a worried glance, her mother thinks as quickly as she can.

"Yes, of course. Hello, dear."

Much better. Though it was anything but genuine, it was still done.

"Sal, Lorenzo?" I turn my attention to her brothers. "As men, you'll respect the head of this house." I sneer, my lip furling.

"Sis," they say in unison.

I shake my head. Okay, they want to play like this, do they?

"Wow, what great men you've raised. Smart, cunning, and wise," I mock.

"They never really got along with her. Can't blame them." Giuseppe shrugs.

"You can and you should. Those are the future leaders of your outfit, and they still hold on to childhood grudges? Emelia greeted

151

them after welcoming them into her home. Next time, have them come better prepared. I wouldn't allow myself nor Emelia to act with such distaste in your home. Show the same respect. Sit."

He does, and I look up at Emelia, and I can tell she's holding back a smile. "Ricardo, my chef, has prepared a nice dinner. Please." I gesture to Ricardo, and he rattles off the menu for the night. The staff serves us our first course, followed swiftly by a filet mignon and asparagus with sliced lemons.

"So, Giuseppe, how's business all the way on the East Coast?" I take a bite of my meal.

"Let's not talk business. I would much rather see how you two are doing and catch up with Emelia."

I chuckle."Now, don't be modest. I insist. Besides, Emelia doesn't have much she cares to say to you or catch up on. Isn't that right, principessa?"

Taking a sip of her wine and swallowing, she nods."That's right. Nothing as of now, Father."

The way she still shows him respect when I have given her full approval to treat him however she likes in our home is remarkable. I understand the dangers of disrespecting other bosses, but Giuseppe? His specialty is attacking with cowardly behavior.

My father let me know how weak and spineless her father was while I was growing up. This explains why he treats his wife and daughter so awfully. It's easy. But when I'm done with Emelia, he will quake when she enters the room. She will not bow her head to her family anymore.

Then again, she won't have any family left but the one we create here soon enough.

"Really? We text, and you tell me you miss me all the time. I'm here now."

Her brows draw in with clear confusion, and she looks at him, then to me, and I lift my brow at her.

"Father, I don't message you. Please don't do this tonight."

Good girl.

I cut in before he can respond to her. "Giuseppe, I feel like you're avoiding talking to me. What are you so concerned about in regard to Emelia?" I implore, smiling with my cockiest grin.

"Is it wrong for a father to miss his daughter?"

"Miss *her*, or miss using her as a punching bag?"

The table goes quiet, and her father and I enter a staring match. I won't be the first to back down. This is just getting fun. This right here is what fuels me.

War.

Enemies.

Winning.

Long moments go by, and he finally breaks.

"Emelia, I would like a word with you." He looks back at me. "Alone."

I meet her eyes, and she nods. Reluctantly, I give her a nod of approval, knowing I'm on guard and ready to strike if he tries anything.

Isabelle starts asking me about the penthouse and saying how much it reminds her of the one they have in Manhattan. To be honest, I tune her out and make sure my hearing is focused on where Emelia is. If I hear the slightest bit of duress or anything along those lines, I will be there to step in and handle Giuseppe like I want to.

This was supposed to be a time for me to bait him, but clearly I will have to be patient tonight.

"How is married life, Nico?" Isabelle continues to ramble, and I just lean back in my chair and sip my whiskey.

"It's wonderful. Your daughter is quite the woman." My response isn't a lie. I've never met a more intoxicating yet infuriating woman.

"Is she? We all worried she would make you want to rip your hair out."

I swallow the last drop and smirk. "Sass is the zest of life. She's intelligent and witty. Wouldn't you agree?" I ask with purpose. I'm curious if she has the nerve to disrespect Emelia again after the first warning.

That's something I enjoy, watching people fold and learn how to behave in the way I like.

"Y-Yes, she is." Isabelle's stutter is like the sound of a victory bell.

"Sal, Lorenzo. You are enjoying the food and my wine. How about you two? Is your father training you on how to run an army the right way?"

Her oldest brother, Sal, looks at me, and he scarfs down the bread roll like he's never eaten. Seriously, how has the Notelli household been run?

Manners? Fuck those.

Respecting women? What's that?

Having a sense of how to run a business? Never heard of it.

How has Giuseppe never been voted out?

My dad had an enemy in that coward. But there are times I see why my father never saw him as a threat—until he did. Nepotism was his way into his position and his way of keeping it. How else would someone like him gain any power at all?

New York should be led by a deadly weapon. Right now, it's just simply existing. If any power were added behind it, then the outfit would have so much more. New York is a ruthless city with a spineless ruler. His men must do all the work, and I mean *a lot* of work. Sure, usually, we have our armies do things for us, but I have watched life leave the eyes of so many. I am a part of every damn thing I run. I do not delegate the majority of the work to be done. There is nothing that happens that I am not at least made aware of, so I can decide what to do, how it should be done.

I call the shots, and when you really fuck with me, I come for you personally. And Sal and Giuseppe? They came for my fucking jugular.

"Please! Stop!" Emelia screams, and I hear scuffling.

I'm up before she even finished the second word. I move through the kitchen and into my living area. Giulio is on my tail as we enter the room. He rushes to separate Giuseppe from Emelia. Her father has his hand around her throat, and there is a fresh red mark across her cheek.

"Don't touch him, Giulio." I move past my underboss and grab the back of Giuseppe's neck, yanking him off my wife."I told you, you pathetic little man, that if you touched her again, I would handle you like I would any other man."

Isabelle, Sal, and Lorenzo come rounding the corner, and when they start to run up on me, Giulio stops them, my other guards showing up and helping detain her brothers.

"Please, this is just between her and her father. Surely you understand." Isabelle panics, begging me to show mercy.

"No." I tighten my grip, and he buckles a bit. "I don't understand cowards who hurt women for fun."

"You are going to make this worse for yourself, if you don't think this through," Giuseppe says, attempting to move, but I keep a tight hold on him.

"Oh, I'm counting on it. I have been waiting to watch you bleed in the name of my father." His eyes widen, and suddenly the room falls silent.

"How do you know about your father and me?"

Oh, it's all coming together, and when his eyes falter for less than a second to Salvatore, I see he understands exactly what I know.

"Because my father taught me how to properly run an outfit, not like the two fucked-up, brainless sons you raised. From day one, I've wanted to take it all from you. I never wanted an alliance. I've wanted revenge. Take your daughter and take you down," I confess what I haven't told anyone, and then I throw him hard against the opposite wall.

He slides down to the floor, groaning in pain. Isabelle lets out a cry, and it's overly done. The queen of dramatics.

"Let us at him, Dad!" Lorenzo yells as he and Sal try to fight against my guards, but they fail.

Opening my jacket, I pull my gun from its holster, and the sound of that hammer clicking into place nearly makes my cock hard. I lift it to Giuseppe's head, and all his family cries out. I ignore them and almost pull that fucking trigger... when I hear Emelia.

"Nico. Please. Just let them leave, and never let them come back." Emelia's soft plea breaks through my rage, and I look at her over my shoulder.

I've seen her cry. I've seen her emotional and almost crack. But this? This is something else. Emelia is broken in front of me. Something even I know must be hard for her to do.

"Emelia, he hit you. I won't let him do that. Besides, I have my own reasons to watch his brain splatter these walls. Might even keep it there as fucking wall art."

"Yes, but if you do that, you'll start another war."

No, I would end one. My father's.

"And every outfit is in my fucking pocket," I remind her. She has no clue what I know nor what I have planned.

"You will start a war for *me*. Just... please. Make them leave, and I will be an obedient wife."

Is that what she thinks she needs to be?

"I don't need you to be obedient, Emelia. I need you to be powerful."

She looks at me, her brothers and mother, then her father. I assess her, waiting for her next words or next move. Finally, she steps closer, and once she takes her place next to me, she takes the gun from my hand. I hesitate at first, but when she meets my eyes, I see she wants my trust. And for whatever she is about to do, she needs it.

I feel like I'm seeing a version of me in her. When I relinquish the gun to her, she slowly steps in front of me and lifts the gun to her father's head.

"Emelia!" Isabelle screams, and I feel fire rushing through my veins.

Is she going to kill her father? Oh, that would be even fucking better. That would turn my best laid plans into a fucking wet dream.

"Emelia, I'm your father. Don't make this mistake."

"You are dead to me." She looks at him with the rarest, deepest form of hate, and that's when I see her... change.

There it is. There is the partner I wanted. There is the daughter I wanted to steal from him and turn against him. Little did I know how easy it was going to be, because he was never a father to his daughter.

"Get the fuck out of my house. And if you try to go to war with my husband, I will not hesitate next time to have him torture you. Not just end you, but fucking *torture* you. Do you understand?"

He just swallows and glares at her.

"Do you understand!" When she yells, I swear the walls shake and the ground quakes beneath us. My chest swells with arousal and the deepest sense of pride.

"Yes," he concedes, but she still waits a moment, holding the gun to his head.

I'm not a man who makes wishes, but in that moment, I wish she would just do it. I want to see her really join me, in marriage, in war, and in fucking death. What's better than a wife? One who is your partner in crime. Tonight, she gained my respect, my devotion, and my alliance. No longer a pawn, she's now a partner.

"Get out." Slowly lowering her arm, she turns, walks down the hall, and leaves us all there.

"Looks like you raised *one* child worthy of being in this world. Giulio, get them out. Oh, and Giuseppe?" I pause, turning and placing my hands in my pockets. "If I find out it was you who fucked with my shipments, I will not only end you, but I will make sure I am voted boss of New York. Your sons will be shining my fucking shoes when you're gone." And with that, I leave to find Emelia.

My blood is beyond hot. I could melt anything I touch, including Emelia. I can't be the only one riding that high. Fuck, seeing her finally put that piece of shit in his place. And what's more, it was his own flesh and blood turning against him, and that was a master-fucking-piece. Emelia has earned her place next to me.

I couldn't care less this started the opposite of an alliance—an all-out war with the Notellis. My wife and I just became a team, and in the heat of that, I want to make sure she feels it and that it's a lasting burn. The hatred she feels for her family should never fizzle out; I want it to burn like acid inside her.

"Emelia?" I look in our room and don't see her. Checking the bathroom next, I spot her standing in front of the mirror, eyeing herself over, her face a scowl.

I don't approach her. Instead, I admire her. A vision. She is a vision standing in front of me. Close enough to touch, but it's more tempting to wait. The longer I hold back, the angrier she will become, and the anger will boil over. Her body will thrum to life, and she will claw at me. Emelia will want to tear us both out of our skin.

Fucking her like this will be like two caged animals set free after being locked away from water and food. Her eyes finally leave her own image and travel hesitantly to mine as I lean against the doorframe.

"You married me to hurt him. Not to make an alliance?"

Did I read this wrong? How could she possibly be mad at me? She wanted a safe place to land and get back at her father, and I created that for her. Giuseppe can't touch her. No, he can't go anywhere near her. Emelia is the ruler. The checkmate.

"That's what you're focused on? I gave you fucking freedom."

"Answer me. Did you use *me* to hurt him and settle some score?"

Slowly rolling my head from side to side and popping my neck, I fixate on the cracking before I speak.

"Yes, I used you as a pawn. What are you going to do, Emelia? Run back to him? You're fucking free. Besides—"

"Fuck me," she orders, cutting off my words and gaining on me. I'm stunned but prepare for impact.

Her hungry eyes tell me all I need to know. We collide, and I bend, wrapping my hands violently in her hair. The same violence bleeds into each other's kiss. We fight, dual, both wanting the upper hand. I tilt my head to get a deeper taste. Not even air can slip from between us, and it still isn't close enough.

"Emelia." I separate us, leaning down farther and taking her full, luscious ass in my hands and squeezing it to the point of bruising.

"Yes, God, yes!" she cries, leaning and nipping at my chin and my neck.

"What do you say to me?"

She isn't mad. No—far from that. The question she posed was for surety that I in fact gave her what she never knew she could have. Even if she was a pawn, she broke out and got away from it, and now she has the backing of more than a thousand men.

She loves the fact that *she* was the weapon used against her father.

If she told me tonight that she wanted to go after him and end his life, ruin the legacy of her grandfather, and destroy and take over everything he claimed was his, I wouldn't hesitate. I would go without a backward glance. That might be the battle I would enter with the most excitement than any other I ever have before. I never thought revenge would be this sweet.

"What do you mean?" she pants, trying to push back enough to get to my tux jacket.

I grip the hair at the nape of her neck and yank her head back. Through gritted teeth, I ask her again, but this time with more force. "What do you say to me for getting you out of that family?"

Not a second's pause. "*Thank you.* Thank you, sir."

"Such a good girl. Open your mouth for me."

She tilts her head and raises a brow, but because I demand her to do it, like an obedient fuck toy, she does it, opening her mouth wide.

I spit down her throat, and she moans.

"Swallow it."

She does, and a wicked gleam dances in her eyes.

"Go to the bed. Take the dress off and put on a fucking show," I tell her, biting her lip and making sure she bleeds. Yelping, she steps back, takes her pointer finger, and touches the painted red tip to where blood is now seeping from her plump lip.

"If you stay still, I will spank your ass till that bleeds too. Go."

She jumps into action, her eyes sparkling with desire.

With a harsh tug and pull, I am out of my tie and jacket while I watch that silky material slide down her body. A bra and no fucking panties. Her ass, God, it's so damn thick I want to bite it.

"Like this?" She bends over to untie the bows of her heels, and her cunt is in full view. So clear I can see it glistening.

"You're doing such a good job, preparing for your husband."

"Do you want to fuck me? Like this?" Stopping the work on her heels, she reaches back, separates her legs enough I can watch, and slides two fingers beautifully into her slick, sweet center. If I could die with this image, I would. In fact, I would like to take a picture of her just like this and hang it above our bed.

"Fuck your pussy. Because I'm not holding back tonight. You're taking it all. Everything. I will even fuck that heart-shaped ass and claim it. You'll be too damn sore to do anything but lay in bed."

Emelia cries out, but it sounds more like a needy whimper than fear, all while her fingers simultaneously fuck her cunt, the sound of her wetness as loud as our heavy breathing. I love knowing that even though she is soaked, her cunt is still tight. That body was made for a man like me, built to take a husband who could fuck her into oblivion.

Unbuttoning my pants, I reach in and pull my cock free, gripping it with as much tightness as I know only her beautiful pussy can. No hand or other cunt on this earth can compare to the sweetness between her legs. Emelia and I may not know one another, and we are still in a loveless marriage, but when we fuck, it's like we've always known one another. That's the only time we can agree on anything. Lust and getting off.

We temporarily hang our daggers and pitchforks up in the corner, and we are lost to the insatiable need that eats people alive.

The devil is in the details, in every curve and inch of her body. What we do would make grown men cry just by witnessing it. But tonight, I'll fuck her with respect. Not physically, but mentally. She is my ally, and we are now partners, and when she's ready, we will take down her father. Who knew this could come from our deceptively arranged marriage. In fact, I convinced myself for weeks leading up to the wedding that she would never take my side and all she'd be is the portal for my heir before she'd run at the first hint of my plans.

"Faster. Fuck yourself faster. Don't you dare go easy on that cunt," I bark at her.

"I want it to be you. I'm hurting. Aching!" she cries, and I growl loudly. I don't even recognize the sound coming out of me.

"Yeah, you are. Ass up on the bed, baby."

With enthusiasm, she rushes to the bed, working quickly to take her heels off when she gets there.

"No. Leave them on," I groan, gripping the tip of my cock as I approach her. "Shoulders to the bed, and if you move, I stop," I threaten. Watching her head bob an eager yes, I praise her, "Good girl."

"I love it when you do that. But I also like it when you treat me like I'm filthy," she confesses, and I grin and line my cock up with her entrance. Without hesitation, I enter her like a feral beast.

"Shit!" she squeals.

The image of her being impaled on my thick cock will never get old. Smacking her ass, then immediately pinching her thigh, I make her yelp.

"Nico!"

I fuck up into her, thrusting with purpose. I still have my shirt and my dress slacks on. The stark difference between her open and bare and me still hidden behind a mask, it makes it that much more thrilling.

"This means nothing more than fucking," I remind her.

Or am I reminding myself?

Shaking my head, I try to rid myself of that thought. This is nothing. She is nothing. We are nothing more than business partners and really good at fucking each other. That's all.

But even thinking about this throws me off.

"Nico? Please don't stop."

But I do. I need to get my fucking head in the game. I'm riding a high and getting my dick wet by really good pussy. That's it.

Needing a minute, I think up something quick. When I pull out, she cries out for me, *"Il mio re."*

Did she just call me her fucking king once again?

Fuck.

"Principessa, don't talk until I tell you to. Put your face into the mattress. Understand?"

"Yes. Just please—"

I slap her ass, watching the thick roundness move with the strength of my touch. Emelia wants to beg, but she fights it, putting her face in the mattress and gripping the sheets. I move to my nightstand and pull out some lube. Watching her shoulders rise and fall in tandem with her desire, I move back behind her.

I bet this is killing her, not being able to talk. In fact, I would bet my life on it. However, Emelia and I are both passionate in the bedroom, and clearly, we are passionate about our enemies as well, but I can't let that be mistaken as some unspoken bond.

It's an alliance.

Alliance is business.

A bond indicates something more, even love, and I will never love her.

I tilt my head from side to side, admiring her pussy, full ass, and stunning back, all while I trail my hands from her shoulders and back to her ass. I touch every inch of skin I can along the way, pinching, grabbing, and prepping her for what's to come. No moans leave her, and for that, I am proud. I want to watch her anticipation grow. See her shiver under my touch and build the excitement.

Her silence is more telling than her words could ever be. The reactions of her skin and the jolts of her body speak louder than even the city life below us.

Each inch of skin is covered in goose bumps, and her cunt is dripping, her juice moving from her center and down her thighs. "Sweet, such a sweet taste you have." I bend and lap up the wetness. I wouldn't dare let any of that go to waste. A faint—and I mean an ever-so faint—sound leaves her, and I smirk against her thigh, nipping it in response, and she jolts forward.

"Nico. I can't. I can't be silent. I need to hear you, and I need you to hear me. Please."

"Anything for you, but one thing first."

She pushes up on her arms and tosses her blonde hair to the side, looking deep into my eyes over her shoulder. "Yes?"

Holding the lube up for her to see, I open it, and I pour some onto my fingers. Emelia's eyes widen, and she looks almost scandalized.

"You like to have your pussy and sweet ass filled at the same time?"

She shakes her head, indicating no, before she responds. "No, but I want you to do it. Please." I love it when she begs.

"Good. Relax and take some deep breaths. Let me in."

Nodding with a deep swallow, she does as she's told. Watching her visibly relax and lean in to trusting me, I take my middle finger to her tight asshole and line my cock up with her pussy, and in unison, slowly—so fucking painfully slowly—I enter her. My finger in her ass and my cock in her pussy. I can't tell which is tighter. They both feel like heaven, and after she soaks my dick, I'm going to coat her walls with my cum when I claim her ass.

I've never been a fan of anal. It takes too much time and care to do it without causing pain. I prefer a fast blowjob or a steady fuck in the pussy. But with her, I feel as feral as an animal in heat, wanting to mark all of her as mine.

"Oh my God! Nico! Fuck." I use my free hand and grip her hip hard.

"Watch your mouth, Emelia. That's not very ladylike."

"I don't want to be ladylike. Fuck me like a whore, Nico."

My head lulls back, and I start pumping, growling. Damn this woman and the curse she has on my cock.

"You naughty slut. So greedy," I reward her the way she wants.

"Fuck my ass, please. I love it when you touch me there." She doesn't have to ask me twice. Adding a second finger, I start to fuck her with my lubed fingers in unison with my thrusting cock.

My fingers are facing down, and my thick forearms are lined in pronounced veins. That's the lust that takes over me when she's naked and wrapped around me. The blood in me thickens, burns, and tries to burst free.

"Emelia. I need you to come so I can get off in your ass. Can you do that for your husband?"

She nods, and this time, she matches up with me, pushing back with force onto my cock and fingers. That's when I stop and enjoy the show. So much effort and hard work from my impish wife.

"Look at you. Such a good job, baby. So greedy for this cock."

"Yes! Yes!" she cries, picking up the pace. Her asshole starts to tighten, as does her cunt, and I can tell she's close as she does all the work.

"Fuck yourself on my dick just a little harder, baby, and you can come on it. Come on, baby, just like that," I encourage, simultaneously trying to keep myself from getting off.

"I'm coming! Nico!" She screams my name through her euphoria, and it is fucking paradise.

"Go ahead, baby. Come for me. Right there," I coach her. "Yes, just like that." I knead her ass, and just like that, my touch and words get her off. She comes hard. "Fuck, Emelia!" The tightening is nearly too much. She's going to milk the come right out of me. I'm impatient and want my time with her now, so the moment her pulsing slows, I tap her ass. "Over. Turn over."

Spent, she does as she's told in a thoroughly fucked and satiated manner, making me smile. I squeeze out more lube and cover my cock, then take her ankles and place them on my shoulders. Once there, she watches me in wonderment, her eyes appreciating my built frame and large cock.

"You ready, pretty baby?"

Biting her lip, she nods.

Grabbing a pillow from beside us, I place it under her ass, and it puts her at just the right height, ready for me. "Breathe slowly, and let me in."

"Anything."

I lick my bottom lip and slowly start to enter her. Her sphincter tightens at first, but I remind her to relax, and inch by inch, she welcomes me. Once I'm fully in, I groan. "Your body is my personal paradise for pleasure."

I grab the softness of her stomach in one hand, then lean forward, shoving my middle and pointer finger into her mouth.

Emelia cries out around them, and I slide in and out, languid at first, enjoying every sensation.

I push my fingers deeper and watch her gag. This causes tears to spill from the corners of her eyes and into her blonde hair. She lifts her head just a bit, trying to watch my hips work up into her.

"Choking on my fingers, so pretty, wife," I compliment, and muffled words vibrate on my fingers, but they're unintelligible. "Enjoy the pleasure. Cry for me more. Show me how thankful you are for this life."

As she nods, her eyes keep watering. My hand leaves her hip, and I keep her impaled on my cock. Sliding my hand from her stomach to her clit, I circle it with the pad of my finger, and she moans over and over. When I see her orgasm building again, I eagerly wait for the finale.

"You ready?"

"Yes," she says around my fingers, and I remove them but quickly grab her throat and resume fucking up into her hard. Right as I start coming, I squeeze my hand around her neck and come down hard on her clit with a harsh slap.

"Fuck!" she screams, and her juices squirt from her pussy as she comes, splashing my abs. She fucking marked me with all her appreciation.

"Good girl." I coat her ass with my cum, emptying into her, and our eyes lock for a long moment. The tears are still falling from her, and that feeling I avoided earlier starts coming back.

Push it back, I inwardly scold.

Lust isn't love.

I don't blame myself for being unable to tell the difference when we're in the throes of passion, because I have never had sex as good as I have with Emelia.

Our bodies are coated in sweat, and I lift my hand and move my hair from my forehead, her eyes locked on her initial on my arm.

"I still can't believe you carved it into your arm."

I glance to where she's looking and shrug. "What's mine is mine." I pull out of her once I've softened and fall over next to her. Emelia moves the pillow from under her and curls up next to me. She faces me, and once she's all settled, I can feel her watching me as I stare up at the ceiling.

"What?" I finally ask, catching up my breath .

"What's the history between your father and mine?"

I expected her to eventually ask me this, and I don't have a reason not to tell her.

"Your father is a coward." I want to approach this delicately. Telling her everything right away isn't the route I want to take. We have only just begun what will be the demise of her family. Baby steps are needed to ensure it doesn't get messy.

"Agreed," she inserts and laughs.

I give a slight chuckle but continue on. "Anyway, our fathers were both raised by some of the strongest men in the mafia, and the rivalry between New York and Seattle started there. It just kept passing down through the generations, and my father and yours were no exception." I pause, swallowing thickly.

I don't like to talk about my parents. They're the only people I've kept sacred.

"They crossed paths, and one day it ultimately led to a bloodbath." Emelia and I weren't touching, but as I keep talking, she slowly moves closer until she has her head on my chest.

I sit up fast. "Anyway, before we could find out all the things your father wanted to do or had plans to do, my father died."

Standing, I move toward the bathroom. I don't have to look back to know she must be staring at me with confusion. I'm not ready to tell her that her father killed mine. That can wait. Besides, my cock is freshly satiated, and I don't want the high to be suffocated by the loss of my parents.

"Nico?"

I stop in the doorway and turn my head slightly. "Emelia, you knew your father was a bad man, and we don't need to spin around in circles to talk about it. He fucked with my blood, so I took some of his," I refer to her, and she doesn't respond. I leave her and head to the shower.

I never planned on telling Emelia everything. I was just going to give her the basics and then execute the majority of my plan on my own. But now she can help me.

My parents' story isn't her business. She knows the general outline, and that's all she will ever need. Besides, the look in her eyes when we shared that orgasm felt too deep, and I can't have her or me getting confused on what this is.

Distance. I have to create distance.

Which lasts a mere hour.

I showered and left the room so Emelia could take her turn, then headed to my office to get some work done. I'm balls-fucking-deep in paperwork for the club, when there's a knock on my door.

"Sir, I think you need to see this." Giulio steps inside with a folder in his hand, and I pinch the bridge of my nose.

"What fucking now?" I yank the folder from his hands and plop it down on my desk. That's when I open what I wish I'd never seen.

My wife.

My wife naked.

My wife naked in bed with another man.

My wife with Damian during intimate acts, and attached is a list of all the websites these photos currently reside on.

"Who put these up?" I growl, my skin heating and my mind becoming nothing but fog. The only thing I can see clearly is revenge.

Bloody fucking revenge.

"Damian Rafael, sir. He's in the warehouse as we speak."

I stand, and my chair flies backward, slamming into the

window so hard I'm truly surprised it didn't shatter or even crack. I want to tear him apart. Remove each finger one by fucking one. And then when I'm done with that, I will cut his throat.

I will do all this with Emelia watching. I want her close enough the blood will splatter her clothes.

"Go ahead. Emelia and I will be there shortly."

I make my way to the bedroom. That's where I find her in just a towel, preparing her clothes for bed.

"Get dressed. We have plans." I leave the room, and she frantically calls after me, but I ignore her.

"Nico! Where are we going? It's late!"

That's the last thing I hear before everything goes silent. I only see red.

CHAPTER TEN

Emelia

I'M LEFT THERE ALONE IN THE SHOWER AFTER NICO took one himself, standing beneath the water in my nakedness with my wayward thoughts. Confused, hurt, and worried.

Tonight, I chose Nico over my father, and while I know what that will cost me, I had no idea he was using me just like my father was. They both wanted me as some sort of chess piece in their match. Before tonight, Nico never let on that he wanted me to be the demise of my father. It was always "be strong," "be the wife of a mafia boss," and "don't show weakness," but never anything about taking down my father.

I was always supposed to be *Nico's* downfall.

What was I supposed to do though?

After what my father did to me, I reclaimed my power in the most monumental way.

And then I was overtaken by lust.

I was filled with pride for taking my life back from my father, but I know the adrenaline-fueled lust is fleeting—because it already is.

Plus, my father will come after me, or worse, he'll tell Nico the truth about why I married him.

Then, tonight. The look. God, the look in Nico's eyes while he took me to places and showed me things only he can was beyond maddening. It was almost like he felt a closeness with me that he has never had with anyone else. There was... vulnerability... and dare I say genuine care for *me* and not just what my body can offer or what being his enemy's daughter could do for him. I was something to him.

But I read it wrong—all of it. I was seeing what I wanted to see.

Am I falling for Nico? No. No way. I don't know him. We don't know one another. But I do care for him. I think. I have to, right? Especially after tonight.

Now, I'm naked and feel ashamed of what we just did. We ride this high, we have sex, and it's an out-of-this-world, untouchable type of sex, then it turns dark. You can't see the spark anymore, like a blue flame. It's difficult to see, but you feel the burn. Even when I attempted to make conversation to see if he would let me in more, he shut me out almost immediately.

There are snippets of him I see, and that's when I try to get in, but before tonight, it was always in the form of banter, mocking, or bickering. Tonight, there was hope of white flags truly rising and the laying down of armor, but then he built that wall back up.

And this time, regretfully, it hurts me. It doesn't cause me anger. I feel... sad. Why can't we just get to know one another? Talk and connect like we do when flesh meets flesh and the sensitive skin becomes a tender thing we treat delicately? Why can't our words be delicate too?

Who am I kidding? Nico could never. He is a killer. A boss. A ruthless man who has no regard for life except for what it can offer him. And tonight, I choose not to be angry. In fact, it's like looking into a mirror. Nico was *made* to be cruel and filled with hate. Just like I was made to think I was nothing to anyone. We are both heirs of the mafia life. There is no escape. You either embrace it or run from it, and we both only had one option. I can't blame him for how hardened he's become because of the only life we've ever known.

The devil in a power suit is just a naked man with scars no one can heal. Not even me. Who even is he? I'll never know. Because Nico will give me the cover but nothing under the surface.

I do my best not to think of Nico during the rest of my shower, but I can't help it. He's all I can think about, and I scold myself. Stepping out, I towel off, put on my nightly moisturizer, brush my teeth, and then make my way into the bedroom to get dressed. I pick out my clothes, but before I can step into them, I'm interrupted by the man I didn't want to think about for the rest of the night.

I swear he must have known.

When I see him, I see exactly what I was ruminating on earlier—I see the devil in the flesh. Nico has transformed into something I have never seen before, an evil that haunts only nightmares.

"Get dressed. We have plans," he bites out and turns fast on his heel, leaving me in the dust.

"Nico! Where are we going? It's late!" I call after him, scared by the look he just gave me.

Did my father call?

Does Nico know, and now I'm going to die?

My stomach turns, and I feel it bottom out and bile rising to the surface. I feel so much fear in this moment that I don't even remember how to breathe in and out, and I choke out a cough, gasping for air.

"No." I continue to grasp onto what feels like brief intervals of oxygen I may not get another chance to take. Dressing in jeans and a white tee with some slip-on Converse happens all in a blur. I don't know how I did it, or recollect any moment of it, but I'm dressed.

On shaky legs, I step out into the hall and make my way to

the elevator where I know he will be waiting for me. I didn't even bother to brush my hair or dry it. I just tossed it over my shoulders and tried to get to him before he came looking for me again.

When I see him at the elevator, I take in what he's wearing. He must have dressed in his office. I know he has a wardrobe in there, because he isn't in the sweats he was wearing when he left the room. He's now in shiny pointed shoes and dress pants. His top half is covered in a white button-up that is tucked into his pants, and his sleeves are rolled up to his elbows, his gun holster completing the look. My heart rate continues to rise, never once falling or leveling out. I think I might just have a heart attack.

"Relax, Emelia. You look like you just woke from the dead," he tells me, and I swallow thickly.

"And you look like you want to kill me."

He chuckles, and it's menacing."Far from it, Emelia. Tonight is all about taking care of you and protecting you. So you can take a breath."

I literally do that. I gasp so loud and bend over, dropping my hands to my knees and sucking in as much air as I can.

"Emelia? What's wrong? Are you all right?" Nico's voice is worried, and accompanied by his gentle hand on my back, I almost start to cry.

I've never been more afraid in my life, and now I have to think up a lie.

"You looked at me like my father always did before he would hurt me. I was worried I upset you somehow," I say through my panting. And it's not a total lie. I have seen looks almost as painfully terrifying on my father's face.

"Emelia, breathe, principessa." He moves the hair that has fallen in my face and kneels down on his haunches. Our eyes lock, and I swear I can see humanity in there.

He has to be developing a soft spot for me. He has to. I know this, because he went from looking like I was his next target to maim, to genuinely worried. I keep my eyes on him, and I finally say it.

"I don't know how to trust anyone," I admit.

"You can trust me. As long as I can trust you."

Guilt builds in my stomach. I'm lying to him by not telling him that just like he had plans, so did I. It wouldn't matter so much if he never confessed his, but now it does. The playing field isn't even.

"In fact, tonight, I will prove how much you can trust me," he adds, and I want to inquire how he plans to do that, but I need a fucking minute. I can only reply with a simple nod. That's all I can muster up at the moment.

The elevator opens, and when we step inside, I take a place next to him.

"Tell me about Damian. How long were you two together?"

That was a curveball. Where is this coming from?

"What? Why does it matter?" I ask, looking at him with an incredulous expression.

"I want to know what he meant to you, Emelia. Answer the question."

I shake my head and roll my eyes. "We got together when I was nineteen."

He has his hands in his pockets, and his feet are planted apart, his eyes focused on the ground. God, he looks so damn handsome. What is it about sleeves rolled up and a strong jawline that makes me so wet for him? The way his black hair is slicked back except the one strand that has fallen in front of his eye—my hell.

"Elaborate. How you met and the entirety of your relationship, Emelia," he growls.

"Uh, okay. Well, we met when he was hired to work in my dad's army. He was my bodyguard, and we spent a lot of time together. That time turned into a friendship and then a relationship." The elevator opens to the garage, and he takes my hand, leading me to his Maserati. I follow behind him, my shorter stature not allowing me to walk side by side with him.

Once we get to the car, he opens my door and ushers me inside, and I buckle myself in as he rounds the car.

Where is he taking us?

He slides in effortlessly and hits the button, the engine roaring to life, and the seat under me vibrates.

"Nico, where are we going?"

"Don't change the subject." He reminds me of what I'm supposed to be talking about.

"It was my first relationship. I don't know what you want me to say!"

He revs the engine and pulls out of the garage, and I brace myself, gripping onto the center console and the door panel.

"Did you love him, or did you just say that to piss me off that day?"

All right, how do I answer this?

If I tell him I loved him, is he going to snap, or is he going to take it like it's no big deal?

He caught me in a room simply talking to Damian, and that led to him carving his ownership of me into his skin. So really, how do I answer that?

"Is that relevant? We are married. He's not a threat," I point out.

"Really? You don't think he's a threat? Did he ever hurt you?"

I look down in my lap, recalling the crying I did for weeks in private when he left. "Only when he left," I whisper.

"So he ended it? Why?" He gets on the freeway, and I look at the cars next to us.

"He said he got another job, but I think he was scared of my father finding out about us. Maybe my father did, and he just bowed out. I really don't know the truth."

"Do you still love him, Emelia?" His words are like a gunshot to the heart.

"What? Nico, you are acting insane. Where are we going, and why do you suddenly care about Damian so much?"

Shit. Did Damian show up? Did he do something stupid and cross Nico, and now he's going to kill him? Fuck.

My palms start to sweat, and my spine turns painfully cold. "Nico. Please."

"Do. You. Still. Love. Him?"

My eyes water, and Nico continues to accelerate and weave in and out of traffic erratically.

"It doesn't—"

"Do you still love him, Emelia!" he yells, and he slams his hand down on the steering wheel, making the answer fall from me like word vomit.

"Yes, I do! He was the only man who truly loved me and protected me." It comes out fast, and I wish I could take it back, but it's too late. I look up at Nico as one tear slowly falls, and his grin is not charming.

It's wicked.

"Nico? Is he here? Did he come here and do something?"

"He is the only man who has ever protected you?" A gust of air mockingly releases from his flared nostrils.

"Yes. He was there to comfort me after my father would hurt me, and he loved me."

"Really? Did he ever hit your dad back or get you out?" he asks.

"No," I admit, dropping my head.

"But I did. I got you out. And I almost killed your father. Stopped only because you asked. But that's the man you still love and defend? So am I just nothing to you?"

Where is this coming from?

"Are you asking me if I love you?" I blurt out.

"No, Emelia. I don't love you, and you don't love me, but you seem to think there is a man still superior to your husband out there and that is something I don't like."

The way he said he doesn't love me shouldn't have hurt, but it did. I don't expect him to. In fact, I never even thought he would one day, but for some reason, it stung.

"I didn't say he was superior."

"Oh, but you did, principessa, just in lesser words, and I don't like it," he growls, looking over at me.

I swallow thickly. "And you've never loved anyone or wished I was someone else? There was never another woman you wish you would have married instead of me?" I flip the tables. Nico has the nerve to ridicule me over something I can't help. Especially when it is apparent it isn't really about love. It's about fucking power.

"No. I fucked women, and that's it. If I didn't want to ruin your father, you wouldn't be sitting here, and you would be off with the traitor," he hisses.

"The traitor?"

"Yes. Your perfect little lover, Emelia." We exit the freeway, and the road we are on is bleak. There are no houses, just a couple of abandoned buildings.

"You're scaring me, and I want to go home. I think you've gone mad and need to take it out on someone else."

He laughs as he pulls up to what looks like a rusted, empty, broken-down warehouse. I know the type well. Who doesn't in the mafia?

"Oh, I am. You're going to love this. You're going to watch it, and I think you just might enjoy it."

My mouth is left slightly ajar and my brows a confused mess as he leaves the car and makes his way around to me. Opening my door, he leans in and unbuckles me before standing back up outside.

"Let's go," he tells me, and I shake my head.

"No. I'm not going in there to do whatever sick thing you're planning. Take me home, Nico." I turn stern and try to act unafraid.

"Fine." He grabs my arm with enough force to get me out of the car. It doesn't hurt, but it's startling.

"Nico! Stop!" He pulls me to the front door, and I dig in my heels the whole way.

"Stop fighting this, Emelia!"

"You stop scaring me and let me go!" I fight back.

"No, not going to happen. Now get in the fucking warehouse," he says through gritted teeth.

Those eyes reappear.

The ones that terrify me to the bone.

I shut down, self-preservation kicking in, and let him lead the way.

We first enter into darkness, the only light coming from an open door at the end of what looks like a narrow hall.

"Walk to the door," he instructs, and I gulp and slowly start moving, with Nico hot on my trail. The closer we get, the more nauseated I become. When we're only a few feet from the door, he says, "Go ahead and enter. Enjoy the gift I got you, *wife*." He draws out the last word with sarcasm and some sort of sick pleasure from whatever is waiting.

With a deep breath, I take a step inside, and the moment I do, I hear muffled pleading. I look to the left, where there are a bunch of lights set up in a circle, but that's not the part I linger on for long. Tied up and bleeding from different parts of his face...is Damian.

"Damian!" I run to him, not caring what happens.

He lets out pained pleas for help around the cloth in his mouth.

Damian has his arms tied behind his back and to the chair, and his ankles are tied to the legs. Giulio stands in the corner stoically. He doesn't even look at us. His eyes stay focused on the wall to the left of us. I'm on my knees and looking for a way to untie Damian, all while waiting for Nico to intervene and pull me off, but he doesn't.

When I fail to untie him, I turn to Nico, who stands next to a table with various medical instruments, knives, a gun, and brass knuckles. He stands so cockily, with his arms crossed, in that now familiar stance. But the worst part is how amused and intrigued he looks. Like he's watching caged animals trying to fight their way out of captivity.

This bastard.

But if I fight him, I will have a significantly lower chance of getting Damian out of here alive.

"Nico. Please, let him go. Why are you doing this?"

"Don't worry about it. Just sit back and enjoy the show." He admires the assortment of knives on the table next to him and glides his hands slowly over each one before picking one up.

"You're an asshole! I have not spoken to him, and you're do this because of what? An alpha pissing contest! Fuck you, Nico! Let him go!" I scream. I look to Giulio to see if there is any sympathy from him, but he is still staring blankly at the wall. I guess that answers my question of if he ever had a soul at all. He is just as heartless as Nico.

"Oh really? So you think he is worth sparing and this is all because I have to claim dominance?" Nico questions, stepping up to Damian and me.

I peer up at him through angry eyes. If I could kill him with a look, I would."Yes. That's what you have been alluding to since we got in the damn car. Why else would you hurt him?"

Nico looks to Giulio and gives him a nod, and I hear Giulio's steps before I see him, and suddenly I'm pulled away, but not without kicking and screaming. I thrash around and yell for him to let me go, but he ignores me. And my pleas mold together with Damian's as we both watch in horror when Nico brings the knife to the trapped man's pinky. And with what looks like no effort, he starts to slice, slowly removing his finger.

I scream so loud my heart skips, and my ears and head throb."Nico! Please! I love him! Please stop! Don't be like my father! Please!" I resort to a last-ditch effort to stop him. I look at the tears pouring from Damian's eyes, and his muffled screams will be a sound that haunts me forever.

Once his pinky is removed, Nico turns to me, blood on his hand and all the way up to his crisp white shirtsleeve. He wears a sinister grin, and I bend over and vomit at the sight.

"Good girl, let it all out. Vomit the rest of him out of your system."

"Why are you doing this?" I cry harder, and he steps up to me calmly, the knife in one hand and the other reaching into his pocket. I still struggle to release myself from Giulio but to no avail.

"Would a man who loves you in the same regard betray you like this, principessa?" He holds up his phone, and my eyes try to focus past the tears.

When they do, my heart stops in my chest. I swear it.

The image comes into focus, and when I see photos of Damian and me naked and entangled with one another, my body on full display, I realize they aren't ones I ever knew he took. In fact, I *never* let him film us or take pictures.

He did this... behind my back.

How could he do this?

Nico keeps scrolling. Each image getting more and more intimate and showing my entire body in ways I wouldn't want anyone to see.

"This is just the start. They were on over a dozen pornography sites, Emelia." Nico sneers. "Do you still fucking love him now? Am *I* still the monster, wife?"

I don't answer him. Instead, my head just slowly shakes, the reality of what is happening sinking in second by second. Each moment that passes, I try to think up a million reasons of how it could be something else, or a genuine mistake, or someone else who did this. It just *had* to be. Damian was the love of my life.

Damian was the first man to see my body. To touch me. To love me. This betrayal would mean none of it was real.

"No. He wouldn't."

"Emelia, you think I would just do this on a whim? All of these were found linked to his IP address. He posted them all. I don't know much about love, nor do I care to, but I'm assuming this isn't something it would entail. Am I wrong?"

Damian starts to move again and speaks behind the cloth in his mouth. He keeps struggling against his restraints, but he fails to loosen them. I look from him to Nico, then back Damian again, and I ask him what I need to know.

"Did you do this?" My voice is low, and you can hear the heartbreak in it. Anyone could heed it in my voice just as clearly as I can feel it in my soul. He looks at me with a petrified look, but I don't see remorse. He is more regretful he's in this situation than he is about putting our sex tapes and images all over the internet.

"You were supposed to love me." My body goes lax, and Giulio loosens his grip on me.

"Are you ready to let me finish the job?" Nico holds the blade up and admires it... and now, so do I.

"Yes."

Damian screams like a weak fuck, and that just fuels me on.

"Good." Nico starts to turn, but I place my hand on his shoulder. He stops and looks at me. "Yes?"

I swallow thickly, and then I speak. "Can I help?"

His brows rise, and Damian's pleas are drowned out by my pulse drumming in my ears. Nico pivots just slightly, his body not completely facing me, but his expression is etched in surprise. "You want to help, wife?"

I nod slowly, glancing at Damian and then to Nico.

Damian does his best to plead his case with just his eyes and pathetic tears, but something in me... darkens... and my heart turns to stone. A feeling I have never felt before. But I welcome it. He betrayed me. He left me. He used me. Was it ever love?

"Yes." I reach out and grab the knife, and Nico doesn't stop me. I circle Damian then, learning finally what it's like to be the hunter and not the prey.

"You never loved me, did you?" I ask, and he starts to rattle off some incoherent words. I look up at Nico and notice he's standing there with a shine in his eyes as he crosses his arms and keeps his focus on me.

"Pathetic, isn't he, Giulio?" Nico asks. "It's nice to take out the trash."

"The best part of this job, sir," Giulio says.

I interrupt them, "Nico, remove the cloth."

He looks at me, and without pause, he does what I ask with a smirk on his face. When he rips the cloth off, Damian starts spitting out words.

"Emelia, baby, it wasn't like that. I needed money. I stole some of your father's goods and sold them, and he almost found out. I needed a way to make some money so I could buy more to replace what I stole. It was a stupid—"

"Shut up!" I scream, stopping in front of him, and I place my empty hand on his forearm and bend to within inches of his face. "You're the worst liar I have ever met. I can't believe I trusted you. Do you do this still? To other women?" I tilt my head and watch him intently.

He stares into my eyes, and I just know he's searching for another lie to tell me.

"Nico, does he do this to other women?" I ask, without breaking eye contact.

"Yes. Dozens, Emelia."

I stand tall then, and without even a brief pause, I bring my hand back and swing it downward, making contact with his cheek so hard his head whips to the side, his neck popping with the movement.

"You sick fuck! Men like you deserve your dicks ripped off.

You used me."

"Emelia, I loved you."

"You *loved*?" I laugh with all the sarcasm I can muster. He's such a bastard.

"No, I didn't mean that. I still love you, and I want what we had."

"That will never fucking happen," Nico chimes in, his voice low and menacing.

"No, it won't, and I was stupid to think that one day, after I gave Nico a family, he would let me leave and we could be happy." I slap him again, and Nico growls behind me. What I said must have upset him.

"Never would have happened," Nico inserts.

I don't respond, because the only person I want to focus on is Damian and his betrayal. I take the knife and admire the blade like Nico did, and Damian begs.

"Emelia, please! I won't do anything like that again. I'll stop it all." The power I feel when he begs, it's almost as if I understand the power the mafia men hold when they're getting revenge.

"I finally have the control to take back all the things that were stolen from me by men like you." I lower the blade and bring it to his hand, specifically his middle finger. Just call me metaphorical. Cutting off his middle finger as a big "fuck you" for being like every other man who's crossed me.

I start gliding it across his skin slowly, the blood seeping out. He screams for me to stop, and I absorb every single second of it. In fact, it fuels me, and the more he begs and yells, the more my chest swells, and the feeling of victory consumes me. I feel vindicated.

I get to the bone and stop, leaving the knife in his finger.

"You deserve everything my husband does to you." I turn and look at Nico. He doesn't look happy anymore, nor is he gloating like he did when I started, but I don't care.

I made Damian bleed.

"I don't want him dead. I want him to walk around with no fingers. That's not a request." I walk away, and Nico yells at Giulio to follow me. The underboss does, and I make it out of the warehouse.

Giulio leads me to the car he came in, and he opens the back door for me. I slide inside and settle in.

"Take me home," I demand as he shuts his door.

"I need to ask Nico. Give me a moment."

"Giulio, take me home. You don't need his approval if I'm just going home. He can finish business."

He eyes me in the rearview mirror, and I tilt my head, challenging him to test me.

"Yes, ma'am."

The entire way home, I think of Nico and what he just gave me the opportunity to do. I even let a tear fall over the betrayal and the embarrassment of knowing others have seen me in those videos and pictures. But I mostly focus on my husband and what he was willing to do for... for me.

"Giulio."

"Yes, Mrs. Valiente?" He gets off the freeway.

"Did he...? How are the photos and videos getting taken down?"

"Nico is taking care of it. We have people working on it. Everything should be taken down before you wake up in the morning." His phone rings over the car's speakers as we pull into the garage.

"Sir," Giulio answers.

"Is she home now?" Nico's voice comes through, and I can hear Damian struggling in the background, followed by other voices. I'm assuming he called for his backup to come finish the job.

"Yes."

"Good. I'll be home soon."

Why did he call to check on me? He could've just tracked me.

The call ends, and Giulio parks. I let myself out, and we head to the elevator and make our way to the penthouse. When I walk off to our bedroom, I climb into the shower and scrub my body. Not just wanting Damian's blood off me but all the times he touched me. I want to erase him from my body and forget him. I feel filthy—from his touch and the exploitation he submitted me to without me knowing. I scrub until my skin is nearly raw and beet-red before stepping out.

I grab the towel and wrap it around my body, stepping up to the mirror and looking myself over.

I should feel disgusted for cutting his finger and for allowing Nico to continue, but I don't. The only thing I feel disgusted over is what he did to me.

I would ponder more on this, but I hear the bedroom door open.

"Nico?" I have so many questions.

"Yes." His low timbre echoes in the room.

I rush out of the bathroom and see his white shirt is stained red, and his hands are splattered as well. "Did you...?"

"No. I need him to send a message to your father. I heard he was working for him again, and I want to make sure your father knows what I'm capable of." He undoes each button of his shirt, and I watch him intently.

"Okay, but what will that mean? How do you know he's working for my father again?" I ask, tucking my wet hair behind my ear.

"It's amazing what you can get out of people when you're torturing them, Emelia."

I gulp, shaking my head and trying to process it all. "What message is it you're trying to send?"

He shrugs. "A reminder that he betrayed someone in my outfit, his own flesh, so he should keep his trash in line."

"No," I snap, my brain no longer functioning on some autopilot program.

"Excuse me?" he prompts, now shirtless. His brows draw in, and he challenges me with just a look.

"That's not why you did it. You care about me, Nico! You do. You wouldn't have done that if some part of you didn't care about me. This isn't a pissing contest or anything other than you wanting to care for me."

What am I saying? We are enemies, practically, except when our clothes are off.

"Emelia, I'm not in the mood. Stop reading into shit." He shakes his head and moves past me to the bathroom. I follow hot on his tail as he starts washing his hands.

"No, I'm not reading into anything. You care, Nico. You want to get to know me. My challenging you at every corner has earned your respect, and the way we touch in the bedroom has made you want to know *us* more. Admit it!" I yell, and he slams the handle on the faucet down and briskly turns.

"You are acting like a fucking child. I did you a favor. I handled a threat like any mafia boss would if someone fucked with his wife. It was protocol."

"Oh, bullshit, Nico! That's crap and you know it!" I come up to stand off with him.

"Emelia, I don't know you, and you don't know me."

I throw my hands up in annoyance. "What do you want to know? My favorite color is yellow, but I look like shit in it. I hate deep bodies of water, because something will eat me. I hate men who don't respect women. I had a terrible childhood. I love to read and watch stupid, corny movies where the humor hardly makes sense. What? What do you need to know about me to admit that you care!"

"I don't fucking care about you, Emelia, and I will never love you! If that is what you're wanting from me, forget it. I don't love you. I will never see this as anything other than just a transaction!" he yells back, and his words cut me to the bone, truly hurting me.

I don't want him to love me... do I?

No, I just want him to like me. To show me I'm not alone. That I have a friend. But that's clearly all in my head, a way-off dream that will never come true.

"You are an asshole. You had a chance to be my friend. We could have been something. I didn't need your love. I just wanted *something*. Something monsters aren't capable of." I leave him and grab my clothes off the bed before leaving the room. I dress in one of the guest bedrooms, and that's where I fall asleep. I have nothing to give right now but my silence. And somewhere deep inside, there is something brewing, and I fear what she is.

When my eyes shut, I dream of what my father said to me. I dream of the chapter of my life I closed and the new one that's starting with yet another letdown.1

"You are failing to do your job, Emelia. The family can't keep waiting while you play house and become his whore."

Those words made my stomach turn. Then he hit me when I told him I didn't want to do his dirty work. I was angry with Nico still, but more so with all the other men in my life, and I wasn't interested in doing anything for anyone anymore. I came home from Greece prepared to be on my own little island until Nico needed something.

"Father, this isn't going to work. He's smart and doesn't plan to tell me anything. So you'll have to do it yourself."

That's when he began to choke me. Nico stepping in when he did was a saving grace.

Or so I thought.

CHAPTER ELEVEN

Emelia

For days after that... I'm a sitting duck, not knowing what my father's planning after what I did to him and what Nico did to Damian.

How come Damian never told me he was working with my father again?

Why am I even surprised?

He lied about more and hid things far worse. So maybe staying inside for a while is the best thing. Getting ready for the day, I decide on a pair of light-wash boyfriend jeans and a loose-fitting white tee. My hair is down in its natural state, wavy and long. I do the bare minimum of makeup, and after that, I head back toward the living room.

It would be nice to have a friend in moments like this, but I've never really had a real one. I think about the fight with Nico the other night. That's all I was hoping for, that he would admit he cared so I could have someone in my life. Someone I could trust and confide in. But I was so fucking foolish.

Nico said I could make friends with the other wives in the outfit, and I decided at the time that would be a hard pass. Now?

Maybe it wouldn't be the worst idea. How do I even start? Is there a hotline or a directory that tells me who they are and their contact info?

I chuckle to myself. Farren and James, my two bodyguards, are standing stoically at the elevator doors when I walk into the living room.

"At ease, boys. I don't plan to go anywhere, and you both look like you're wound so tight I could give ya a soft nudge and you'd just fall right over like a chess piece."

They don't move. Are they even blinking?

"Seriously, guys? Hello?" I wave my hands in front of Farren's face. "Blink once if you need saving," I tease.

"We've been instructed not to socialize with you, Mrs. Valiente," James says, and my head turns toward him.

"Really? Anything else the boss tells you to do? When to take a bathroom break? How to point and shoot?"

"We can take you anywhere you want to go today, Mrs. Valiente," James avoids the questions.

"No, I will be staying in today. I have no desire to go anywhere." I release an annoyed breath. I thought they would at least provide some conversation. Maybe I should take up ventriloquism and make some friends with myself.

"Sounds good, ma'am." James remains stoic and doesn't look at me.

"Isn't there somewhere you can retreat to, since I won't be needing you today?" I ask, heading over to the couch.

"We're ordered to guard the entrance at all times." Farren's voice is much stricter and denser than James's. I'm convinced he's actually a robot.

"Fine. I don't feel like being watched, so I'll take myself to the bedroom."

That was a waste of time, I think, entering my room. I should have stayed in here to begin with.

Pulling out my cell phone, I'm surprised I don't see anything from my father, not even a threat.

Not being one for social media, I don't even have those to check. Seriously, I need to get a hobby. Well, I do have one hobby, and Nico did mention it would be arranged. I quickly message Giulio, knowing I will get nowhere with Nico, and there's the huge fact that we haven't talked once since the fight after the Damian situation.

Can't say I'm shocked. He was cruel, and I was hurt. Neither of us is going to wave our white flag again anytime soon.

Giulio lets me know all my skating supplies will be delivered in a couple of days and that I will be able to return to the ice. I give a curt thank-you and toss my phone on the end of the bed.

God, I miss the ice. Miss the sound of it under the blades on my feet. The wind moving through my hair as I get lost in the music playing in my headphones. Like I did back in New York, I will have to go a few times and see when it's more or less busy. When it's too busy, I don't get to take up the ice like I prefer. I took skating lessons my entire childhood and young-adult life, learning how to not just glide on the ice but how to do toe loops, axels, and different types of spins.

That was my escape, and the days where the rink was nearly empty were the best for me. There were days I would spend upwards of ten hours skating to my heart's desire.

The day drags and drags, seeming never ending. Alone, I eat the pasta Ricardo made and take a bubble bath before I head to bed. I turn all the lights off, open the curtains, and let the city lights draw dreamscapes on the wall, and within thirty minutes, I am out to the world.

Walking around the corner, my palms begin to sweat and my heart rate kicks up a few notches. My father is behind me, and I'm scared of what is going to happen. Once we're completely out of the room and away from Nico, my arm is yanked, and I'm shoved into a wall. I'm surprised the thud of my body didn't make as much noise as I assumed it would, alerting Giulio or Nico.

"You have failed to provide me one single fucking piece of insight. And that just won't do, Emelia."

I try to walk away, but he pushes me back into the wall.

"No, you are going to stay right here and listen to me." His eyes bore into me, and years of fear and pain come flooding back to memory.

"You are failing to do your job, Emelia. The family can't keep waiting while you play house and become his whore."

"I don't want to do your dirty work." He slaps me so hard my vision blurs.

"You will do it. Or so help me, Emelia, I will kill you both myself," he threatens.

"Father, this isn't going to work. He's smart and doesn't plan to tell me anything. So you'll have to do it yourself." I try to sound like I'm not afraid, but that doesn't work.

He begins to choke me, and before he smashes my windpipe, I cry out.

But unlike before, Nico never comes.

No one does.

My father's eyes turn a darker hue, and the evil grin on his face widens as he squeezes tighter. My hands claw at his as I fight for air, but I fail, and with each second, his face becomes more and more blurry.

Suddenly, I'm floating above myself, looking down at my lifeless body and my family laughing sinisterly.

I jolted out of the nightmare. My entire body is covered in sweat, and I look over at the time. Seeing it's 11:00 p.m., I turn to Nico, but he isn't there. Curiosity hits me, overtaking the awful dream, and I go in search of him, checking his office, but it's locked, and I don't see light seeping from beneath the door. The living room and kitchen are next, and it's empty except for James and Farren.

"Ma'am, is everything okay?" Farren asks.

"Yes, um... has Nico come home yet?" They shake their heads at the same time, and I drop mine. "Okay, thank you."

Why am I so upset that he's gone? I wasn't planning to apologize or talk to him; I just wanted to see if he came home or if my suspicions were right. He's most likely at the club, doing God knows what.

Making my way back to bed, I slide under the thick comforter and wait until I can't anymore. I swear Nico never made it home by the time dawn comes, the bed empty still. He has to be with other women or avoiding me.

Either way, neither option should bother me, but they do, because I'm stubborn and know I don't deserve the treatment he's dishing out. I deserve respect after what I did to my father. There was a small glimpse of hope with him, and I clung way too tight to it. I looked deep in his eyes as we had sex and thought I saw something there. Then he took me to watch him torture my ex-lover for doing terrible things to me.

But I was a fucking fool.

I won't do that ever again.

The line has been drawn.

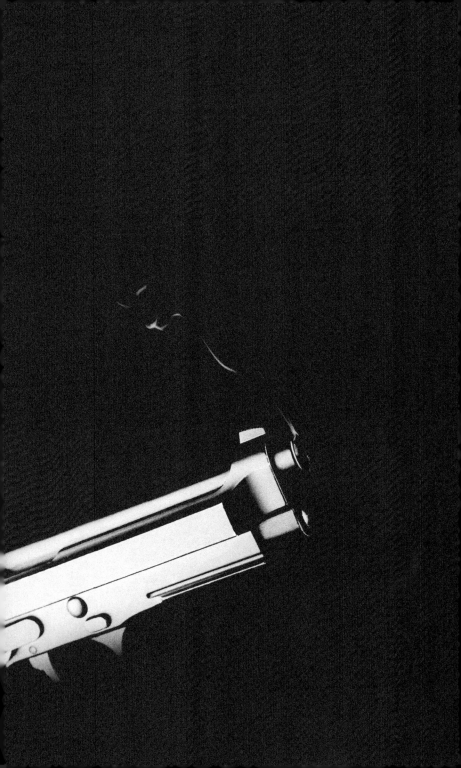

CHAPTER TWELVE

Nico

I'M AVOIDING EMELIA. I DON'T WANT TO SEE HER WHEN we are both fully alert, because whatever I saw in her eyes the other night is something I don't want to happen again. And until I can get control of myself, I will avoid her while she's awake.

The fight we had showed me she felt the same thing I did when we had sex. The sensation that scared me. And clearly I wasn't a complete idiot for feeling it. But we both need to be able to differentiate between lust and love. If we don't do that, then we will just keep fighting.

It's noon, and I am in an abandoned warehouse on the docks. This is a building I own to conduct the kind of business that requires a lot of clean-up and easy access to my boat. It's also close enough to the highway so we can get rid of any... problems. I have cops in my pocket and on my payroll, but I try to only utilize them when the time calls.

It was just days ago that I was here watching Emelia take control of her life. It aroused me, and I know it aroused her too. I thought I would come home and we would chase that high together, but she turned it into something... something that left me feeling confused and messed up over.

Do I care about Emelia?

Could I learn to feel for her in the ways she wants?

Fuck. I need to focus. I have to shake her. She is all I think about. Day and fucking night. But business is calling.

"You betrayed me, Levetti. You made a big mistake with that one." I look at my once most-trusted man. He oversaw the dock shipments, and this entire time, he was double-crossing me. His eyes are already bruised and swollen, and his lip has a deep cut that blood seeps from. I am standing over him, his body tied to a chair, and my rolled-up sleeves are stained red, my dress shirt covered in what I have done to him, and it's only just begun.

"Why don't you tell me who you're working for, and maybe we can just make this quick."

He looks up at me with disgust."I'm dead if I tell you and dead if I don't. I want you to get what you deserve and everything ripped away from you, Valiente."

This is news to me. I treat my men very well, pay them more than most bosses, and give them protection and loyalty—until they fuck it up. He secretly came into my outfit as an enemy and played his cards right, until he didn't.

I grab the chair behind me, flip it around, and straddle it. Placing my arms on the high back and intertwining my hands, I shake my head.

"Is that right? Why don't you tell me what I deserve then, Levetti. Because you're right. You are dead either way. So, get it out. Let's hear all your woes, since you're so torn up inside about them." I belittle him, lessen his worth, and it shows on his face. He can tell what I'm doing.

"You killed my brother! You didn't think I would turn on you? Thought I would stay loyal?"

"Giulio," I call to my right-hand man, and he approaches. I'm about to dig this dagger deeper.

"Yes, sir?"

"Who is his brother again? I don't recall."

"Fuck you, you son of a bitch." He spits, and it doesn't reach me, but it's enough to have my knee-jerk reaction kicking in, and I punch him so hard his neck cracks, and he groans in pain.

"Sorry, Giulio, I won't be needing the name. Not worth worrying about." I nod at him, signaling for my knives. Giulio steps over, grabs my kit, and places it on the table behind me, setting my tools up the way I like.

"Who do you work for, Levetti?"

He spots the knives, his eyes widening. Maybe he will crack. But where is the fun in that before I can have mine?

I stand and pick up my filet knife. I like to start with the fingers, then work up to hands and arms. This knife is my sharpest and cuts the skin smoothly.

"Fuck man, listen. Please."

"Don't beg, Levetti. It only makes this game more fun for me." I look over at him, tilting my head. "I will ask you one more time, and if you don't give me the right answer, this knife—" I hold it up, the light from the high windows bouncing off the sharp instrument and reflecting against the opposite wall. "—will be doing the rest of the work for me."

"Fuck you! I will die for my family. Do your worst."

I laugh and look at Giulio. "What a way to start the day."

I advance on the traitor, doing what I do best. Retribution and revenge.

We make it to the club a few hours later, where I plan to shower. Most times, I go from one job to the other, and having a place to clean up that doesn't require going home is ideal. I have a meeting right after, and this one, I'm looking forward to. If there's one enemy in the group, more aren't far behind. I will not let my outfit be run like it has no leader.

This is not the little leagues. And for some reason, some of these men may have tripped and bumped their fucking heads to think I wouldn't catch on or would just let this go.

I am about to undress and shower, when I look myself over. I'm covered in the blood of a man I just ended for crossing me, and I'm about to sit at the head of my table and weed out more, if there are any.

I decide against showering. Let them see one of their fallen soldiers' blood all over me. I want them to know I'm not only keeping an even stricter eye on outside enemies, but I'm also looking inside my own army.

"Giulio!" I holler, and he comes to the door and knocks.

"Sir?"

"Come in." Opening the door, he squares his shoulders.

"Yes, sir?"

"Call them in." He looks at me in the mirror, and I nod. Giulio has been with me long enough to know exactly what I'm planning. "They need to fear what's going to happen."

It's all I say, and he nods, dismissing himself. There is still blood on my hands, my arms, and even spatters on my face. I run my hand through my longer black hair, one single piece falling and hitting my forehead.

At that moment, I think about Emelia. I want to slip into our bed tonight and fuck her lazily as she slowly wakes and then lets me fuck her right back into slumber. I don't care if we are in the middle of a faceoff with one another. I crave her cunt. Her thick body. Her goddamn taste. All of her.

My phone dings, and I check the messages from Giulio.

GIULIO

They're ready, sir.

Putting my phone back in my pocket, I crack my neck, look at my green eyes that resemble my father's, and remember what legacy I'm carrying on. Slamming my hand against the light switch, I leave for my conference room. As I step out of my office and into the hall, Giulio follows behind me.

No one else but my men are allowed up here. No dancers, no security for the club, just made men. And when we reach the door, I take another deep breath, trying to keep my composure. Being calm is my strength. In fact, it's my greatest scare tactic.

Opening the door, I see them all sitting, their heads turning toward me. You could hear a pin drop, and you nearly do. The room is soundproof, so the music, dancers, and patrons can't be heard.

"Stand. All of you."

They all rush to their feet. I stare at a dozen of my closest men and eye them over one by fucking one. I will spot it. It takes just a look to sense deception. All I need is one shift of the eyes when we lock for me to tell there's a snake in my house. But not one moves. They all look back at me, heads high and chests out like they were trained to do, and I stand at the head of the table.

"You see this blood? Do you know who it belonged to?" I pose the questions, placing my knuckles on the mahogany wood and leaning forward.

"Levetti," Jeremiah says, and I look over to him and smirk.

"Correct. Tell me how you know that, Jeremiah?" Walking to him, I grab the back of his neck hard and slam his cheek to the table. He doesn't fight me, which is in his best interest. I know Jeremiah, and I know he isn't an enemy. My father and his were close friends. But I have to set an example.

No one is safe.

I don't care what connection we've had in the past or what loyalty they've once shown.

No one is safe if you cross me.

"He's the only one not here, sir."

I keep his head down and look at the other men. They kill for me every day. Fear isn't something that often comes over them, or shock for that matter, but I can see it building in them now.

Harshly, I let him go, and he rises slowly, massaging the back of his neck.

"What happens when you cross me?" I look to the next person, Danny. Moving to him, I punch his stomach hard, and he grunts, bending over and letting out a wheezy cough.

"We cross you, and we leave in a body bag," he croaks, struggling to get some of the words out after the sudden impact.

"Good job." I pat his back.

This time, I really need to drive it home. They need to remember who I am.

Moving to Giulio, I look him in the eye before removing my gun from its holster. Flipping off the safety, I place it right between his eyes.

"Who has immunity from me, Giulio?"

Without a bat of his lashes, he speaks. "No one, sir."

I make a show of pulling back the slide of my gun, checking to make sure a bullet is chambered, and then closing it with a loud click before putting it to his forehead again. This time, he blinks and swallows.

"Who?"

"N-No one, sir," he stutters, and I know if I turn around, every single man in this room will have their heads down. Lowering the gun slowly, I turn and see just that. Each man has their head low, and they don't even attempt to steal a glance at me.

I trust Giulio with everything, and I know he would never cross me, but I needed them to know that if he ever did, he is not granted immunity from me. It had to be done.

Giulio stays standing behind me, and I turn back to my men. "You all remember who you work for. If you know anything about Levetti and who he was in business with, you better speak up and do it now." I look around the room and give them ample time, but no sound is made. Not one man moves.

"Good. Now, back to fucking work. Jeremiah, you are now

dock manager. You can get with Giulio to go over plans and all the shipment details." I leave the conference room and move back to my office, slamming the door and locking it.

And in a fit of rage, I finally snap.

I slide everything off my desk, glass shattering and papers flying through the space. The men don't get to see this part of me. If they knew I was showing any sense of agitation or worry about what's happening in my outfit, they could use that as a way to blindside me.

I tear my office apart, every fucking inch of it. And when I finish and there's nothing left but me breathing heavily, I grab my phone and check the cameras.

I find Emelia in our bed, reading. Her eyes fly over the words, and I look at her body, barely covered by flimsy material I could shred in my bare hands, it takes everything in me not to go to her.

I have to put some space between us. If we're going to fuck, then it has to be just that. When we work together and put on a show at events, it has to be just that—work. A job and nothing else.

I will go to her tonight when her eyes are slowly closing, and we will fuck while she's too tired to try to talk to me or get inside my head.

Emelia can't be a goddamn distraction! I all but throw my phone, then run my hands back and forth through my hair. What the fuck is going on in my head? Slamming the meat of my fist into the side of my skull a couple of times, I shake it off, trying to get her off my mind so I can finish the day. But it doesn't work. I check the cameras over and over, watching her move throughout the house for the rest of the day. I'm secretly there with her as she eats dinner alone, and I get hard and stroke my cock to her showering. Once her head hits the pillow, I finally leave.

I need her. Need my distraction. And fuck me for giving into it.

CHAPTER THIRTEEN

Emelia

THE FEEL OF ARMS ENCAPSULATING ME AND PULLING ME into a warm wall of muscle wakes me.

"Nico?"

"Shh, I want you. Let me work us both back to sleep." His raspy voice thrums against the shell of my ear.

I could cry with relief when he lifts my leg by gripping the front of my thigh and slides his cock into me.

"Yes, such a good wife. Ready for me." He lazily begins to fuck into me, and I moan out his name, holding on tightly to the pillow. I want to ask him where he was all day, and up until now, I realize I can't, because the feeling of him controlling my body feels entirely too good to stop to talk. That and the fact that would be me surrendering first.

For now, he's here, and we're in sync. I meet his movements and get lost in what it feels like to be fucked by the most dangerous and powerful man in the world.

My husband. That man is my husband. Suddenly, I cry out, screaming his name when the sensation hits hard. His finger is on my clit, working it delicately, and I detonate around him, squeezing and pulsing on his hard cock. Moments later, he bites my shoulder and comes inside me.

I feel the hot spurts, filling my insides and reassuring that I am his and his only.

But is he mine?

Am I ever going to be afforded the same luxuries of owning him and knowing him and who he is? Or will he be just a thief in the night, coming to claim me and leaving before the sun hits the horizon?

I guess tomorrow will tell me. Until then, I'm too tired to ask, and I doze to his words of praise.

"Good job. You did such a good job taking me, principessa." The delicate way he brushes my now messy hair from my face and kneads at the muscles of my neck is almost too intimate, a crack in his rough exterior. I fold and lean into yet again and pray that tomorrow we can start building at least a friendship.

But tomorrow comes, the morning light breaks through, and the only warmth in my bed is the side I occupy by myself. Not only did he leave without a word or an attempt to speak to me, but he also made the bed on his side. Almost as if to remind me that he is not anything or anyone other than the man who gets to use my body.

That hurts more than his absence.

It's the purposeful way he put a visual reminder that he's never fucking there.

This sets the tone for my day, and I wear that like a badge of honor, filled with unspoken rage and a sense of being used. Something changed in me a few days ago, when he not only nearly took my father's life but let me have the option to, and then again just hours later with Damian.

We have spent days apart. He comes in the middle of the night like a phantom of passion yet a ghostly reminder that to him it's just another day. Feelings are sprouting in me, but from what? I don't even want to be around him—or do I?

God, this is a personal hell to be in. My mind is a minefield of possible pain, and I can't escape it. And up until a few weeks ago, I hated him. Now, I have this need and longing inside me to become something to him.

How desperate do I sound?

To crave the simple act of friendship from a man who knows no such thing and has made it clear he won't even try. All he's ever known is how to hate. How to use. How to kill. And I expect him to make an exception for me? Because I hold the title of being his wife and carry his last name? How foolish is that? How pathetic of me to think something so naïve and trivial.

That anger doesn't stay dormant for long, not even close. Each minute and passing hour makes it grow like a hungry beast, clawing and fighting to find a way out of my skin. I sit with it, try to control it, ignore it, and combat it, but it festers and broils and burns me from the inside. Then I simply... snap.

First, I take three shots of whiskey, and then I grab a sharp kitchen knife and cut out my fucking tracker. It hurts like a bitch, and I'm surprised no one hears me crying out around the washcloth I bit down on. I'm able to stop the bleeding, but it takes some time. I have retribution on my mind, and I believe there's nothing that can stop a madwoman.

I place the tracker in the closet in my underwear drawer and then keep on going like a dog with a bone. With three band-aids on my open cut and a makeshift tourniquet around my arm. I go into Nico's office, a room he rarely leaves open. But that's the housemaid's fault, who forgot to lock up before she was done, and I now take advantage.

Rummaging through some papers on his desk, I find it almost instantly. The club. I rip off the corner of the paper where the address is printed and stick it in my pocket. Next, I go in search of my purse, finding the credit card he gave me. Before I step into the living area, I remove the tourniquet and replace the band-aids, and that's when the first real obstacle I need to overcome presents itself.

"Mrs. Valiente? You all right? Do you need something?"

I turn and hide the card behind my back. Doing my best to hide all the negative emotions fighting for supremacy inside me, I plaster on a fake smile and shrug. "No, Farren. I was looking for my birth control. Can I have some privacy please?"

Like any man who has never understood women, he backs down quickly, the comment obviously making him uncomfortable. "Yes, ma'am."

"Where is James?" I hadn't taken notice of my guards much today, but at this moment, I need to.

"He's on a run for Mr. Valiente," he responds, and I inwardly gloat.

"Hmm. Well. I will need to take my medicine with water. Would you mind going and getting me some? Make sure it's filled with ice."

He eyes me over, almost as if he'll refuse, because he's my watchman and not my helper. I stand firmly in place and don't bat a lash. I dare him to challenge me.

"Yes, ma'am." He leaves me and goes to the kitchen. Turning, I go to pick up my phone, but my anger doesn't overshadow my wisdom. There is no way this phone isn't being tracked. If I bring it, he will find me. I have all I need—address, money, and my vengeance.

I hurry then, no looking back and no hesitating. Making it to the open elevator, I hit the button for the ground floor, and just moments before the doors close, I see Farren come out of the kitchen, and he yells as he drops the glass of water and starts running.

"Mrs. Valiente! Stop!" I hear his fist connect with the closed door just as the elevator jolts into movement, a muffled "fuck!" along with it, and I hold my breath. I wait for the elevator to stop at his roar, but it doesn't, and I grin wickedly.

Watching each number as it goes down, I know I'm in the clear.

But as the doors open on the ground floor, security for the building is there.

"Mrs. Valiente, please return to your penthouse. Farren has informed me that you're to be sent back up."

My eyes nearly wander, but that would be too much of a telltale sign that I'm trying to escape. Used to having to be quick on my feet, the lie comes easily.

"My husband, *Mr. Valiente*," I emphasize his name and watch the security guard swallow thickly, "asked me to meet him for coffee at the café next door. Alone. Now, I would hate for him find out that not only did my guards feel the need to stop and question me, but so did the building staff. You know Nico, right?"

We both know damn well he knows who my husband is. And if this were all true, the man would be right in stepping aside, if he values his head, knees, or fingers.

I place my hands on my hips and look just to the left of us, where a Victorian style clock sits, the time showing 7:00 p.m.

Releasing a sigh of annoyance, he finally steps aside."My apologies, ma'am."

I nod, leaving him then. I take long yet steady strides, holding in a deep breath until I can get away. The moment the revolving doors close in behind me, I release the breath, and then I rush to the corner out of sight of the guard, move to the edge of the sidewalk, and hold out my hand for a cab. One pulls up, and I climb in, but before I shut the door, I hear my name being called.

I yell at the cab driver, "Go! I will tip you a grand if you get us far away from this building as fast as possible." And that he does.

"No problem, ma'am. Where would you like to go?" He darts into traffic, and I look behind me, seeing Farren and the security guard yelling at one another. But I see Farren pull out his phone and snap a photo quick.

Fuck. The license plate.

"Take me two blocks and then a left. That's it."

He looks at me through the rearview mirror like I'm mad, but I don't care. "Miss?"

"Do what I say. Here's my card. Hurry and run it for the grand and whatever the two blocks is." I hand it to him and keep looking back. No car yet, but I'm sure Farren will find me in minutes if we don't hurry.

We turn left, my twitching leg as I watch him run the card and wait for it to load. Paranoid, I keep looking out the back window. Still in the clear.

"All right. All clear."

I say nothing, just grab the card and go. Bolting from the cab, I run a block. My chest hurts from the chilly evening air and the anxiety building in my chest. I'm the daughter of a mafia boss; I know what I need to do to get away, but I have no idea where I am. All I know is I need to find a new driver.

Getting a block away from my last cab, I hail another one. This time, it's a sweet older woman, and she greets me instantly, taking notice of my distress. "Sweetie, are you all right?"

I nod, trying to catch my breath. I lean my head down and attempt to regain some composure. "Yes, um...my husband is looking for me, and I just need to get away."

She slowly pulls into traffic and hesitantly asks, "Do I need to take you to the police station?"

I shake my head vigorously. "No, no, it's not that. I just need a break; that's all. I am not in danger," I say between heaps of heavy breathing.

"Really? Why would you be running and looking over your shoulder if you just needed a break? I would say danger is exactly what you're in, sweetie."

I finally meet her eyes in the rearview mirror and shake my head. "Valiente. Does that name mean anything to you?"

Instantly, she stiffens and slams on the brakes. Her shoulders lift, and her head practically tucks. Her brunette hair is up in a high bun, so I can see her face clearly.

"Ma'am, if I may say, I don't feel comfortable having you in my cab." It's not rude the way she says it. No, it's fearful.

"I just need you to drop me off at some sort of clothing store. I won't let anything happen to you. I will tip you well."

She waits, and I look at her name tag hanging from her mirror. "Lenny?"

She looks at me, her eyes hollow and petrified. I don't blame her. There is a risk in helping me, especially as it's helping me escape *his* men.

"I can drop you off a block away from a boutique close by, but I won't take any money. I can't be tied to this. I'm a single mom and...." She pauses, and my heart sinks. I don't want her to fear what could happen, and it's then that I realize being involved with me comes with a risk, and I am to blame for making this kind woman afraid.

"I understand. You can do that. And I will make sure you are safe. Nothing will happen. I promise." I will see that no one is hurt in my parade of getting back at Nico. It would destroy me if something like that ever happened.

The rest of the ride is silent, and I can't help but notice her repeatedly checking her mirrors to ensure there is no one following behind us. Moments later, we pull up to the sidewalk outside a building. "One block up"—she nods north—"is the clothing boutique, CC Chic. They are very nice there and can help you. Just be careful, and good luck, Mrs. Valiente."

I climb out and shut the door. Rushing forward, I tap on her window with my knuckles, and as she lowers it, I hurry to tell her, "You're safe. I promise. And thank you. I appreciate you, Lenny. Please, do not worry about my husband."

She nods, and I see a little bit of the anxiety leave her face. I tap the roof of the cab, and she leaves. Waiting a moment, I assess all the cars that pass and make sure she is, in fact, not being followed. When I'm sure she isn't, I head in the direction she advised until I find the clothing store, and when I step inside, I'm cheerfully greeted.

"Hey, friend! Welcome! I'm Shayla. What can I help you with?"

Finally able to focus on my end goal, I look at her and release a deep breath. Her green eyes sparkle, and they contrast beautifully with her burgundy hair. "You ever heard of the revenge dress?"

She smiles and nods, knowing exactly what I mean. "Boy do I ever. We have a lot of clients who have come in searching for that type of look. Let's make him feel really, really stupid for whatever he did." She winks and takes my hand.

This is going to be so good.

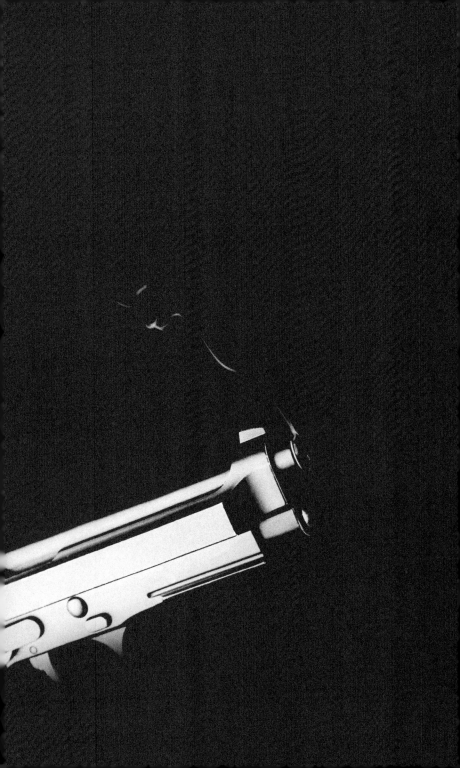

CHAPTER FOURTEEN
Nico

"We jumped thirteen percent in sales this month, which is quite an improvement, given the shit show that happened these past couple of weeks." I pause and look over the numbers on my paper in front of me. "But—" I look up to the same men who sat at this table last night and took my threats. "—do not let that make you believe you can slack on what needs to be done. We are still looking for anyone who may have been working with Levetti."

The door opens, and Giulio enters.

"Sir," he inserts, "I need to speak to you in private."

Knowing my underboss would never interrupt a meeting for anything other than an emergency, I close the folder in my hand and drop it on the table. "Get back to work. We will meet tomorrow," I tell the other men in the room, and they all stand and follow behind me, going the opposite direction as Giulio and me when we leave the conference room.

We head upsta`irs to my office that overlooks the club, and the second they're all out of earshot, I ask, "What's going on?"

"It's Mrs. Valiente, sir. She's seemed to have run off."

I halt and turn toward him. "Excuse me?" My teeth grind as my jaw clenches.

"Yes. She escaped both guards."

I turn once again and continue to my office, my anger growing stronger with each step. "Tell me, how does my wife just get away, Giulio?"

"I'm not sure. I asked Farren to brief us both."

"Is he in my fucking office?" I yell in his face.

"Yes, he couldn't find her, and he didn't want to tell us over the phone."

I scoff. "He isn't going to win fucking brownie points for coming to me in person. He let her out of his sight! What does her tracker say? We should be able to find her with that. Did he forget how to do his job?" I growl, and finally, we make it to my office. When I throw open the door, Farren jumps and starts backing away as I gain on him.

"That's part of the problem. They found it... in your closet. She took it out," Giulio tells me, and my head nearly pops off.

That crazy fucking bitch.

"Sir. I'm sorry. She slipped out."

My hands are on Farren's neck the moment he finishes that sentence, and I push him hard against the glass wall that overlooks my club.

"You are a trained fucking assassin, and my little five-foot five wife got the better of you?" I mock him.

This is a joke, right? How do these men keep fucking up like they don't know their heads from their asses?

"Sir, she had a plan, and I made a mistake."

Tilting my head, I look him deep in the eye, that feeling of needing to hurt and drain breath out of someone creeping in. The part where humanity leaves me and my dark side completely captivates me.

"I think we need stronger men, wouldn't you agree, Giulio?" My eyes never waver from Farren's. No, they continue assessing as I breathe in the fear exuding from him.

"I agree, sir."

Farren grits out, "Sir, I'm tracking her card. She used it on a cab, and I have the driver down in the basement. He swears he dropped her off two blocks away, but after that, her card was used at a clothing store. It was closed when we got there."

The boiling in my stomach, simmers over."Fuck you and your stupidity!" I punch him hard, his head flying back and hitting the bulletproof glass so hard his brain must rattle. I release his neck, and he falls to the ground.

I turn, rubbing the throb between my eyes. One hand on my hip, I think about what to do.

Why would she run from me? Where is she going? Something in me feels different, and that just adds to how beyond angry and out of control I am. Regardless of where we stand currently, I still hate the knowledge that she's out there in the night, a moving target.

Why do I care? If she wants to act stupid and like a madwoman, then I should let her. But—I can't. Why is she crawling in my skin and affecting me? I am spiraling into fucking madness.

"Her phone. Check her phone."

"She left it at home, sir," Farren groans out, standing slowly.

Smart woman. My wife isn't a fool and would know better than any other woman in the world how to outrun the mafia... for now.

I will find her, and when I do... goddammit, when I do—

"Sir! There she is," Giulio cuts in, pointing out the window and down to the dance floor.

I spot her instantly, dressed in a sequin dress that catches the strobing lights. I can see nearly all of her back, the material only covering her ass, and the front dips low, showing all her cleavage and hanging on by a mere scrap around her neck. Her hair is down and curled, her makeup soft, but her lips are painted a bold red. But the biggest concern above all of that is who she's dancing with.

"Are those the Dean brothers?" I grit out.

Watching my wife dance and grind her body against three men I have been looking for brings on a whole new level of insanity I have never felt. They stole from us, roughed up some of our dancers, and killed a few of my men, including Giulio's brother. We have been hunting them since they took off from Seattle. Now, here they are, in my club, dancing with my fucking wife.

They must be fucked up on hardcore shit to think coming to my place of business was wise. Did they think they wouldn't be caught? God, I swear men like that take all the fun out of the job by making it so easy to find them.

"That's them, sir. They must not know you own this club. Or they're high out of their minds and have no idea."

"They just stepped into the lion's den." I watch them dance with her and take notice of my entire body tensing and growing angrier with each passing moment.

"They're touching her, sir. She's in distress. Want me to stop them?" Farren's voice seems to come from far away as I watch her try to fight them off.

I'm on the dance floor in what feels like minutes, but really, it's less than one. I push through the crowd, hearing Giulio and Farren ordering people to leave, but I have my eyes on Emelia. She's yelling for the brothers to stop, and I pick up the pace. When I reach them, I wrap one arm around her waist and pull out my gun, extending my arm straight out beside her head. She looks up and back, finding it's me, and I feel her entire body go lax for a moment before she tenses once again.

People start to scream when they see my gun, and the Dean brothers suddenly realize where they've landed themselves.

In fucking hell.

"Nico!" she cries.

"I will handle you in a minute."

The three skinny, crackhead brothers turn to disperse and run, but Giulio and Farren are right behind them. Realizing they're stuck in place, they begin to apologize, but it lands on deaf ears. They were as good as dead when they messed with my business and Giulio's family, but now they've messed with what's mine.

They touched my wife.

They made her feel unsafe.

And this provoked me.

"Shut up." More of my men now surround each exit as the club empties. The dancers have left the stage and head back to their dressing rooms. Now, it's my wife, me, half of my closest army... and some of my very unfortunate enemies.

"Nico. Please," she begs, and I tighten my grip on her waist.

"You will receive your punishment when I'm done." The three men in front of me all look at one another and around the room—trying to find an escape, I'm sure.

"We can get you back what we took. Just give us time. Please," Charles, the oldest, says.

I scoff. "You think giving me back the drugs you took will mark you safe? Giulio, did you hear that?" I laugh loudly, the noise thundering through the club. The music still plays, but at some point, it was lowered.

"Stupid men play stupid games. You killed my brother," he answers me and then addresses them.

"Yes, exactly," I reply and begin to sway Emelia a little bit back and forth. Her breathing is loud. As it should be. Her entire body trembles with fear.

"We can let them go. They didn't hurt me. Please."

"Hurt doesn't matter, wife. They touched what's mine. That was the stamp on their death certificate."

She shakes her head, but then the first loud bang rings out, followed by a thud. Emelia screams, and I hold her tight as she begins to cry. His brothers start to panic.

"Quiet!" I silence them, and they still. "You killed Giulio's brother," I repeat, and Emelia suddenly stops, finally registering there's more going on than with tonight's incident. Her body stiffens in my hands.

"We didn't know he was one of your men."

"Lies. You knew who he was. You knew exactly whose boundaries you stepped in."

Eric tries to speak next, but I silence him with a bullet. He falls to the ground, and Emelia shakes.

"You touched my wife. You fucked with my most valued possession." I nip Emelia's ear, and she shivers in response.

"I don't like when someone fucks with what's mine, so you must pay. But since Giulio has his own vengeance, I will let him have his fun with you, while I go and handle my wife." I pull Emelia with me, but she keeps looking back, watching as Giulio and a few of my men take them away. The last brother standing kicks and pleads as he goes, but it fazes no one.

"Farren! You and the others clean up the mess, then the club can reopen."

They obey, and Emelia walks up the stairs on shaky legs, and I watch her from behind. She takes a few glances back at me, but I bark for her to keep going.

She tested me. Angered me.

Scared me.

I don't feel fear, but the knowledge that they could have taken her and hurt her... that caused me a sensation I have never felt in my entire life. She weakened me, and I have to remind her that I am not a man who will let anyone overrule him.

"To the left," I tell her when we hit the top of the stairs. She hesitates, and I tsk at her. "To the left, Emelia. Now," I demand, and she keeps walking.

My office door is at the end of the hall, and she continues on until we reach it.

"Here?" she whispers.

"Yes. Inside."

This time, she stumbles, and I catch her before she hits the ground.

"Goddammit, Emelia!" I growl, and once she's stable, I let her go and lock the door.

"Nico, I'm sorry. Please."

Pinching the bridge of my nose, I shake my head."No. You don't speak until I think of what to do with you."

"What to do with me?"

There's sass in her tone, and I turn to look at her."Yes! What to fucking do with you. You ran off, then you came here and could have gotten killed. They are dangerous men!"

"Were!" she yells back. "They were, but you killed them! Without even blinking! You monster!"

I gain on her and wrap my hand around her neck, just enough to get her to hear me loud and clear."I did, and I would do it again. How many damn times do I have to tell you that life means nothing to me, Emelia? I have no regard for it, and you seem to think I do. That you married some prince, when I'm the fucking devil. When will you get that?" I seethe.

"Why couldn't you let them go? Why did you have to do it in front of me? I don't want to be a part of that."

I grin, chuckling sinisterly."You seemed to love it the other night when you were cutting into the flesh of your ex," I remind her, and her jaw drops.

"That's different. I didn't *kill* him."

I just laugh at what she says, knowing damn well there is no difference.

"Emelia, you are a part of it. You are married to a boss in the world's largest criminal organization. And with that comes death. Next time you want to run away and play some fucked-up game, you should think about that."

Her eyes water."It is not my fault you killed those men. They were already a target. I just happened to stumble into it."

"Yeah, and I saw the way they tossed you around, and now you have fucking bruises."

"I don't..." She pauses and looks down at her arms, seeing the bruises forming.

"Exactly. Someone hurt you. That is more than enough to kill them, Emelia. Plus, they had priors. It is what it is."

"No! You didn't just do that because it is what it is, Nico!" She starts to bring back up the fight from the other night, but this time, something in me goes along with it.

"And you didn't come here just for nothing. You wanted attention, and you fucking got it! So what do you need, Emelia?" I yell back.

"Why am I such a burden to you, and why do you fucking hate me so much that you'd rather avoid me than ever come home and attempt to get to know me? Is it someone else? Are you sleeping with the women here? Are they who you think about when you're with me at night?" Her words pour out one after the other with what feels like no breath between.

"Because you are getting under my fucking skin, Emelia!" It finally comes out, and we sit there quietly, nothing but our angered breathing filling the room.

"I what?" she finally prompts.

I turn and face the club, watching people come back in. Rubbing my lips together, I place my hands on my hips and debate what to say next, because even I don't understand this softness that is forming around her for me.

"You make me want to know you, Emelia. Just like you said the other night. You make me want to have something here, and ever since that happened, I've been fucked in the head. My business dealings are getting all fucked up, and I blame you."

"Why would you blame me?" She sounds wounded, and when I turn and look at her, I hate what I see. She's so goddamn breathtaking, but she looks like she's been hurt far past repairing.

"Because you're making something in me... soft. You drive me mad, but you test me in a way I fucking crave." I claw at my chest before punching my heart.

"No! Please don't hurt yourself," she cries, rushing to me."Nico..." She caresses my face, and I lean into that feminine, caring touch only she can give me.

"You make me mad, Emelia. You make me want to do things—"

"You make me just as mad, Nico. You are so closed off, and cold, and I just want *something* from you. Even if it's just your friendship."

I stop and grab her wrists hard, bring them around my neck, and smash our bodies to one another. A gush of air leaves her mouth as we slam into a violent kiss, and I catch her hair in my hands, tugging her head back so I have her at the perfect angle.

"We could never be just fucking friends. You awaken too much in me. You make something warm spark through the coldness inside me."

Her face softens."You don't know me. We don't know each other."

"I want to fucking start. That's all that matters, baby." I admit things I would never admit to any other person. But Emelia isn't just anyone else anymore, and I curse myself for this. She's the closest I've ever let anyone other than my parents get to my darkness.

"Give me something then. Make me believe it."

"What do you want? My fucking heart? I will rip it out my fucking chest and give it to you. I will give you ownership of me."

"That's a start. But I need more." How long has she been craving this softness from me?

"You saw what I'm willing to do for you, Emelia. I would kill for you."

"But could you love me?"

"I couldn't love. Love isn't enough. If I can't have something untouchable and unmatched, then I want nothing at all."

Her breath hitches.

"Can you give *me* that?" I counter.

"We both have to try."

I grasp her chin with my free hand and run my thumb across her plump red lips.

"You're a mess."

"The mess that you want," she responds, reaching up to try to take my lips in a kiss, but I stop her.

"You did something bad tonight, Emelia. You need to tell me what your plans were and why you misbehaved."

"I wanted you to hurt."

"Really?" I lean in and bite her lip, and she cries out.

"Yes, I thought you were cheating or trying to make me feel like you really didn't want me around."

"I didn't," I admit. "I didn't want you around, because you were making me feel things I didn't want to feel."

"And the women?" Her eyes drop.

"Emelia," I warn.

"Please," she pleads.

"Stand against the window, legs apart, hands flat against the glass."

Her eyes fly back to mine. "But I need—"

I put my thumb to her lips again to shush her.

"I will answer you. Show you. Now do what I said."

Nodding, she steps back as I release her, and I watch her ass sway as she moves to the window. "Can they see me?"

"No."

"Could they if I wanted them to?" She looks over her shoulder at me.

"Yes. I can change the setting. But that won't happen, Emelia. I won't share you."

"Exactly. Don't share me. Warn them. Show them what is only

yours to have."

My cock grows hungry for its mate. She wants me to put on a show, the ultimate way to let them know they will never be able to have her. The jealous man in me is furious, but the animal in me is starving.

"Please. Let them watch. Let them know. Those women need to know you desire a woman like me."

This angers me. Emelia never questions her body. She's always exuded confidence, and if I'm being honest with just myself, I haven't even laid eyes on another woman anywhere, especially this club, since I first saw her.

"If you doubt this body ever again—" I step up to her and start caressing all her curves. "—I will withhold this cock for punishment."

She whimpers when I lick the column of her neck and bite it."Nico, please."

I like when she begs. But I have other plans. Stepping back, I pull my gun back out and take out the clip, ejecting the bullet in the chamber. The sound alerts her, and she turns so fast I feel the wind of her movement as I set down everything but my empty handgun before pressing a button on my desk. "Wh-What are you doing? Nico, please."

Does she think I'm going to hurt her? That this was all a ploy?

"Easy, principessa." Attempting to calm her, I drop to my haunches and lift her dress. I kiss each thigh, then over the see-through fabric covering her delectable pussy. I then reach under the sides of her dress and grasp her panties before slowly lowering them.

Her smell fills my lungs, the scent of her and her cherry body wash. Fuck me. The material lands in a puddle at her feet. The white lines that take up the inside of her thick thighs are kissable, and I do that, trailing over them with slow, lazy, wet kisses. I bite the thickest part of her thighs, and she cries out, gripping my hair. I don't have to look up to know her head is thrown back in pleasure.

"Nico, what are you doing to me?"

I laugh softly against her skin, and the vibration makes her quiver. "You're going to experience lust in a way you haven't yet, sweet principessa." Then I take her over, not just telling her what I plan to do but immersing her in the feeling.

With the gun in my hand, I slide it between her pussy lips, and she gasps, looking down at me as my eyes wonder from the placement of my weapon to her expression.

"Fuck the gun, baby. Get off on the weapon that protects you."

"Nico," she breathes. It's not hesitation. No, she's asking me if this is real.

"Yes, Emelia. You are mine. You can do it, baby. Be a good wife and do what your husband asks of you."

"Oh God." Throwing her head back against the window, she starts to slide against the ridged metal of the barrel.

I praise her, "Good girl. There you go, getting it so fucking wet." The black weapon starts to slicken with her wetness. It catches the dim lighting in my office, and I feel it start to drip down onto my hand. Fuck, I can't wait to drown myself in her slick heat. Her pussy was made to fit my cock and mine only.

"They're watching," I tell her, leaning to the side and spotting some people who have taken notice. She gasps in delight, not having realized until now that I made the glass transparent when I set my clip down. My chest burns, and I start to fill with rage, yet she works herself harder against my weapon. Me acknowledging that people are watching her only makes me angrier and her hungrier.

"Enough." I pull the gun away and stand.

Emelia cries out for me, nearing her orgasm before I stopped. "Nico, w-why did you stop?" She braces her hands against the window and looks at me. Her chest rises and falls rapidly, and my eyes bore into hers when I reach my desk. I hit the button to fog the glass and block not just others from seeing us but us from seeing anyone else. I pace the office, and she just watches the caged animal roam before calling to me again.

"Nico?" She finally gains footing and bends to pull her panties back on, but I stop her abruptly.

"Put those on and I will turn your ass red," I roar into the room.

Her shoulders stiffen, and she shakes her head. "What happened? I thought we were... connecting."

I run my hands through my hair, then down over my face, and that's when her scent fills my lungs again. It still lingers on my fingers, and it calls to the male in me. The animal. The crazed lover who wants to destroy her for anyone else.

"I can't share you. I want to walk down there, lock the doors, and burn the fucking place to ashes with everyone inside who just got to see that." I stalk to her, and she stays pressed to the glass, worry in her eyes. "But that's not before I personally remove every single man's eyes who watched you take pleasure."

She gulps and nods, her eyes slowly softening. "I don't want others to have me. I don't want anyone to touch me like you do," Emelia whispers, and I place both hands on the glass beside her head and drop my forehead to hers.

What the hell has she done to me?

"You make me insane," I tell her, closing my eyes. Suddenly, the most delicate, softest hands cradle my face, and I groan.

"You make me furious," she replies.

"And what are we going to do about that?" I ask her, so fucking lost in what I'm feeling and equally as pissed that I'm letting walls down and showing some semblance of vulnerability to the woman I have fought so hard to remain untouchable to.

But I just. Fucking. Can't.

I want her to take whatever good that is left in me and claim it. Secretly keep it as her own and nurture it when I come home to her every night. I want a fucking wife. I want a friend. I want her to take the roughness from my days and toss it out nightly so I can breathe again. It's then that I realize I haven't really released a full breath since losing my parents. No, not until Emelia, and this is just the beginning.

"You can start by letting me in there. We just have to try. You don't have to be a mafia boss when it's us, Nico. We can just be us. That's what a wife and husband do." She leans in and kisses me, wrapping her hands at the nape of my neck.

I try to mentally resist it one more time, my face twisted in pain. But when that sweet tongue of hers touches mine, I am rendered defenseless. My hands leave the glass and tangle in her hair, gaining my ability to deepen the kiss. We fight each other, kissing more and more roughly.

I move us toward the couch in my office, but I don't break contact. Bending, I wrap my arms around her waist and keep our lips sealed. The second we get to the couch, I reluctantly have to pull away as I step back and unbuckle my belt, and Emelia's greedy hands make work of undoing my pants and pulling the zipper down. Once that's done, her hand reaches into my briefs, and she wraps her warm palm around my hard cock, somehow making it stiffen more.

"Let me taste you," she whispers against my neck.

"Just for a minute. I want to be inside you, Emelia. I need it."

She nods eagerly and drops to her knees fast. Pulling me out, she immediately wraps her plump lips around my cock, staining it with what's left of the red lipstick she wore.

"Fuck, you are so damn good at sucking cock, baby." I watch her, moving her hair to the side so I can see my girth stretch her mouth so fucking wide. Her eyes water as she looks up at me when I start to fuck her mouth, and we don't break eye contact while I do it. Me still in a suit and my queen on her knees for her king. The only time she will ever bow before anyone is to me. On her knees before I repay the favor.

"I won't come until it's your cunt, pretty baby," I warn her as she tries to suck my fucking soul out of my body. I see what she wants, but I want it deeper. There isn't a chance in hell I'm wasting a drop of me for anything but her warm pussy.

"Mmm," she whines in disappointment, and I laugh, tugging at her hair a bit. But this has her moaning instead, and I tug it again, this time hard, and she groans louder against my cock.

My pretty wife wants it rough.

Anything for the queen of the Seattle mafia.

Yanking her hair harder, my cock pops out of her mouth, and she screams in pleasure."Oh God!"

I see it then. Her hand is between her legs, and those delicate fingers are touching my property.

Get a fucking grip, I inwardly scold myself. I can't possibly be jealous of her fingers.

But I am. Goddammit, I'm jealous of anything that occupies her intimate parts that isn't me. If I ever found her masturbating with her hands or toys without me... I just might snap.

"Do not come until it's on my cock, wife." I pull her up by her hair, and she makes a sound I've never heard before, but it's pure pleasure. It's as if she invented it, and I would like that to play at my goddamn funeral.

"Call me that again."

"My wife," I grit out through my teeth, practically growling with my possessiveness over her.

"Tell me how you want me. I'll do anything for you." The obedience she shows me will never go unappreciated. I will reward her for being submissive with me exclusively.

"I want you to ride my cock."

She nods, biting her lip.

"What is it, principessa?" I ask, grabbing her chin and tilting it up for her to look at me.

"It's nothing." She tries to shake her head, but my grasp won't let her, and that answer won't do.

"Tell me," I warn, moving my hands to her neck and squeezing.

She swallows thickly before she responds. "I'm always worried I'll be too heavy and it won't feel as good for you. Or that it's not my best angle."

"Emelia?" This isn't her. Her body has never been a problem. She has flaunted it, owned it, paraded it around for me to salivate over.

"The women here... they are beautiful. That's why I came. I wanted to see.... You don't have diversity in body types. You only hire... thin.... At least, that's what I noticed tonight." I never thought of that, and to be honest, she's right. It wasn't something I purposely did. I just never thought about it.

"First, you're right. More bodies like yours need to be showcased here. Since I know what I have, I know what the men paying high amounts of money for are missing. Second, Emelia Valiente—" I pause as she hangs onto every word. I've never really called her by her name with my last name attached, and it's captivating. "—I want you. I crave you. I want to claim, own, and mark all of you as mine. Your body is nothing like the women's down there." Her eyes lower, and I tighten my grasp, making her look back up. "To me, it's fucking superior. Why do you think I don't want anyone seeing it? Tasting it? Fucking you?"

I wait a moment, thinking back to our wedding night and that lowlife scum of an ex and her in that room. And I remember the images and videos of her that he took, replaying them over and over in my mind. My body tenses.

"When I saw you with Damian on our wedding night and then in those fucking...." I can't even say it, and I can tell she doesn't want me to either, because that was a huge betrayal to her. "I wasn't just being a fucking prick who was claiming ownership. I was mad with the idea that he could have access to you. That he did. That he tasted the lips of perfection and the body of a goddess. Don't ever compare yourself to any woman before you. It will be pointless, a waste of time, trying to make it add up, because you will always reign over any of them." I kiss her smiling lips.

"Now put all that weight on me and fuck me like you know who owns you," I tell her, moving around her to sit on the couch. Her back stays to me, and I give her a minute to realize my words hold truth and that she has nothing to fear. My loyalty is to my wife. My arousal is in the palm of her hands.

Turning slowly, she places one leg on either side of my hips, my cock hitting her center. God, I'm desperate for her. "Sit on my thick dick, wife. I'm growing impatient," I growl.

Biting her lip, she does just that. Slowly, she slides down my cock, taking inch after inch like a champ. I'm large, thick, and hard for her to take, but she does it so fucking well. Once she's fully seated, I see there's still something missing. Bringing my hands up to the dip at the front of her dress, I rip it right down the fucking middle.

"Oh my God! Nico, that was expensive."

I laugh."Really?" I palm her gorgeous breasts and pinch her tight nipples in between my fingers, eliciting a sweet yelp.

"Ahh! Yes. It was four thousand dollars." This stops me, and I laugh hard. "What is so funny?"

"That's not even pennies to me, Emelia. If you're going to complain about how expensive something is, then at least make it less comical."

Rolling her eyes, she blows me off."Maniac."

"I am. Now how about you get this maniac nice and fucking wet and ride his cock? Wives have duties."

She giggles, a slight blush scattering over her cheeks and her nose.

"I'll never get tired of watching you respond to degradation like it's your first language."

Slowly, she begins to rock her hips, adjusting to my size and positioning me just how she wants me. The act alone might make me come, but I do my damn best not to. I want this shit to last. I watch her breasts wobble slightly with each calculated movement, and my eyes fixate on her beauty mark just under her right breast above her ribcage. The intimate way I know it's there is something I hate to admit I take great pleasure in. I rub it with my thumb almost too much.

I am comfortable with someone I barely know and feel a connection and longing to know her, and that's a place I've never been with anyone. There is a difference between fucking to get off and fucking to connect, and this is us trying to connect.

Where will we fucking go after here? Because it can never be the same.

CHAPTER FIFTEEN

Emelia

His eyes pay close attention to my breasts and the mark on my ribs. It's almost like that's where his pleasure is focused instead of the soft rising and falling of me on his cock. Tonight, we turned over a leaf, called a truce, agreed to stop being enemies and give this marriage a fighting chance. All this pent-up lust and even more pent-up anger unraveled, and we couldn't do it anymore.

There was a softness—dare I say a weakness—in Nico as he let me in tonight. I would never admit that in detail to anyone, especially him, because I fear it would shut him down, or worse, put us back at odds. Nico has to move at his own pace, to exist in a world where he feels he can be himself without others seeing a weakness in him. For me though, this vulnerability is his most powerful strength.

I need more.

I pick up the pace and brace myself for the orgasm I'm going to have. Because this angle and the man are both too much for me to wait any longer. What he did with the gun... that was—well, that was intense and raw and sensual. The way I know that gun will, in fact, protect me in our world—and protect even more so the man behind it—added a new level of sexual intimacy.

Then he brought up Damian and how that made him feel—

"Come back to me, principessa," Nico pulls me from my wandering thoughts, and I catch the way he admires me.

"Sorry, I just.... It feels good, and I don't want to leave this space. It's safe. It's like nothing I've had before," I admit, and he sits up, sliding his hands under my arms, up my back, and into my hair so he can bring me in for a kiss. We don't need the words right now. We just need to feel. And feel, we do.

The room fills with moans, groans, and heavy breathing, and we fuck hard and with ferocity, trying to see who can claim their orgasm first. Who can claim one another more. Our foreheads touch between messy kisses. The longer we go at one another, the less coordinated it gets and the more freeing it becomes. We just want to get as close as possible. Touch each part of one another all at once.

We crawl underneath each other's skin, and together, we orgasm.

"Fuck, fuck, fuck, Emelia!" he groans out with each pump of his hips.

"Yes!" My voice is raspy and breathy after all the yelling and moaning.

"Take every drop, Emelia." With choppy but hard thrusts, he pours into me, and I kiss his forehead, letting him take what he needs in this moment. The calm will come, and I just hope this will be the same man.

Will I be met with a new outlook on us, a new version of Nico, or will he be the old, callous, and cold man I married? Will it always just be sex for us?

I'm unable to tell right away, because I fall asleep within seconds of him laying me down. His phone rang when the dust settled, and he kissed me gently and said he had to take it. I nodded, and once I snuggled down onto that surprising comfortable couch, I was out, the adrenaline of the night and the passion we shared exhausting me.

I'm woken up what I assume isn't much later, but we're home, and I'm being placed in bed. How did he carry me here? I look up at Nico's profile as he pulls the blankets up and fixes my pillow, and I smile at the sight. He's still being soft.

"Nico?"

"Shh, baby, you have to sleep, and I still have work to do. I will be to bed soon. Rest."

I want to argue for him to stay, but the truth is I'm exhausted. Looking down, I see I'm in one of his dress shirts. Did he dress me? How did I fit in one of his shirts? He's muscular and built with a large frame, but how did I fit? Oh, whatever. I'm too tired to play riddle me this.

And once I shut my brain off, I fall into slumber, the night carrying me away.

THE MORNING SUN COMES THROUGH LIKE IT DOES every morning, but this time, there is a heat I haven't felt before. A wall of warmth, muscle, and strength.

He stayed.

Nico has been gone before I've woken every morning and comes home after I've fallen asleep for a while now. But this morning, he's here. I turn my head slightly and see his hair is a mess from what I'm sure was good sleep. When was the last time he went to bed at a decent hour and slept in?

"I thought I was the only serial killer in this marriage." Nico's voice is hoarse and deep, and my core tightens. God, he sounds sexy.

"What?" I laugh.

"You're watching me sleep. That's a very serial killer thing of you to do, my wife."

I giggle and turn to face him. He opens one eye and smirks, opening his arms to invite me into his chest.

"You stayed...." I trail off.

He nods."Yes. We have to start somewhere. I gave you my word."

My heart feels like a swarm of butterflies is inside it, flying rampant.

"How do we even start?" I ask.

"Afraid you'll have to navigate that one, Emelia. This is one thing I'm not good at," he admits what we both already know very well. This is uncharted territory for him. But it is for me too. Only difference is I had a relationship before. Has he ever had a relationship that was more than a sexual payoff?

"Nico? Am I your first?"

He laughs loud. There is still as rasp to his voice, and I look up at him."What? I'm serious." I smack his chest.

"Emelia, I didn't learn how to fuck you to sleep by being born with the skill."

My smile fades then, but I hurry and hide it. Made men don't have low body counts, neither in fucking nor in killing. We can't go back, only forward.

"You know what I mean," I tell him. He senses my unease, and I appreciate that he just lets me have it and moves past it.

"You're my first and only wife. So, yes. And no, I haven't had a romantic relationship outside of what you and I are trying to do here," he admits.

"Well, we have to get to know one another *outside* of the bedroom," I add. Because as of today, that's all we know about each another. Oh, and how to royally piss one another off.

"Okay. Is there a list of questions we should ask?" He plays with my hair, and I draw shapes and words on his chest with my finger.

"No, we want it to be authentic. I'm sure there are plenty of books on how to get to know someone, but that seems counterproductive."

I feel him nod."Agreed."

We stay silent for a little while. This is a lot harder than I would have thought. Just ask questions.

"There is a picture in your office. It's of a man and a woman and a little boy. It looks like you. Is that your parents?" I guess we can go straight for the jugular. I tightly shut my eyes and scrunch my face, scolding myself for this one.

"Yes." He sounds cold. I sit up and look at him, and he doesn't look back at me. He keeps his eyes focused on the ceiling, and I realize I have about two seconds to change the subject.

"A sex club. That's interesting." It takes a minute, but he laughs.

"Yes. A sex club. And I still need to handle your guards. I want the name of any of the people who helped you get away yesterday," he says with such ease, changing the course of the conversation.

My back tenses. I remember Lenny then and the fear in her eyes when she realized who I was and who I was trying to get away from. The way she feared for her family. I made a promise, and I don't want to break that.

"Nico." I tighten my hand on his chest, so afraid he won't hear me.

"No, Emelia. You will tell me names, and they will be dealt with. Lucky the first guy is in our hands."

I shoot up."But they didn't do anything wrong. They didn't know I was running," I blurt out, doing all I can to make sure they don't get hurt because of me.

"I don't care, Emelia. They could have helped my wife run away from me."

I think up something fast and soften my body, forcing the

tension to leav. I kiss his chest first before speaking. "They didn't though. They were helping me get to you."

"Nice try, Emelia. Names."

Fine. He wants to play tough, then I can be tougher. Moving my hands down his defined pecs and chiseled abs, I go under the sheet and find his cock. He slept in the nude, which eliminates barriers. I need to get to it, so I bite the taught flesh above his rib as I get him hard.

"Emelia," he warns, but I ignore him.

Once he's rock-hard and ready, I lower the sheet to his thighs and climb over him, straddling him. I work at the buttons on his dress shirt I'm wearing, and I lower onto his erection. Once free, I throw the shirt to the floor and start circling my hips, adjusting to his large cock.

"Please, baby, don't be mad at me. I promise I won't do anything like that again," I whisper, my voice low and siren-like. He bites his lip and tries not to give in, but I know what my body can do to him. I slide up and down slowly, gasping on the fall. "God, you feel so good. You're so big." Stroke his cock and his ego.

"You're playing dirty," he warns, resolve slipping second by second.

"I know. I really think you should forgive me though. I can be better." I bite my lip and move my hands to my breasts, giving them the attention he normally would.

"Emelia," he tries one more failed attempt, and I apologize again, but this time, I lower on him, bare down, and circle. When his eyes roll to the back of his head, I know I've won this time.

"You're such a naughty little slut." He flips us and fucks into me harder and harder, and the information he demanded is now a thing of the past.

Thank God.

And I am able to get him to agree to let the first driver go within minutes.

We go at each other for a good two hours before he finally gets up from bed. The talking will have to come another day, I guess. But at least I know Lenny and the others are safe.

He stands, moving to the bathroom, and I feel cold then. Like I was used. Because usually I am. We make love, and then he's gone until the next time. Sure, he kissed me and said he was going to shower, but I can't help but feel that loneliness creeping in.

Instead of letting him see me like this, I get dressed in a lounge set, the long-sleeved top hanging off one shoulder. I decide I will shower when he leaves for the day.

Stepping into the kitchen, I see breakfast was already made and the table is set. I'm sure Nico gave them a time, and the staff followed it strictly. Giulio is having a coffee at the kitchen island while reading the paper, and I walk by him to head to the coffee machine.

"Morning, Giulio."

"Mrs. Valiente," he says back. I have had some conversations with Giulio, but they were sparse, as he goes where my husband goes.

"Did you sleep well?" I ask.

"Never do, but yes. Thank you, ma'am."

His answer makes me smile. I pour some coffee with a dash of creamer and turn to look at him.

"That's an interesting answer. A bit of an oxymoron," I point out.

He matches my smile and laughs a bit. "I guess you could say that."

I grab a piece of bacon and climb onto the kitchen counter. I should sit at the table, as it was set so nicely for us, but I'd much rather sit here and talk to him than move to the dining area.

"Are you married, Giulio?" He can't be over fifty-five, so I assume he must be. Unless he's like other underbosses and chooses the life like Nico had before our arrangement.

"No, I was, but sadly she passed away."

"Oh, Giulio, I'm so sorry." I place my hand over my heart, and I fall silent. I never know what to say when someone tells me they've lost a loved one.

"It's fine. It's been a couple of years, but after her, I didn't want anyone else. Besides—" He pauses to sip his coffee. There is some gray starting to come through his dark shoulder-length hair. He wears it either in a low bun or slicked back. Most men couldn't pull that off, but he does very nicely. I will say, he is very handsome. "—I'm married to the job." He shrugs.

I remember everything that happened last night. Who am I kidding? I don't think I will ever forget all that happened last night. But one part that sticks out to me is one of the men I was dancing with killed Giulio's brother. Should I bring that up? Most likely, I shouldn't, and for the first time this morning, I avoid a complicated question. Giulio doesn't owe me any answers.

"If it makes you feel better, I have always been married..." I click my tongue and look up, thinking about the irony in my statement. "I have always been married to the mafia as well, even before Nico. We all are, in some way, right?"

Giulio nods with a knowing humorous smile. He seems so kind and levelheaded. It's hard to think he has a mean bone in his body, but clearly he does, and I have seen it.

"Yes, we are. Also, James and Farren have been—" He pauses, and it isn't the good kind of pause. He looks at me, and I put down my coffee, my body going cold. No. Please, no. "—moved. For now. Until Nico knows what he would like to do. I will make sure your new guards are here before you and Nico come back this afternoon."

I'm about to get up to go to Nico, but he steps into the kitchen. Once again, my breath catches. He's dressed down, nothing like his tailored suits he wears daily. He's in jeans and a white V-neck shirt that still somehow looks expensive, which I'm sure it is. It hugs his arms, torso, and hips perfectly, and he styled his wet hair in his signature slicked-back look.

I forget for a moment what Giulio just said as he approaches me.

"Giulio," he greets his underboss but doesn't stop his gaining on me. Once he reaches me, he cages me in, putting his knuckles to the white marble countertops on both sides of my hips.

"When I take a shower, you are to be there. It's not a question or up for debate. You are to be naked in the shower with me. Got it?" He tilts his head, just inches from me but loud enough for Giulio to hear.

I would be embarrassed, but when he gets this close to me and tempts me, I can't help but get tunnel vision. Now add the attention he is giving me as more than just his wife of convenience, and I almost let it slip my mind what I want to talk about.

"Nico." Finally, I snap back to it once he leaves me with a kiss on my neck, and he makes his way over to pour some coffee for himself.

"Emelia."

I straighten my shoulders and hold my head high. "I am more than okay with you reassigning my guards as a punishment to me, not them. They did their best. I ask that you please do not do anything to hurt them. They are not to blame."

He looks at me over his shoulder, and I gulp. He looks amused but deadly. As if the punishment is a sick, twisted part of the fun. Watching them suffer would bring him fulfillment.

Turning with his coffee in hand, he leans against the counter and looks to Giulio and back to me again. "And tell me why I should do anything other than break their hands and knees for letting the one thing I pay them a lot of money to protect slip away."

I shake my head. "Nico, you promised. I don't care if you punish me, but I won't let you hurt others in my name. Unless they are awful. Then I won't stop you," I add. Those men were bad last night. They got too comfortable, and when I found out they hurt some women and killed Giulio's brother as well as others, I wasn't exactly jumping up to plead for their mercy.

"I don't need to punish you. In fact, I like *not* punishing you. But threatening men who should have protected you, and others who shouldn't have helped you, has only benefited me in ways I thoroughly enjoy." He reminds me of the way I used my body to get him to agree to keeping Lenny and my other driver alone. This is going to lead to an argument, and it has to. That doesn't mean we have to be cruel. We can argue, no matter the status of who we are trying to become together.

"Nico, I don't want to fight about this. Please. You agreed that I have a say, and I ask that you reassign them and that be that. Okay?" I cross my arms and give him a sincere look of pleading.

He stares at me for a long minute, assessing me and taking a few sips of coffee. He finally breaks his eye contact with me and turns to Giulio. "Permanent clean-up duty."

Giulio nods, takes out his phone, and types something before he puts the phone to his ear. I go to leave the room, thankful it went in my favor and that we didn't have to throw everything in the kitchen at one another, but he halts me by calling out my name.

"Emelia, your skates are in. I will be taking you myself to the rink today to see you on the ice. Be ready in an hour."

Turning, I shake my head, confusion taking over me. "What?"

"I want to see you on the ice. Consider this a staycation honeymoon. I took the next week off to be with you, wife. Don't waste a minute."

My stomach flips, and I suck on my tongue, trying not to let a smile break free. Nico wants to try. We really just might have a shot at being free from misery.

"Fine. I can do that. I will be ready in thirty. I don't wear makeup when I'm on the ice," I tell him as I retreat from the kitchen. With my back now fully to him, I crack a giddy smile. He doesn't say anything, but I know he's watching me leave, and I add an extra sway to my hips. My way of saying thank you for everything today.

WATCHING THE WAY HE HANDLES THE WHEEL WITH such confidence and an essence of ownership makes my stomach flip. In a good way. How could I have hated this man and loathed the idea of being married to him, and now I'm in a car, going on... a date? Is that what this is?

Nico wasn't wrong when he said we never had a proper honeymoon. God, that feels like ages ago, when really it was only a little more than a month. But he isn't wrong. We didn't get a proper honeymoon. Are we ever going to address just how bad the start to this was? Or are we going to move forward and start anew?

I don't think we can until we really talk about it.

And... how and when will I tell him about my father and what he originally wanted me to do? Everything in me knows I should, but I can't. What if it ruins what we're attempting to build here?

There is more to Nico than a tough exterior. I see it in small glimpses of his gentle touch, his profound love making, the way he has shown possession, and his very unconventional and mostly annoying way of wanting to keep me safe. In no way do I think this is okay or the right way to express things, but I have to remember the world we're surrounded by. Gentleness and words of affirmation are not the norm.

Why hasn't my father called? I wonder for the millionth time since that last dreadful yet liberating night, when I told my father to leave, the gun to his head, as I reclaimed power. All while I shuddered in fear deep, deep inside, because I knew he would want to retaliate. His silence isn't a sign of my victory. No, it's a warning. He's waiting, planning, and plotting, and I have no idea when my life will be cut short.

I guess this is why I want to make each moment left of my life count. Because my father will come to claim his revenge on me. Until then, I might as well absorb what's left.

There is fear in me, but there is also contentment. I knew what he would do to me one day. Knowing my father would ultimately be the reason I died, I've grown accustomed to that idea. I've prepared myself for it. Death doesn't scare me anymore. So I choose here and now, and that is with Nico.

I look up at Nico, and I realize he's on the phone. My thoughts took me so deep I blacked out on reality.

"Yes, I will be back to work in a week. I will check emails periodically, but I'm leaving you and Giulio in charge. Good work, Randeno." He ends the call.

"Who is Randeno?" I ask.

"He's one of my most loyal men. He was the youngest in my father's army, and now he's the oldest in mine." He smiles.

That smile, it's sparse. A sight you want to capture, because you never know when you'll see it again. Not his smirk. Not his cunning and mocking grin. But his real smile.

"That's sweet. What did he do?"

Nico reaches over, places his free hand on the thickest part of my yoga-pant-covered thigh, and kneads at it. I love when he touches the parts of me others ridiculed.

"I told you, he's in my army."

I shake my head. "No, I mean you told him 'good work.' What did he do?"

He shakes his head, "Tsk, tsk. No, principessa. You don't get involved with the business."

I nod. "Hmm, I just show up to all your events and support you and *seem* as though I'm your partner."

"You are my partner. You are my queen. You make this a kingdom. You don't need to be involved with the dangers of my business."

I look out the window. His words aren't harsh, and they do make some sense.

I sigh. "I guess you're right. I'll just keep thinking it's all sunshine and rainbows and charity work that you do," I tease, and he smiles again, this time with a little laugh.

"I do some charity. You will be doing more soon too."

I look back at him. "Do you do charity for a sense of redemption?"

He peers at me briefly before adjusting his shoulders as well as his hand on the wheel. "No. I do it because I can. I don't need redemption, Emelia."

"You don't ever feel like this life is killing you from the inside out?" I cautiously ask the question, adding my physical touch. I place my hand on his on my thigh, and I trace the rough skin over thick veins.

He shakes his head. "It's all I know. That's all I'll ever know. Besides, redemption came already."

My brows lift, and I'm curious as to what he means by that. "When?"

"We're here," he cuts me off, and I know that was deliberate. Nico shares only what he is ready to share. And that redemption isn't something I'm going to be afforded the luxury of knowing.

Time. Slow, painful, annoying time. That's what we will have to give one another.

CHAPTER SIXTEEN

Nico

Randeno and Giulio found some more of my shipments, and luckily most of it was there. It was docked along the Oregon coast in the middle of the night. I'm sending some of my men out to investigate further, but this reeks of the Notellis.

Maybe that's who was backing Lavetti. Giuseppe wants revenge, and he's knocking at the wrong door. Emelia is now on my side. She isn't a treaty anymore, or a physical object of alliance; she is now a part of my reign.

I haven't told her all the details of why I want to end her father, just bits and pieces. Now isn't the time. I'm not ready to strike. It's too soon. After this incident at my house and sending that sick fuck Damian back to him with my message, they will be too on guard. They can't know when we're coming.

I hop out of the car, rounding it and opening Emelia's door. Extending my hand to her, she takes it and steps out. I open the trunk next and take out her bag with her skates and a change of clothes for her to wear to dinner tonight. She reaches for it, but I take her hand instead, earning me a snort and an eye roll.

"That's one tongue lashing for you," I tell her, stopping us and pulling her into me.

"What is that, Nico?" Her voice is raspy yet soft and sensual.

"Each time you act like a brat, I will give your greedy clit a tongue fuck, baby."

She moans and leans in closer. "Then I won't behave all day, *il mio custode.*"

Fuck me.

"Emelia. I will fuck your cunt with my tongue the number of times you act like that today, but I will only bring you right to the edge," I threaten.

She goes up on her tiptoes and bites the side of my jaw. My cock starts to grow hard, and I look around, making sure no one is watching my wife take intimacy from me.

"I love the idea of you eating me and withholding my orgasm from me for hours. Sounds like the perfect date, husband."

My eyes roll back, and my cock is now fully hard. I have to have her. I need to feed my cock the meal it's grown to crave morning, noon, and night.

"But we will have to wait until tonight, I suppose." She shrugs, wiggles from me, and leaves me standing there hard, horny, and now ready to pounce. That dirty little wife of mine has no idea what I will do for that tonight. I also can't believe I'm here playing fucking house and letting Emelia into my personal space as more than just a wife of convenience and a fuck of a lifetime.

Giulio was surprised when I told him I wanted the week with Emelia and with minimal to no involvement with work. Is it a bad idea, given we are most likely going to war with the Notellis and starting problems with possible other outfits if they do not agree to this? Yes. But I'm not afraid of a little fuel on my fire. In fact, I welcome it. The buildup to war is almost—*almost*—as satisfying as fucking. I'm fucked in the head, and in my line of work, I embrace it.

Emelia disappears inside the building, and I catch up to

her a few moments later. When we're inside, she looks around curiously. "Where is everyone?"

Placing my hand on the curve of her back, I urge her toward a bench near an entrance gate to the rink. "I wanted you to have it all to yourself. I rented it out."

She halts abruptly and turns to look at me. "Nico, that is insane. That must have cost a fortune!"

"Emelia, I own Seattle. I have enough money you could drown in it." I shrug, and she shakes her head, rolling her eyes. "Another orgasm withheld," I say, and she smirks.

"You're an ass."

"If you think this behavior is me being an ass, I would hate to know just how bad you thought I was before today."

"The worst," she admits nonchalantly.

"Good, because—" I stop her, needing her to hear this. I grasp her chin and pull her face to me, and she looks softly into my hard eyes. "—there will be times, Emelia, when I won't be able to be a charming prince. I will have days where business will interfere, and I will have to set boundaries and lift walls for those moments. I need to know you understand that and won't let it set back whatever we build."

Hesitation is glaring at me like the sun would. This is a different tone than the one we've carried since last night, but it has to be done. I'm not a soft man. I may be able to give her a gentle side when needed, but that isn't going to be me every day, all day, and I still have to be Nico outside of our marriage.

"I understand." Blinking, she agrees to my terms.

"Good." I don't know what she's thinking in that moment, but it can't be the worst thing, because she hasn't pushed me away and told me to go fuck myself. But she does free herself and walk ahead of me, not keeping physical contact.

I can give her that. If she is to respect the boundaries I set, then I need to reciprocate, even if it makes me want to pull her in and smack her ass. Having a wall put up by her is worse than the walls I place. Mine are to protect her. Hers are to keep me at a distance. That is something we will need to learn to understand and compromise, something I know almost all marriages require. Give and take and an even greater amount of sacrifice. But in our world, those stakes are higher, and the sacrifices are much bigger.

Keeping a good distance from her, I follow Emelia to the bench. I resist touching her and pulling her to me, but we're in her element now, and I will let her lead. She sits, and I place the bag next to her before leaning against the plexiglass and half wall of the rink. Folding my arms across my broad chest and crossing my ankles, I admire her precision and the delicate way she puts on her skates, lacing them up.

Her hair is slicked back into a low bun, her face free of makeup, showing the faintest sign of freckles. Emelia is wearing tight yoga pants that hug every inch of her like a second skin and a long-sleeved top that is just as tight, but it's cropped, showing me the slightest amount of skin. A peek of her upper stomach shows, and I see that freckle, the damn thing I want to kiss and lick all the time.

Focus, Nico. This is Emelia's place.

She moves past me without a word and opens the gate to the rink. Before she steps in, she looks back to me, her eyes somehow looking brighter against her cold cheeks. "Do you skate?"

I shake my head. "No."

Giving me an incredulous, curious look, she glides onto the ice and keeps talking to me. "So, you came here today just to watch me skate?"

"Yes."

"Because that's not creepy. That would make you a stalker."

"I kill people and sell drugs and weapons. Stalking should be nothing to you," I tell her, and she shakes her head, but as she does this, she does some sort of turn and slight jump in the air before landing on one foot and letting her other move easily behind her.

"What was that move?"

"A clockwise toe loop. It's a simple jump." She does it again, but this time, she does two circular movements in the air, before landing gracefully.

"Simple? I would fucking break my skull if I ever did that."

"So if I ever wanted to kill you, I would just put you on ice?"

This time, I shake my head, my tongue gliding against my inner cheek to my bottom teeth before responding, "Funny, Emelia."

She glides along the ice, alternating between facing forward and backward. It looks effortless for her, even as she starts a conversation. "I went to an ice skating competition with my mom, and I just fell in love. It looked liberating, freeing, and complicated all at once. Of course, I was only four at the time, so I just thought it was magical." She smiles so damn wide, and I nearly match it.

"How come you never went professional with it?"

One brow quirks, then she is in the air again, doing three spins, making my jaw drop I'm so unexpectedly impressed.

"I'll give you a guess. His name starts with a G, and he is the world's biggest fucking asshole. Besides you." She winks.

"Fair enough." I will take that title. Means she doesn't think I've gone soft, when clearly I have. She melts me inside all while adding fuel to a never-ending flame that was once just a sparking ember.

"He still let you do it as a hobby though?"

"Only because he thought it would be a good workout and that I would lose all this weight and be some skinny little thing, like all the women men desire. Joke's on him. It only made my muscles bigger too."

My insides burn. I feel the sting start in my head and travel viciously down my spine. Her body is perfect. It feeds men like me who are hungry, insatiable, constantly starving. That body was made to keep me coming back again and again, and though she radiates confidence and thrives in her skin, it still doesn't make it okay that her father made her feel like she was something not worth desiring.

"How often did you do it when you lived back in New York?"

Emelia gains speed as she takes off for the other side of the rink, and before she gets there, she jumps up, lands, and starts spinning in place at a fast pace. Her back is arched, and one leg is angled at her other ankle that is attached to the foot still on the ice. My God, she is fucking good at this. She looks at peace, in her element. Fucking centered.

"I would go five days a week for three to sometimes ten hours each day." She is now a little out of breath, and I see why. "Anything to get away from my family. They were suffocating and demanding and overbearing, but if I said I was going to work out at the rink, they practically leaped out of the way." She meets me back at the half-wall door, and I watch her intently. She's beautiful. Makeup-free. Flushed cheeks. And glowing in her element. Carefree... and just—free.

"Nico?"

I shake my head, Emelia pulling me from wherever the hell I just went. "Yes?"

"Can I have music on? I want to skate to my favorite song."

"Sure. Where's your phone?"

"In my bag, back pocket." She pushes off the glass and starts skating backward. "It's Lana Del Ray's 'Young and Beautiful,'" she hollers, and I look over at the employee in the box who has his head buried in his phone. Walking over to where he is, I sort through her songs and find the one she asked for. Tapping on the glass, I alert him, and he stands fast, coming to unlock the box.

"Yes, sir?"

"Plug this in and play this song." I show him, and he nods. He's young and will know how to use an iPhone. I walk back, but this time, I take a seat at the top of the bleachers. I want to take her in, all of her. See her become one with the ice.

The humming sound of a low, feminine voice and a piano starts, and Emelia closes her eyes where she's positioned in the middle of the rink. She doesn't move at first, and I swear I'm on the edge of my seat, waiting for her next move. The second the woman starts singing, my wife's eyes open, and she sets into motion, gliding effortlessly, the faint sound of her blades on the ice almost adding to the music.

"Will you still love me when I'm no longer young and beautiful?"

The words accompany a haunting melody, and Emelia's face shows it. It draws in tight with pain, but her moves don't falter. She never misses a jump or landing, executing them at the perfect time, in tandem with the music. Music isn't really something I've paid much attention to or realized how much of an impact it has on someone. Or how it can accompany something so painfully beautiful like it does right now.

This song will be burned into my memory, as will the image of Emelia skating to it. The song crescendos, and goose bumps rise on my body as I watch her. Fuck me. She's taking over my head. Emelia is beautiful, sensual, challenging, talented, and she is making her way into my fucking soul.

Panic rises up in me. I don't know if this is something I can do. Let her in. Have something with her. The only people I believed could love one another were my mother and father. After my father died, I watched my mom slowly waste away until she took her last breath. Broken hearts can kill, and that's what took her. The idea of living without my father put her in her grave, and I swore that type of love was made solely for them and them alone. That was a once-in-a-lifetime kind of thing.

"Emelia!" I holler out when the song stops, and she looks up at me from the center of the ice, both of us breathing heavily. She nods, knowing what I want.

I need her.

I look to the booth as I stride down the bleacher stairs, and the young man working glances at me. I tilt my head toward the exit, flashing my gun just so I don't have to worry about him interjecting. He does what I silently told him to without a moment of hesitation. Emelia glides to the edge of the rink as I hit the bottom landing, and the second the door closes behind that now faceless employee, my hands are in her hair and our mouths are on one another. We claw at each other, the passion seeping out of us both.

"My skates." She breaks our seal, and I shake my head.

"Keep them on," I tell her.

"But they could hurt you."

"I fucking hope they do. Mark me up. Make me fucking bleed for you."

"Why do we always have to have pain? Why do you crave the harshness, Nico?" she whispers, running her hands through my hair and piercing me with her gaze.

I don't know how to answer her in the way I think she needs me to, but I do the best I can with what I know. "Because the pain means it's real. It's the only way I know how to let you in."

Tears well in her eyes, and she grips the hair at the nape of my neck and brings my forehead to hers.

"You don't have to be tough with me. You can breathe, Nico. Just breathe. I need to know you are capable of love."

Does she love me? She didn't directly say it, but I suddenly feel the earth tilting on its axis, and the air from my lungs feels like it's being sucked out of me by the Grim Reaper himself. I can learn to like her, but am I capable of love?

"Nico, it's okay. Breathe. We just need to focus on the now. Come back to me." Emelia kisses the tip of my nose, then my lips.

"I don't know how to love, and I don't know what it will do to me if you teach me how."

"Don't let me teach you anything. Just exist with me. Learn who I am, and let me learn you, and whatever happens, we will figure it out." The way she is still so soft when the entire foundation of us has been hostile and built on the vilest form of disrespect and disdain blows my mind.

"Take us home. Take me to bed. Just let me and you have time. That's all I ask." I almost feel... jealous... angry... that she isn't telling me she loves me. That's a part of her I don't have yet, and I want it all, even if it's suffocating me and scaring the living fuck out of me.

I found the one thing in this world I am afraid of. Nico Dante Valiente, the boss of the Seattle mafia, fears the love of Emelia Rene Valiente. My own fucking wife.

"I can't wait for home."

"If you want to have me at all, you will need to let me in emotionally, Nico. I can't just keep giving you my body to mask our feelings. They have to rise to the surface," she tells me, moving back enough to separate our touch. I want to pull her back in and demand she let me show her what I'm feeling, because I can't show her with words. I only know how to speak with my body.

"Take me to lunch," she urges, soft still.

"Yes, let's eat."

She nods. "Okay."

Stepping onto the foam-padded floor, she moves to the bench, and I grip the wall and drop my head back between my shoulders, breathing in and out deeply. Trying to regain some equilibrium, I hear her feminine voice tell me she's going to use the restroom. I nod and give a slight smile before she disappears. I would watch her walk away, but I'm afraid if I do, I will be a weak fool and crawl after her on hands and fucking knees.

I had planned to take us to a few more places after she got to show me how she skates, but maybe I need to step back and let us take a second. She emerges a minute later and smiles softly at me, pointing to the booth, then putting her hand to her ear in the international sign for telephone.

I nod and watch her make her way over to it, and then she's

by my side once again, her phone in hand. I grab her bag, and she slides her cell into the pocket I found it in earlier, and then I take her hand, a gesture I would normally only do if we had people watching us, but this one happens out of habit. I go with it, not wanting to be a complete dick and yank my hand away from hers.

We get to the car, and she climbs in. When I reach in and buckle her up, she laughs. "My hands aren't broken. I can do that."

"I know you can, but I want to do it."

She rolls her eyes.

"Third denial."

She remembers our conversation before we went in, and she giggles. "Third time's the charm. I bet the payoff will be... explosive."

"Nice play on words, principessa." I shut the door, round the car, and climb in. Music plays in the background, and I ask her where she would like to eat.

"Anything you're craving? I had dinner reservations, but clearly it's too early, seeing as it's not even noon," I tell her, driving into downtown Seattle.

"We can have dinner in bed." She winks, and I smirk, biting my lip and gripping her thigh hard.

"Naughty."

"You aren't complaining," she retorts.

"Nope. Never will. Food. What are you craving?" I bring it back in before we end up fucking in my sports car.

"I don't know. Why don't you pick it? I want to eat somewhere you love."

I don't usually go out to eat, so I can only think of fancy restaurants where I have entertained guests or conducted business.

It hits me then. "Are you picky?"

Emelia shakes her head. "Not one bit."

"Perfect." I drive a few more blocks, then take a right, landing us at Pike's Public Market Center.

"Oh, this is awesome! I read about this place. I also remember that scene in *Free Willy,* when they threw the fish! Is that real?"

I park the car and laugh. "Yes, that's real. You want to see that while we're here?"

"Um, yeah! That sounds like fun. You think you could use your big, bad mafia power to let them let me throw one?" she exclaims, clapping her hands.

"I'm sure I can do that." I smile, looking at her eyes light with excitement.

"Okay! Perfect. Now take me to this place where you like to eat. I'm starving."

"Me too. But I have to warn you, you might not like it."

"Try me," she challenges.

All right.

I slide out of the car and help her out next. She accepts my hand, but this time, she pulls me in and wraps her other hand around my bicep as she looks around the entire place with wonderment in her eyes.

"Is that the gum wall?" She points as we enter the start of the path through the market.

"Yes, it's pretty popular... and disgusting if you ask me," I tell her.

"Are you afraid of germs?" She laughs, looking up at me.

"And what if I was?" I question.

"You literally get people's blood splattered on you for a living, but a gum wall is pushing limits."

That's fair.

"We all have our things. I'm sure you have one."

"I do. I hate deep bodies of water. That is a no for me." She shivers.

"Really? So if I would have taken us swimming off the back of the yacht, you would have thrown a fit?" I ask, getting in line at the place I chose to eat.

"Not a fit, but I definitely would have pushed you overboard and took off to hide somewhere on the boat." She lays her head on my arm, just above her hand, and I notice now more than I did before the difference in our heights.

"I would have chased you down and thrown you in."

"Animal," she retorts.

"I can be." I lean down, grip her chin between my thumb and pointer finger, and give her a deep kiss. She moans into my mouth, and I have to pull myself away, because I don't want others hearing her sexy noises.

"So what do they serve here?"

"The *best* fucking sandwiches. It's worth this line." It's an indoor sandwich shop, but the line is always out the door and starts on the cobblestone path.

"I love a good sandwich. I always get the works." She smiles.

"Good, because there are a lot to choose from." We talk about the different types of meat they have, and when it's our turn, we decide to get two different kinds to split and share. We then hit the cobblestones again and eat while we walk.

She takes a bite of the Philly cheesesteak and moans. "Oh my God, Nico, this is so good." She wipes the corner of her mouth as she chews it the rest of the way and swallows. Damn it, she's fucking gorgeous, even with her mouth full.

"I know. That's why it's my favorite. Let's try this turkey club. I've never had it." I take a bite and remember why I love this place so much. I used to come a lot more when I was younger, but when I took over the business, I didn't have time to make pit stops at a sandwich shop in the city.

At this moment, I feel... normal. Something I haven't felt in a very long time. The responsibilities I have and the power I hold all dissipates, and it just feels like a normal fucking day with an extraordinary woman. The woman I get to call my wife and take home tonight to fuck until we both can't take anymore.

That's a fucking legacy I would proudly die with.

We keep walking and making small talk. She wants to stop at every tourist spot, and I indulge her. You'd think this is her first time out in the wild. This day feels like it will never end, but this is the first time in my life I can say with confidence that I never want it to.

CHAPTER SEVENTEEN
Nico

By the time we have hit every shop, she has a bag filled with Seattle merchandise and a hat she is now wearing as we walk down to the dock.

"Nico, this is awesome. Thank you. I feel like such a tourist." She laughs, and I take her bag from her and resume holding her hand with my free one.

"You look like one." I chuckle.

"Shush, I am enjoying it. Let me have it." She lightly slaps my arm, and I just shake my head. "You clearly never get out. Are you having fun?" she asks a moment later.

"I'm having fun, because you look like you've never been outside before," I tease.

"Ha-ha," she mocks. "But really, what do you like to do for fun?"

"I told you. Work."

"Boring. Come on, Nico," she urges, nudging my shoulder.

"Fine. I like reading and swimming. It's relaxing, and it's the only time my brain shuts off."

"I like to read too. Do you have a favorite genre?" she implores, and I will admit, this feels weird. Getting to know her is easy, but me sharing things about myself? That's not something I can say I like doing. At all.

"Horror."

"Shocker." She laughs. "Gore and all?"

"Yes. And mystery," I add.

"That checks out. I like mystery too, but I have to have some romance in it."

"Shocker," I use her word against her.

"Well, I do. Nothing is sexier than solving a mystery and having wild, passionate sex." She shrugs, and I stop us, this time turning and pulling her into me.

"Really? You like that? Mystery and toe-curling fucking, baby?" I hold her tighter, and this forces her to stand on her tiptoes as I lean in at the same time. As I put my lips only inches from hers, she nods, her body tightening in my grip. She wants me. Wants us. And I want to get us home so I can give it to her.

"I do. I love it. I like the idea of being chased too. To be caught and fucked hard," she whispers, her eyes watering with arousal, and I wonder if she's remembering that day in Greece. My cock is hardening in my jeans, and I know now I need to get us the fuck out of here.

"Is that right?" I question, and she simply nods. "Do you remember where the car is?" She nods again but more eagerly. "Good. I want you to go straight to the car, and I'm going to follow you. I will give you a head start, but if I catch up to you, you owe your husband those pretty fuck-me lips on the way home. Got it?"

"Y-Yes," she stutters, her cheeks flushing red before she grins. I let her go and wait for her to move, but she doesn't at first, so I lean down to her ear.

"Run," I growl, and suddenly she's gone, taking the alley and hurrying as fast as she can. I count to ten, and then I'm off. Passersby don't pay too much attention, seeing as it's the middle of the day.

They must assume we're in a friendly race, since she was smiling, but little do they know I'm chasing her to fuck her like a beast.

She keeps looking over her shoulder and sees I'm getting closer, and I almost want to slow down so I can watch her beautiful ass as it bounces. But I want those lips on my cock. When she's within feet of the car, I close in on her, and I push her against the passenger door, my front to her back, caging her in, both of us out of breath.

"I got you, wife."

She groans, and I can't wait to let her suck me off. I open the door, and she and I both remain calm so we don't draw too much attention and so we can reclaim our breaths. When she's in and buckled, I slide in my seat and start the car.

"Suck, baby," I demand, and she eagerly obliges, turning to face me and bending down. My windows are tinted, so no one can see, but I start driving the second her lips touch my cock.

Fuck me, that's good. So fucking good.

"Right there, baby. Oh yeah, such a good girl. Be a good little cum slut and take it all," I praise and degrade her at the same time, and she moans around my cock. I nearly come. Fuck. She is sucking with a vigor that I haven't seen from her before. It made her hot being chased like that, and that was just minimal effort. What would she do if we had more time and privacy to have fun with it?

I keep my eyes on the road and one hand on the wheel, but remembering this car has an option I've never bothered using before, I put it on autopilot, touching the screen for Home. When I get a hold of the back of her head, I push with force, and she gags loudly, my cock hitting the back of her throat, causing a new gush of saliva to coat me.

"That's right. Get it nice and wet, baby. Soak it for me. Suck me like your pussy would."

She tightens her lips and pushes herself past the gagging stage, bobbing her head up and down fast, and that's when I lose it. I let go of the wheel, reach behind me to grab the head rest, and drop my jaw, moaning her name.

"Fuck, Emelia, swallow it all, baby." I empty my cum down her throat, and she chokes over and over but never lets up. So fucking good.

When I have nothing left to give, she drops me from her mouth but doesn't resurface. No, she stays there and licks my entire cock clean, even the few drops that hit my balls.

I twitch, already getting hard again.

"Shit. Emelia, come up, baby. Come here." I want to save my next hard-on for her cunt.

She sits up, takes the tip of her wedding ring finger, and wipes at the corner of her mouth. Somehow, we are now in the parking garage of our building, and I am ready to take her inside. But she does something I don't expect.

"Not yet. I don't want this to go to waste."

Looking at her confused, I suddenly realize what she means when she lifts her hand and shows me the cum that leaked onto it as she jerked and sucked me. Leaning back in her seat, she reaches that hand into her yoga pants and starts to finger herself.

"Holy fuck, Emelia." That is the hottest fucking sight—her taking my cum and pushing into her cunt while she plays with herself.

"Jerk yourself off. Come again. Get off with me. Please," she begs, tear stains now drying on her face as her hand works inside her pants. I grip my cock, and its already hard from the sight of her.

"You like this cock, baby? Like that it gets so fucking hard for you?"

"Mmmhmm," she moans out.

"God, yes."

"My fingers are too small. I need your big cock, *il mio re*."

I sweat when she calls me her king in Italian, I jerk harder without thought. I pick up speed to match her. She is working that pussy so fucking fast that I know she nor I will last. I want to look at her bottom half, but the real pleasure is in her eyes, and I can't stop looking into them.

"*Vieni per me, moglie.*" I don't usually speak Italian to her, but this time when I do, she cries out. Her chest starts to rise and fall in choppy breaths, and then her thighs begin to shake, and before I know it, she's gasping loudly.

"I'm coming. Fuck. Yes!" She fills the car with sensual cries of pleasure, and I come again, my cum pouring out like it didn't just minutes ago.

This fucking minx. She can make me do things I never thought were possible. I clean myself up the best I can, putting myself back in my pants after a few moments, then I lean over and reach my hand into her yoga pants. I go straight for her center and circle her hole, collecting her juice. She watches me intently as I pull my hand out and bring her sweet taste mixed with mine to my lips.

"Mine," I say when I lick her from my finger. I dip my hand back in and repeat the motion, but this time, I don't bring it to my mouth. Instead, I lift it to her lips and smear it all over them.

"Mine," I reiterate, and she responds instantly.

"Yours."

Damn fucking right.

The day doesn't end after that. No, we spend another hour fucking and clawing at one another like depraved animals. The sun hasn't even set yet, but we have calmed down enough to offer each other some reprieve.

We are lying in bed, lazily touching and sharing open-mouthed kisses, when my phone rings. We both groan our protests, but I lean over and see it's my underboss so decide to answer. We could use a minute of separation.

"Giulio."

"Sir, sorry to bother you, but I have something to report."

"All right. Out with it," I snap.

"We got word that not even twenty-four hours after you and Mrs. Valiente left your honeymoon that the boat was hit."

I shoot up in bed. "What?"

"Yes, the boat exploded. They found a bomb in a hidden chamber at the bottom." My heart speeds up to an alarming rate, and I realize that if we hadn't left when we did, Emelia and I could have died.

Emelia.

Emelia could have been dead. Someone knew we were there and wanted to hurt us and didn't care that my wife was on the boat. Men are out for me all the time, at every corner, but my wife? She is sacred. Off limits. She is the part of me that will flip everyone on their heads and ruin their worlds if I find out who would dare do that her. Emelia is not to be harmed. Ever. There is no return if you mess with mine.

"There's more, sir."

"What else?" What could possibly top that? Nothing, but I need him to tell me everything so I can instruct him on what to do next. Emelia sits up, pulling the sheet up to her chest and touching me softly on the shoulder.

"The Notellis. Giuseppe hasn't moved. He isn't sending men out or anything. They are all lying low, so we can't for sure tie them to anything, but I did get word that he has his own shipment coming in."

"Good. I want one of our moles—unmarked, never been sent to a job outside Seattle—on the ground. He can keep a safe distance, but I want him to take pictures of all the men who are there getting the shipments. We will investigate all of them and see if there's anyone new that could be doing the dirty work."

"Yes, sir." He pauses. "Are you going to tell Emelia?" he asks, and I peer at her over my shoulder and see her face is twisted with worry.

"No. Keep me informed as that progresses." Before he can get a word out, I end the call.

"What's going on, Nico?" She sounds terrified, and that is exactly why I have to lie to her.

"Giulio's just keeping me up to date on things." There is a way she looks at me that I can tell she knows something is off, but she doesn't push. I told her already that I will not talk about business with her.

In the meantime, I have to put my game face on, wait for a new report from my men, and try to focus on Emelia. The waters are so fucking dirty in my outfit right now, and we're under attack. All since Emelia came. There is no way that is a coincidence.

How could her family want her dead? If they wanted to come after me, they could have. But to sacrifice their daughter at that cost, without her knowing? How fucked up. My poor wife was placed in my life as a casualty, and she didn't even know it.

Emelia breaks our silence and stands. "I'm going to take a bath, if that's all right."

I nod and let her leave. I will join her in a minute, but I need a fucking moment alone. I listen to the water run, and I go into a deep trance as I think about my next move.

Today was going too fucking well. I wanted to spend it with Emelia and not worry about this shit, but like always, business will always be my first fucking wife.

Finally, I get up and make my way to the bathroom. Emelia is sitting in the tub and looking out at the Seattle skyline as the sun falls behind the buildings in golden hues.

"Nico, what's going on?" She doesn't even look at me when she asks this. She keeps her head on her folded arms on the lip of the bathtub.

"Nothing. Let's not focus on business or anything but us right now."

This has her shifting in the tub, and I can tell she's annoyed. "Fine. I can do that, on one condition."

"What's that, principessa?" I ask, stepping in and sitting down opposite her.

"I want to know about your parents. About what happened." She softens her voice, but my back stiffens. I don't talk to anyone about my parents. That is a hard fucking limit for me.

But if I don't give her something, she's going to withhold all of herself from me again. And today was enough to make me realize I can't do that anymore. I can't push her out; my body and soul won't fucking let me.

"What do you want to know?" I ask, my eyes now wandering to the same skyline she was admiring.

"What were they like?"

That's an easy question. I can do that.

"My mother was kind. Patient. Doting. Everything you imagine a picture-perfect mother and woman to be. It was like she was out of a story book, to be honest." Glimpses of her smile, the same one I have, flood my memories.

"Really. So you two got along?"

"She was my best friend. Both my parents were, but my mother had more time to spend with me."

Emelia hums a sound of interest.

"What?"

"Nothing. It's just you are so hardheaded and cold, but you say your best friend was this loving and soft mother."

I nod. "True, but I said both parents were my best friends. My mother, Lealena, was able to teach me patience and how to keep my cool when things got a little... messy. That's why I'm so good at negotiating and keeping calm. That's why I am the devil to most."

"I wouldn't know about business dealings, but I will take your word for it," she adds. "Also, your mother's name is beautiful."

"Thank you. She was born in Sicily and moved here with her family when she was six." I take this chance to ease my twitching palms and reach my now soapy arm out to her to pull her in. She doesn't reject it. This tub could fit four people, and that makes it easy for her to lie flat against me.

She places her head on my chest and continues."And your dad?"

"He is where I get my—" I tilt my head back and forth and think of how I should phrase this. "—business side from."

"Nice. Phrased that beautifully. Was he as feared as you?" she questions.

"No. He was feared, but the game has only become more ruthless, with higher stakes, and more evil since he died. I had to adapt to that. He just gave me the tools."

"Did he ever, you know, hit you?"

"No. My father never hit me. He had me fight men double my size and train with them, but never did my father hit me." I look down and see her eyes drop. Seeing her feel the pain of her own parents treating her so poorly only makes my quest to end them that much stronger.

"Emelia, my parents were rare in this world. When my father died, it was because of me and...." I trail off, and this has her eyes back on me.

She moves and straddles me quickly before wrapping her hands around the back of my neck. She begins to softly rub the hair at my nape, as if she knows her touch can fucking center me, which it does.

"Nico, you don't have to tell me if you aren't ready."

"No. It's important you know." If she is going to see me take down her father and his empire, I need her to know that not only did he hurt her and destroy her life, but he also took my parents from me. This is the first time I have told anyone. Not even Giulio knows the full story of why I hate the Notellis so badly and why I was persistent in refusing to make them an alliance for so long.

"I was supposed to be at the warehouse to train that day, but I decided going out and drinking with my friends would be more fun. But I didn't realize that one of those friends happened to be an enemy. He was a mole. The youngest one the Notellis ever had."

She pauses her caresses on my neck, and I can almost feel her hand go cold. "What?"

"Your brother, Sal, and I were friends. He was sent to the private school I attended here in Seattle. Simply told me his shitty parents back home sent him here to teach him how to be independent and be a man."

She's looking up at me as I adjust us a bit and try to find my next words.

"That day, I got so drunk nothing really made sense. I wasn't as on guard as I usually am. But I was still aware enough. Sal thought differently. He thought I was so far gone that I wouldn't remember." I take a deep breath, roll my shoulders, and wipe at my lips for a minute, looking out my bathroom window again.

"Sal asked me where my father was, and I told him he was waiting at the warehouse for my training. Most of it is vague, but I remember enough. He laughed, and I joined him, saying my father would just train me harder when I'm hungover as a punishment. Sal disappeared a few minutes later. Something about going to the car to grab more drinks."

This time, I slowly turn my head and prepare to tell her what I never fucking thought I would.

"Then, two hours later, my distraught mother told me the warehouse had been raided. My father was left for dead."

Emelia's eyes are wide and filled with tears. They overflow after another moment and cascade down her cheeks.

"I got there in time... to be there when he took his last breath," I say, getting choked up at the memory of his last words of wisdom to me.

"Take care of your mother for me, son, and remember when you marry to protect your bride with honor."

"At first, we thought it was our closest enemies, Los Angeles, so my father's men were on them. But then I learned the truth months later." This part makes my chest burn, because this was the one and only time I felt heartbreak and weakness. I hold back as best as I can before I tell her.

"Then my mother died. Losing my father was her death sentence. She couldn't live without him. She breathed for him, Emelia, existed for him. Every ounce of her belonged to my father's soul. They loved each other so deeply that they tethered together in death. Where he went, she would follow."

Holding her stomach like she may be sick, she looks around the bathroom and shakes her head. "Nico, how do you know it was my family?"

"Well, just like your father, Sal was messy and didn't cover his tracks well. One night, we were celebrating graduation. I mean, *they* were. I was mourning the loss of the only family I had left. But in a drunken stupor, Sal confessed to someone what happened. He didn't know I could hear him. I was just on the other side of the door."

I remember hearing those words leave his mouth.

"I got him drunk, found out where his poor little daddy was, and told my father. I killed my father's enemy and a mafia boss."

He was gloating to some girl, but little did he know he was signing a death warrant.

"Nico, I think I'm going to be sick." She climbs out of the tub quickly and runs to the toilet. I am out just after her and hold her hair back as she loses what little contents she has left in her stomach.

"Emelia, breathe," I tell her, and she wipes at her mouth, trying not to puke again. I take this opportunity to grab her robe and my towel. I help her into it, and I wrap the towel around my waist as I get her to the bedroom. Her entire body is shaking.

"My family killed yours. And then you agreed to marry me? For what? Were you going to kill me?" She backs up slowly, losing her balance a bit. I reach out to catch her, but she holds her hands up and signals me to stop.

"No, I wasn't. I was building an alliance with *you*. Not your family."

"What does that mean?"

"It means what it meant the day we said I do," I tell her, but this time I'm harsher than I mean to be.

"We married so we would ensure that war was over between our families."

I shake my head. "I never once agreed to anything but an alliance. *With you*."

She watches me closely as it all starts falling into place for her. "You wanted to turn me against him as revenge?"

I nod. "I told you that the night your family came here," I remind her. We are too far into this to hide anything anymore.

"Right, but then what?" She slowly backs up to the bed and takes a seat on the edge.

"Then when the time was right, I would take down your family, and they would see you standing beside me as they burned."

"So, I was the revenge for my father killing yours," she reiterates to herself. "I thought, when all that came out when they were here, that I was revenge for their mafia feud. I thought I was just your way to finish your father's life goal of taking over New York, if that was the case. I had no idea it was your plan to kill—"

"At first, yes, you were only a pawn, no matter the catalyst for my plan. Now, you are revenge *and* my redemption," I answer what she asked me just hours ago. Charity work isn't my redemption. Emelia is.

"What?" She shakes her head, and I drop to my knees in front of her and take her shaky hands in mine.

"I wanted your father to see you fall in love with me. I wanted him to see you would take my side and that you were mine. You belonged to me and had no choice but to turn on your own. Then..."

"Then what, Nico!" she screams, tears streaming, and I want so badly to lick up her tears and make love to her. Tend to her wounds and heal her. But I have to make her understand.

"Then we would take them down together, and when I met you and knew just how fucking badly your family treated you, I knew you would want that too."

"You don't know me! You don't know that! It is my *family*, Nico!" she yells, placing her hands on her forehead and closing her eyes as the tears pour.

"Emelia, listen to me." My voice turns stern. She has to listen.

"Your family treated you like garbage. They took your value and crumbled it. They hurt you. Do you honestly think they love you?" This hurts her. I can tell, because she weeps.

"Nico—"

"Tell me, baby, do you love them? Do you think they love you? What about that three-week hospital stay when your father threw you down a flight of stairs?"

Her head shoots up. "How do you know about that?"

"Emelia, I know everything. I'm part of the largest fucking criminal ring in the world. I did my research. You were treated poorly, and now that I love you, I will seek revenge and make sure they bleed harder than they ever made you. Do you understand?" She's stone-cold then, but I am running hot. My breathing is heavy.

"You love me?" she prompts, and it's then I realize what I fucking did.

Shit. It came out. I didn't plan it or mean to; it just came out. Naturally.

Fuck. I was right. She made her fucking way in. Damn it! I curse myself.

"Nico?" I look at her, and she wipes at errant tears. "You love me? Or are you just trying to get me to forgive this?"

I wait a long moment, trying one last time to push back everything I feel, but I fail miserably. I am like my mother more than I thought. Where Emelia goes, I will. Fucking. Follow.

"Yes, I fucking love you, Emelia," I snap out, more at myself, not her. "I fell so fucking fast for you. I need you every second. I avoided you, because even when we were in our rage, I fell for you. Your hate made me love you. The way you would touch me and then push me away, it drew me in."

"Then why didn't you come home and be with me? Talk to me? Tell me?" She cries still.

"Because I needed to distance myself. I don't want to fucking need you. I don't want to love you, but I can't stop myself. If you aren't breathing, neither am I. And I feel like a madman, because you have only tested me up until last night. You made me angry every day, but I saw through you, and I spotted something I knew I had to have forever these past couple of days."

"What? What did you see?" she yells hysterically.

"I saw my parents. I saw that love could exist and I could fall for someone, and if I ever fucking lost you like my mother lost my father, I wouldn't recover. You scared me!"

With that, she is on me. Grabbing my face, she kisses me with all she has, the water droplets from her hair mixing with the salt of her tears. It all fills my taste buds, and I can't get her close enough.

I grab her thigh and nudge her, so she will let me in closer. "I love you, Nico. I do. I fell for you the second I knew I hated you." That would make no sense to anyone else, but to us, it does. Everything about us makes sense to us. Nothing in the world could understand the force that is us.

"You drive me fucking crazy. You know that?" I grip her neck and push her top half back enough so I can look at her. See her. Feel her.

"So do you. Nico, take me. I need you."

I lay her back on the bed and open her robe, then drop my towel.

"I'm sorry my father killed yours. I'm sorry you lost your mother because of him." She apologizes for something she owes no penance for.

"Emelia, don't apologize for other people's mistakes. But I need you to understand something. Your father is a very dangerous man. He himself may not be able to do much, but he will have others do things for him, and you are at risk."

"I understand. What are you planning to do?" she asks with a shaky voice.

"I will take care of him. For good."

"You're going to kill my father?"

I shake my head. "No, Emelia, I'm going to end the bloodline. Only you will be the last remaining heir."

She gulps. There is no other way. I thought I would have a couple more years, but with each passing day as Emelia's husband and seeing the way my business has been messed with, I have to do it sooner rather than later. I have my father's legacy to carry and my wife's protection to keep.

"Emelia." I gain her attention. I can't believe I am going to fucking do this. "Is this going to push you away?"

She looks at me, her brows furrowed with confusion. "What?"

"If I get revenge on your family, is it going to fucking hurt you, my love."

Her eyes flutter rapidly, and the tears start to come back again. I come to tower over her, using one hand to cradle her face.

"I don't know. I don't have a choice. You are the ruler of this marriage, and my life is now yours to decide what to do with. What will my opinion matter?"

Fuck.

"Emelia, you have a voice in this marriage. I know we were at each other's throat at the beginning, but I have told you time and again that you have a voice and a stand in this marriage."

She shakes her head. "No, I don't. Because if I ask you to spare my family's life, then what am I asking you to do to *your* family? Your parents are dead because of my father. So, I'd be asking you to sacrifice the retribution you deserve, that your parents do."

She has a point, but at the end of the day, things have changed. Our marriage is evolving, and we are not the Emelia and Nico from the day we got married. We are the Valientes, and we are partners. I will honor Emelia in the way my father told me I should honor my wife.

I just never knew how and never thought I would have to. But now... now, I do, and now, I want to.

"You asked me about my parents...," I trail off, rerouting my question.

"Yes."

"My parents taught me one thing I never used. Until now. They taught me that when I found a wife, I was to treat her as an equal and give her a place next to me. I am giving you a fucking place, Emelia. I am giving you the choice." That's the number one way I can honor my parents. More than vengeance. I can be a husband they would be proud of.

Emelia says nothing, and that leaves me just as silent.

What now?

CHAPTER EIGHTEEN
Emelia

WHAT NOW?

My father killed my husband's father. And now he's lying above me, with the words "I love you" still fresh from his tongue and the knowledge of how twisted our ties are. Nico's family and my family were meant to merge, but not for alliance, for war. And I am in the center of it all.

Knowing what I do now, I feel more guilt than ever by not telling him about my involvement. I can't be mad at him, because my father planted me here to do the same thing he is asking of me. But the difference is, he is giving me a choice. He isn't forcing me to do anything or to let him do this. I have a choice, and this eats at me all while making me feel more conflicted yet appreciated and respected at the same time.

I'm so fucking confused. I'm scared. I'm worried. I'm... in love.

Nico stills hovers over me, and I don't know what to do. So I just slightly push on him and sit up. He doesn't fight it. Standing, he grabs his towel and moves to the closet. He emerges dressed a few moments later, and I think my silence has upset him.

"Please don't leave. I just don't know what to say or do, Nico.

Please."

He hurries over to me and takes my hand. Pulling me up from the bed, he brings me in close and holds my face. "I'm not leaving you. I'm taking you somewhere special so we can work this out. I need you to get dressed. Okay?"

My heart settles a bit—not a lot but just enough that my hands stop shaking.

"Um, yeah, okay. Give me a minute." I hurry and dress in jeans, a sweater, and put on some sandals. I put my hair in a wet twist and hold it together with a claw clip. He takes my hand, and we silently make our way back out again, the sun just now fully set.

The drive feels long, and we don't speak the entire time. It felt like another hour, but it was no more than twenty minutes. We pull up to this beautiful Victorian style home, with ivy growing along the side of the house and some of the front-facing windows that overlook a lake.

"What is this?"

"This is my summer home. I never use it, but it's where we'll be staying for a while." Nico doesn't let me ask anything more, because he is out of the car and rounding to my side. He takes my hand and helps me out. The second my feet hit the gravel, I look around at the white house with black-framed windows and Victorian posts leading up to the front door, these painted black as well. I've never seen something like this before. It's like a modern twist on an older home. I expect that the inside is filled with luxury, but there's also deep history with this place.

I follow him, his hand in mine, guiding us to the door. He opens it, and immediately we are greeted with a double staircase and a grand foyer. The floors marble, and everything is in shades of black, white, and sage. It's stunning. Truly stunning. I wouldn't peg this for Nico's style at all. It looks like it was recently redone with a woman in mind.

"Nico, this is beautiful. It looks untouched." I admire the

abstract paintings lining the walls going up the stairs. I see a room to the left and another to the right. One looks to be a formal living room, while the other looks to be more of a casual sitting area. I can see a glimpse of the kitchen directly under the staircase. The arch of the steps frame the entry to the kitchen, and we walk toward it. When we enter, the entire room is white, from the marble counters to the cabinets. The only color in there is the silver appliances. But the real view is the floor-to-ceiling windows that look out into the forest, tree-lined with moss and deep shades of cedar wood from the constant rain and humidity.

"I had it redone last year and haven't been back to see it since. I have a cleaning staff that comes in and keeps it dusted. Speaking of staff, our teams will be here soon. Giulio included."

I am overwhelmed. Truly, I am spiraling in not only my own turmoil but the heaviness of the pain my husband carries and the power I wield over what he will do with that power, or not do.

Suddenly, I feel faint.

"Nico, I feel sick. I need to rest."

He nods. I wanted him to bring me somewhere to make love, but I just can't think straight right now. I need to clear my head and think about what choices I should make, and worse, I have to find a way to tell Nico about my involvement in all this.

"I agree. You can rest upstairs. I know it'll be late, but dinner will be ready when you wake up. So just a nap for now, wife."

I shake my head. "I'm not very hungry."

I can tell he wants to dispute that and tell me I need to eat, but after a moment, he nods.

"Anything, principessa. Let me show you to our room."

I am overstimulated, exhausted, and beyond overwhelmed with the amount of information I've consumed today.

Consumed? More like been fed with a spoon covered in poison. Except for when Nico said "I love you." In the same timeframe, I learned Nico loves me and my father is the reason for the death of his parents. Originally, all along while my family was plotting to use me as his demise, Nico was plotting to have me aid him in his mission to kill my entire family.

So I never really had a safe place to land. If I was brought into this marriage in all the ways deemed wrong, then what do I really have?

Nico's love.

I have his love. A man who was incapable of love handed it over to me without batting a lash. Then he told me that I can basically tell him to leave my family alone, and he will. So I wield power yet feel powerless. My fuck. My head begins to pound, and the air is thick. It's starting to suffocate me. I need to take a pharmacy-worth of drugs to knock myself out for a week.

"You all right in there, Emelia?" Nico's voice breaks through my fog.

"Yes. Is there a chance you have some headache medication here? My head is pounding," I ask. And why are we here? This place is stunning, but I have a hard time believing he brought me here for a "second honeymoon."

"Yes, the staff has arrived. I have your suitcase here, and I will get you some water and some medicine." His feet don't retreat, and I assume he wants me to say something, but I'm all tapped out. Is he wanting something more from me? Me to tell him it's all okay? It's not.

I wanted to be made love to after his love bomb, but the option he laid at my feet may have been the least effective and counterproductive thing he could have given me. I don't want to be near him. I need space. I need a moment to process and to breathe through this. To find out where to go from here.

Finally, his steps leave, and it feels... freeing. I love Nico. At least I think I do. Goddammit. Was it all just passion? Lust? And all the pent-up joy from this truly amazing day that took over? Maybe we both just believe it from experiencing all that.

I don't fucking know. I almost scream this into the room, but I refrain.

"Here's the medicine and water, and I have some pajamas I will get for you," Nico says as he returns, and I don't say anything.

"Emelia?" I still don't answer, and tears start falling down my cheeks. He takes the hint and softly states, "I do love you. Come find me when you're ready." His leaves, and I feel a deep ache in my chest as my tears fall rapidly, then soft sobs leave my chest.

How did I end up here? I should have ran. Ran for the hills the second I had the chance. All those years growing up... I should have found a way out.

I get up and step into the bathroom. I undress and get into the pajamas he pulled from the suitcase he must have had the staff pack. I stand in front of the mirror and look at my face, not recognizing the woman looking back at me. She's lost. Confused. Alone. This is like an episode of some sort of special on how a woman went mad.

I take my clip out, shake my hair loose, then reposition it higher on my head and place it in a messy bun. My face is still makeup free, but there is no mistaking the darkening of the skin surrounding my eyes. I just need rest. I will wake up, and this will all just be a dream. Right?

Stepping back into the bedroom, I expect him to have abandoned his words and come back. But the room is empty, so much so that it cannot only be seen but felt. There is a desolate feeling to the room, and it loses all coziness. The pajamas he gave me consisted of his shirt and my panties. A long-sleeved comfy shirt I lift to my nose and take a long sniff of. It smells like him, and I can't keep the tears from falling again.

I didn't want to feel him. I didn't want to feel anyone or anything when I came in here. I wanted to sleep and forget what would be waiting outside these four walls when I awoke. But now I yearn for him, long for Nico's touch and his shelter. But if I call him in here now, it will just add to the confusion, and that's not what I need.

I can't take it anymore. There isn't enough of me at the moment to give any part of me to anyone. Including myself. I resist the urge to go in search of him or call out his name. I even remove his shirt and stay in just my panties. His shirt will be just as real as his arms around me in my sleep if I keep it on. I need a clean break from him.

Stepping to the side of the bed that contains my pills and water, I take them and down the entire glass. The moment my head hits that silk-covered pillow, I am taken by much-needed slumber. No dreams come, and no clarity seeps in. Just sleep.

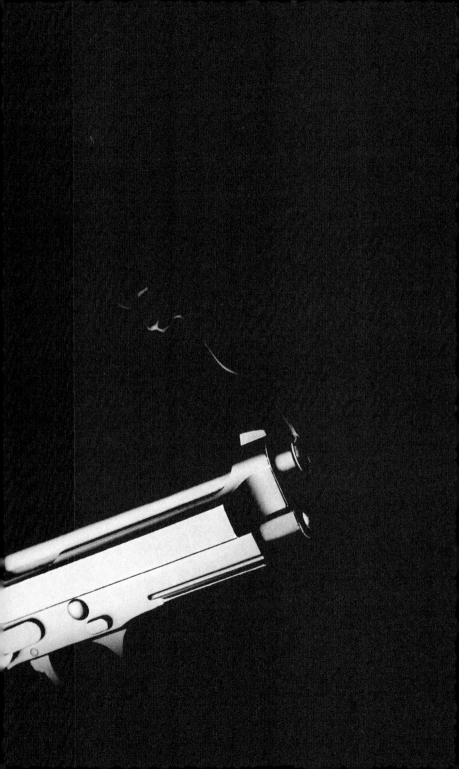

CHAPTER NINETEEN

Nico

SITTING IN MY OFFICE, I stare out the window and look at the rain that begins to hit the glass. I hear the staff preparing dinner just down the hall, but Emelia is the only thing I can think about. The way I blurted out I love her without even thinking still has me more lost than anything. I can't believe I'm even capable of feeling it, let alone saying it.

It takes all of me to not go to her and wake her up with soft touches and eager lovemaking. I need her like I need to breathe right now. Luckily, Giulio knocks on my office door and distracts me.

"Come in."

He steps in and shuts the door behind him. "Sir. We have men in the air and set to land in New York in a few hours. I also looked into the yacht explosion. Luckily at the time, all staff and the captain had been off-site. No one was hurt. But the damage is significant and will have a high price tag to replace it."

Giving him an incredulous look, he nods, understanding what I'm giving him that look for.

"Will do."

Money isn't a fucking problem in our world, and my yacht isn't something I care enough about to spend a high price fixing. I'll just get a new one. My only concern is finding out the information I need so I can build my case for Emelia.

"It was her family?" I prompt with conviction.

Giulio waits a moment. "The bomb was one that most of the outfits carry, sir. It wasn't a generic one. In fact..." He pauses, and I bark at him.

"Get it out, Giulio. Enough pussy-footing around."

"It was traced back to ours. It was one of the unaccounted weapons we lost in the stolen shipment."

Standing, I slam my hand down on the desk. "Fuckers!" I turn and face the windows, placing my hands on my hips and letting out a string of curses. "It was her fucking family, Giulio. I know it. This man wanted my father dead, and now he wants me dead so he can reign."

"So we take them out. We have enough to do it, sir."

"We are missing one thing," I murmur, staring intently out the window.

"What?" Giulio sounds dumfounded.

"My wife's approval," I grumble.

"Excuse me?"

I turn to face him. "You heard me. I need Emelia's approval to go forward with this."

You'd think I just told him the most insane story he has ever heard. I don't blame him. When did having anyone's approval be a requirement in any of my choices?

"Sir, what does it matter? This marriage was all a part of using her as a last-minute 'fuck you' to her father. Given the recent change in events, I would say you got that. You have her wrapped around your finger like some brain-dead idiot."

Without fucking hesitation, I pull out my gun and stride up to him. Grabbing him by the collar of his dress shirt, I pull him within inches of my face and put the gun harshly against the underside of his chin.

"Don't you ever fucking disrespect my wife, Giulio. I don't care about our fucking history or your loyalty to me. I will empty a fucking clip into your thick skull. Do you understand me!" I yell, spit flying from my mouth.

"Yes, sir. I'm sorry. I didn't know things had progressed on your end," he admits.

I push the gun harder."I don't care if I hate every breath she takes. You don't talk about her in that way. Ever."

This time, he remains silent. Smart fucking man. I release him with force, and he slightly stumbles back.

"Get the fuck out of my office until you have news to report about the Notellis's delivery tonight."

Without a word, Giulio departs.

Fuck me! I slam my fist into a wall and watch it go straight fucking through.

I know a snake when I see one and I can smell a skunk from miles away. I know her father has everything to do with this. And now I have to wait for Emelia to either agree to my choice or betray my father's legacy.

What would my dad have done if my mom's family were the enemy?

Tonight, I will send my men into the den, and if they find anything that belongs to me, then this will be the end. I will tell Emelia that not only did her father kill mine, but he had plans to kill her and me both without a look fucking back.

"I have no choice, my principessa," I say into the empty office.

Hours pass, and Emelia still hasn't woken up. I spent most the night on the phone, answering emails and text messages, trying to get some work in without ruining any time I will have alone with Emelia. I found myself thinking back to the way I blurted out I love her without any warning or hesitation.

I know many things about Emelia already. Know when she's angry. Know when she's vulnerable. And now I have seen and known her when she has felt free. On the ice, I learned so much about her. She was in her element, lost to the forces outside that rink that were built to destroy us.

She forgot about the pain her parents caused. The abuse she took her whole life. I think she even forgot about me and everything we have. It was like there was her, the music, the ice, and nothing else. I've made a living out of learning people and what they're thinking without ever having to hear them say a word. Emelia spoke loudest when she said nothing at all. She wears every emotion she has on her face so clearly, and that heart bleeds openly on her sleeve, even if she pretends it doesn't.

She reminds me of my mother. Emelia would sacrifice all she has for those she loves... but I don't think she has ever truly loved or been loved. Yet, I see she would still give up everything for those she cares for.

Hell, I saw the turmoil when I gave her the option to keep her family alive. Something I would never do, but with her, I did. For nearly my entire life, I lied to myself. Convincing myself I didn't fucking want love, when all along, I knew deep inside I didn't want love if it couldn't touch the type my parents had. And more than that, I felt admitting that even to myself made me less of a man and too emotional. Too sensitive. Something I never want to be.

But if I ever had a chance to tell my mother that, hell, my father, they would laugh in my face and tell me to man up.

"Love is the only thing that can save your soul. It's the only thing that can bring you peace and solace, my sweet boy." I hear my mother's voice so clearly it almost... hurts.

My father told me the only softness inside him was my mother.

"I will only ever lay down the façade and armor for that creature. That divine angel, son. She is the heaven on earth and redemption I will have to cling to when death takes me and drags me to the underworld."

I never believed redemption would come for me, but it did, with hair in golden hues, curves crafted by the gods, and a heart meant for every good thing in this world. Nothing to do with me. Yet she's here, and she is mine.

It's been hours, and I have honored the space she practically screamed at me for with silence and tears. I need her. Have to touch her skin and center myself. I need her to need me. I need her to crave me and let me in.

Leaving my office, I head up the stairs and down the hall to the master bedroom. When I open the door, I see her lying on the bed, the sheet covering just up to her hip while her bare skin is out on display for my hungry eyes. My shirt still sits at the end of the bed, and I wonder if she didn't see it.

Climbing onto the bed, I lie behind her and start to kiss her shoulders, her bare back, the softness of her skin above her ribs. I knead the thickest part of her hip with my large, calloused hand. The imagery of Hades touching his Persephone comes to my mind, the dark soul seeking the light from her heavens.

"Wake up for me, my love. Let me feel you," I whisper against her softness.

"Nico?" She sounds pained, and when I peer up, she's looking at me with a weakness in her eyes, a hurt so deep that I caused and only can cure.

"Emelia," I groan out her name is desperation. In that moment, I know we are in love, but I also know it's not only the kind my parents had, but it's something much darker. We are going to become one. If I could sell my soul to the devil to be intertwined with her, I would. The battles, crimes, and more that I would commit to keep her safe and to keep her mine—I wouldn't hesitate to do it.

"Nico," she whimpers again, turning on her back, and I grab her breasts and squeeze them, then rub them softly. Grazing her puckered nipples, I feel my cock grow so damn hard I can't help but grind against the bed. I need a release. I need to feel something, the restriction unbelievably painful.

"I'm not going to resist you anymore. I gave you space, and now I need you to invade mine." I beg her to let me taste her, fuck her, love her—anything. I just need her.

I reach under the blanket and touch between her legs. She is soaking through her panties, and I growl. I'm so damn hungry for her. Ripping the panties as if they're merely paper, I breathe with relief as she automatically lets her legs fall open for me.

"Good girl," I praise, kissing the roundness of her stomach, her thighs, and then my lips land on her clit. Fuck me, she tastes like mine. It's like she has grown so accustomed to me that she tastes like her with a dash of me. Maneuvering between her legs, I settle myself there, and she leaks for me. Licking from her hole to her clit, I kiss her there, and she cries out my name.

Peering up but leaning my head down, I grin at her like the devil himself. "You taste so good, baby."

She starts to rub her breasts, and I envy those hands, so I reach up and grip her breast, pinch the nipple, and dive between her legs again. I nip each of her pussy lips, then lick circles around her entrance, before I start to fuck her with my tongue. Taking my hand from her breast, I wrap it around her thigh and use it as leverage, so I can gain friction on my cock and still fuck her pussy with my pointed tongue.

"It's not enough, Nico. This isn't enough!" she cries out, and I stop... reluctantly. I sit up and remove my shirt, and she admires my body, taking in all the ridges.

"This is more than enough. In fact, it's too much, Emelia. The way I need you."

She starts to cry, and I hate the sight of her losing her fucking mind. She doesn't understand love, not that I do either, but I have seen love enough to recognize it between us. Emelia has never had it, and that makes this so fucking hard on her.

"You are too much for me."

"No, Emelia. We are just right. You're scared of this, because you don't understand it. Let me fucking show you. Let me spoil you with *me*. With fucking love."

For a minute, she keeps her eyes on mine without a word, and I wait on the edge of my seat the entire time.

"Please," she gives in, a longing so deep in her soul that she needs to feel it. I stand and move to the side of the bed to finish undressing. We watch one another, and I see the tears falling from the corners of her eyes. There is so much I want to do to take the stress away from her, but I only know this way. The words don't come naturally to me. The emotions, they are limited, but the physical touch, that is endless. I can give her all of me in our sacred fucking. Finally naked, I climb back between her legs, and I align myself with her entrance.

"You ready, pretty baby?"

"Yes. Please," she begs. As I enter her slowly, her head slides back against the pillow, and we both let out sounds of pure relief. We aren't fucking; we're connecting. Solidifying our destiny. I kiss her chin and neck while they're exposed to me. I hit so deep in her that I know she can't take any more.

"Tell me this." I move in and out slowly, the sound of our joint arousal mixing in the air. That erotic sound will never be one I tire of.

"Yes. Anything."

"Why aren't you wearing my shirt, Emelia?" I wasn't going to let that slide.

"Because..." Her head snaps back up, and she bites her lip as she reaches down to my lower back.

"Because why?" I start to pick up the pace.

"I needed space. If I put that on, I would've felt you drowning me," she admits through a moan. This makes me hurt and angers me all at once.

"What a way to go. If you're going to die, I would like it to be from you drowning in me." And then I warn her, "Don't you ever try to put space between us again. Understood?"

"Nico, please." I know what she's begging for, but I need to hear her confession.

"You have to say it, baby," I tell her.

"I don't know how to move forward. I don't know what we will do from here."

I start to exaggerate my thrusts, making sure she feels it all. "You let me have control. You give up the fight. You have fought this since day one. We both have. Just give me the control to show you what life is going to be for you."

She finally nods, and I cup her cheek as she does. Her eyes search mine, and she sobs, not stopping her nodding.

"Shh, principessa. You're mine now. You can surrender to us."

She closes her eyes, giving in to the pleasure. I push up on one arm, so I can look at her body and watch her enjoy the gratification. My other hand firmly grabs the headboard, and I give her slow but very pronounced thrusts.

"Promise me something, Emelia." I break through the heavy breathing and moans.

"Yes. God."

I hit her just right, that tender flesh inside her that will have her coming so fast if I hit it too many times.

"That you'll never leave me. You'll love me with enough passion that it fucking suffocates me."

"Choke me," she demands, and I slow my pace.

"What, baby?"

She nods. Is she really asking me that?

"Choke me. Show me how bad you want me to take your breath from you."

I wait a minute, but then something comes over me. "Straddle me, Emelia."

"But—"

I cut her off. "Trust me."

"Okay."

Moving to the edge of the bed, I sit up and take her hand, helping her down to stand in front of me.

"Easy, baby." I grab the back of her thigh to make her straddle and take me in.

"Your body is beautiful, Nico," she says as she sinks.

"As is yours, my goddess."

She smiles and slides up my length. "What do I do now, *il mio re*?"

Once she is fully seated on me again, I take her hands and bring them to my neck. "Take the air from me."

"Nico, no." She stops, growing uneasy.

"Emelia, I asked you to do something. You do as I say, remember?"

She shakes her head rapidly. "No, I don't want to hurt you." She starts to grow emotional again, so I cup her face.

"My principessa, you won't hurt me. You trust me?"

"Of course. I trust you with all of me. But I don't want this to hurt you."

"It won't. I promise," I assure her. I have never been into breath play, but I want to try it with her.

"Okay." She holds her hands up for me to take the lead and place them where I want them.

"Good girl." I put them around the column of my throat. It's so thick she can't wrap her small hands completely around my neck. "Now squeeze, gently at first. I will tell you when to tighten it, okay? When I'm ready for you to let go, I will spank your ass, okay?"

Hesitant still, she takes a deep breath. "Okay." She starts to add pressure. And I begin to lift her up and down on my cock by her hips. Her hands are tight, but she's holding back.

"More pressure, baby. It's okay. I will tell you when it's enough."

She swallows thickly, moaning as I purposefully bring her down at an angle that will hit that spot inside her. "Fuck, Nico." She adjusts and wiggles, fighting hard not to orgasm.

"Tighter."

Emelia adds more pressure, and I start to feel a difference, my breathing a tad restricted. She starts to fuck me now, wanting her pleasure while giving me mine, and my neck becomes her holding place.

"Good girl. Fuck, baby, keep fucking me like that." She squeezes my neck harder, and it's like her cunt. Tight and greedy.

"Yes! Nico."

"Say it," I breathe out, my words restricted.

"Say—shit, right there. Oh God, right there." She keeps fucking me, and when she nearly cuts off my air, I bite out.

"Say you love me."

"I love you, Nico. I love you!" She orgasms hard then, and I smack her ass, my vision getting foggy, and when she releases in the middle of her orgasm, she screams, and I gasp for air and in pleasure as I empty inside her.

"Take all of me, every drop, pretty baby." I fuck up into her with choppy movements, and her thighs shake and quiver as her back bows, and she drops her head to me, jolting as the aftershocks of her orgasm hit.

We settle, and I cradle her face as she starts to cry.

"I love you too, Emelia. Whatever that means to us, or however it works, I know I have it with you."

She nods, and I carry her to the bathroom. I want to take a hot bath with her stuck to my skin like glue.

We have a battle ahead, and I don't know what will come out of it. All I know is I want her to be waiting for me on the other side.

CHAPTER TWENTY

Emelia

M Y HEAD LAYS ON HIS CHEST, AND WHEN I LISTEN CLOSE enough, I'm able to hear his heartbeat. The warm water of our second bath tonight aids our sore muscles and tired bodies. Waking up to him after falling asleep without him held a different meaning this time. I was used to that—going to bed without him and being woken to make love before falling back into slumber. But this time, it was a call for each other. A desperate need to solidify our relationship. There was an emptiness that we both felt and so badly needed filled by one another.

"I feel different," I say finally.

"So do I."

"What do you need from me?" I ask, sitting up.

"Everything."

"That's not telling me, Nico. I need to know what this means for us."

He smiles, scooping water from the bath and pouring it on my shoulders. "What do you need to know?"

"I don't know. That's why I am so scared and confused and feel different."

"Good or bad different?"

"Both."

We stay silent for a moment.

"Seeing you in the rink today... that is what I have with you."

"What?" I question. A talent? I'm perplexed.

"The way you feel free on that ice is how you make me feel. I feel free when I'm with you. Even when you're pissing me off. I've never felt more like myself than I do now, and my world is flipped upside-down as we speak."

That may have been the kindest, most romantic thing I have ever heard. "Did I flip your world?"

"Yes, but in a good way. But my business is being fucked with. I am spiraling out of control, because I am distracted by you. You are the only thing that has ever consumed me so fucking much that I'm literally putting my entire outfit in danger. Don't you see the power you wield?"

I don't know how to take that.

"My parents told me to find love one day, and I laughed in their faces. Now, I'm in love, and I'm eating my own fucking words, Emelia."

I turn and place my back on his chest. Every time he speaks, I lose my words. It's as if there's nothing I can say that makes sense.

"My parents never loved each other. I know they didn't love me, so I never knew what love looked like." My hands graze over the top of the lavender suds. He hums a light response, and I continue. "He cheated. He hit her. He hit us kids. Then he taught my brothers how to be the same way. I don't think I even heard the words 'I love you' growing up."

He kisses the top of my head.

"I thought what I had with Damian—"

He cuts me off then. "Do not bring him up, Emelia. I already gave him enough passes. If you dare tell me you loved him like you do—"

"I don't love him, and now that I feel what I feel for you, I know nothing ever came close, and that scares me." I don't chance a glance over my shoulder. Instead, I keep my eyes ahead and stare at the tiled wall.

"Did your brothers hit you?" he asks, and I choke back a sob. I don't want to cry anymore, and I especially don't want to give those tears to my family.

"Yes. They started hitting me after my father began hitting them."

Nico grips my shoulders and growls, "Tell me one reason worth keeping those sick fucks alive, Emelia, because my will to let you choose is hanging by a thread."

I bring my knees up as I sit up and wrap my arms around my thighs.

"Because I want to believe there is love there. I want to believe my family can love me." I do sob then, so hard. Wasted tears or not, my pain is real, and it eats at me, carving away pieces of my heart every single day.

"Emelia." He leans forward and kisses the top of my spine. "They don't deserve you. And you deserve real love. You deserve to be treated like a human and not a caged animal."

"But I was their daughter." I cry harder, and I feel him tensing as he pulls me in.

"I know, baby. I know." I've been vulnerable in many ways before, but this is a new one. There is intimacy involved now, and there is the fact that my heart is on a platter for him to take and use against me.

"I won't do it." He breaks through my sobs.

"What?" I turn to look at him. His face is like stone, and his jaw tics, but he isn't mad at me. No, he is laying down his armor.

"I won't kill anyone in your family. I will let them be free. I will fly us to New York, and I will shake hands with him and call a true peace treaty. For you."

"Nico." I straddle him, the water around us sloshing and some falling out onto the floor. "No, please, don't go to them. Just let them leave our lives. You don't have to say sorry or be anything to them. I don't just respect you. I also respect the people who made this man." I place my hand over his heart. "The one that can be soft, loving, and gentle with me. Who can show vulnerability in the silence. In places where he and I exist alone." I kiss his heart over and over.

"Emelia, my father would want me to do this right."

"No, he wouldn't. He would want you to trust and do as your wife begs of you. And I ask that you just let them go and let it be. Just focus on us and on your outfit." There is something he isn't telling me, and I see it in his eyes—the only place on him that always tells me the truth.

He thinks he can hide his secrets and his pain, or whatever feeling he's experiencing, from me, but he can't hide it in his eyes.

"Don't do that. You can't use that," he warns.

"I'm not. I want my husband to let go with me. I will move on and heal with you loving me like this. They are out of our lives. *Right?*"

He doesn't respond, and that's all I need to tell me my suspicions are right.

"Nico, what did they do?"

"Nothing." He turns stone-cold, and I shake my head.

"No, you don't get to do that. You don't get to shut me out, *especially* when it comes to my family."

"You just said it yourself. You let them go, and they aren't family anymore, so don't worry about it, Emelia."

He could have slapped me and I wouldn't have winced as hard. "No, you don't get to do that either. You don't get to hurt me with my own words and turn them on me. I am your wife and partner. You tell me. Is my father doing something to our outfit?"

He turns his head and rubs his lips with his hands. He is

debating telling me something.

"Nico. Tell me!"

"Yes! I know your fucking father is the one who stole my shipment and tried to have us killed on our fucking honeymoon!" he yells and removes me from him before standing and climbing out of the tub.

"What? Nico!" I call after him when the shock wears off, and I see him leaving the bathroom hastily. Climbing out, my brain is filled with questions, concern, and downright shock.

"Nico!" He is half dressed with his jeans on as he grabs his shirt. I hold the towel to me and breathe heavily."Nico, what are you talking about?"

He doesn't stop and keeps getting dressed. He reaches for the door handle, and I yell.

"If you open that damn door without speaking to me, I will leave you. I will leave this marriage."

He turns fast and is on me in a heartbeat. His hands wrap around my neck, and he pushes me into the wall."Don't you ever threaten to leave me, Emelia. You are mine, and I would hunt you down to the ends of this fucking earth if you ever tried to hide."

He isn't hurting me, but I see the spiral. He doesn't know what to do, and I know I have what it takes to settle him.

"Then talk to me. I can't help you if you don't talk to me. Please," I plead, my voice a whimper at the end.

"Get dressed and meet me in my office. It's downstairs and down the hall to the left. I will tell you what I know."

"Okay." He lets me go, and I watch him leave, his entire body tense. I dress fast after I find my suitcase in the closet. I put on some yoga pants, an off-shoulder white tee, and some fluffy socks because my feet are freezing. The second I'm clothed, I all but run to find his office. It takes me a moment, but when I do, he is sitting in his chair. Giulio is there, sitting on the couch against the wall opposite the desk. I give him a nod before stepping up to Nico's desk.

"I am only letting you in on this information because this is your family, but you will not get involved with business going forward. Is that understood, Emelia?" My mafia husband is back. The lover I had moments ago is now gone.

That is the give and take I agreed to, so I don't mention it. "Yes. Now tell me what the hell is going on."

He opens a drawer to the left of him and pulls out a folder, then tosses it on the desk. "Soon as we got married—and by soon, I mean within days of our engagement—a large shipment of my—" He pauses. "—imported goods... was stolen."

Nice choice of words. So, drugs, weapons, and who knows what else.

"And you have evidence it's my father?" I sort through the papers. There are lists of what was taken, tracking numbers, and pictures. None of it makes sense, but I get that it clearly adds up to someone trying to play dirty with the Seattle outfit.

"No. But I find it convenient that it all started happening right at that time. Then..." He pauses again, and I look up at him. He's staring at Giulio, and I follow his eyes.

Giving Giulio a look, then Nico, I ask, "Then what, Nico?"

"The last picture will show you what's left of my yacht. Our honeymoon yacht. Less than twenty-four hours after we left."

I get to the picture, and it shows water with floating pieces and some random shots of a metal object with numbers stamped on it. My heart drops to my stomach. "We were supposed to be there when that happened."

"Correct. We were. Meaning someone knew where we were and when we were supposed to be there. And to top it off, those numbers on that piece of metal pictured—that is from my stolen shipment, Emelia."

Suddenly, I feel like I'm going to be sick all over again, because I have no doubt my father was up to this. I need to call him. I need to get away from Nico and call him to tell him we know and that I will declare a war on him my damn self. I didn't do my part, but that didn't matter, because he was never going to wait for me to even try. He was marrying me off so he could kill us both. So my brother could reign over Seattle, as my husband has no family, no legacy, but I do. That son of a bitch.

"I need... I need a minute." I drop the folder and take off to the bedroom. I grab my phone from the nightstand and start pacing as the line trills, the ringing seeming never-ending.

"Ahh, my daughter. I see you came around. To what do I owe this pleasure?"

"You tried to kill me and my husband. What happened to the deal? You wanted me to tell you his routines and infiltrate his business so you could take over, but you tried to *kill me* before I even got the chance. You bastard!" I yell.

"Emelia, what did you think would happen if I let you live? You could have become pregnant with his legacy, meaning your brother would only get temporary control over Seattle. What needed to be done had to be done. It's a shame my men failed to mention you left early. What a stroke of fate. Lucky you."

"I hate you. I married him so I could help you kill him. But you never needed that. You're sick, and I will watch him kill you. I will make sure you get what you—" My phone is ripped from my hands, and I spin to see Nico. His face is red, his neck thick with veins, and the rage in him is like nothing I've ever seen before. How much did he hear? He grips my phone so hard it cracks in his hand, the glass breaking before he drops it to the ground and stomps on it.

"Nico... I can explain." As these words leave my mouth, he takes the gun from the back of his jeans and lifts it straight up to my head.

"You liar! You fucking lied!" he yells, the entire room echoing with it.

"I didn't, Nico. I promise. Just let me explain." Tears stream down as I hold my hands up in surrender and back into the wall he's cornered me in.

"No need to explain, *wife*." The way he says it holds the utmost disdain. What was once used as an endearment of ownership and love is now once again filled with hate. "You are a rat, and what happens to rats in this world, baby?" he growls, his lip furling, and I begin to shake uncontrollably. I knew this day would come, but I really thought it would be my father holding the gun on me.

"Nico, please. I had no choice, but I immediately knew I wouldn't do what he asked—"

"Shut up! You betrayed me, Emelia. And traitors, you know what happens."

I nod and beg for mercy. "Please, Nico. I knew early on that I wasn't going to betray you."

"Liar! You made me open up to you. I told you things, because I loved and trusted you! I should kill you!" I flinch and close my eyes when he cocks the gun. But when nothing comes, I open them slowly. That's when I see the gun pointed at his own temple.

"Nico?" I ask, horrified.

"I won't kill you. In fact, I should do something much worse." He pushes the gun harder against his head, and his eyes darken.

"Nico, what are you doing?" I cry.

"You said you love me."

"I do, Nico. I love you more than anything. I would never hurt you or betray you. Please believe me."

He gets closer to me now. "Yeah, baby, you love me? Huh?"

"Yes, Nico! I love you! Please come back to me. I can explain everything."

"No. I don't believe you'll tell me everything, but I do know one thing."

"What? Tell me, please, what?"

He smiles sinisterly. "I know you love me, but it's too late, baby, and I know a punishment much worse than killing you."

"What?" I repeat, confused out of my mind and terrified.

"I watched my mother die slowly when she lost my father. Her love for him was so deep that she couldn't bear to be without him. I should pull the trigger and end it all. Kill myself. And then you can suffer like she did until you die and join me in the fucking afterlife."

I see him slowly putting pressure on the trigger, and I scream out, "Nico! Please, stop. Please. It's us. You have to let me tell you! I love you. Don't do this to us." I cry so hard I feel it deep in my chest.

"I won't live life without you, baby. I love you too much. So what do you say? How about I meet you in hell, my wife?" He tightens his hand on the trigger, and I call out for Giulio.

"Giulio, help! Nico, please! I love you. Stop!"

"Yeah? You do?" Spit flies from his mouth, and his face is so red it matches the shade of blood I fear I'm about to see.

"Yes, please, I love you!"

"Good!" He clamps his eyes shut and I scream, dropping to the floor with my eyes closed as he pulls the trigger.

Someone enters the room hurriedly, too late, and I don't need to look up to know it's Giulio.

But it's then I realize I didn't hear a thud in front of me after the blast.

Crying and gasping for air without any sense of control, I slowly look up and see Nico standing over me, breathing hard. His gun is now at his side, and I fall back against the wall when I see he shot the one to the left of us.

I scream through my cries.

How could he have done that to me?

I wrap my arms around myself and wail so hard I don't think there is an end in sight for me.

"Giulio, get my plane ready. I'm going to New York."

He walks away, and I begin to choke, coughing so hard I can't catch my breath. The door shuts, and I try to stand, but my legs give out and I fall, still sobbing and choking. Soon enough, my body gives out completely. Everything goes black, and I pass out with a whimper for my husband.

"Nico...."

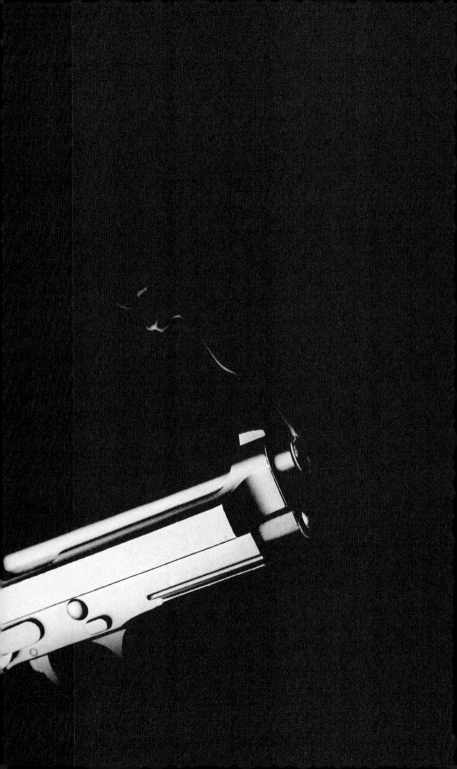

CHAPTER TWENTY-ONE

Nico

I WATCH HER SLEEP IN THE BACK OF MY PLANE. SHE looks tortured even in slumber. But I don't feel remorse. I want her to feel pain for betraying me. Is it hypocritical, as I hid my plan from her all along? Yes. But nowhere in that plan did I even consider her death an option. She was put in this marriage to make sure I only made it out in a fucking body bag.

But that ship has sailed, and Giuseppe's plan has backfired, because I will be the one who ends him. When I heard those words leave Emelia's mouth on the phone, I felt everything in me disintegrate into a rage so deep I could taste it and feel it traveling through my blood.

I knew her father was behind it, but I never thought Emelia would have known or been in on it. Even if what she said back home was true, it still didn't sit with me as the truth. When she passed out, I carried her to the car and onto the plane. She hasn't woken since, and I'm thankful for that, because I don't know what the fuck I'm going to say to her when she wakes up.

What happened before we left was insanity. There were two sides of me that collided and couldn't overrule one another. The killer in me who would end anything and anyone who fucked with him. And the man who loves the woman who hurt him.

I would have rather killed myself than her. Because I couldn't watch the life leave her, and I couldn't imagine a life where she wasn't in it. The twisted, fucked knowledge of that ate at me since I pulled that trigger. Now, I watch her sleep and have no idea what to do when she wakes. But I do know what I plan to do when I get to New York.

Start. A. War.

Emelia doesn't get a say anymore.

Leaving her to rest, I head to the front of the cabin and sit next to Giulio. The whiskey I asked the stewardess to prepare is waiting for me, but instead of downing it, I take my sweet time. Looking out the window at the dark vastness of the night, I think about everything that has played out in the past couple of weeks.

"You trust that she didn't plan to do what her father asked, right?" Giulio implores.

When I first heard what she told her father, I would say yes, I did believe she would have done it. But once the dust settled, I remembered how much Emelia despises her father, and she wouldn't hurt me to help him.

I shouldn't have reacted so madly, but I couldn't help it. Something took over me, and I had to do what needed to be done. The only way I would be able to see her true loyalty was in the way she begged with the fear of losing me in her eyes.

Fuck, I'm a prick.

"Yes, I know she wouldn't," I hiss.

"So what is the plan then, boss? We just going in, guns blazing? You know that won't work. We have to have a plan."

"I'm aware. I'm working on that, but I can't think with you incessantly talking, Giulio."

"Sorry, sir." He goes silent, and a few moments later, I hear the back door open.

I stand, fixing my suit jacket I changed into once we got on the plane, now fully in business mode.

"Nico?" Emelia's voice sounds raspy.

"Emelia." I turn and walk toward her.

She holds her head, rubbing at it. "My head is pounding. Do we have any medicine?"

"Yes." Giulio stands without needing direction and goes to find the stewardess.

Once we're alone, she sits on the couch and puts her head down. I move over to dim the lights a bit, so they aren't so harsh.

"Why am I here?" Emelia asks but doesn't look up at me. Her tone is firm, and I know a fight is coming.

"We are going to New York. I have business to take care of."

"Meaning my family?" She finally looks up as Giulio approaches with water and some pills. She takes them from him, then sips some water before taking the pills and swallowing them down.

"Yes, I have to attend to some business with your father."

"And you don't think he knows you're coming, Nico?" she asks matter-of-factly.

"No, he does. I just sent in our last-minute RSVP to the annual ball. All outfits were asked to attend, but seeing as I was planning on being on yet another attempted honeymoon with my wife, I had withdrawn our names from the list."

"I'm not going to that ball with you. I don't want to see my father, and after what you did back at the house, I don't want to see you either." Her chin quivers.

"Emelia, I lost it back there. I was hurt, and I was angry."

"Angry? You call that anger? That was cruel."

"I know. But your betrayal was just as cruel."

"What betrayal, Nico! I didn't do anything. I tried to tell you that I never did what he asked, and you decided to go mad on me and almost take your—" She stops, holding back tears. I swear I have caused more tears for her today than she has shed in her lifetime, and for that, I hate myself.

"I know we're figuring things out and trying to navigate something neither of us understands, but I can't have you without trust, and vice versa."

"Why didn't you tell me sooner then, Emelia?"

"Because I didn't want you to do what you're doing now. I didn't want a war. I didn't want to lose you," she admits, and I drop my head, releasing a sigh.

This is all so fucked.

"I know. But that doesn't make it okay. You have to tell me things like this, Emelia."

"I thought we didn't talk about your business?"

"This is different and you know it." I tilt my head and give her a stern look.

"How?"

"Because this could have had us killed."

"As could anything in your line of work! We are moving targets, Nico, and I knew that since I didn't do what he asked he was going to kill me. And I wanted to breathe and see what life was like free for just a moment, and I saw that in you. Now, I don't know what I see!" She stands and moves to the bedroom.

I follow her, hot on her heels. "Or you could have told me sooner, and he would've already been dealt with," I retort.

She turns and pierces me with a look. "I don't know what I'm doing! I've been controlled my whole life, and then I was with you, and we were arguing and having beautiful sex I just thought was lustful hate, but it was really our way of communicating our wonderment and excitement for one another. I was falling for you, and nothing felt like it was going to get in the way." I can tell she wants to throw, hit, or break something, but she holds it all in.

"I felt free, and I wanted to revel in that. I had a voice. I could tell you how angry I was. I could speak without being hurt. We may not have had the perfect start, and we may not have been playing twenty fucking questions, but you were learning me, and I was learning how to be alive. You were giving me space to breathe and live for the first time, Nico."

Each word is filled with pain, and I feel her hurt in my soul, the way she whimpered every other word out of that sentence.

It was true though. We weren't getting to know each other in the conventional way, but we were getting to know each other in a way that was unique, freeing, and new to us both. We created our own fucking love language.

"You're right. I fucked up. I'm sorry. But we can't act like this didn't happen, and we can't let your father do this to us. He can't take you like he took the only other people I loved. I won't let him have you, Emelia." This time, my voice cracks.

Fuck. I don't cry. I never have. Not even at their funerals. But for her, for Emelia, I would crawl on hands and knees and beg for her to love me. To take me as hers. To own me.

"*You* almost took you from me, Nico! You almost pulled that trigger and took away the one person who sees me. Who knows I exist. How could you do that to me?" She sits on the edge of the bed, and I do exactly what I knew I would.

I drop to my knees in front of her and beg for her forgiveness.

"I'm sorry. I will say it a thousand times if I need to, but I am sorry, Emelia. And we are here. Breathing still. I'm at your feet, and you have me, baby."

She nods into her hands. "I will make you say it every day. Every day, you will apologize for ever doing that to me." She grabs my face and pulls me onto her, and I nod.

"Every day. You and me." We kiss, our tongues colliding, and I apologize. I say sorry so many times for the entire next hour.

"So beautiful, baby."

She rides me slowly, and I rub her thighs gently. We have been at it this whole hour, and I can't stop having her. I have held off my orgasm, making sure she has plenty before I take mine. Besides, there is pleasure in watching her take hers. I would argue it's better than my own orgasm. I roam from her thighs to the thick, plush softness of her stomach. I knead the skin there. Every inch of her is breathtaking, especially from this angle, because I can see almost all of her.

"Say it again," she whispers, rocking her hips.

"I'm sorry, baby. I'm so fucking sorry."

"In Italian."

"Mi dispiace tanto, piccola mia."

She smiles, biting her lip. The tears have long gone, and that spark in her eye slowly returns.

"Come for me, my love. Come inside me!" she cries out.

"You need that? Do you need me to come to feel me, baby?" She smiles again and nods. "Good girl. Can I take control?"

"Always, *il mio re*," she practically purrs, and I don't think I'll need to after that.

"Scream that while you ride me good, principessa."

She braces her hands on my chest and starts to rock harder, alternating between that and her rise and fall, and I am there.

"*Il mio re!*" she screams, coming with me.

"Fuck, baby! Fuck!" I come so fucking hard. She squeezes down on me and milks my cock with her orgasm, and then she falls beside me on a deep breath.

"Shit," she says, and I laugh.

"Yeah, shit."

"That for sure got me pregnant." I look over at her when she says this, and she winks at me. "Calm down, I was kidding. Kind of." She looks at the ceiling thoughtfully.

"Are you ready for that?" I ask, rubbing her stomach in the way I would if she were pregnant with our child.

"I just realized I never got my pills refilled in all the chaos. So... I could be at any time. I mean, I could now. I won't know until my period comes or not."

"A week then?"

"What?"

"A week. That's when it's supposed to come."

She sits up and turns to lay on her stomach, but she stays propped up on her elbows. "Have you been tracking my period, Nico?"

I smirk. "Yes. I track everything you do, baby."

"You are twisted. But yes." She laughs. "One week. If I'm late, I will take the test."

"God, I want to fuck you again just to make sure you are," I growl, turning and biting her shoulder.

She yelps. "Sex fiend." She laughs, her blonde hair falling all around her. I go to respond, but there is a knock at the bedroom door.

"Flight is to land in thirty minutes, sir," Giulio says from the other side. Both me and Emelia groan before standing. We make our way to the shower to rinse off quickly. Once we're done, we start getting dressed and prepped for landing. We are in our seats just shy of ten minutes beforehand. Emelia takes my hand and rubs my knuckles.

"Are you going to kill them all... Mother included?" she whispers, and I shake my head.

"No, I won't be killing them. I will just make sure they understand I know, and if they try anything again, I will see that every outfit on my side helps me take down his kingdom."

She looks surprised.

"Why, Emelia? Do you want me to take care of them?" I will do anything she asks. I would love to kill them. In fact, just hours ago, that was the plan, but I don't think Emelia can handle that right now.

At least, I didn't think so. Until now.

"I..." She trails off and looks around.

"Emelia, speak up. I will do what you say in this situation."

Her eyes come back to me, and they show so much loss yet hate.

"They tried to kill us, and they could try again, and I could be pregnant when they do." She stops for a moment, really thinking the next part over. "Yes. But not my mother."

"She was awful to you, Emelia," I remind her.

"Yes, but now she will have nothing, and I won't let you kill a woman in my name. Call me sexist, but I won't. She hurt me most anyway. I want to watch her live a poor life. Empty and alone. Don't kill her."

Giulio and I look at one another, and we both share a shocked yet proud grin.

"Anything you say."

"Take care of your mother for me, son, and remember when you marry to protect your bride with honor."

The plane lands, and we prepare for what's to come.

CHAPTER TWENTY-TWO

Emelia

NICO AND I GOT TO THE HOTEL ROOM AND IMMEDIATELY went to sleep. We each had nothing left to offer in those early-morning hours. And we didn't wake until nearly noon the next day. Breakfast, or lunch, was waiting for us already, and that first sip of coffee was what I needed to start the day.

Nico showered first, as he has business to attend to before the big night tonight.

I can't believe this is going to happen. My brothers and father will be gone. Their reign of terror will be over, and for my mother, well, her terror will truly just begin.

Part of me knows that if they hadn't attempted to kill us, then I wouldn't have let this take place tonight, but when my father admitted it on the phone and with so much hate in his voice, I knew what I had to do to not only protect Nico and me, but to protect the future of us. Meaning my children. My father would never stop. He cannot be stopped unless he's dead.

I will be free forever. And something I truly never thought I would say—Nico will also be free. Just a short time ago, I wouldn't have cared about his freedom. But now, that's all changed. Feelings developed, love blossomed, and I want his parents' retribution.

Nico emerges from the suite bedroom, and he's dressed in a suit, as always. Never a workday he would be in anything else.

"You're so handsome," I say unprompted. I'm so lucky. Nico is the epitome of God's gift to women, over six feet with black hair slicked back in a way only he can pull off. His green eyes compliment his strong facial features. He is a work of art, and I am merely a woman.

"You're beautiful, principessa."

I am still in a robe, and my hair is a mess on the top of my head. But I take the compliment, because it's coming from him.I open my mouth, and what comes out next seems to come out of nowhere, but we never talked about it after it happened.

"Nico, I want to thank you for what happened with Damian. Thank you for protecting me and getting rid of all the pictures and videos," I tell him, and he eyes me over curiously.

"Where is this coming from? And you don't need to thank me. That's my job."

I roll my eyes, because even after all the emotions we've shared, he will keep some sort of nonchalant, "this all business to me" energy.

"I just keep thinking about the past couple of months and how we got to where we are, and I never thanked you. For your *business*," I add, teasing him.

He understands what I meant, and he instantly corrects me."I didn't mean it was my mafia responsibility. It's my job as your husband to always protect and defend you, Emelia."

"Oh, well thank you," I reply bashfully.

"I will do it again and again." He doesn't say it outwardly, but he's insinuating what he's planning to do tonight.

"Are you going to eat?" I change the subject. This is all a bit much for brunch talk. We will be knees-deep in it soon, and I want to try to make every last minute count.

"Yes, I am, but I'm going to take it to go. I have something I need to do before I come back here this afternoon to get you. The makeup artist will be here in an hour, and your dress should be here soon as well," he tells me, grabbing an apple and toast before leaning down and kissing me.

"Oh, okay. Well, I will miss you. See you tonight?"

"See you tonight, baby." He starts to walk away, but he stops. "And Emelia, please wear my mother's pearls tonight. They mean a lot to me." He leaves like a gust of wind that came and went.

My heart starts to flutter. So he did give me those pearls because he was falling for me. It was intimate. It did mean something to him. And now, knowing how much he loved his mother, they will hold a special place in my heart.

I realize I've daydreaming about Nico and what those pearls mean for longer than I meant to when there's a knock on the door and I'm pulled back to my regular state of mind.

"Ma'am, your makeup artist is here," the guard Nico brought alert me, and I move toward him as he opens the door. I see a young man who is maybe five-foot five, and he looks terrified of the three guards watching my room.

"Hi, I'm Francisco. I'm here to do your makeup, Mrs. Valiente."

"Yes, come in, and don't let them intimidate you. They're all bark and no bite." I give him a wink and move aside for him and one of the men to come in. I don't ask questions, knowing Nico most likely told them I'm not to be alone with anyone and to double up with security when my makeup artist got here.

"Where would you like me, friend?" I ask, trying to make Francisco more comfortable. Seriously, he looks petrified.

"Um, the chair by the window is fine."

I look at the comfy chair and round table by the large open windows, and I move to it. Francisco sets up shop and gets to work. Soon enough, with just the right amount of small talk, we get to chatting like we know one another. He tells me he has a partner and two sons they adopted. I told him we're thinking about having kids, and of course he tells me all about why I should and the ups and downs of being a parent. But all in all, he reiterates how amazing it is. I wish I could bring him back to Seattle with us. He's seriously one of the kindest people I've ever met.

I'm sad when we have to part, but when I see how lovely he did my makeup, my stomach flips at knowing how much my husband will be salivating over me tonight. I work on my own hair, something I told Nico I prefer to do. I blow dry it halfway, then add curlers. Letting those set for a bit, I sit and call Nico.

"Wife, is everything all right?" he answers.

So serious.

"*Husband*, everything is great. I just miss you. Wanted to make sure you're safe and okay."

He chuckles."Emelia, I'm safe. This isn't my first time. You don't have to worry. I want you to relax today. It's been a wild couple of days. Just enjoy it. Room service is on its way up now with champagne and strawberries. Indulge."

I pout."Well that doesn't sound like much fun, since you aren't here. I would love to eat strawberries. Off of your cock," I seduce him through the phone.

"Baby, I'm in a room full of men right now."

My face goes red."Oh my God, I'm so sorry!"

"It's all right. They can't hear you, but I'm afraid I can't engage in the way you and I both want to. I will be back soon though, so save some for that?"

I nod, even though he can't see me. I'm still mortified.

"Yes, will do. Bye." I hang up fast and roll my eyes. God, I'm an idiot. The phone rings almost instantly, and it's Nico. I debate letting it go to voicemail, but knowing him, he will just keep at it.

"Hello?"

"I stepped out. Seemed my wife couldn't bother saying she loves me. Do you need attention, principessa?"

"No, no, I can wait. I was just embarrassed."

"Two things. You always say 'I love you' before we end a call. And two, don't be embarrassed about your needs. They couldn't hear you, and if they had, then they would've all lost their ears by now. I don't share. Remember?"

I blush. "I do."

"Good. Now do you need some attention? I can take a few minutes for my wife to get her fix."

He wants to help me get off, and as much as I want that, I just want to wait for him.

"No, go to work. You can give me all of you when you get back."

"Good."

"Wait, before you go. Can I get a phone like my old one? This new one you got me is huge. Seriously, it's the size of my head, Nico." After he broke my phone, he gave me a replacement, and I genuinely despise the outrageous size.

"You've handled something bigger."

"Ugh! Nico!" I laugh.

"I will see what I can do. See you soon. I love you." His voice lowers, sounding sincere.

"I love you," I say back just as genuinely. We end the call, and I get back to finishing my hair.

The dress came, and it is breathtaking. The satin fabric is a fire-engine red, and it catches the light stunningly. It ties around the neck and drapes in a swoop at my breasts, giving me ample cleavage. It's an empire waist, and it flows down the rest of my body effortlessly, but the most eye-catching part... the large slit up my right leg. The opening ends at the center of my thigh, and I have never felt more beautiful.

The final touch is the pearls, and when I put them on, I slowly run my hands over the classy white globes. I close my eyes and feel for Nico and imagine the pain in his heart when he lost his mother.

"A fucking vision, my love," his voice catches me off guard, and

I jump a bit, but I lock eyes with him in the mirror. He is in a three-piece suit I haven't seen before. He must have had one picked up. He's leaning in the doorframe of the bedroom with his hands in his pockets, and he looks at me with an expression that says he wants to eat me alive.

"Right back at you." I giggle, turning and sauntering toward him.

"Your hips look like a delicacy in this dress." He grabs my hips once I'm within reach, and he pulls me in flush against him. Hitting a wall of muscles and man, I cling to his lapels.

"Everything in this suit makes you look like a delicacy," I remark.

"I shouldn't have bought a dress I'd just want to take off."

"I think that's exactly what I should have on. Imagine it at my feet tonight, after you conquer all our enemies," I remind him of tonight, and the mood shifts.

He admires the pearls around my neck, spinning them between his fingers, and I can see he's having some sort of moment. I almost address it, but he beats me to it.

"You sure you want me to do this, Emelia? This is your family, and once it's done, it can't be undone."

Without an ounce of hesitation or even a moment of pause, I answer, "Yes. Nothing is going to hurt my new family. They were never really my family at all."

I think of a future Nico and a future me, running around barefoot and laughing in our home, and I want to protect that. That life is the only thing I'm thinking of and the only thing I want to protect.

"Okay. Then let's do this." He gives me his arm, and I wrap mine around it.

We make our way to the elevator with the three guards and Giulio in tow.

Once the doors to the elevator shut, Nico leans down to my

ear and whispers, "I can't wait to see that red lipstick smeared on my cock and around those pretty little fuck-me lips."

I have to resist the moan that bubbles inside me. I grow wet and rub my thighs together, and he smiles down at me, knowing what he's doing to me."Ass."

He winks but doesn't respond, enjoying the arousal he elicited in me. He lets me in the black SUV and slides in next to me. The driver pulls out into the downtown traffic, and we make our way toward the ball.

"Plan? Do I get to know?" I ask.

"Some of it. You will go tonight, smile, dance with me, and just enjoy time with me. When your family is ready to go, I will instruct you on what to do from there."

I nod. He wasn't lying. That was the bare minimum.

"Promise you will be safe. Please." This is not a small task he's carrying out. This is dangerous, and he's had less than twenty-four hours to plan it. Anything can go wrong.

"I will. I'm starting to take offense that you think I'm some amateur here."

"No, I don't think that, but you've had less than a day to plan this out, Nico. God knows what my family's been planning for months now."

He looks at Giulio, and they both share a knowing laugh.

"What?" I question, looking back and forth between them.

"Emelia, we once took out thirty-three men with six of our own, and only two were slightly injured. I think I got this. I've gone through many things like this, and it's a rinse and fucking repeat task. Trust me, okay?"

This does nothing to calm my nerves, but I have to do what he says. I have to trust he can do this.

"Okay. Giulio?" I turn and face him.

"Yes, Mrs. Valiente?" he responds.

"Do not let anything happen to my husband. You bring him

back home to me. Understood," I say with authority.

"Yes, ma'am." He nods.

"Good."

Nico rubs my thigh, gaining my attention back."You're sexy when you're bossy."

"Don't you forget it." I kiss his lips, and when we part, I wipe away the lipstick I left behind.

Pulling up less than thirty minutes later, we get out and walk into the fancy downtown hotel. Strolling through the lobby, we make our way to the large ballroom. Entering, I admire just how stunning it is. Chandeliers hang in what looks like a thousand shimmering lights. The floor has been turned into a marble-like dance floor and seating area. The tables are draped in cream cloths with red runners, and glass vases filled with water, roses, and floating candles at their center.

It takes me some time to notice the people in the room. I'm so captivated by the beauty of the setup that I almost forgot we're at a party. A lot of these faces, I recognize, as we're back in New York, and I have attended many of these balls before. But there are some faces I do not know.

Nico immediately starts greeting people, some by their first name and some by their last. I assume he does this based on how long he's known the people or the status of their business partnership.

He introduces me proudly, telling everyone I'm his bride. We've been married for a couple of months now, but it still feels like I'm his new bride. Although this time is different. This time, there's no bitterness when he says bride or wife. Instead, there's pride. I never thought there'd be a day we'd be this close, let alone in love.

My heart warms at the knowledge I have finally fallen in love. I was never in love with Damian, not even close. What I had with him was naïve, a twisted hope that he would help me get away from my family someday. And for him, I was his own personal sex tape for money. Little did I know fate would put me in the hands of the man on my arm. My husband.

I fell in love with the man I was forced to marry. The man I despised from the moment we laid eyes on each other. But under that dislike was his redemption and my salvation. Nico is going to protect me tonight, as well as protect the future of our children and his parents' legacy, and his own.

All of these happy thoughts drain from me in an instant, when I see my father, mother, and two brothers. And they look at me with hate and dishonor. When really, the only dishonorable ones here are them. We are in a room filled with trained killers, surrounded by the most elite people in organized crime, and here I sit, knowing that the worst of them are the people who gave birth to me. Not because of what they can do, no. Because Nico could do far worse. They are the worst of the worst, because they turned their back on family, on blood, and that is the one thing in the mafia you're supposed to honor the most—your flesh and blood.

"Nico," I whisper in my husband's ear, and he tells the gentleman he's talking to to please excuse him.

"Yes, Emelia?" He looks at me, and with my eyes, I alert him to my parents' presence. He follows my look, and his eyes land on my father. I wait for something to happen, for Nico to tense up or to react, but he stays eerily still until he gives my father a curt nod and leads us to our table.

"How are you so calm right now?" I ask as he pulls out my seat.

"Does a lion pounce on his prey before the opportune moment?" he asks.

"No."

"Exactly. For the last time, Emelia. This is what I do. I am known for my deadly ways for a reason. I can remain calm even outside the eye of the storm, wife."

"You are annoyingly arrogant, and yet it's somehow hot," I tell him.

He smiles wide, showing his beautiful white teeth. It's the smile I rarely get to see. "Also another talent of mine. You're welcome." I'm about to make a smartass rebuttal, but the speaker cuts us off. The lights dim, and they begin.

"Familias, to see you all here in one place makes me so happy." The man speaking is much older, short, balding, and has a really impressive mustache.

"Who is he?" I don't recall his face from anywhere.

"He was the boss of the Chicago outfit. He retired, and his son took over. His name is Paolo Francesco." I nod, and the guests begin to clap at something I missed, including Nico, so I follow suit. He goes on about the night, how we can donate to any of the charities we would like, and to enjoy the dinner and drinks prepared for us.

Nico and I eat our food, and he talks to the other guests at our table, but I stay to myself for the most part. Occasionally, I will smile, nod, and answer a question, but to be honest, I'm riddled with nerves and anxiety. I can feel my family watching me, but I don't dare look back at them. If I tip them off, we're screwed.

I came here to be with Nico, and I told him I would trust him. I will stick to the plan, and then all of this will be over soon.

"Nico?" I interrupt, saying sorry to the others at the table.

"Yes?"

"Would you like to dance with me?" I ask shyly for some reason. But I've never gotten to dance with Nico the way I wanted. When we danced at the wedding, all I wanted to do was knee him in the balls.

"Of course. Ladies, gentlemen, I owe my beautiful bride a dance tonight. It was good to talk to you again. We'll speak soon." He gestures to DeLuca, the man next to him, then stands and helps me out of my chair.

He moves us to the dance floor where the lovely band plays a melody that is slow and sensual. We get into position, and he takes the lead. He slowly moves me across the floor, and it's effortless. He's in control tonight; there's not an ounce of weariness in his body.

I lean into that and let myself believe this is going to be okay. It has to. It just has to. We dance for two songs, until Giulio interrupts us. He whispers in Nico's ear, and Nico doesn't move his gaze from me, like he's purposefully trying not to let his eyes wander. He pulls me in and dips down to my ear.

"I need to brief our men. Giulio said your family is leaving soon. Head to the bathroom. I will text you when we're ready, then meet me at the entrance, and we will make our departure."

I nod, and with that, I leave him and go in search of the bathroom. Finding it instantly, I step inside, and that's when the anxiety really hits me. My stomach is churning. My mind is racing, and I'm starting to sweat. I have my hands braced on either side of the sink, and I drop my head between my shoulders, trying to compose myself and not succumb to vomiting.

"You okay?" a voice asks from the stalls behind me.

Peering up, I see a beautiful brunette. She has straight hair that slightly curls in at the ends, and she wears an emerald-green dress that compliments her eyes. Her body is sculpted like a model's. I envy her beauty for a moment, but the anxiety overrides that brief lapse.

"Yes, I just had too much to drink tonight." I fake a small laugh, and she laughs too, stepping up to the mirror next to me.

"Same here, and all the men have been ruthless tonight. Old pigs don't know how to back off." She pulls out some lipstick and starts to reapply the stunning red that enhances her plump lips.

"Sorry to hear that. Are you not here with anyone?" I ask, hoping this small talk will distract me enough until my phone signals that Nico is ready.

"Nope, I come to these things hoping I will find someone, but not one man out there is even remotely attractive." She smacks her lips, then puts her lipstick back in her purse and continues to rummage through the small clutch for something else. "Well, there is one. One I've been with and had my eyes on for a while."

"Oh yeah?"

"Yeah, except there's some bitch in the way." Her voice is hostile, and suddenly I realize she's talking at me and not to me. I turn to look at her, and she gives me a malicious, mocking smile. "Hello, Emelia. I'm Natalia. Nico's ex. And you're in my way of getting back what I want."

I go to open my mouth to tell her to leave or I will call Nico in, but she rips her hand from her clutch, and I feel a sharp stab in my neck. The room becomes fuzzy, and my eyes grow heavy until there is nothing. Nothing but blackness.

CHAPTER TWENTY-THREE

Nico

"You will make sure to take her to a new hotel. Do not go back to the other one until I give the all-clear. Your only job is to keep my wife safe," I tell Giulio and Phillip, her newest guard.

"Yes, sir."

"You three, with me. In and out. You get the car, and you two hold them hostage in the back. Take them to the warehouse, and I will be waiting."

"Yes, sir."

"Good." Taking out my phone, I text Emelia that we're ready. I head to the entrance with my men and wait for her. I can see her father and brothers coming, and I curse, knowing we have mere seconds to make this work.

Fuck.

I call Emelia, and it goes to voicemail. I look back again and notice that Mrs. Notelli isn't to be seen, and my stomach drops.

"Giulio! Watch them. If they leave before we do, follow them. Get to the car now. Keep me posted."

"Yes, sir." He hurries out before the Notellis see him, but I pass them on the way to the restroom, that feeling in my stomach growing worse.

"Looks like we both lost our brides tonight," Giuseppe says with malice, but I ignore him.

I keep my cool, because if he knows we're going to follow him, it will be the end of this plan. I pray Emelia's merely knocked out and can be taken to the hospital or that her mother has her locked in there until her father can get away. He probably thinks I will have my men distracted finding Emelia. Wrong. The only one who will find her is me. I will not let them outsmart me.

I get to the bathroom and throw open the door. I kick in each stall, and they're all empty. That's when I see Emelia's clutch on the floor alongside her phone.

"Fuck!" I pull out my phone and call Giulio." They have her. They fucking took her. Did they see you? Do you have eyes on them?"

"They saw us. But not before I could mark their car with a tracker. We're following but keeping a far-enough distance. We didn't want to let them know we're onto them, sir. I had to change the plan. Emelia not being there put us back."

"Fuck, Giulio, listen to me. They fucking have her. They got Emelia."

"What?" he hisses.

"Yes. I need you to get to her. I'm tracking you now. I will get there as fast as I can. Do not let them hurt her. Do you understand me, Giulio?"

"Yes, sir." He cuts the call, and I rush out. I see the nearest SUV and take it. I don't give a fuck who it belongs to. The valet hollers after me, but I'm already gone. I weave in and out of traffic, following the tracker on Giulio's phone.

I can't speed fast enough. I can't get to her quickly enough. My phone pings then. It's a message from an unknown number, and I almost don't open it, but I see Emelia's name in the body of the message.

UNKNOWN

**With Emelia gone, you have me
and I have you. Love, Natalia.**

Fucking bitch! Is it her? Did the Notellis not have a part? I hit the Call button, and Natalia answers.

"Baby," she coos, and I cut her off.

"You fucking bitch. Where is my wife!"

I hear Emelia scream then.

"Emelia!" I yell into the phone, nearly sideswiping a car in my pursuit.

"Aw, so cute. You two like each other. That's sweet. Anyway, with her gone, I can come back." Natalia's voice is like nails on a chalkboard, and I will not hesitate to put a bullet in her delusional skull.

"Where are you?"

"Nico, it's my family! Don't— Ah! Ow! Please, stop!" Emelia screams in the background.

"Oh, that looked like it hurt."

"I will kill everyone in that fucking room, Natalia. You included. You just watch."

"Good luck finding us. Your men couldn't keep up. We will talk tomorrow, when the problem is solved. I will change your mind about us."

I go to yell back at her, but the call ends, and I slam my hand down hard on the dashboard.

"Fuck, fuck, fuck!"

I call Giulio, still tracking him. "It's Natalia. She was in on it. They used her to get to Emelia. How close are you?"

"No more than three minutes, sir. Where are you?"

I see Giulio on the tracker right in front of me, and I flash my lights. "Move faster."

"Yes, sir, we have to take a sharp right in less than a mile. She's in an underground parking lot in a new development that looks to be under construction still. We can't drive in. They will hear us. We need to go by foot."

"Fine. Just hurry."

He ends the call, and I ride his ass all the way there. When the hard right comes, we almost take out a row of cars at a light. Abruptly, he begins to slow down, and I do too. I see the construction and know we're almost there.

"I'm coming, baby. I will get to you."

Rolling to a stop, we all leave the SUVs and draw our guns.

"Giulio, I want you to come in this entrance with me. Phillip, you three, go around the back and see if there's another entrance. I want to come from both angles, so they aren't prepared. Nodding, they head around the building, and I take the lead into the garage. Being as stealthy as we can, we stay against the walls, and that's when I hear Emelia yell.

"He will kill you! What is your plan now? Kill me, and then what? You can't fucking hide from him, you coward!" I hear a sharp slap, and she cries out, and my teeth grit. Careful now.

A lion doesn't pounce until the opportune moment.

"Stay here. Wait until you hear gunshots before you come in. I don't know what to expect down there, and if we storm in all at once, they may shoot her, and we can be outnumbered."

Giulio nods and pulls out his phone to communicate that to the other men. I make it to the third level and peek around the corner to the fourth landing, and that's when I see her. She's tied to a chair, with her two brothers on each side of her. Sal has a knife to her neck, and Lorenzo has her hair in a tight grip. I clutch my gun and release a slow breath. Looking back, I see Natalia standing in the corner, enjoying the show. That fucking bitch has it coming. Giuseppe stands in front of his daughter, some type of knife in his hand beside his waist.

"I hope he comes here. In fact, Emelia, I'm counting on it. It seems you have fallen in love, all while fucking up the plans. So, when he gets here—" Her father leans forward, coming within inches of her face. "—I will kill him first. I will watch you cry over the enemy's body, and *then*... I'll kill you." He shrugs.

Coward. He is a fucking coward.

"I hate you. I will haunt you until the day you die. And then I'll meet you at Hell's gate and watch you burn." She's so confident and brave when she says this, and my chest swells with pride. Her father turns to walk toward a table filled with tools for torture, and that's when I make my move.

Pointing my gun straight at Salvatore's head, I pull the trigger and quickly move to Lorenzo's, firing again without pause. Emelia screams, and her father looks up, pointing his gun. But he doesn't see me.

"Come out, Nico!" he yells. "You want a war, and I came ready for one! You killed my fucking sons! Come out!

I move around and keep my gun pointed at him. He goes to shoot, but Giulio pops out from the other side of the garage and shoots the hand holding the gun.

Giuseppe cries out in agony while bending over. "You fucking son of a bitch!"

I rush over to Emelia, as does Giulio, and I begin to untie her. Her neck is bleeding, and my mother's pearls lay all around us. When I shot Salvatore, the knife must have slipped and nicked her neck. But the pearls stopped it from hitting her jugular. My mother's pearls saved my wife.

I hear a gunshot, then turn to see Giuseppe with his gun in his good hand and Giulio on the ground. I reach for my gun but am stopped when her father points his right at Emelia.

"Stop or she's fucking dead, and you will be wearing her brains."

"What is it you want? Your sons are dead now. You can't take over Seattle. You are in too deep, Giuseppe. You fucked up, got too messy, and thought you could outsmart me."

"I did once, remember?" He tilts his head and looks at me with cold eyes. He steps closer, keeping the gun extended.

Mine is on the ground where I placed it before I untied Emelia. I see her hands moving slowly in my peripherals, untying herself the rest of the way. I don't bring attention to it.

"You do remember, right?"

I give him the look the Grim Reaper would. "No. I don't recall a time where you ever outsmarted me, Giuseppe."

"Really, how about when I killed your coward father?"

Suddenly, Emelia moves fast, and she grabs the gun. While Giuseppe is distracted and looking at her, I kick the gun from his hand, and then I grab him, wrapping one arm around his neck while my other restrains his arm behind his back. He weakly tries to make his way out of my grasp, but he doesn't succeed.

"Don't you ever speak about his father like that again. You have always been weak, Father. You hit me and Mother to make yourself seem bigger. Hell, you sent your teenage son in to do the hard work for you to kill my husband's dad." Emelia holds the gun straight out, pointing it at him.

She is covered in blood from the punches and smacks to the face, and her dress is torn in places, but she manages to still look like she's unbothered and in control. There is the power I wanted from her all along. From day one, I told her I needed her to look strong, be strong, and gain power, and here we are full circle, and she is the representation of the most exquisite creature in the world.

"I never wanted a fucking daughter. I begged your mother to get rid of you."

Emelia laughs, but it's a delirious, unhinged laugh. It even puts *me* on edge.

"Oh, *Daddy*, what ever will I do, knowing that?"

"Baby? Give me the gun. I will take care of him."

She shakes her head. "No. This is my time, Nico. I want to earn a place in this world. Why not now? Make my father proud. I will be like the son he never had, because those two fuckers were just as pitiful as him."

I don't expect what happens next. She points the gun down and pulls the trigger, shooting him in the foot. I let him go, and he falls to the ground, screaming.

"That's for the day you pushed me down the stairs." She shoots his other one. "That's for the day you hit me with the butt of your gun and made me bleed, then didn't let me go to the doctor. And this..." She points the gun at his chest. I hold my hand out and warn her, but she ignores it. "This is for killing my husband's family."

She pulls the trigger, and he falls to his back and lets out guttural noises that pull her lips into a wicked smile. He isn't dead yet, but there is no way he's getting up anytime soon.

Phillip and the other men come rounding the corner, and I'm on Emelia, taking the gun from her hand. I put the safety on and slide it in my holster.

I grab her face and see her eyes glazing over as she looks at her father on the ground. "Emelia? Baby, are you in there? Baby!" She is zoned out and completely gone.

"Phillip, get Giulio to a hospital, and you two, take care of her father. Somewhere he can't be found." I bark out my orders before I pick Emelia up. I carry her out of that garage and to the car.

Starting the engine, I keep trying to pull Emelia from her dazed state, but I get nothing. I drive to the hotel and get her inside and in the shower. It isn't until then that she snaps, and with the loudest scream I've ever heard from someone, she unleashes everything built up inside her.

I hold her tight as she screams, not trying to stop her or contain her, just to keep her safe. I let her feel, let her breathe, let her be free.

CHAPTER TWENTY-FOUR

Emelia

I WAKE UP TO THE LIGHT COMING THROUGH THE window. My face aches, and my body feels heavy, like I was hit by a car. I look around the room and see I'm alone. I look down at my body, and I'm covered in scratches and bruises, and I'm completely naked.

Slowly, the memories of the night before come flooding back. I remember blacking out in the bathroom, then coming to with my father, brothers, and Natalia surrounding me. I remember Natalia calling Nico, and me screaming for him not to come. I wince remembering the pain from each hit from my brothers and father.

Then... I remember shooting my father. Did he die? I don't know. I remember the sound of the gunshots and seeing him fall to the ground, but after that, it was like a haze overcame me, a black haze, and I couldn't hear or really see anything.

Slowly, I get up, moving to the door where a robe hangs. Pulling it on, I tie the belt around my waist and open the door. Nico stands, ending the call with whoever he was speaking to.

"Emelia, you should be resting. Come sit." He rushes to me and takes my hand, then walks me to the couch. I sit gingerly and look around.

"Where is everyone?"

"The guards are outside the door, and Giulio is at the hospital."

Panic sets in. Did I shoot him?

"Did I—?"

"No, you didn't. Your father did."

"Is Giulio alive?"

Nico nods. "Yes, he will need physical therapy, but he was only hit in the shoulder. He will be fine."

"And..." I pause, swallowing past the lump in my throat. "My father?"

"He's gone. My men took care of him, and he is no longer an issue."

"Did I kill him?"

"No, you got him good, but I stopped you, and he was taken away and handled."

I start crying then, overwhelming emotions overtaking me.

"I'm sorry, baby. It had to be done. He was never going to stop, and he was a danger to us and his own outfit. Okay?"

I look up and I shake my head. "No. I'm free. He's gone. The pain is gone." I release a deep breath, like it's my first time on earth and I've never breathed before. I inhale and exhale so rapidly I almost hyperventilate.

Nico holds me close, rubbing my back and kissing my head all over. "Yes, you're free. Forever."

"But what about Natalia? And my mother? They surely won't be okay with all this. What if they do something or go to another outfit and turn them against you?"

He shakes his head. "My men caught Natalia as she took off. That's why it took them so long to get to us. And your mother..." He hesitates, looking out the window.

"My mother what, Nico?" I lean to get back in line with his vision.

"She killed herself, Emelia. My men showed up with your father's body to show her, and she grabbed a gun and shot herself. She's dead." I look around the room. I should feel pain and remorse, but I don't, and that scares me.

"Nico, why isn't this hurting me?" I ask him, because I fear for myself.

"Because they were evil, Emelia. They would have killed you. They tortured you all your life. You are free from that hell." He rubs my thighs.

"I'm sorry." My lip trembles, and I drop my head to his shoulder.

"Why are you sorry? You're safe. I'm safe. Everything is okay."

I look up and cradle his face, rubbing my thumbs along the stubble on his chin.

"No, I'm sorry you lost your parents because of my father. I'm sorry they aren't here. I'm sorry for everything."

"I'm not. That revenge brought me you. It gave me you, baby." He drops his head to mine and wipes at my tears. "You fucking avenged my parents last night. You get that?" I shake my head, unable to see through much right now.

"You don't need to see it now. All you need to see is we are both free, and we did it together." He grabs my hands and kisses my knuckles and bruised wrist from the ropes I was tied up with.

"Turn around." Nico growls.

I turn around slowly, my body already heating up with anticipation for what is coming. I feel his hands come around my neck, my sex gushing with want until I feel the cold weight of something on my chest followed by the snap of a clasp. I spin around in excitement as I stare into my husbands beautiful green eyes.

"HOW?! I thought they were gone forever!" He smiles, as he cups my face affectionately.

"I had our men scour the garage for every last pearl and had them restrung while you slept. I cannot think of a more beautiful and deserving person, *mi principessa*, to wear this piece of my mother. And then, in time, we will pass them down to our daughter when she finds her *soul* in someone like I have found in you. "

"I was supposed to hate you."

This causes him to laugh, and that big smile he saves for me makes my heart flutter back to life again, and I smile.

"You did. It was the best kind of hate."

"What do you mean?"

"We created our own love language, Emelia. We didn't do anything conventional."

I shake my head in disbelief. "We are crazy."

"Yeah, we are. But it's right. And I hope you never stop hate-loving me."

"I hope you never stop hate-loving me either." We kiss. His taste and mine becoming one. I vow to love him like I've never loved before and hate him in a way he's never been hated before, because that hate was all wrapped up in a pretty bow. The second we unraveled it, we got lost in one another. We became one.

"I love you," he whispers.

"I love you, husband." I seal my words with a kiss.

THE NEXT FEW MONTHS, I HAD TO SPEND TIME LEARNING how to live without my parents. Not in a way one would think. I had to spend time learning how to be me without the trauma they caused. I had to learn how to navigate, knowing I had nothing to fear anymore. But most of all, I had to learn how to heal the scars they left.

The outfits were a mess for a long time after that. In fact, there were many close calls, and I almost lost my husband. Nico and I also had to learn new things about one another. I had to learn how to balance his soft side with his overdominating, ferocious side. And he had to learn how to let me in and continue to tear his walls down for me when he shut the mafia world out.

But out of everything, I had to learn who Emelia was. This new version and how to love her and accept her for all she was. I never had to give much thought to freedom, thinking I'd never have it, and now I do. It took time, but this arrangement that started as deception from both of us turned into a love for the ages. One I dreamed about and only ever read about in novels.

Nico and I became something we both didn't understand but could never go back from. We created our new love language. The kind of love that you love to hate.

And me?

I survived.

EPILOGUE

Nico

10 YEARS LATER

"Come on, baby. Just give me one more," I groan out, sliding in and out of her snug cunt slowly, before reaching between us and pinching her clit.

"No." She laughs through her moan.

"One more. Give me a daughter. Come on." I sit up and pull her hips off the bed to fuck into her.

"I gave you three sons. It will most likely be another boy," she hisses when I hit her cervix. "Fuck, Nico. Please, let me come."

"No. Not until you agree to give me another one."

She bites her lip, and I know I'm about to win this one. I've had her on the edge of coming for nearly two hours now, and if she doesn't soon, she may burn from the inside out. I hit that spot of hers, and she screams.

"Yes! Fine! Yes, I'll give you one more. Please, let me come!"

"Good girl. Such a good fucking girl." I hit that spot three more times, and she comes so hard. And I let go inside her. We ride that high for minutes. Long, toe-curling fucking minutes. We collapse, and I pull her into me.

"Good. I will have the doctor come tomorrow to remove that fucking birth control."

"You're crazy. If it's another boy, you owe me."

"Yeah, I will owe you another baby."

She slaps my chest. "You're insane, seriously. You kill people for a living, and this tops that on the scale of insanity."

"Yeah, and...?" I suck on her neck.

Ten years and three sons later and she's still under my skin and in my soul. Emelia wasn't supposed to mean anything. She was an arrangement. But then she changed something in me with her deceptive ways. She cast a fucking spell on me. No one sees me in the same light she gets to when we shut that door. But for Emelia, I am at her mercy. She was my redemption. And I was her salvation.

My parents' love was something I looked at with admiration but thought of as a horrifying thing if it ever happened to me. Then Emelia happened. The idea of me falling in love fast and with a softness I didn't know I could possess took me years to fully be comfortable with, but in time and with Emelia, I did.

I stay hardened outside the walls of our home, but when I see her at the end of each night, my armor falls to the ground, and I feel a weakness for her that I used to ridicule myself over. But now, I honor what she can do to me. I see my father in me. He was the strongest man, the most ruthless man, but with my mother, you'd think he was a dad in the suburbs, obsessed with the ground his wife walked on.

Emelia gave me that. Emelia gave this madman with no remorse a soul. And I never want to lose it again.

—

ABOUT THE AUTHOR

USA Today Bestselling Author, CC Monroe spends her days working and her nights writing spicy romance novels, that will leave you blushing during the steamy scenes and crying when romance gets a little angsty! Living in the snowy state of Utah with her husband and two sons, she enjoys reading, music, movies and the outdoors.

When she isn't writing or working, she is making people laugh with her mad sense of humor and tip of the tongue one liners.

Printed in Great Britain
by Amazon

31643745R00195